For my mom, who taught me to live with laughter, love, and music.

THE SONGS OF LORALAN

OF STARLIT BLADES AND HALLOWED FLAMES

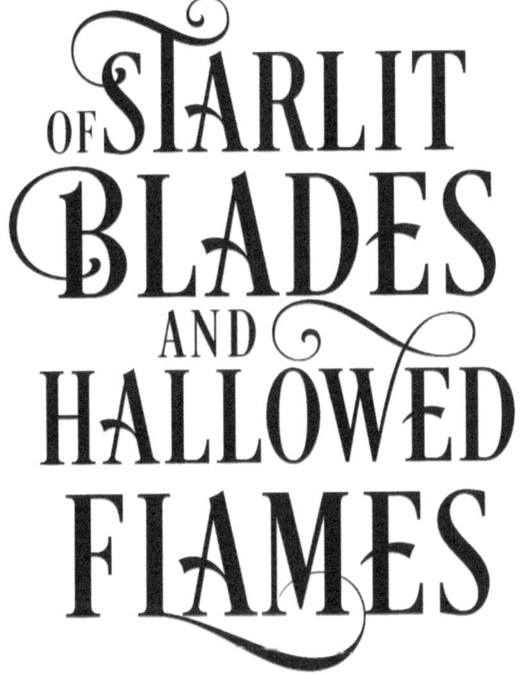

A.L. LORENSEN

CONTENTS

THE DRAGON SCALES
THE GOLDEN GROVE
MONTERRO
ARCHITECT'S HEART
VASTET
CALDRECH
LORATE
THE PHOENIX RIDGES
BAEL
WESTERN LORALAN

PROLOGUE

Stars flooded Aspen's eyes, stretched out like a sea of glinting silver against the smooth midnight backdrop. The golden light from the Golden Grove trees cast the sword in a rich, gilded hue. Aspen let her fingers hover over the black blade, afraid to touch it. "This is..." She shook her head. Words failed to encompass everything the weapon was. She cast a skeptical glance at the two large men that held it. "You're sure *you* made it?"

The younger of the two—Will—scowled and showed her his bare forearms, where he had a tapestry of angry red marks. "I've certainly got the burns to prove it! Do you know how hot we have to stoke the fires to forge galatite?"

"Hotter than a cup of tea?" she asked with a wry grin.

Will rolled his eyes. "And ma says *you're* the smart one."

Aspen brightened. "She does?"

"Not any*more*."

"All right, that's enough," Aspen's oldest brother, Tarragon, said, shouldering between them. He offered Aspen the sword. "Why don't you try it out?"

Aspen's eyes widened. She wanted nothing more, but the weapon's glossy beauty felt above her. "Why don't you do it?"

"We all know you're a better swordsman than the rest of us," Tarragon said, his green eyes—brighter than a lightning flash—watching her with quiet pride. Aspen used to swear they glowed in the dark.

"Well, not *all* of—" Will began before Tarragon elbowed him in the ribs.

"Just try it," Tarragon said again.

Despite her reservations, Aspen reverently took the blade from him. As soon as she weighed it in her hands, it settled in as if an extension of herself. She swung it, the movements fluid and perfect. She gasped in delight, a smile of pure pleasure splitting across her face. She had never wielded something so stunning, cutting its dark arcs through the air so seamlessly she hardly felt it. Every twitch of her wrist had it leaping into action like an animal eager to please its master. "It's incredible!" she said, unable to tear her eyes away from it. She took a few whacks at their pile of firewood, wincing at how barbaric it felt to do with such a beautiful sword. But when she inspected the blade, it was still just as glossy and perfect as it had been before.

"It won't break," Tarragon called. He and Will had settled themselves into the grass beneath the golden trees, and grinned as they watched her. "Galatite is the strongest metal across the kingdoms of Alchilon. It won't chip or dent, either, so it won't need to be sharpened."

"And if it *does* break," Will chimed in, "That's something outside of our control, and you're better off running from whatever broke it."

Tarragon shook his head. "It's *not* going to break."

Aspen smiled at them and offered the sword back, her heart twinging with envy and remorse that she had to return it. "You really outdid yourselves with this one," she said. "I wouldn't be surprised if you're both comfortably set for life when you sell it."

Neither of Aspen's brothers moved to take it. She pushed it closer to them, but they just smiled up at her from their seats in the grass.

"It's for you," Will said.

Aspen's eyes went round, and her face blanched. "No, I couldn't possibly...you put so much work into it. You deserve to profit from it or, at the very least, keep it for yourselves." Even as she said it, though, her fingers curled more tightly around the weapon.

Tarragon must have seen the gesture, because he gave her a knowing look. "Our profit," he said gently. "Is making sure you can protect yourself. We know we can't keep you from throwing yourself in danger."

"Sister Earth help anyone that tries," Will muttered with a wink.

"But we can give you a weapon that will never fail," Tarragon continued. "So long as you have this sword, it will protect you and everyone you choose to defend until it's time for you to retire and pass the fight to someone else."

Aspen pressed the flat of the blade close to her chest, unable to speak past the lump of gratitude in her throat. Tarragon's blessing resonated through her.

That resonance turned to crushing, paralyzing guilt as she stood before the Council of Elders months later.

She had never understood what "exquisite" pain meant—not until the soaring Council Room benches roiled and bucked in her vision, stars of every color imaginable adorned the darkness behind her eyelids, and the Council of Elders wavered like gossamer threads as they watched her from their pulpits. It was beautiful, in a way. And it made her want to vomit.

Fire raced along the still fresh wound on her back, making her break out in a cold sweat and shivers. The ground swayed beneath her. She choked back bile but kept her gaze firmly fixed on the Elders —on the cold, dead hatred in Inula's eyes as she held the golden orb of Aspen's memories in her palm. Aspen deserved that hatred, every bit of it. The invisible wounds fractured across her heart buried themselves even deeper as Ro, Tarragon, and Will flooded her mind.

Tears threatened, but she bit them back. She didn't deserve to cry. Not when it had been all her fault. Her sword had not failed them. *She* had.

Elder Inula's voice was as sharp and frigid as ice when she spoke. "Aspen Tanner," she said. "If you are to be understood correctly, you are telling me that you ignored the counsel of a ranking official—causing deaths that should not have happened—because you were *afraid?*"

The words slammed into Aspen like blows to the face, but she straightened her shoulders and spine and took them.

"You saw the context, Elder Inula!" Another elder cried, too blurry in Aspen's pained vision to make out properly. She recognized the voice, though. Hemlock. "You know that is nowhere near what Aspen —"

"Context does not matter, Elder Hemlock! Only the facts," Inula snapped, her eyes never leaving Aspen. "And the facts are that this girl took her men into battle when she was ordered not to and *left them on the battlefield*, which resulted in the deaths of her entire party, including the *prince*." She slammed the golden orb down. It bounced over the railing and rolled to a stop at Aspen's feet, swirling with images of blood and carnage. The same ones she saw in her dreams every night.

"The rebellion—our final hope of reclaiming our kingdom—has lost its champion and heir to the throne," Inula continued. "And it is all. Her. Fault."

Inula could not have hurt Aspen more if she had run her through with a sword. She swayed as the world spun around her and the blood fled from her face. It was true. It was all true. As much as it haunted her—as much as she wanted to take it all back—there was no changing it. The least she could do was take her punishment with dignity.

"Better people have been sentenced for far less," Inula said, waving off Hemlock as the other elder moved to speak. "The Council of Elders is bound to a rule of unbiased equality, no matter the person or circumstances." Inula stood and pointed a single, accusatory finger at Aspen. "Precedent made by one is rule for all, and the precedent has been set. Aspen Tanner is sentenced to the only punishment suitable for cowards of the highest order."

"No!" Hemlock was on her feet in an instant, her outrage echoing through the room.

"Aspen Tanner shall now and forever more be known as a shadow walker."

The words thundered over Aspen. The tears finally fell, silent and horrified. Her knees buckled. She pitched forward, her only thoughts of the swirling memories in the orb, and then the world went dark around her.

CHAPTER

ONE

The wind shrieked through Aspen's ears, swirling inside her and turning everything it touched to ice. Her chest heaved. The deep wound in her shoulder seeped blood down her arm, and her broken ankle throbbed inside her boot. Agony raced through her throat anytime she tried to draw breath. The rain pelted her like daggers and thunder and lightning clashed overhead as she collapsed, choking on blood.

"Aspen!" Someone caught her, huddling their shoulders over her to protect her against the worst of the storm. Her eyelids fluttered as she tried to open them. "I just got you back," they said. "You're not leaving me again!"

With tremendous effort, Aspen managed to get her eyes open. A face swam in her vision, indistinct in the darkening storm. However, the figures gathered around him were stark and vivid. Dozens of faceless figures dressed in blood-covered armor. They loomed over her, their faint, tumbling whispers flooding every portion of her. She closed her eyes and gritted her teeth, willing them away—*begging* them to leave. When she forced her eyes open again, they were gone. The person hovering over her swam into view instead.

"Tristan?" she croaked, her words slurring in her mouth. "What are you doing here?"

He shook his head, rain drops flinging from the dark hair plastered against his scalp. "Remember? It's me. It's Ro."

Aspen shook her head, which only sent the world spinning. She shut her eyes again. "No, you died," she said in a broken whisper.

He clutched her closer. "I *didn't.* I just forgot who I was."

Aspen clenched her fists. The prongs of a key dug into one of her palms, and a single tear slipped down her face, whipped away by the storm. Something was wrong with him being there. She grit her teeth as she tried to string coherent thoughts together. No. *No.* It was too good to be true. Ro was dead. He was *dead*! She had finally accepted that fact.

He pressed one of his hands against her shoulder to stop the bleeding. "Remember? I was stupid and let General Laire throw me into this storm. You even warned me to be careful."

Aspen moaned from the pressure against her wound. Memories slid back to her through her fog of pain and blood loss. Finding Tristan at Fort Lorate. Escaping together. Traveling to the Dragon Scales and fighting off sorcerers and crazed generals. Leaping into the perpetual storm. And Tristan finding her through the torrent, gripping her face in his hands, and telling her the words she thought she would never hear again.

For evergreens and aspen trees.

Before she could form any coherent thoughts around the images, a shadow circled above them, cutting through the storm clouds. A roar pierced through the thunder and the massive shadow descended from the sky, streaked with lightning. As it grew closer, Aspen's dread grew. She tried to pull Tristan or Ro or whoever he was away, but her arms just twitched uselessly at her sides.

"Move," she croaked.

He leaned closer to her. "What?"

"*Move!*"

But it was too late. A mottled dragon the color of the storm landed in front of them, tail lashing and horned head held high above them. The ground trembled with its weight, its talons digging into the ground to keep it steady against the storm. It was about the size of a horse, and regarded them with slitted eyes the color of lightning.

You were foolish to brave the storm, her voice—rich and rumbling—spoke to their minds.

"It...wasn't by choice," Ro responded weakly. He laid Aspen down and shifted himself in front of her, arms outstretched as if that would stop the dragon if it attacked. "Aren't dragons extinct?"

Aspen let out a manic, half-delirious chuckle. Ahh, yes. There was the man Aspen knew. Full of stupid questions.

Very few of us survived, the dragon responded, *And we are but a shadow of the race we once were.* The dragon flexed her wings, the paper-thin membranes glowing with each flash of lightning. *But that is of little importance now. I am Storm Chaser. Who bears the key to the Midnight Fens?*

"I thought the Fens didn't allow beasts of burden?" Aspen asked, her mind deliriously latching onto that minute, ridiculous fact.

The dragon regarded her coldly. *Do I look like a beast of burden?*

Even Aspen's blood-deprived self couldn't argue with that logic. Aspen extended the glowing key in her hand, her arm trembling with the strain. "I am Aspen Tanner," she rasped, the words lurching from her mouth between gasps for air. "Here with a plea from Commanding General Dallowyn." The effort set her coughing, more blood and phlegm filling her mouth. She turned her face and spit it out, grimacing and heaving.

Storm Chaser regarded the key but did not take it. *I'm afraid my masters do not permit your kind access to their domain.*

Aspen settled her head back with a thunk, scoffing even as she cursed her half-blood birth. "Your Gate Keeper said much the same thing before I bested him and took his precious key." She fumbled with her sword and used it to push herself to her feet, despite Ro's protests and her own body shrieking at her. She straightened her shoulders as best she could, blood trickling down the side of her body. "For the sake of my people, I'm not leaving before I claim an audience with the Fens."

Storm Chaser crouched on her haunches with a rumble in her throat, like a jaguar ready to pounce. She eyed Aspen's sword. *Your dedication is admirable, and I am loath to resort to violence, but I am at the mercy of my master's whims. You will find I am not so easy an opponent as one lowly Gate Keeper.*

"*Enough!*" Ro leapt between Aspen and the dragon, teeth bared in a snarl. "These petty squabbles over bloodlines end *today!*" he said, his voice thunderous. "She has your stupid key, threw herself into this goddess-forsaken storm, and has done everything you asked. It's time your people actually honor that!"

Aspen could only gape at him. That was *not* the man she knew. That was someone with authority and confidence. It sat well on his broad shoulders.

"I am *getting* you into the Fens and to a healer," he said to Aspen, not taking his eyes off Storm Chaser. "It's about time I started earning my keep around here." He cast his voice back out to the dragon. "Well?"

Storm Chaser growled and paced a few steps, her tail lashing about her. *I did not say it is because you are a half-blood,* she snapped, her voice terse in their minds. *You are an outsider. The people of the Fens hide themselves for a reason. But you carry our key, so I will take you, as is my duty. Do not say I didn't warn you about the reception you will receive.*

THE STORM REARED ITS HORRIFIC, undulating head at Aspen and Ro as they clung to Storm Chaser's back. Rain and hail battered their exposed skin, leaving angry welts. Lightning and thunder battled each other in the steel gray clouds, leaving them blind and deaf, and the wind wrenched at anything it could touch. It was a miracle the dragon's delicate wing membranes weren't torn to ribbons. It took all Aspen's strength just to hold on, her face buried in the warm, iridescent scales.

The turmoil of the elements paled only compared to the turmoil wracking Aspen's mind. She had lost everything in this Sister Earth forsaken place five years ago. Her brothers. Her best friend—the rightful heir to the throne of Loralan. The images had sealed themselves to the insides of her eyelids. She had been too weak—too *stupid*—to do anything to save them. Now she was supposed to believe the man sitting behind her—arms wrapped tight around her waist, warmth leeching into her skin, his chattering breath sending gooseflesh along her spine—was the same one she had watched crumble beneath a mace? The one she had watched die in every moment of her sleeping hours? No matter how desperately she ached to believe it, she couldn't bring herself to. The fear of losing it all again, and what that might do to her already tenuous sanity, loomed all too close and all too real.

Ro pressed his mouth to Aspen's ear to be heard over the din of the storm. Even then, he had to shout. "What exactly do you intend to do once we get to the Midnight Fens?"

Aspen laughed to herself at her sheer wretched luck. Not only did she have to deal with hallucinations of her dead friend; she also had to navigate the stupidity of elven diplomacy. The letter of request Commanding General Dallowyn had sent with her was back at camp with Ash and Styrax—she hoped Ash wouldn't kill her *too* badly when they got back. Not only had she come without proper documentation, she was a half-blood on top of it. If even *one* pure elf took her seriously, she'd consider it a miracle.

She curled her fingers tighter around the scales beneath her. If she needed a miracle, then she would force one to appear. She refused to fail. The base of her left thumb throbbed. She had already failed too many people in her life. She refused to do it again.

The Fens are just ahead, Storm Chaser said. *Hang tight. This will not be an easy landing.*

Aspen didn't have time to register the words before they plummeted. The screaming wind pounded against her ears and pressed her head as if it intended to crush it. Ro yelped and nearly broke Aspen in half as he fought to stay seated on the dragon. Aspen's consciousness fled to the edges of her mind, just present enough to keep her grip, but not much else. And her grip was slipping.

Just before her consciousness abandoned her, Storm Chaser snapped open her wings and jolted as she landed. Aspen and Ro tumbled from her back. Aspen sucked in a hiss of pain as her wounded shoulder and broken ankle rioted against the abuse.

Ro helped her to her feet. She swayed, her eyesight fading in and out. Sister Earth, how much blood had she lost? She didn't need this now. She had a mission to complete. Not even death would stop her at this point.

"Are you all right?" Ro asked, shouting over the din.

She waved him off. Mistake. She teetered off-balance and nearly fell.

Ro gripped her tighter. She wished he would stop doing that. It made him seem even more real, and she couldn't have that. Not if he disappeared the moment she got her wits about her.

Before Aspen could voice her protests to him, Storm Chaser's chest glowed bright and fierce before she snapped open her jaws and roared. She blew a pillar of fire into the clouds above. The whirling torrent whisked it away like a twirling ribbon.

A crack opened in the storm, like massive doors opening. Warm firelight spilled from it, stark against the sopping darkness of the storm. Aspen's frigid muscles ached to be wherever the light was coming from.

Quickly! Storm Chaser ushered Aspen and Ro toward the light. *They won't be able to leave it open for long with the storm still active.*

They staggered and stumbled forward, fighting numbed limbs, exhausted bodies, and the wind bent on knocking them flat. As they drew closer, two tall, lithe figures appeared in the light, which did indeed end up being a doorway.

"By the Phoenix, Chaser! What half-dead rats have you found this time?"

She bears the key, Storm Chaser responded when they reached the door. *It's my duty to show them safely here, no matter the circumstances.*

Those words felt pointed—probably referring to Aspen's half-blood status. Aspen readied herself for another uphill battle. It seemed she existed for nothing else.

"What sort of fools try to enter three days before the storm sleeps?" One figure—an elf with long white hair and beard, singed black on the ends—groused as he waved them inside.

"Desperate ones," Aspen said, her tongue heavy in her mouth. Her body cried for sleep, but she knew she would not get it. Best to forget it existed until later.

"She's wounded, she needs..." Ro's words slid to a stop. Aspen glanced at him, and his eyes glazed over, his mouth dropping open. They had entered what appeared to be the inside of an ancient, cavernous tree—one that continued to thrive and grow despite the elves within it. The walls, floor, and ceiling all blended together in perfect curves as smooth as fresh-churned butter. The host tree's grains danced in the shadows cast by a monstrous hearth. Young branches, sprouting silver and velvet black leaves, intertwined to form a mantle. Various pillows, chairs, and blankets were arranged in front of the fire, perfect for weary, sopping wet strays to sink into.

"Desperation that gets you killed does no one any favors," an elven woman tutted as she gathered up blankets. She had long black hair tinged with white, which she spent a good majority of her time sweeping out of the numerous pockets adorning her clothes when she bent over, until she gave up the fight and tied it all up in a haphazard bun. "Thorn, stoke the fire. These two are soaked through."

Thorn, the other elf, let out a long, growling sigh. "Yes, Thistle." He coaxed a growth of new log from the wall, his eyes glowing a deep forest green. The log plopped into his hands. He tossed it with little regard into the already roaring fire. Sparks hissed as they jumped from the wood. Some landed in Thorn's beard, where they ignited, burning more black patches into the hair. He patted out the miniature blazes as if swatting at flies.

"I...remember places like this," Ro said almost to himself, his eyes misty. "This is what the Golden Grove is like, isn't it?"

"Parts of it," Aspen said with a pang in her heart. She traced the grains of the wall with her palm.

"Don't mind Thorn," Thistle said as she approached with blanket laden arms. "My husband's joints act up while the storm is out. It makes him grumpy and miserable most of the time, but I still love him."

Ro nodded as he took a blanket. Thistle helped him dry off his hair and took his wet socks and boots. "What was so urgent that you had to come three days early?"

Ro shrugged and looked at Aspen for help. His utterly lost look struck a tender chord in her. There was the Tristan she knew from the past several weeks. He always had more questions than he ever seemed to know what to do with. Somehow, they had grown to be endearing rather than a nuisance to Aspen. Not that she would ever tell him that.

As she watched him, dangerous questions floated through her mind again. *Could* Tristan and Ro be the same? Did she dare to hope?

Whatever the answers to those questions, Ro needed her to provide an answer to Thistle's question first. Explaining the story of Ro's former general rendering him nearly paralyzed with a warlock's memory-eating spell, and then Ro getting sucked into the storm and Aspen jumping in after him would have taken ages. So she went with the simplest answer she could give. "We've come from the Golden Grove to request aid from your queen."

Aspen expected resistance—the gate keeper she had won the key from hadn't been thrilled about her pleas—but instead, Thistle smiled. "I'm sure Queen Holly will be delighted to help," she said. "She used to visit the Golden Grove as a child, and has many fond memories of the place."

Aspen felt the tension in her shoulders slowly, tentatively relax. "What a relief to hear," she said, her voice cracking. Could it be so easy? Had all the struggles to get to this point been worth it?

"Before anyone goes anywhere, though, we need to get you both warm and dry." Thistle wrapped Ro tightly in a blanket and sent him off toward the fire.

"What a handsome caterpillar you make," Aspen said to him, feeling slightly giddy from the warmth of the fire and excessive blood loss.

"Just you wait. I'll be the most beautiful, toasty butterfly you've ever seen when I'm through," Ro shot back with a wry grin.

Thistle chuckled as she approached Aspen with another mountain of blankets. Her mirth quickly gave way to horror, though, when she saw the sorry state Aspen was in. "You're wounded! Why didn't you say something earlier, child? I could have—" Her words and footsteps stopped in an instant. Her slanted eyes narrowed. "I'm afraid my senses are getting duller with age, so pardon the question, but...do you happen to...to be a half-blood?"

Thorn turned from the fire to watch the exchange, his face set in hard, impassive lines.

Ro tuned in as well. "So what if she is?" he growled.

Thistle took a deliberate step back, as if Aspen carried a disease. The tension in Aspen's shoulders returned. They pulled tight and back, pulling her spine straight. Bleeding and barely able to stand on her ankle, she watched her hosts, saying nothing. She didn't have to. They knew. The inexplicable kinship of shared magic pushed them away from her. She didn't have enough of it. Her eyes were too round, her ears not pointed enough. Too short. Too *breakable.* Too human to be elven, and too elven to be human. She was filth, and everyone made sure she never forgot it.

Thistle dropped the blankets like a protective barrier between her and Aspen. Before Aspen could react, Thistle charged at her.

CHAPTER
TWO

Aspen braced herself, shutting her eyes grimly against the blow she knew was inevitable. Her senses were too dull to stop it.

"Thank goodness you've come here instead of someplace like the Golden Grove!" Thistle practically swept Aspen off her feet as she half-carried, half-led her to a cozy room tucked in the corner of the inn's main floor. "The Phoenix knows they would just let you bleed to death if you went to them in such a state!"

"I...what?" Aspen asked, biting her tongue to keep from crying out at the elven woman's jostling and touch.

Thistle helped Aspen onto the bed and checked over her injuries, her face growing more alarmed with every passing moment. "By the Phoenix, how are you still conscious? Who *did* this to you?" she asked, more a question to herself. She waved Aspen off before she had time to answer and pressed the back of her palm to Aspen's forehead. "You're burning up. Thorn, call the healer!"

Aspen heard the faint sound of a door opening and shutting in the main room.

"I don't have time for this," Aspen protested, even as her eyelids threatened to droop and her body shivered with cold sweat. "We have to see the queen."

"Queen Holly won't be holding audiences for several days," Thistle said, applying just enough pressure to keep Aspen pinned to the bed. "So there's no point wearing yourself out until then."

Thistle stripped Aspen down to her undergarments before Aspen could protest. Aspen's blood was stark against the thin linen, and Aspen's head swam at the sight of it. There was more of it than she had expected. Thistle reached to remove the bracer from Aspen's left hand, but Aspen flinched and pulled it closer to her and out of the elf's reach. The blood drained from her face at the thought of what Thistle would do if she saw the mark she hid beneath the bracer.

Thistle pursed her lips but didn't press the matter. She pulled some clean rags from the bedside table, dipped them in the room's washbasin, and dabbed away at the filth and crusted blood. "You just rest," she soothed as Aspen arched reflexively away. "The healer will be here in a few moments, and then I'll make some tea to help with the pain."

Aspen dueled with the urges to fight Thistle's fussing hands away or give her a hug. She waited for the facade to fade—for the horrible prank to be revealed that Thistle was going to lock her in the room to rot alone, or cart her off to a prison somewhere. Half-bloods were the curse of the earth. Abominations that defied the Ancient Laws.

But Thistle didn't do any of those things. She just gently washed Aspen's wounds, watching her with genuine care and concern.

"Why?" Aspen asked, unable to keep the wariness out of her voice. "You don't even know me."

Thistle gave her a sad smile. "We have sheltered enough half-bloods here to know that morsels of kindness are hard to come by." Tears filled her eyes, and she blinked them away. "My brother and his human wife lived in Brahmon for a time with their children. They left before the...incident. But they knew many others that didn't." Her words hung stagnant over the room. She cleared her throat and patted Aspen's hand, shaking her head. "The Phoenix came to the Fens centuries ago and taught us that half-bloods are not the curse the world makes them out to be. And now we finally have a Queen that rules by those teachings."

Aspen pressed her lips together in a frown, blinking back the darkness that threatened to overcome her now that she was laying down. "Your gate-keeper didn't share that mindset."

Thistle grimaced. "Some are taking…longer to adjust. The teaching's of the previous Council were a contagious plague, and we most likely won't be rid of them for a long time. But we won't banish anyone with ties here unless they are outright harmful to the others living here. We do find other duties for them outside of the Fens, though. I suppose it's been so long since we've had visitors that we had forgotten those elves could pose a problem to those that wanted to find us."

Aspen snorted. "Problem is an understatement," she said, still bitter at the spear-wielding elf that had tried to skewer her when she had found the entrance key to the Fens.

Someone knocked on the room's door frame. "Will she be all right?" Ro asked, wide-eyed and still wrapped in his blanket.

Aspen tried to sit up, pulling her own blankets up to cover herself. "*You* should be over here. You were cursed and hurt and—" Her movement caused the world to rock around her, and stars swirled through her vision.

"Absolutely not!" Ro and Thistle said in unison. Thistle shoved Aspen back onto the bed and waved Ro over to a seat beside her. His face turned white when he saw Aspen's wounds.

"She'll be better now that you're here," Thistle said, shooting Aspen a warning glance. Aspen got the message loud and clear. *Stay. Put.* "I'll go check on where that healer's at."

"We have two other friends outside the storm," Aspen said to Thistle, her voice weak as her injuries and exhaustion caught up with her. "Another half-blood and a naiad. They'll have an injured sorcerer and an older man they're holding prisoner."

Thistle's eyebrows shot up her forehead, but she didn't comment on the motley assortment of people Aspen had listed. "I'll have Chaser bring them back." She left Aspen and Ro alone.

"You *captured* Laire?" Ro asked, his voice both awestruck and strangled. She couldn't imagine the warring emotions that must be competing for his attention. After all, the man had posed as a mentor and father-figure to him for five years.

Aspen rubbed her neck, the bruises left by Laire's fingers still swollen and tender. "Styrax did," she said. "Laire nearly killed me." She kept the 'again' that floated through her mind to herself.

Ro tensed. He hugged her to him, arms shaking. "I'm so sorry."

Aspen closed her eyes and just listened to his heart thrumming against her ear, warm and solid.

"Thank goodness for Styrax." His breath skated across her hair.

Aspen nodded once, the movement jolting through her neck. "And Ash."

"And Ash," he agreed. He pulled away from her and took her hand in his. "Not the sort of reception you were expecting from Thistle and Thorn, huh?" His smile was bright, but his eyes were hollow, as if he were trying to force lightness into the conversation. His smile quickly faded, though, and his brows knit together. "Are you going to be all right?"

Aspen slipped her fingers from his grasp, guilt weighing on her chest. "Shouldn't I be asking *you* that?" The words grated against her throat. Her head pounded, and she struggled to keep her eyelids open. "Someone you trusted turned a curse against you and threw you into the most heinous storm in existence. Not only did you survive, but now your lost memories are back, too? Are *you* going to be all right?"

Ro slumped back in his chair, the hollowness in his eyes spreading across his face. "I can't describe how happy I am to have these memories back," he whispered. "But more keep coming and I just—" He ran his hands through his hair, looking lifetimes older than he should have been. "It's a lot. I need to process, but I'll be fine.

Eventually." He leaned over and brushed a stray strand of hair away from the corner of her mouth. "And *you* need to sleep."

He fluffed the pillow behind her head and tucked the blankets closer around her chin. Aspen felt horrible for the blood she was getting all over them.

As unconsciousness floated around her vision, a small, terrified question slipped out before she could stop it. "Will you be here when I wake up?"

Ro squeezed her hand. "I'm here to stay," he said. He gave her a weak smile. "For evergreens and aspen trees."

Aspen fought back the pain and nausea coursing through her until exhaustion finally won out. Ro's hand in hers was the last thing she felt when sleep finally overtook her.

THREE

Sedick slammed the tower door behind him. It almost flattened the acolyte following Sedick through the doorway, fluttering like a nervous hen.

"I told you these talismans had to be finished by *sundown!*" Sedick thundered. "How will you feel when I tell Osmen that our troops fell to the Golden Grove because you had to *sleep?*"

"I'm sorry, my Lord, I'm sorry!" The acolyte blubbered, wiping sweat from his brow and ringing scalded hands. His cloak pockets sagged with earring studs, bracelets, and rings, but only half of them glowed with the touch of magic.

"Sorry does not pay the debt you owe me for teaching you magic!" Sedick said, smacking the back of the acolyte's head.

"You're right. I am sorry, my lord," the acolyte whimpered and winced as he realized he'd apologized again. "There will be no more delays. I will complete them by the end of the day."

"See to it, before I put you under inquisition."

The acolyte paled and tucked his fingernails into his palms as if to protect them. "Yes, my lord." He practically fled down the passageway.

Sedick paced around the workspace, massaging his temples and growling to himself. So much to do. *Too* much to do. And incompetent help was only adding more to his already overflowing list of responsibilities.

This is how you use the power I gave you? A voice asked in Sedick's mind. *Wasted on bullying insignificant whelps?*

Sedick swore under his breath. On instinct, he looked down both ends of the hallway, even though he knew he wouldn't find anything. Even so, the shadows still seemed to grow and writhe into living beings.

It had been years since Sedick had heard that voice, and he had hoped that he had rid himself of it forever. But demons always slunk back where they were least wanted.

Master, the word rankled Sedick's pride as he projected the word back, but he swallowed back his ire. *What do you need from me?*

Meet me in your gardens. I have a task for you.

The connection ended. Sedick cursed again and hastened to his estate. He ignored all the serving girls he usually lingered on and shoved past guards without a second thought. A task? Was he not already controlling an entire country from the shadows? What else could his master *possibly* need from him that he could not pass on to his acolytes? The question irked him, but also left a hollow sort of excitement in his chest. It had to be something that required immense power. And missions like that had the best reward. Would his demonic master finally grant him his own power, and not some borrowed farce?

The thought preoccupied so much of his mind that he walked too near a solid door in an isolated corner of the castle. Something slammed against it and made the handle rattle.

"Release us!" a strident voice cried from inside. "If nothing else, return the girl to her mother!"

Sedick sneered. His wife, Milaia, had always possessed an uncanny knack of knowing when he was near. He threw one of his bangles at the door. A shock-wave of orange tinted magic shuddered through the wood. He heard a shriek of pain, and then silence. Sedick smirked and continued on his way.

It was dark when he reached his estate grounds. Torches guttered along the walls, passing uncertain, ghostly shadows across Milaia's neglected, dying garden. A dark figure sat silently on a crumbling stone bench, its shape as uncertain as the shadows. It did not move when Sedick approached, but Sedick felt his flesh crawling —the telltale sign it was looking at him. Even after three decades, and for all his power, Sedick knew he was nothing compared to his master.

"You are slow, Sedick," it said to him in a deep, hissing voice.

"I would have been faster if you would come to the palace." Sedick said, sucking in a long, controlled breath through his nose to calm his irritation. "For all your power, you could go anywhere you pleased."

The demon stood slowly, its features flickering into view in the torchlight. Black, curling markings snaked around its ageless face, and fire smoldered in its sightless, darting eyes. It loomed over Sedick, and he unconsciously took a step back. "Baffling though it may be to you," it ground out through clenched teeth. "There *are* some things even *you* could not understand. I cannot enter the palace. Not yet."

It stood that way, silent and watching and radiating power, until Sedick couldn't hold its gaze anymore. He curled his lip in disgust at himself as he looked away.

The demon sat again, its face expressionless but its presence still radiating hints of ire. "I did not bring you here to listen to you whine. We are here to discuss *you*." It took a trailing vine into its hand, weaving it through its fingers even as the vine's thorns tore into the demon's hand and drew white, milky blood. "I hear the attack on the Golden Grove is already shaping up to be a brutal failure."

Sedick's blood boiled even as his heart hammered in his chest in fear. That stupid, idiotic mission would never leave him in peace. "You would be correct," he said, a growl leaking out even as he tried to remain neutral. "But the fault does not lie with me. It was a plan doomed to fail from the beginning. Osmen should have known that. If you would let me overthrow him and take the throne, I—"

"*No*," the demon spat. "We have discussed this. The *moment* you move against the king, I will revoke the power I have given you."

Sedick bit back a retort, frustration and rage shaking his limbs.

The demon smirked. "It's good to see that you are still learning, even without my hand to guide you. Sit." It gestured to another bench beside it. Sedick ground his teeth but complied.

"I have a job for you," it said.

Sedick said nothing.

"My mistress needs an item. A single flame closely guarded in the phoenix caverns at the heart of the Golden Grove."

Sedick bristled. So, even after all his years of service, dedication, and achievements, his master still relegated him to little more than a slave. "I am no errand boy!"

"You are whatever I tell you to be," the demon said in a quiet voice that was more terrifying than its anger. "And you *will* get that flame. The job is practically done for you with this charge against the Golden Grove. Even *you* will be hard-pressed to fail this assignment. Use whatever means necessary, and bring the flame back to me." Without another word, the demon vanished into the night, the shadows seeming to follow it like starving dogs.

Sedick flipped over the stone bench the demon had sat on and screamed. The bench crumbled. The moment Laire's sword granted his wish, his demon master would be the first to fall before him. Sedick would no longer be a slave to *anyone*.

FOUR

Vinea had never been so happy—or so terrified—to return to Lorate. Everything was both familiar and alien. Her body expected to fall back into routine and comfort, when her mind knew that things could never be the same. Her entire life had shattered in what felt like moments, and she doubted she would ever finish putting together the pieces.

Vinea had considered circumventing the town entirely and heading straight to Lorate. She was tired and filthy, and her mostly healed wounds still ached. But her need for a sense of normalcy won out. She needed to see the familiar streets and quiet, happy faces—needed to feel like maybe her whole life hadn't fully crumbled around her. She had her home and her daughter. If Laire chose not to be part of that, the ragged hole in her heart would eventually heal. It had to.

As she passed through the streets, though, dread settled like a cloak of thorns over her. The roads were silent, even though people still milled through them. Their steps were slow and aimless, their expressions blank. They walked by Vinea, but didn't seem to register her at all.

She reached her hand out to get someone's—anyone's—attention, but someone snatched her into an alleyway. Before she could scream, a hand clamped over her mouth. Vinea balled her hand into a fist and rammed her elbow into her attacker. They grunted, but their grip still held fast.

"Vinea!" they said, the word a hiss through clenched teeth. "Vinea, it's me!"

Vinea stopped struggling at the familiar voice, her eyes wide. When her body relaxed, her attacker released her. Vinea turned and took in the young, dark-skinned spy. "Chaedra?" she asked.

Chaedra looked at Vinea as if she were a long-forgotten spirit. "What are you doing here?" she asked. "I haven't seen you for *weeks*! I thought Sedick or Laire had caught you. I thought you were *dead*!"

Vinea's heart plummeted. She didn't want to tell Chaedra how close all her assumptions had been to the truth. Her wound still ached from Sorren's magic, and Sedick's threat of reporting her for treason still loomed over her head. "Why are we hiding in alleyways?" she asked, glancing around but not sure what danger she was looking for. "What happened to everyone?"

Chaedra pressed her lips together until they were a pale, thin line. Vinea noticed the exhausted bags under the woman's eyes. "They found out where Osmen's sending the Lorate soldiers."

Vinea's stomach twisted into a painful knot. "Oh." She looked out at the streets again, anger swelling in her when she remembered her husband had done this. Laire had sentenced Lorate's husbands, brothers, sons, and friends to death when he assigned them to march against the Golden Grove. But even amidst her righteous fury, a small sliver of hope still burned. The Vanguard—King Osmen's elite soldiers—would accompany the Lorate forces. Maybe the Vanguard would...

Vinea jolted. The Vanguard! She had to tell Chaedra —

"Why aren't you in Monterro with Linae?" Chaedra asked.

All thoughts of the Vanguard and the rest of the world at large lodged in Vinea's throat. She froze, all the air in her body rushing out. "Linae's in Monterro?" she asked in a heady voice that somehow didn't connect to her body.

Chaedra's face paled. She reached out to Vinea as if preparing to brace her. "You didn't know? Sedick took her there weeks ago."

Vinea didn't even let her finish before she was out of the alleyway. She didn't know if her feet touched the ground. The stares and open hostility from the townsfolk rolled off her back. Her aches and pains slipped away to a back corner of her mind. The only thing she saw was the road toward Monterro. The only thing she felt was the storm of fury and terror raging through her.

"Where are you going?" Chaedra called after her.

"The Pit," Vinea said, the words burning like venom in her throat. "And I'm taking Sedick with me."

CHAPTER
FIVE

Aspen woke to hushed voices, muffled through the blankets that had inexplicably ended up over her head. Everything hurt, physically and mentally. She couldn't move without something in her body twinging, and with each new stab of pain came another memory. The Dragon scales. The storm. Tristan...Tristan...

Not Tristan, he had said. *It's me. It's Ro. For evergreens and aspen trees.*

Aspen lurched from her bed, heart pounding and body shaking, feeling as if her mind had caught itself in a torturous loop. The mark on her thumb burned. It couldn't be true. The storm, the dragon, the kindly elves, and the inn all had to be a dream. Now that she was awake, it would all have disappeared, just as dreams were supposed to.

Why, though, did that dream feel so real?

Still delirious with pain and exhaustion, she stumbled out of bed, taking the blanket with her. Where *was* she? Tall ceilings rose above her, ending in a smooth, seamless finish of warm, stained wood.

Torches crackled merrily throughout, casting everything in soft light. High, vaulted windows revealed dark leaves of blue and purple outside, flecked with spots of silver. The Midnight Fens. They were—she had—how did?

She shook her head, gritting her teeth against the way the movement sent her vision spinning. All that would come with time.

Her sword leaned against the wall. She strapped it on and drew the blade before padding toward the sound of the voices. They were speaking in low tones, so even when she was practically on top of them, she couldn't hear what they were saying. Aspen pressed her back against the wall, took a long, bracing breath to calm the nausea and pain rolling through her, and rounded the corner, weapon at the ready.

"Aspen Tanner, you put that sword away *right now*," Ash sniped as she came into view, her expression steely. She sat on a couch beside a large hearth, Styrax beside her, and had dark circles rimming her eyes.

Aspen looked at her in consternation. "What are you doing here?"

Ash tutted. "Well, I'm *certainly* not here to make sure my addle-brained cousin hadn't killed herself. That would just be ridiculous." She crossed the room and plucked Aspen's sword from her hands. "Because who would be stupid enough to throw themselves into a storm while bleeding to death?" She turned on her heel and sat back down again, glaring daggers at Aspen.

Aspen furrowed her brow. Had she really thrown herself...?

By the Architects, she *had*! To save—"Where's Tristan?"

"Sleeping," Styrax answered. "At least, that's what a *dragon* told us after it scooped us up like a few slabs of holiday roast."

Not holiday roast, Chaser said, her talons clicking on the wooden floors as she walked into the room and curled near the fire. *Those have much more fat on them.*

"Thank you?" Styrax responded, as if unsure of what else to say.

Chaser looked at Aspen critically. *You might want to sit down,* she said.

Aspen's legs trembled beneath her weight, and she had to agree with the dragon, but something still felt...Off. Something that set her senses alight with warning bells.

"I'm going to *kill* you, *wench*," a voice seethed from a dark corner of the room. "You'll regret not killing me. You should have *never* touched my family."

Ah. Yes. There was the danger.

"You brought *Laire* with you?" Aspen asked, peering into the corner to see him bound to a support post. His eyes roved wildly in his skull. His sword was well out of reach beneath a pile of knapsacks. Aspen still shuddered when she looked at it.

Styrax shrugged. "We couldn't very well leave him. He'd just run off and be a general danger to everyone around him."

Aspen absently brushed her fingertips over the bruises on her throat. "Fair. Is there a reason he's not gagged?"

"The savage nearly bit my fingers off when I tried." Styrax glared daggers at Laire, who snarled in return.

Aspen sat down, positioning herself so she could see Laire from the corner of her eye. "You didn't destroy his sword?"

"Do *you* know how to break galatite, cursed or not?" Styrax asked with a raised eyebrow.

Aspen conceded the point and fell into a deep silence. So far, everything from her 'dream' had been true. That had to mean that... Her heart thudded in her chest. No. She couldn't believe it. Not until she saw him again with her own eyes and wasn't delirious with pain and shock.

"Have you spoken with...Tristan?" She asked.

Styrax shook his head. "You've both been asleep since we got here about a day ago. We were hoping maybe *you* could shed some light on what happened?"

"Thistle and Thorn have been very kind, but knew just about as much as we did," Ash said, her lips pressed so tight together they almost disappeared. "What would you have done if they *weren't* kind, Aspen?" Her hands balled into fists. "If they *hadn't* found a healer for you, or, worse yet, refused to find one for you altogether?"

Aspen knew where this conversation was going. She pinched the bridge of her nose. "Ash, I—"

"You're going to listen to me, Aspen, because this is the last time I'm having this conversation with you," Ash snapped before Aspen could finish.

Aspen and Styrax both looked at her in surprise. The venom in her voice had been palpable. Styrax shifted a few inches away from her to get out of her line of sight.

"You. Cannot. Survive. On luck alone," Ash said, the words shooting from between her clenched teeth like arrows she had kept drawn for too long. "I am *tired* of chasing you down and cleaning you up after you throw your life around like it's some cheap shield for others to use and abuse."

"Ash, we're at war, that's what people—"

"ASPEN!" Ash's voice thundered through the sitting room. Thistle and Thorn poked their heads in, but as soon as they saw the look on Ash's face, they retreated back into what smelled like a kitchen and closed the door behind them. Ash's face was filled with so much rage that all the blood had left her cheeks. When she spoke again, her voice was so quiet Aspen almost didn't hear it, but it pierced her to her very core. "I did not sacrifice my old life to watch you throw yours away." She looked Aspen directly in the eyes, her face more serious than Aspen had ever seen it. "If you *ever* do that again when I am *right there* to help, I will leave. Do you understand? I won't stay and watch you get yourself killed anymore."

Aspen wanted to vomit. Her arms trembled as she saw the conviction in Ash's eyes. She would do it. Aspen knew she would. And the thought of Ash no longer being in her life—of the emptiness it would leave behind—terrified her.

She dropped her head, studying her hands. "I understand," she said, her voice quiet with regret. She met Ash's gaze again. "I'm sorry."

A shudder ran through Ash. "You should be," she said, a new waver developing in her voice. Aspen could still see the hurt that lingered there, but some of the tension left Ash's face. She leaned back against the couch with a sigh, and after a few moments of silence, Styrax inched his way back over.

He interlaced his fingers with Ash's and cleared his throat, looking tentatively between the cousins. "Is the air cleared enough in here for us to talk about what exactly happened?"

Before either Ash or Aspen could answer, another one of the inn doors opened. "I...I think *I* might be able to do that," someone said in a quiet voice from the doorway, squinting as if even the muted fire glow was too bright for him. The young sorcerer that had nearly killed Aspen in Vastet. Sorren.

Aspen's still tender side twinged. She slowly stood, reaching for her sword before realizing Ash still had it. Although he was only a boy, his magic was powerful enough that it radiated its own presence around him. He had nearly *killed* her, and she had no idea where his loyalties aligned. But, here he was, wrapped in a blanket and peering out at them like an owlet with a migraine.

He gestured at Aspen with the corner of his blanket. "You don't need to..." He grit his teeth and shook his head, rubbing his brows. "I'm not going to hurt anyone...Most likely."

"That's a true balm for our confidence," Styrax said in an undertone.

Aspen regarded Sorren carefully. The magic she had sensed swirling through him—powerful and wild—was still there, but it was quieter. Calmer. She remained standing, but motioned for him to join them.

Sorren did so cautiously, watching them all as if they might lash out at any moment. As his attention roved around the room, his eyes eventually fell on Chaser. His jaw dropped, and a gasp escaped his lips. "You're a great dragon, aren't you?" he asked, his tone reverent.

Chaser shifted, looking uncomfortable. *In a sense,* she said, her voice reluctant. *That is my species, but, as you can tell by my size, I am...deficient.*

Sorren looked outraged. "Deficient?"

Aspen share a look with Ash and Styrax to see if they were following along. Styrax looked just as perplexed as she felt, but Ash's attention had locked solely on Sorren, her brow furrowed and a frown on her face.

Chaser looked behind her, as if searching for an escape route. *My original master was a sorcerer that found my egg and hatched me. He died when I was young, though, and since a dragon's growth is tied to the nurture they receive from their hatchers, I'm stuck like this. Forever.* The bitterness in her words was unmistakable.

"You are absolutely incredible," Sorren said with as much reverence as the most ardent of worshipers. "You look like a thunderstorm. And you can *talk*! I thought your kind were extinct, but..." he babbled on for some time, not leaving a single detail of Chaser's form and beauty—the perfect specimen of a great dragon, apparently—out of his shower of words. Chaser at first appeared bewildered, but Aspen saw that quickly change to fondness and a hint of embarrassment.

Aspen's unease lessened as well. The more the boy talked, the more secure she felt in that he truly meant them no harm. And, if she was honest with herself, she didn't have the energy for a fight, anyway. So, she sat down again and watched the exchange.

Eventually, Chaser gently flicked the tip of her tail on Sorren's ear. *I thank you for your high praise, little one,* she said. *But I believe the rest of your kind are waiting for some answers.*

"Oh." Sorren pulled his blanket tighter around himself, a look of trepidation creeping onto his face as he turned to face Aspen and the others. "You're right." He sat, settling himself at the edge of their circle, and looked at them expectantly, as if waiting for their questions. He tucked his blanket until the only part of his body showing was his head.

Aspen glanced at Styrax and Ash to see if they had anything to say first. Styrax just watched on with interest, but Ash continued to stare at Sorren with knitted eyebrows, face drawn in concentration.

"Ash?" Aspen asked quietly.

Ash didn't look at her, but waved her off.

Aspen compressed her lips with concern, but supposed she owed Ash some time to her own thoughts. She turned to Sorren. "You said you know what happened to—" her tongue stopped the word before she could speak it. "...Tristan?" She said instead.

Sorren tucked his knees to his chest and blew out a long sigh. "I can take an educated guess, based on what happened to me. After Laire said...That word—"

"*Betliaoter,*" Laire snapped.

Sorren flinched like Laire had struck him. He kept his eyes shut for a moment, breathing deeply, his face white. After a few moments, he opened his eyes again. "Yes, that one," he said, pointedly not looking at the captured general. "Did Tristan collapse like I did?"

Aspen nodded.

"Was he ever awake and alert after that? Or has he been unconscious this whole time?"

"He was awake for a while," Aspen said, if her hazy, dream-like recollection of the events was anything to go off. "That's actually how we got here. He handled most of it."

Sorren looked as if he had expected that answer. "And when he was awake, did he mention anything strange about an old self or forgotten memories or anything like that?"

Ash and Styrax both looked at Aspen, mouth agape and eyes wide.

"Yes," Aspen said slowly, not looking at the others. Her heart hammered in her throat. So that *hadn't* just been a dream. He really was—he really believed himself to be—

Sorren nodded, far too knowing for someone his age. He swallowed, as if hesitant to share his next few words. "The same thing happened with me." He pulled on his earlobe, where a ragged hole was healing. "Sedick specializes in mind magic. When I was younger, he cursed me and took my memories because I disobeyed him. I think he probably did something similar to Tristan."

Styrax leaned forward, hands clasped between his knees. His golden eyes were wide. "Tristan had a cursed ring around his neck."

"I had a stud in my ear." Sorren rubbed at the spot again. "On top of wiping our memories, the spell also made us see monsters that weren't there and lash out at anyone Sedick deemed a threat." He glanced at Laire again before looking away quickly, hunching his shoulders like a shield. "It also had a failsafe if we ever broke most of its effects. An 'obliterate' spell that would eat our minds if we didn't obey." He ran his hands through his hair, a small, sad smile on his face. "It looks like Sedick's not as powerful as he thinks, though, because I remember who I am." He gave Aspen an earnest look. "I hope Tristan was the same?"

Before Aspen could answer, Ash joined the conversation.

"Who are you, then?" she asked Sorren, her arms crossed tight over her chest.

Sorren's smile melted off his face. "My name is Sorren. I'm...Well, Sedick is, unfortunately, my father."

Ash was out of her seat in an instant. Her fists and arms were tensed so tightly at her side that Aspen saw the scars from the time she had spent as Sedick's prisoner years ago. Ash had only escaped because...

The realization plowed into Aspen as fiercely as the storm outside.

Ash rushed to Sorren with a barely repressed sob. "You amazing boy! I thought I would never see you again!"

It was Aspen's turn to gape. No. It couldn't be.

Sorren looked just as stunned and mildly terrified. He extricated himself from Ash's grip, his face white. "I think you have me confused with—"

"Do you remember rescuing an elf from Sedick's dungeons?" Ash asked before he could finish.

He looked at her, still uncomprehending. "That's why Sedick cursed me. How did you…" His eyes widened with realization, and he looked nearly ready to faint. "*Ash?*"

Ash nodded slowly, her eyes brimming with tears. "I'm sorry I couldn't go back for you that day. I tried."

Aspen choked back her own emotion. She remembered that day—remembered Ash stumbling out of that estate, battered and bleeding, with a haunted look in her eyes. Ash never told Aspen what Sedick had done to her in there, but Aspen knew the only reason Ash had made it out was because of one brave young boy. Sedick's son.

Someone cleared their throat in the doorway. "Did someone die?"

A jolt of warm lightning raced along Aspen's spine at the voice, causing gooseflesh to appear across her skin. She turned, unable to draw in a full breath. He stood there, balanced on the fine line of possibilities. Could Tristan really be…?

Ash and Styrax looked between him and Aspen expectantly, not saying anything.

He furrowed his brow. "Did *I* die?"

"I think you're about to if you don't come over here and explain yourself," Styrax said in a tone obviously meant to lighten the mood.

He took a seat, hovering on the edge as if waiting to flee at a moment's notice. "What did I do?" He caught sight of Aspen, and the worry lines on his face smoothed with relief. "I'm happy to see you up and about."

Aspen nodded mutely.

"Well, apparently, you went and found your memories without telling me—the person who told you to go find them in the first place—about it," Styrax said, putting his fists on his hips. "So, to say I'm peeved is an understatement."

"Oh, that." He smiled sheepishly, but there was a hint of trepidation in his eyes. "My name's actually Ro, and I guess I'm a prince? Or something?"

"Is that all? I thought you were going to be someone important." Styrax said with a grin.

Aspen touched her fingers to the floor, making sure it was still solid beneath her as her vision spun. He wasn't a dream—wasn't a phantom that would disappear the next time she closed her eyes. He was as real as the breath in her lungs. Ro had returned.

SIX

A few days later, Chaser returned to the inn. They had all just sat down to breakfast, but Sorren was on his feet in moments when he saw the dragon, an unabashed grin on his face. He fished a plate of eggs off the table and laid them at Chaser's feet. She gave him a gentle cuff over the ear with the tip of her tail.

Thank you, little one, she said. She turned to the room at large. *The storm has abated, and Queen Holly is accepting petitioners.*

Aspen didn't realize she had moved until she was on her feet, her fingers gripping the edge of the table until her knuckles turned white. Anxiety rushed through her like a great ocean, drenching her in cold sweat.

Thistle hustled over, wiping flour and grease on her apron. "Now, you just hold on a moment," she said, her face stern. "Healer Fungus may be skilled."

Styrax covered a snort of laughter by coughing into a napkin.

Thistle proceeded as if she hadn't heard him. "But he can't replace a good meal and *rest* for recovery. Audiences with Queen

Holly will be open for several days. The *least* you can do is finish your breakfast."

Aspen's stomach roiled at the thought of food. It was true, the elven healer with the unfortunate name had done an excellent job in stitching her up and speeding the healing process along—although it still ached to move and sent her head spinning if she bumped one of her injuries—but, as the thought of finally meeting with the queen loomed over her, her vision swam as if all the wounds had reopened. Aspen still couldn't help but feel she had doomed the mission by being there.

"We've waited too long already," Aspen said, her voice hoarse. No matter her fears, she had to see the mission through to the end. "We need to see the queen *now*."

Thistle pursed her lips. "Well, you'll at least need to wait for a Queen's Guard to be summoned, and—"

I've already done that, Chaser said as she devoured her plate of eggs and sized up the rest of the breakfast on the table. *A guard should be here in the next few minutes.*

Aspen cast Chaser a grateful look. Thistle scowled, but didn't voice any further protest.

"Ash, will you—" Aspen began.

But Ash was already on her feet before Aspen had time to finish. "This is the *one* exception I will make to you refusing to eat," she said with a wink.

Aspen gave her a relieved smile.

"I'll come, too," Ro said, stuffing a few bites of buttered bread in his mouth first.

Styrax let out a heavy, long-suffering sigh as he drew the leftover food closer to him. "I *suppose* I'll stay here to watch over the lunatic general and his creepy sword," he said, helping himself to a plate of sugared fruit.

Ash smirked at him. "We appreciate your noble sacrifice."

"Yes, yes, I know. You can write ballads about me later," he said with his mouth full.

A fair warning, Chaser said before they left. Sorren had tucked himself underneath one of her wings and was also helping himself to a plate of breakfast. *Even though you have been Thorn and Thistle's guests, not everyone will be as accepting of outsiders. Most of the Fens believe outsiders bring barbaric ideas and prejudices. Do not expect the same level of hospitality that you have received here.*

Aspen nodded her thanks and headed out of the inn with Ro and Ash in tow.

As Chaser had promised, a Queen's Guard met them just outside and led them toward the center of the Fens. He said nothing, but maintained a perpetual scowl on his face, also as Chaser had promised.

As they walked, Ro lagged, gaping at the village and deep-colored leaves as Aspen walked beside Ash, lost in thought.

Aspen hated diplomacy. Mincing words, stroking egos, nurturing frail vines of 'friendships' that could choke her at any moment—it all felt so under-handed, so mentally treacherous. Although a battle-field promised more threat to life and body, she preferred the simplicity of its politics. If someone came at her, weapons swinging, she'd found an enemy to cut down. If a government leader approached her, slinging words often sharper than blades, she had to smile and endure in the off-chance they might supply her a minor favor at some point. Sometimes, she almost preferred a sword to the face.

The guard led them inside a large central garden. "Wait here," he said before leaving them. No explanation. No 'please'. He simply left. Aspen tried not to clench her jaw.

"Hand off the sword, Aspen. You look like you're about to decapitate someone," Ash said with a long sigh.

Aspen hadn't realized she'd wrapped her hand around the pommel at her side. She released it and forced her knuckles to relax. "I hate all this 'hurry and wait'," she said, the words a low, frustrated growl in the back of her throat. "If it had been a Council of Elders, we wouldn't have had to wait for *days* through all this pomp and circumstance."

Ash splayed her hands. "What can we do, though? We're not exactly in a position to argue."

"That's the problem. We *should* be," Aspen said with a frustrated growl. "That treaty is binding, no matter if they have a Council of Elders or a queen. If they try to say otherwise, I'll shove it down their queen's throat."

Ash snorted. "Don't you think you're in *enough* trouble with our council?"

Ro snorted and grinned at Aspen. "That doesn't surprise me one bit."

Aspen rolled her eyes. "When have I *not* been on their last thread of sanity?"

"Making it a habit doesn't make it any better," Ash said.

"Makes it more entertaining, though." A thread of a smile pulled on Aspen's mouth, despite her anxiety. "Did you see Inula's last fit?"

Ash grinned. "You think I would miss that? It's my favorite part of her charming personality."

Aspen chuckled. The conversation let some of the tension melt from her shoulders. For the moment, she could tune out the thoughts of how horribly the meeting could turn out.

The guard returned, looking just as dour as before. "You three, follow me," he barked.

"That's something I've loved about traveling," Ash said under her breath. "The locals are always so warm and inviting."

Aspen smirked, grateful again that Ash and Ro had agreed to come with her. They had an uncanny knack for easing her anxiety— at least Ash did. Ro could often be a comfort as well, when he wasn't attracting danger at every turn.

The moment she thought about it, though, the weight of her mission settled more heavily on her chest, making it difficult to breathe. This negotiation *had* to be successful. Not only for the Golden Grove, but for Ro, too. If the Golden Grove fell, he would lose a foundational piece of the Rebellion and could never reclaim the throne. Hundreds would die if they failed. If *she* failed.

Aspen straightened her spine and dug her nails into her palms. She would smile and mince words and put on an act with the best of the diplomats before she allowed herself to fail again.

The walk to the throne room would have been beautiful if Aspen didn't have other things to worry about. The thick, twisted trees around them carved intricate patterns around the village huts. Warm firelight caught the edges of the deep, black leaves above, speckled with white that looked like stars. Vines with silver flowers —similar to the ones around the free-standing arch Aspen had gotten the entrance key from in Lorate—dripped from the over-hanging branches and curled around the edges of every pathway. The Midnight Fens had always contended with the Golden Grove in its otherworldly elegance.

The throne room laid nestled deep into the heart of the largest tree. Opulent carvings swept away from the entrance, alive with bright-colored lichen and flowers. Aspen recognized a depiction of the legend of the elven races' birth—the earth goddess cradling the leaves of a majestic tree and breathing life into each—but after that, the images blended into a history not her own. She caught brief glimpses of a phoenix as well.

Though the carvings were immaculate, the opulence hinted at arrogance and entitlement, and Aspen found dread taking deeper root in her stomach. She didn't feel equal to dealing with either at the moment. Her back cried out, her other wounds ached and sapped the strength from her, and a headache throbbed behind the bridge of her nose. *Sleep,* her body begged, despite the several days of rest she had already given it.

"How are you holding up?" Ro asked quietly, sidling up next to her.

She inwardly winced, cursing herself for being so transparent. She couldn't show that type of weakness to the queen. "I'll be much better when this is all over."

Ro gave her a skeptical look, but she strode a little ahead of him to avoid further questions.

The guard swung open a single, unassuming door and ushered the group inside. He motioned for them to stay put and then approached a simple raised dais where a woman wearing a soft jerkin and light-colored trousers sat. Other than a circlet made of braided tree branches settled across her forehead, she wore no other adornments.

"My queen," the gate keeper intoned, kneeling. "These are the outsiders Thorn and Thistle spoke to you of. They wish to interrupt our new era of peace—"

The queen waved him to silence. "That is enough, Currant. I would like to speak to them first, before I make any judgments." She leaned forward on her throne and waved Aspen, Ash, and Ro closer to her. "Please, what brought you so far from home? Currant tells me you are from the Golden Grove."

"It is the Golden Grove that has brought us here," Ash said. She hesitated a moment, as if unsure how to address the woman, before settling on, "Your majesty." She gave a slight bow before continuing. "We have received troubling reports that King Osmen plans to deploy an attack-force against us."

Currant sneered at them. "Surely the *mighty* Golden Grove can quickly dispatch of one measly attack force."

Aspen's tongue pressed against the back of her teeth as she fought the urge to snap back. Instead, she gave herself a few breaths and answered coolly, "The Golden Grove is nothing more than a farming village at the moment, one of mostly children and the aging. The able-bodied have been on the front lines for the past ten years."

The queen leaned back in her chair and rested a finger on her lips, her expression unreadable. "Do you not have a standing force from the Rebellion there? Why have you not gone to General Dallowyn for help?"

"General Dallowyn is the one that sent us to you for help, your majesty," Ash said. "There is a small army stationed at the Golden Grove, but it is not enough to push back a full-scale attack."

The queen folded her hands in her lap, one thumb trailing over her wrist. "Who heads the army at the Golden Grove?"

Ash glanced at Aspen. "General Shadowalker, one of the best generals the Prince's Rebellion has at their disposal."

Currant tsked.

"Hush, Currant." The queen tilted her head at Aspen and Ash. "I have heard of this General Shadowalker. Certainly an...*odd* choice for a name, but they are quite formidable. If they do not feel they can handle this force on their own, then it must be a dire situation." She straightened, her head held regally. "What is it you ask of me and my people?"

Aspen felt some of the weight lift off her chest. Despite her earlier doubts, this queen seemed like a reasonable individual. Perhaps they would have an easier time at success than she initially expected. "We've come to request your help," she said. "As many fighters as you can spare."

Currant guffawed. "You think we can even spare you *one*? We are in the middle of securing our queen's status, and you—"

"Currant, one more outburst from you, and I will throw you from this room!" Queen Holly snapped.

Currant's eyes bugged out of his skull, as if he still had more to say, but the queen fixed him with a hard stare. He seethed for a few moments, the color high in his cheeks, before he bowed his head and retreated to a corner where he skulked and glared at Aspen. She caught Ro glaring right back at the guard, moving so that he blocked most of Aspen from Currant's view.

The queen sighed, only loud enough for Aspen, Ro, and Ash to hear. "Please forgive him," she said. "He believes he is being protective, but makes a nuisance of himself more often than not." She brushed a stray piece of hair behind her ears and leaned forward. "How many soldiers does the treaty call for?"

"The original asks for five-hundred," Aspen said, "but if that feels too steep a price, I am willing to negotiate."

The queen nodded, her forefinger resting on her chin. "May I see the document?"

"Of course." Aspen nodded to Ash, who dug through her knapsack and produced the parchment scroll, which she handed to the queen.

Queen Holly took it and perused it. She nodded to herself a few times, before rolling it up and handing it back to Ash. "Everything seems in order. Five-hundred is what the Elders promised, and five-hundred is what you'll receive."

Aspen had to force her jaw closed to keep it from dropping to the floor. The world stopped as the queen's words echoed in her ears. All this way—the *fight* they had had to get here—and *finally* something had gone their way on the first try. Aspen narrowly avoided collapsing with relief. Instead, she settled for a deep bow. "Thank you, your majesty," she said, her voice shaking.

The queen chuckled. "You seem surprised."

Aspen winced, the color rising to her cheeks. They hadn't even officially sealed the deal yet, and she was already offending their new ally. "My apologies. Our journey here has been an arduous one, and I believe that is what we have come to expect."

Queen Holly raised a knowing eyebrow. "And that has nothing to do with the fact that Loralan systematically abuses you for being half-bloods?"

Currant coughed and rubbed his nose. A small smile tugged at the corners of Aspen's mouth. She liked this queen more and more by the minute.

"If ever you two tire of being made to feel unworthy of simply existing, you may find a home with me," the queen said. "The last princess of the phoenix clan taught acceptance of all, and I intend to impart those teachings throughout my kingdom." She extended her left hand to Aspen. "Now then, shall we seal this agreement?"

Still weak in the knees with relief, Aspen moved to shake the queen's hand.

Currant gasped in outrage. "You will *not* touch my queen's hand with anything but your own bare palm," he said, his hand on his weapon. "There have been too many attempts on my queen's life, and I will not have you sliding out poison or a blade when she has offered nothing but transparency and kindness."

Aspen glanced at the bracer she wore—the partial glove sown to it. She had almost forgotten about it and the mark it hid. She looked to the queen, praying she would dismiss Currant the same way she had all his other requests.

The queen rolled her eyes, but sighed. "Unfortunately, he is correct. This is a danger we have had to navigate recently within our kingdom."

Aspen's mouth ran dry. She tried not to let her fear show in her eyes. *No. No, please no. Do not let this end here.* "The Golden Grove thanks you for your aid." Aspen couldn't get enough breath behind the words. Her heart pounded against her ribs, remembering all the stares—all the *hatred*—when people discovered the mark on her hand. "Your help will save thousands."

Ash tensed behind her. Ro shifted on the balls of his feet, as if he, too, could feel the new wave of tension.

Aspen removed her bracer, revealing the dark, ugly pattern at the base of her thumb, flashing with names only her eyes could see—Will, Tarragon, Ro, Abran—and a single scar she had dug into her own flesh. She tried to reach for the queen's hand again. *Please. Think of all those you will save.*

Queen Holly's eyes locked onto the mark. It took her two beats before any registration showed on her face. All at once, the welcoming smile ripped off her face. She leapt to her feet as if she had been bitten. Her chair toppled behind her, and she looked at Aspen's mark with petrified eyes, her face white. "*Five...*" she whispered. "I've never seen so many..." she covered her mouth as if to vomit and then turned to Aspen with accusing eyes. "You *are* a shadow walker, in more than just name."

SEVEN

Aspen couldn't feel her limbs. Her heart hammered in her throat. "Your majesty, *please*—"

Currant was on her in a second, blade drawn at her throat as he placed himself in front of his queen. "You *dare* approach my queen with your coward's mark? You dare ask for our *help* with such a sin?"

The world was crumbling around Aspen. She saw flashes of images—bodies littering the ground. Golden trees on fire. Sightless eyes staring at her. Condemning her for being their downfall. Her hands shook. "No, please. I will leave. I will go. Ash can—"

"You should *never* have come to begin with," the queen said, eyes burning. She pointed a finger at the treaty, her magic flaring powerful and deadly around her. The protective charm around the parchment dissolved, and a moment later, the parchment disintegrated to dust. "Guards!" the queen snapped. "Remove these interlopers and tell General Dallowyn that he and his rebellion can *rot* for this act of open hostility."

"No. No!" Aspen's whole body shook. Not another failure. Not again. She could not have the weight of any more deaths on her head. *Would* not. "No, you are condemning the Golden Grove to death! You cannot do that to them! I will leave! You will never see me again! Do *not* kill them this way, *please!*"

"They should have thought of that before putting their faith in a *coward*," she said with a snarl. She spat on Aspen's cheek.

"No!" Aspen felt her insides shatter, the word stuttering brokenly out of her on repeat. She hardly felt the dribble dripping down her cheek—hardly saw the guards coming at her with weapons drawn—until Ro roared and lifted her bodily, whisking her way before a spear impaled her abdomen.

"What is wrong with you people?" He took several steps back, Aspen still clutched tightly to him. Ash followed them, bow drawn. "We came to you on good faith!"

"Good faith does not send a murderer to our doorstep!" the queen cried.

The words shot like arrows through Aspen. Memories of the Council of Elders swam in her eyes—Inula's words resurfacing.

Aspen Tanner is sentenced to the only punishment suitable for cowards of the highest order.

The guards swung at Ro, tearing a piece of his tunic before he lunged out of the way.

That knocked Aspen's stupor aside. "No!" she shouted, this one full of righteous venom. She flung herself from Ro's arms and drew her sword on the guards, spreading herself protectively in front of Ro. "Do what you will to me anytime you like," she said through clenched teeth, her sword arm trembling with rage. "But you have just drawn weapons on the heir to Loralan, and that I will not let stand!"

The room froze, thunderstruck.

Ro took Aspen by the wrist. "We have to go. Now."

They fled down the steps and back into the main square, Ash hot on their heels. A bell rang out across the square, counting the number of enemies with each toll.

One.

Doors flew open as they ran past.

Two.

Elves poured out from their homes with shouts of alarm. The lights from inside blurred past as they ran.

Three.

Onlookers caught sight of Ro, Aspen, and Ash. They called out to their neighbors before giving chase. The shouts and footsteps grew in number with every second.

Four.

Arrows flew past Aspen's ears, thudding into the ground around their feet. Ash fired back without breaking stride. She didn't hit any of the elves, but they faltered in their steps. Blades scraped against leather as they were drawn.

Five.

Aspen's heart hammered in time with the footsteps pursuing them. Five rings, signaling five enemies. Aspen, Ro, Styrax, Ash, and Sorren. And all of it was her fault. Her coward's mark throbbed. Her back burned. She was a curse to herself and everyone around her. She had to get them all out.

"This seems oddly familiar!" Ro said beside her. "Do you always make your exits being chased by an angry mob?"

Aspen knew he was trying to lighten the mood, but her fear only deepened. With the mob behind them, there was no way out of the Fens except through the main doors they had originally entered. And she had no doubt Thistle and Thorn would want nothing to do with them after the uproar they had started.

"Ro, I don't know if we can —"

A roar pierced through the crowd, and Chaser leapt in from above, batting elves away with her tail and outstretched wings, Sorren whooping with glee on her back.

Get on! she said.

Ro hoisted Aspen onto Chaser before Aspen could protest and leapt on behind her. Ash vaulted on behind them both, spitting curses and firing more warning shots at the approaching elves.

"What about Styrax and Laire?" Ro asked.

They're out of the Fens. I got them out as soon as I heard the bell.

"Why aren't *you* with them?" Ash asked Sorren.

Sorren grinned at her, his eyes wild. "Have *you* ever passed up the opportunity to ride a dragon?"

Before Ash could respond, Chaser bunched her legs beneath her and jumped straight into the air, her wings straining mightily to get them airborne. The elves shouted below them and drew their bows to fire, but Thorn and Thistle ran out in front of them.

"Don't shoot Chaser!" they cried.

That hesitation gave Chaser enough time to pull out of firing range, and they were off.

Aspen shook, adrenaline and fear overtaking her. The world spun, and she couldn't get her eyes to focus. Failed. She'd failed. No one was coming to help the Golden Grove. All that work, planning, and hope crumbled around her. It had all failed. And she was to blame. For everything.

"Aspen?" Ro asked quietly. Tentatively. "What was that all about back there?"

But she couldn't bring herself to speak—couldn't even look him in the eyes.

His arm tightened around her and he touched Chaser's shoulder. "Can you take us somewhere they won't follow us?" he asked. "I get the feeling Thorn and Thistle won't be able to keep them away for long."

Chaser was silent for a moment. *I know of a place,* she said slowly. *No one from the Fens will dare set foot in it.*

"Sounds perfect," Ro said.

I would not be so hasty, she retorted. *The place is...Unwell.*

"Just our kind of place," Ash grumbled

"We can sort that out when we get there," Ro said.

Chaser was silent again. *Very well,* she said finally. *The elves call it the forest that never sleeps. I will take you there, but do not expect me to stay.* A shudder ran through her. *Some things are better left untouched.*

CHAPTER

EIGHT

L eaving the Fens was like plunging into a nightmare. Chaser barreled through the inn and shouldered open the large entrance doors. As soon as they were outside, Aspen's entire body froze. The storm had cleared out, exposing the barren wasteland in its place. The ever-churning waves of the scattered lakes glittered beneath them, reminding Aspen of the flash of weapons. Without having to look, she knew when Chaser flew over where Ro had fallen beneath a mace, and then the spot where her brothers had fallen. She could see the crimson blood stains in her mind's eye from all the soldiers she had slain. Her body shook with the memories. It was only fitting that her newest failure led her back here. They always did.

Ro stiffened behind her, as if he had a similar reaction to seeing the Dragon Scales. She didn't say anything, praying that he wouldn't ask her about it. She couldn't tell him. Not yet.

Ro didn't ask her any questions about it, and Aspen silently thanked whatever gods would listen that they had decided to spare her for once.

Styrax waited on the edge of the Scales with Laire in tow. When she saw Styrax, Ash waved.

"Chaser, let me off here. I'll get a little weight off your back," Ash said.

Chaser gratefully swooped low, and Ash joined Styrax. He conjured a floating water platform and followed the dragon as she continued to fly. He couldn't match Chaser's speed, but they were at least able to follow at a distance.

Aspen lost track of how far they flew. The heavy darkness of her failure settled heavily on her shoulders. The only thing that kept her grounded in the present was the wind coursing through her hair and the distant smell of salt from the Dragon Scales coating her lips.

Chaser banked her wings and glided in circles to a clearing several miles off from the Dragon Scales.

This is as far as I take you, she said, her scales twitching as if she had ants beneath them. *My binding won't let me go much farther from the Fens.*

"Binding?" Sorren asked as he slid off her back.

Before the man that hatched me died, he magically bound me to the Fens so that they would have to take me in. She pawed at the ground, her talons digging furrows in the dirt. *I don't believe he anticipated it being this...permanent.*

Sorren's face fell, his eyes full of understanding. He hugged Chaser's neck. "I'm sorry," he said. "If I ever figure out a way to break those bindings, I'll come back for you."

Chaser stood stock still for a moment, as if unsure what to do with the affection. But then she closed her eyes, and something close to a purr rumbled from her throat. *You are very kind,* she said. She pulled away from Sorren and pointed her muzzle at a forest in the distance. *Your destination is there. Be forewarned, it is not for the faint of heart.* She looked at Aspen as if she could sense just how frail her spirit was at the moment.

Aspen forced her eyes to focus and mutely nodded her thanks.

Chaser spread her wings and took off just as Styrax landed with

Ash and Laire. Sweat beaded his forehead, and his chest heaved. "Are we stopping here to rest?" he asked. "Thank Sister *Earth*, these two were *heav*—"

Ash cuffed him over the ear.

"You're right, you're right." He bent over to suck in more breath. "Sorry. I, of course, didn't mean *you*."

Ash arched an eyebrow. "You said 'these two'."

Styrax grimaced. "Ah, yes. I did, didn't I?"

Aspen didn't wait to hear the end of the squabble. Limbs shaking, unable to look any of them in the face, she marched toward the forest Chaser had indicated.

As they drew closer, she heard the rush of trees rustling in the distance, which only grew with every step. When they reached the forest, the voices drowned Aspen, tumbling and breaking over each other like waves in a storm. The force of them beat against her chest and nearly drove her to her knees. Fear. There was so much *fear*. And anger, and a pain so visceral it made stars dance behind Aspen's eyelids. She glanced at the others. Ash's hands were clamped over her ears. Styrax was green as he watched the forest grimly. Sorren's eyes darted around as if trying to hone in on at least *someone*, and Ro just stood with his mouth agape.

Laire, though, screamed like a man on fire.

"Get me *out* of this place!" He bellowed. "Take me away or kill me! I will not stay here. I cannot!"

"You will stay wherever we put you until we find something else to do with you," Aspen snapped. She stormed away, leaving him writhing and moaning manically.

"Aspen, wait!" Ro called after her.

She ignored him. She ignored Ash's worried eyes on her—Sorren and Styrax's unspoken questions—and melted into the forest, her mind as loud and agonized as the surrounding trees.

What was she going to do now? She had failed. She had failed again and people were going to die. *Her* people. The Rebellion. The Golden Grove. All of it would be snuffed out, and it would be her fault. Queen Holly's hate-filled look had burned itself into her brain. She deserved it. She deserved all of it, but it didn't make it burn any less like fire in her throat and behind her eyes. The forest's cacophony of voices shouted more accusations at her.

Aspen's head swam and stars danced in her vision as her breaths came out more shallow—more panicked. She put her hand around her throat, feeling the phantoms of Laire's fingers from when he nearly strangled her. She leaned against a tree to get her balance and calm herself down. The moment her skin brushed the bark, a single voice blasted through her mind as if it had been pent up for decades. She staggered away from the tree, tears that were not her own springing to her eyes. The tree shuddered forlornly, its message brushing through its leaves like claws through gravel.

Aspen clenched her jaw as she looked at the tree and heard its keening words. She may not have succeeded where she wanted to, but she could help this one last soul. She drew parchment and a quill from her knapsack and settled herself cross-legged in front of the tree. Taking a steeling breath, she put her hand back on the trunk, tendrils of magic lacing from her fingertips. The voice did not assault her this time. Instead, it was silent, bark and limbs quivering with relieved anticipation.

"*Guardian spirit.*" The silken syllables of the Ancient Tongue slipped over her tongue as her magic wound its way to her hand. "*I thank thee for preserving the memory of my kin. Relinquish thy burden. Thy work is done. I will carry their words to those they hold dear.*"

A shiver ran the length of the tree trunk like a great sigh being released. The green of Aspen's magic threaded up the bark and through the tree's limbs. The frantic phantom whispers in its leaves vanished, allowing for a single voice to manifest itself.

Why is this happening? What have we done wrong? The children! I have to get—

The voice ended abruptly—a thought cut down before it could complete itself. The sudden, torn end wrenched a hole in Aspen's heart. She wrote the words and read them back to the tree, one hand still pressed against its bark. Another sigh rippled up its trunk, its leaves finally falling silent.

"*Who?*" Aspen asked before the tree could fall dormant.

The tree's branches creaked out a slow, tired response. *Aster.*

The tree fell still and the light of Aspen's magic faded from its bark.

Aspen wrote the name down, tore off the corner of the parchment she had written on, and closed her eyes. For the moment, her mind had cleared. She knew the panic would come back eventually —it always did—but right now she had an opportunity to control *something* as the world crumbled around her. So, she went to the next whispering tree and did it all over again. And again. And again. Time vanished for her as she became entrenched in the tragedy the trees told her—the final memories of the elves that had died beneath their branches. The last vestiges of the half-blood village once known as Brahmon.

Aspen didn't know when Ro joined her, exactly, but she felt his presence as he sat and watched. She didn't acknowledge him—was too afraid of the questions he might ask—and he, in turn, said nothing. He simply followed and observed as she went from tree to tree, sitting closer to her with each new task until their shoulders and elbows brushed together.

She took the messages of dozens of trees—each a new slip of parchment filled with terrified words cut short—before she finally leaned against one of the now silent trees. Sweat dripped from her temples, and her hands shook from the strain of using so much magic. Her skin was coated in green mist. The shreds of parchment in her pocket felt like lead weights.

Ro shifted carefully so as not to disturb her. "You should rest."

"What do you think I'm doing right now?"

"This doesn't count, and you know that." He bit the inside of his cheek, his eyes getting a far-off look. He absently toyed with the grass and leaves beneath him and sighed. "Do you want to tell me what a shadow walker is?"

Aspen stiffened and sat up. Her head swam with the motion and she hunched over, eyes clenched tight against the swirling ground beneath her. "No," she said, her voice flat.

He put his hand against her back, the warm sensation of his palm near her spine helping to ground her. "I figured as much."

He grew quiet, and Aspen chanced a glance at him. He wasn't looking at her, but into the trees still spinning their tales, his face twisted into pale, grim lines. She had forgotten that Ro had grown up learning how to understand the Ancient Tongue.

"What do you hear?" she asked him.

He swallowed, his hand shaking as he balled it into a fist. "A lot of fear. Like everything's been ripped away from them." He looked at her, his blue eyes wide with grief and horror. The color had left his face. "What *is* this place?"

"Brahmon," Aspen said. Through the trees, she saw the withered, overgrown remains of houses, wells, and fences, all crouched like the corpses of ragged beasts. "Or at least what's left of it. This was a half-blood village until Osmen razed it and declared war on all the Ancient Races."

Ro knit his brow as if deep in thought. "I remember Styrax saying something. Didn't the..." He gulped. "Weren't things so bad that the women...Killed their children to spare them?"

Aspen nodded. "That's what the reports said. And the trees say much the same thing."

Ro furrowed his brow. "Why have the trees been telling you about it?"

Aspen picked up a dry leaf, crunching it delicately between her fingers. "Elves have always had a close relationship with trees. As a gift, the trees will carry the last thoughts of the elves that died beneath their branches until someone comes along to translate the words and take them to their closest surviving kin." She threw the leaf away, the brutal lines she had broken into it catching the sun. "It's supposed to be a beautiful, sacred thing. But war and brutality taint everything they touch."

Ro's frown deepened. "But Brahmon was attacked over twenty years ago. If all they needed was someone to translate their messages, then why..."

Aspen shrugged noncommittally, but the bitterness burned a hole in her chest. "No one cares that much about half bloods." She stood, not wanting to feel his pitying look on her back. "You should see if Ash has dinner ready. I'll finish up and meet you there." She left before he could say anything and settled herself to her work again. The last two trees were of an elven woman and her young son—their intermingling voices filled with the same terror each of the others had. The son asked after his father, which quickly devolved into panicked cries for help as he saw his mother with a blade. Those cries were cut short. Aspen's heart wanted to twist out of her chest as she placed the boy's parchment in her pile after writing his name. Ivan.

Her fingers trembled with exhaustion and furious sorrow as she placed her hand on the final tree, whose words sounded like shuddering, aching weeping.

I had no choice, Laire, they whispered to Aspen. *I had no choice. No choice. Oh, sweet Sister Earth, I will rot in the Pit for this. I had to do it. I had to save him from what comes next. I don't know what's come over you, but please, end it now. I can't live in a world where I have killed Ivan. Where I would have watched you do it if I hadn't. You and that wretched sword.*

Aspen nearly broke her quill in half when she realized who the voice had addressed. A deep, bitter, and molten rage seared her vision to oblivion. She almost didn't catch the shuddering, shaking name the tree spoke to her.

Anise.

CHAPTER

NINE

The camp was quiet when Ro came back—almost eerie compared to the roaring forest it had been just a few hours prior. Laire's screams had gone quiet after Ash had given him a mild sedative from her medical pack, and Styrax was watching over him. They had placed the cursed galatite sword far on the other side of the camp. Its sapphires glittered like eyes in the firelight. Sorren had curled himself into a blanket near it, dozing.

Ash looked up from her cooking fire when Ro approached, her face drawn with worry. "How is she?" Ash's attention flickered to Aspen's vague silhouette, visible through the trees.

Ro shrugged helplessly. "Not well, I don't think." He sat across from her as she continued to stir her concoction. His stomach rumbled forlornly, but Aspen's screams from the courtroom were louder in his mind. "Ash, what happened back there?"

Ash's face tightened, and she glared into her stew pot for several moments. Finally, she let out a deep sigh and set a lid over the pot while she sat. "I won't go into details, because that's Aspen's story to tell, but I can at least tell you what a shadow walker is." She lifted her sleeve to reveal a dark tattoo on her shoulder, almost identical to

Aspen's. The only difference was Ash's name scrawled inside in fine print. "This is a replica of Aspen's shadow walker mark," she said. "All of her soldiers elected to get one." She gave him a small, smug smile. "Aspen hates that we did, but since she knows she couldn't stop all of us, she just insisted that we put our names in them so someone can identify us if we fall in battle."

Ro nodded along, smiling as he imagined the barely contained rage Aspen must have felt when Ash, as usual, did what she wanted.

Ash's smile faded. "We all chose where to put our marks, but a true shadow walker's mark starts on the left hand—used for making trades and sealing vows, so that all may know what manner of person they are dealing with." She spoke as if she were reading from an old, dusty tome detailing the finer points of manure distribution—mostly emotionless, with a hint of disdain.

Ro tilted his head. "A mark 'starts' on the left hand?"

Ash pressed her lips together and traced the five curves on her tattoo. "The mark of a shadow walker is also called a Coward's Mark," she said. "Each curve represents a life that ended due to the bearer's cowardice."

An instant, explosive rage ignited in Ro, setting his face aflame. "*Aspen?*" he asked. "How could *anyone* believe that she—?"

Ash held up a hand, her own eyes burning. "Delusional people," she said. "My mother, the head of the Golden Grove's Council of Elders, to be exact."

Ro's ire died as quickly as it had flared. All the color drained from his face. "Your *mother?*"

Ash gave him a pained smile. "My mother has never been fond of half-bloods." She gestured to herself. "*Ironic*, all things considered. But, from what I understand, she has a particular hatred for Aspen. When she found something to blame her for, she jumped at the chance."

Ro splayed his hands in utter disbelief. "But what could Aspen have *possibly* done for someone to think she's a coward?"

"She's got a sword wound on her back," Laire's voice growled from the shadows. Ro and Ash both jumped, and Ro grit his teeth so hard they almost cracked.

"Enough out of you," Styrax barked at Laire. "If we wanted a washed up General's opinion, we'd ask someone else, because you're just a lunatic."

Laire ignored him, his eyes locked onto Ro's. "Scars on the back are a sure giveaway that she ran."

"*You* gave her that scar!" Ro bunched his legs beneath him and lunged, but Ash caught his arm and hauled him back. "She beat you that night, and you couldn't handle that loss, so who's the real coward?"

Laire didn't answer. Instead, his face took on the purest ghost white terror Ro had ever seen as Laire watched something past Ro's shoulder. Ro looked and saw Aspen storming through the trees, her eyes murderous and locked on Laire. Green, hazy magic swirled around her in frantic wisps, and she held two pieces of crumpled parchment in her hand.

"Aspen, what—" Ro started.

But Aspen barreled right by him.

Laire tried to retreat, but there was nowhere for him to go. "No. *No!*"

Aspen caught his shoulder and slammed him against the tree. "I come bearing the final gift from the trees meant to bring you comfort and closure," she hissed. The words burned from so much venom that it made Ro's mouth go dry.

"NO!" Laire's scream deafened Ro and made spots swim in his eyes.

Aspen opened one of the parchment pieces in her hand, reading each one to Laire as he screamed and writhed and wept. Ro's heart clenched painfully in his chest. They were the words of a small, scared child. A child that had *died.*

As soon as Aspen finished the first parchment, she opened the next one and did the same thing. As Ro watched, each syllable hit Laire like a physical blow. When she was done, she released Laire and tossed the messages at his feet. He kicked them away as if they were vipers.

"You killed your *own family*, and you call *us* the monsters?" she asked, chest heaving. "The people that hate us because of the fear Osmen has spread, I can at least understand, but you *knew better*! You knew we had nothing to do with starting this war! How many have *died* because of you?"

Blood started to fill in Laire's pale face. He blinked, and some of the madness left his eyes. Instead, black hatred took its place.

"She. Killed. My. Son!" Laire roared. "What *else* would you call monstrous if not that?" He gave her an accusatory look. "And do not begin to say you are spotless. How much blood is on your hands?"

Aspen froze at that. Ro shook his shocked stupor off and leapt to his feet, setting himself between her and Laire as a buffer before things got more out of hand. "What's going on?" he asked, wary of the righteous fury swirling in Aspen's face and the halo of magic floating around her.

Aspen didn't tear her eyes away from Laire. "The reason things got so bad in Brahmon was because most of the families had at least one member of the King's guard." Her body shook, and her fists clenched so tight that her hands turned white. "Osmen came one day and ordered them to attack their families. And they did it. Brutally and without question. The women killed their children before their fathers tore them apart." She gestured to Laire, her jaw clenched so tightly it made Ro's ache. "And he was one of them."

Ro took a step back. His heart stopped in his chest as he looked at Laire with revulsion.

Laire lunged forward, snarling and spitting like a deranged, wounded animal. "I'll kill you! I'll rip out your throat! I would *never*—!"

"Do you know how many lives you have ruined?" Aspen shouted over him. "Do you know how many people would do anything to get their family members back? The family members *you* stole?" She dumped more sheets of parchment out in front of him from her knapsack. Dozens of them. "These are people that *trusted* you. *Loved* you. And you killed them all." Ro could tell she wasn't fully speaking to Laire anymore. She rubbed the mark on her thumb. "Our choices have consequences, *general.*" She took his wife's and son's scrolls and tucked them into his tunic. "And we have to live with them."

She left as he screamed after her. Ro could only stand, frozen to the spot. It seemed Ash, Styrax, and Sorren had fallen under the same spell.

After screaming until he went hoarse, Laire sobbed, his whole body falling slack. He turned his red-rimmed eyes to Ro. "This is the kingdom you want to lead?" he asked. "One that has been left to shatter and rot?"

"I—" Ro didn't know how to answer that. His heartbeat quickened, nearly choking him as it traveled up his throat. He had Ro's memories back, but Tristan still existed within him, small and fearful. Did he want a broken kingdom? Did he want a kingdom at all?

Laire's sobs turned into low, unhinged cackles. He gave Ro a grin that threatened to pull the skin from his cheeks. "Some broken things are better left to burn."

TEN

Aspen didn't know how long it had been until Ro found her tucked away in the shell of an old barn, where she had intended to be alone. He had an uncanny knack for doing that.

She didn't acknowledge him, but watched in the distance through the rotting doors as the vengeful wrath of the Dragon Scales' storm descended back into the valley. Fingers of swirling, midnight clouds wrapped over the lakes in a vice-like grip that flashed with roiling lightning. A funnel shot up from the center, and soon the mountain of storm blotted out the distant sky. Aspen could almost feel the prickle of lightning from here. They had *survived* that. All for nothing.

Aspen had no more emotions to feel. She had expended them all. So, she just sat with hollowness swirling in her chest. Where did they go from here? She had no idea, and couldn't help feeling like she had now doomed the entire rebellion. There was no one left that could help. Dallowyn's men were several weeks away and occupied with the front lines. The other generals were the same—each assigned to their own tasks and too far to help. She knew Dallowyn should have never entrusted her as a general. Inula had been right about everything.

Ro eased into a sitting position next to her, grimacing and digging his palms into his thighs as if to rub out some knots there. He had the blue journal Aspen had gotten him tucked into his belt, as if he had come out to write.

"I thought you'd be asleep," Aspen said, hoping he'd take the hint to leave her alone. She didn't want anyone to see her this way—as a failure with no options. *Especially* not him. "You've had a long day."

Ro finished grinding the knots from his thighs and moved onto massaging his calves. "I have," he said slowly, his words compassionate but his eyes far away, almost haunted. He blinked, and his focus came back to her. He smiled a little too tightly. "But so have you."

Aspen grunted in agreement and drew her knees to her chest, leaning her head back against the wall. Ro leaned back with her, and they sat in silence.

Aspen supposed he meant it to be a comforting gesture, but her heart pounded more frantically in her ribcage as the memories she kept tucked away shook themselves free. She suspected she knew what he was there for. He wanted to know about shadow walkers. And, inevitably, that would lead him to ask about *that* night. How could he not? She would have to answer, because he deserved to know. But she didn't know what to tell him—where to *start*—or if she even *could* tell him. She wasn't sure if the words would make it past her throat.

"Aspen, today..." he said finally.

Her whole body clenched. She closed her eyes and braced herself.

"I think it's really incredible what you did for this place."

She looked at him in consternation. "What?"

He gave her one of his soft, crooked grins. "You were exhausted and worried and angry, but you still spent your time to receive those messages, something no one in twenty years had cared to do." He gave her a crooked, self-deprecating smile. "It wouldn't have been the first thing on *my* mind, at least. You're always looking after others, and I think you're amazing for it." His face grew serious. "Are you taking time for yourself, though?"

Aspen snorted to cover up her discomfort at the odd fluttering sensation in her stomach. "You sound like Ash."

He rolled his eyes and shook his head. "I'll take that as a compliment." The movements were stiff, is if he had to force them out.

Aspen looked away from him, grinding her teeth in self-hatred. There he was, hurting and still trying to figure out his life after it had crumbled around him, and he was comforting *her*. She really was useless. "Ro, a shadow walker like me's not worth your effort," she said, the words spilling out as if they had been waiting years to be said. She supposed they had, in a way.

Aspen felt Ro bristle next to her. The words he wanted to say radiated from him in their ferocity. She watched his hands ball into fists from the corner of her eye. Heard the sharp intake of breath. But, still, Aspen didn't look at him. She couldn't—couldn't see the pity in his eyes. That would be the last thing to break her.

Ro let out a long breath, his tense body relaxing with it. "Can you tell me what that phrase means?" he asked.

And there it was—the question that would lead to too many answers. Answers she didn't want to give. Answers she couldn't deny him.

Aspen ground her teeth, the guilt pressing against her spine until it felt like it might snap. She turned back to face him, hurt by the concern on his face, knowing it could turn to hatred and blame in an instant. Inula had looked at her like that. Aspen's own *mother* hadn't been able to look at her at all. The memory burned like searing iron through her heart, but she steeled herself against it. Against the possibility that she would lose someone else to the consequences of her own failures. Ro deserved to know.

"How much do you remember about the few months before you lost your memory?" she asked.

Ro furrowed his brow. "Very little. I get bits and pieces here and there, but it's still jumbled." He toyed with the silver ring around his neck, chewing the inside of his cheek. "I remember Dallowyn gave us a mission—you, me, and your brothers. After that, I don't remember much else."

Aspen exhaled. So she would have to tell him everything, then. This was going to be a long night.

"Several months before that mission, you and I weren't even soldiers yet. Gan had just told you about your birthright, my brothers were out on the front lines, and I...well..." she scratched the inside of her forearm, her shoulders hunched. "I was too eager to prove myself, too."

Ro said nothing, but leaned forward, attentive. Too attentive.

Aspen bit back the barbs she wanted to say to make him stop listening and carried on. "I found an opportunity not long after. A shade somehow forced its way into the Golden Grove and killed two children."

"Shade?" Ro asked, giving her a wry smile of apology. "That one's not even a fuzzy memory."

Aspen appreciated his attempt to lighten the mood, but her heart hurt too much. "A piece of a demon's soul," she said. The smile slipped off Ro's face. "They do their master's tasks unfailingly, and they can paralyze you with a single look. They show you the images of their previous kills in their eyes, and that fear immobilizes you."

Ro's body had grown taut, as if his breath had built up in his body and he couldn't release it. "That seems like something intimately specific to know," he said, the light of horrible recognition building in his eyes. "You went after it."

"I did," Aspen said bitterly. "No one else was doing a thing about it. Those children deserved justice, and I thought that, maybe, I could prove my worth as well."

Ro furrowed his brow, lost in thought. "But...something went wrong? Your father...?" His face went slack with grief. He put his hand over Aspen's as his mouth dropped open, his eyes wide. "Oh, Sister Earth, Aspen, your *father!*"

He looked like he wanted to hug her, but Aspen shied away from him, nodding miserably, her face tight from the strain of holding back tears. "I didn't find the shade. It found *me*. It paralyzed me—taunting me with the images of it tearing the children apart. I couldn't breathe." She placed a hand over her heart, remembering the tight, crushing pressure of terror in her chest from that day. "I knew I was going to die." She fiddled with her trembling fingers, her stunted tears choking in her throat. "But then my father was there. He knew I was going out to do something stupid and followed me. He jumped in front of me, which broke the shade's spell, and told me to run. Like a coward, I did." Her voice broke. She gripped her knees, hands shaking. "I can still hear his screams. When search parties went to find him, they...they only found pieces of him."

"Oh, Aspen, I'm—" Ro reached for her hand again, but she snatched it away.

"I wish my failures ended there, but there's more. So, *so* much more." She stood and paced around the ruined barn, arms folded tight across her chest. Before she could get the words out, though, a cry cut through the night.

"*FIRE!*"

ELEVEN

Ro was on his feet in a moment. He met eyes with Aspen.

"Go, I'm right behind," she said.

He nodded, and they ran out of the barn together. Black, acrid smoke billowed from the center of the camp, flames glowing bright and fierce against the stark outlines of the tree trunks. Ash staggered out of the smoke, dragging an unconscious Sorren. She kept glancing back into the flames as if waiting for someone to emerge.

"What happened?" Aspen bounded to her cousin, wrapped her hands around one of Sorren's shoulders, and helped drag him to safety.

"Where's Styrax?" Ro's face bathed in the orange-red light of the fire, sweat beading down his face.

"He's trying to stop the fire!" Ash waved Aspen and Ro away as they huddled around her. "Help *him*! Laire started the fire and is still in there. I'm worried he'll do something to Styrax!"

"How did Laire—" Ro began.

"Later!" Ash snapped. "Help Styrax!"

Grinding her teeth at all the damage Laire seemed capable of inflicting, Aspen ran into the smoke. Ro bounded after her.

Amidst the wash of reds and oranges and the billowing curtain of black smoke, it wasn't difficult to find the stark white glow of Styrax's magic. He stood in the crumbling ashes of what had once been the campsite, a globe of surging water encasing him. As they watched, though, it shrunk, clouds of steam crawling away from it.

"Styrax!" Ro lunged after him. Aspen hauled him back before a flaming branch crushed him as it fell.

"Stay back!" Styrax's shoulders hunched and his eyes glowed. His jaw clenched and unclenched as he reached toward his water-shield. It stopped shrinking for a moment. "He's after you two! Said something about you destroying his family?"

The words hovered over Aspen like phantoms, and she swallowed, hyper-aware of the fading bruises around her neck. Styrax had barely finished speaking before Aspen's eyes were drawn to a figure outlined by flames. He swung at her, and Aspen drew her sword just in time to parry it, her back screaming at her. Something flashed when their blades met—a jolt that rattled through her spine made her vision spin.

Laire jumped back, his eyes wide. The fire roared around him, but never touched him. Aspen wouldn't have seen him at all if it weren't for the fact that all the surrounding light vanished—drawn into the bone white sword at his side, never to be released.

"You should have killed me when you had the chance," Laire's voice, soft and menacing, somehow carried over the flames. The sword throbbed with a grayish light, and his eyes reflected it.

Aspen glanced at her sword, and her face blanched. A single chip along the blade's edge—an edge she had never had to sharpen— flashed in the firelight. It felt like her brothers' promise had been torn from her. It was the Dragon Scales all over again. For the *third* time. She couldn't let him get the upper hand again. "What have you done, Laire?"

"Freed myself from the ghosts of my past." He kicked over a piece of what had once been a cottage roof covered in wisteria. Aspen followed his gaze and realized that the flames burned the hottest over every remnant of Brahmon structures.

Laire looked up at her, his eyes inhuman. "You will be next. I will take everything from you—your friends, your home, your family— and then I will take your life."

"We've already determined your threats don't work." Aspen's lip curled into a smirk she didn't feel. "I am still very much alive after three attempts, at least."

"It's not a threat." Laire clenched his sword and held it up to the firelight, caressing it like he would a beloved pet. "It's a promise." He turned his glittering, wild look at Ro. "You'd better keep her close, boy, before she's taken from you forever."

"You're not taking anything from me again!" Ro's whole body tensed as tight as a bow-string. Before Aspen could stop him, he charged after Laire.

"Ro, STOP!" Aspen tried to shout at him, her heart jumping into her throat. She moved to run after him, but Laire vanished into the smoke before either could reach him. Ro pulled up short and whirled to Aspen, his eyes wild. But then his jaw went slack in horror.

"Aspen! Get Styrax!" He pointed behind her.

Aspen turned to look just as the last bit of Styrax's protective shield evaporated. With a gasp, he collapsed, ashes swirling around him.

Aspen cursed. She looked one more time for Laire, but he was well and truly gone. But Aspen never trusted her luck. "Stay close to me!" she told Ro before running to Styrax, who was pale and sweating and nearly unconscious.

"Fire and...Water," he mumbled. "Not a great mix."

"You call *me* the idiot?" Ro asked. Aspen could tell that his mind was still on Laire, his breath heaving in his chest. But he gave her a single look, and some of the ire in his face smoothed over. He nodded once to Aspen and hauled one of Styrax's arms over his shoulder.

Aspen grabbed the other, and together they ran out as the last remnants of Brahmon burned behind them.

"By the Architects, I thought you all *burned*!" Ash waited for them on the far edge of the burning forest, across a small stream where the fire couldn't reach. She had paced a haphazard track in the surrounding grass. Sorren was just starting to stir at her side.

"Is Styrax all right?" she asked, her voice a few pitches higher than normal.

"He's alive," Ro responded. "The heat got to him, though." They laid him out on the grass, and Ash promptly dumped the entirety of her waterskin over him.

He started awake, spluttering. "What was *that* for?" he asked before he saw the look on Ash's face. "I mean, thank you?" he hastily amended.

"Stop giving me heart-attacks!" Ash smacked him on the shoulder and then glowered at Aspen. "*All* of you!"

Sorren groaned. His hand immediately flew to his head, and he sat up, wincing. He swayed a little as he blinked at all of them. When he got his bearings and saw the fire in the distance, his eyes grew wide. "The sword did all of *that*?"

They all looked at him in consternation.

"Sword?" Ro asked slowly.

Sorren nodded, then winced and rubbed his eyes. "I...I think the sword talks to Laire," he said. "When I was traveling with him, he'd mutter in his sleep to it. And tonight, while Styrax and Ash were making dinner, Laire was saying all sorts of nonsense to it." He blew out a long breath. "I tried to get him to stop because it sounded like he was using warlock words, but then, before I knew what happened, the sword just flew across the clearing to him."

"It *flew*?" Aspen's eyes widened with horror, and she rubbed the scar on her back as a shudder ran down her spine. She already had enough nightmares about the sword as it was.

"I tried to stop it." Sorren shrunk away from them as if expecting to be beaten. "But it cut him loose, and then he slammed me into a tree. That's all I remember."

Ash hugged him and inspected his head for injuries. His body relaxed at her touch.

"That must have been when the cooking fire got out of control," Styrax chimed in. "It leapt up like some angry beast and started burning the ruins. Obviously, it spread." He rested his forearms on his knees but winced as he brushed the raw, burned flesh there. "I stayed behind to try to put the fire out, and here we are." He looked at Sorren dubiously. "Does the sword really *talk* to him, though?"

"It's supposed to steal souls," Aspen pointed out. "So stranger things have happened."

A shudder ran through Styrax. "I don't like how easily horrifying things are drawn to us."

"Agreed." Aspen folded her arms and surveyed the group. "We can't stay here. We don't know where Laire went, and if he's talking to a soul-stealing sword, I don't necessarily want to find out."

"Where do you want me to go?" Sorren didn't look any of them in the eyes, his shoulders hunched close as he seemed to make himself as small as possible.

Aspen tilted her head at him. "What do you mean?"

"Well, I'm not exactly one of your group, am I? I just got tacked on because Sedick is a—" He clapped a hand over his mouth before he could finish the sentence, looking apologetically at Ash and Aspen.

Ash smirked. "We all know what he is. No need to dance around the subject." She ruffled Sorren's hair. "I think you're stuck with us for the time being, if you want to be."

Sorren looked ready to cry tears of relief.

"If we can't stay here, and the Fens aren't an option anymore, what do we do from here?" Ro asked Aspen.

The entire group looked at her as one, and the weight of their trust nearly smothered her. She had failed them so often. She couldn't keep leading them—not if the results were the same as they had always been for her. Defeat and death. "We lost our supplies in the fire, and are out of most of our other options," she said slowly, trying not to let her doubt flood her words. She turned to Ro. "You're going to be the leader of this kingdom one day. What do *you* think we should do?"

Ro's face blanched. He took one step back and cleared his throat, letting out a strained laugh. "How about let's wait until I have a crown on my head before I start making decisions?"

Aspen nodded, but her confidence still shrunk in her gut. "All right, then. There's no sense in trying to find help anywhere else. Everyone is too far away, so it's down to us. With one last long push, we'll make it to the Golden Grove entrance by tomorrow and can take the next steps from there."

"Lead on, General," Ro said.

Aspen smiled at him, but it was a hollow thing. She had no next steps. No plan. They had all placed their faith in the wrong person.

TWELVE

He stayed in that burning forest, the heat blistering his skin, until everything turned to ash and the fire was nothing but a bed of burning embers. Nothing was left.

He stayed there, letting the ashes and smoke blow into his face and reveling in the destruction they came from, until he smelled the tang of sweat carried across the breeze. With a grin, and the sword clenched in his hand, he wandered, following the smell to his prey.

The sun hung low on the horizon when he found the camp of soldiers. They milled about, silent and disciplined, and wore armor that bent and shifted with the light and terrain around them—the perfect camouflage. If it hadn't been for their smell, he never would have found them. They were all young, but carried themselves like hardened, emotionless mercenaries that had seen years of battle.

He smiled, clutching the white sword closer to him. This was going to be fun.

Laire stood, heaving for breath, over the dead body of a man he didn't know. He looked around, eyes wide. Where—where was he? The last thing he remembered was throwing Tristan into the storm, and then nothing. He still had the demon sword in his hand, which was slicked with blood. His boots had become separated from the soles—as if he had walked for days in them without stopping. His clothes were in tatters. He was starving and so, so tired.

But, most importantly, an entire force of angry men with drawn weapons had surrounded him, their forms shifting and hard to focus on in their reflective armor.

The *Vanguard?*

"You've killed a general of the King's Men!" one soldier barked. "State your name so that we may know who to execute today!"

Laire glanced down at his sword. That was the only explanation for how he had gotten into this situation with no memory of it. "What have you done to me?" he asked under his breath.

I have given you your wish, its hissing voice whispered to his mind. *Seize it, and we will see if you are worthy of your next task.*

"What do you know of what I want?" he asked with gritted teeth.

Laire, your family has carried me for centuries. Do you truly believe I do not know everything about you? the sword asked, something in its voice smug but warm. *I have watched you since you were a babe. I have heard every secret you have whispered to yourself in the dark. Of course, I know your every desire.*

Its words shuddered down Laire's spine, just as terrifying as they were true. There was no room to doubt. Not in the sword's pure, powerful certainty.

Laire leveled his gaze on the men, who were inching toward him. He knew the training they received—knew they had been taught to value strength above all else. He tilted his sword—let the sun glint off the blood that stained it—and stepped off the dead man, kicking him aside. "I am General Laire Baison." He stood tall and threw his head back. "You will answer to me now. Any man that dares oppose me will meet the same fate as your former general."

The soldiers didn't move. They didn't sheathe their weapons, but they also didn't approach any further.

"We only serve the king and those who serve him," the lead soldier said. "How do we know you serve the same cause?"

Laire looked around, trying to gage where on Mother Night he was. That would tell him more about where they were in the timeline to invade the Golden Grove. In the distance, he saw the snow-capped tip of a single mountain. A mountain he knew well. "You are two days' ride from Fort Lorate," he said. "You are waiting here for the men of Lorate to join you, and will then march together to the Golden Grove."

The lead soldier appeared unphased. "You could be a spy."

"A spy would not know the word to bring you dogs to heel," Laire said with a growl. He spoke the warlock word revealed to every Vanguard general. "*Ipan.*"

Laire saw the pain flash through every man's eyes. The word activated the studs in each of the men's navels—their gift for being sworn into the Vanguard. But none of them flinched. Laire smirked to himself. They were trained well.

Slowly, begrudgingly, they lowered their blades. Laire still saw the distrust in their eyes, but it now mingled with a healthy dose of respect and discipline. They saluted Laire, their faces wary. "Welcome to the Vanguard, General Laire."

Laire had expected an entirely different feeling when he heard those words again. He had waited *five years* for that moment, after all. But he only felt emptiness—felt the cold in his hand where Vinea's warmth should have been and the icy hollowness around his neck where Linae used to cling to him. He clenched his hand tighter around the sword. He would get them back. With time.

THAT NIGHT, after Laire had commandeered the general's tent and changed into a new set of clothes, he fell into a deep sleep. The sword woke him, though, when the night was at its darkest.

I have given you what you sought. Now, you must help me.

Laire took the sword in his hand, his thoughts empty save for the sword's words. Without question, Laire let it guide him outside. The night was only lit by stars, the moon dark, and the night sky dripped like a seamless pool of ink into the landscape. Laire almost toppled over, not able to discern up from down, but the sword pulled him along and kept him upright. It took him to the body of the dead general—Laire didn't even know his name. The sword touched itself to the man's chest, and the blade glowed a sickly, grayish hue.

The man changed into something so grotesque Laire couldn't describe it. He was grateful the darkness masked most of its form, save for the watery shimmer from the stars and the sword's light. The sword whispered in a hideous language that made every bone in Laire's body sharpen with pain. His vision blurred at the edges, and he staggered a step back just as something dark and nebulous left the sword and vanished into the dead man's chest. Laire blinked, and in a moment he was staring, petrified, into a pair of unblinking silver eyes.

Every fiber in Laire's body screamed in horror. Nightmares that he didn't even know he had flashed through his eyes and threatened to tear him apart from the inside out. He wanted to scream, but the sound stuck in his throat, building until his throat nearly ruptured from the strain.

This is a shade, the sword whispered. *You will never see it again, but it will serve our mistress well.*

Something passed between the shade and the sword. Laire didn't hear the words, but his connection to the sword afforded him an uncertain glimpse into the idea passed between them. A cave. A golden flame. And a phoenix.

The visions ended. The shade blinked and then vanished in a breath. Laire's fear overcame him. He vomited into the grass before his world went dark.

THIRTEEN

Normally, the sinuous form of the ocean beast dragging the ferry across the channel to the island of Monterro made Vinea's stomach twist into knots. The beast was large enough to swallow a person whole, and the waves hacked against the small craft like butcher's blades, smacking against the wood hard enough to leave a few inches of ocean spray at the bottom of the boat.

Today, though, as the white spires of Monterro Castle came into view, looming high over the city like sickly whale bones, she had only one thing on her mind.

The ferry listed to the side as the beast turned itself away from the shore, its handler cracking a serpent root whip over its head so it didn't crash into the bank. The beast let out a moan that rippled through the water, and Vinea felt its own anger and helplessness ripple through her heart.

As soon as the ferry brushed up against the shore, Vinea leapt out of the boat and onto the sandy beach and broke into a run as soon as her feet hit the sand. The sky overhead matched the gray of the water and threatened rain. The city of Monterro—capital and former pride of Loralan—was not much better. Vinea remembered how dazzled she had been as a young girl with the pennants and flowers rippling through the town in every color imaginable. The wooden homes and shops had been painted bright white to stand out against the vibrant colors, and the stone walls and streets had been bedecked with colorful sea moss. The air had been clean and filled with the flowers' perfume. Now, the city looked and smelled like a place where things went to rot. Flowers wilted on their vines. The moss had turned to squelching mud and refuse. The white paint had faded to a sad gray. And at the center, perched at the highest point of the island city, Castle Monterro lorded over the landscape.

Vinea's heart thundered in her chest when she saw it. The pools of scarlet blood that had flooded the halls of the palace flashed in her mind. Her family had been taken from her on the Day of Bluest Blood. She would not let Monterro take her family from her again.

Vinea veered to the left when she reached the outskirts of the city, her goal only a few streets over from the main thoroughfare. Sedick's manor stood like a crooked sentinel, looming silently over the rest of the street.

As Vinea approached, she saw two acolytes in gray cloaks standing at the entrance. She remembered all the trips she and Laire had made to this place all those years ago when they had sought Sedick's magic to help them conceive Linae. She remembered how many women had been allowed to march through the gates unhindered, all under Milaia's nose. At one point, Vinea had felt sorry for her. However, after seeing what Sedick had done to Sorren—after hearing that he had locked Milaia away—she understood the mistresses must have been a blessing. Every night Sedick shared a bed with someone else was one less night Milaia had to spend with him.

And now it would be a blessing for Vinea as well.

She wiped some of the dust from her face and threw her head back. She had lived on the streets for several years after the Day of

Bluest Blood, and she knew how to play a part. Hands folded primly at her waist, she strode purposefully toward the gate.

The guards gave her a cursory once over, and one flung out a halfhearted hand to stop her.

"What is your business here with Lord Sedick?" He asked in a bored tone.

Vinea batted her eyelashes, letting a smirk play across her face even though she wanted to vomit. "I would hardly think Lord Sedick would want me to announce my business with so many ears listening in," she said.

The other guard snorted. The first one just frowned at her, glancing at her shabby skirt and dust covered arms. "How old are you?" he asked. "You don't look like one of his normal girls. They usually seem a bit more timid."

"Oh, I can assure you," Vinea leaned forward conspiratorially. "I am going to give him *exactly* what he asked for." She had many things in mind. Tearing out his teeth individually and making him eat them was her current leaning.

The soldier couldn't look her in the eye. His ears had reddened. "S'pose a man changes his taste every now and again," he grumbled. "Go on through. But be quick. Don't want anyone else to see you."

Vinea folded her arms. "I was under the impression that this was to be a...private meeting. Why the worry? Is the lady of the house about?"

The guards exchanged a look—one that was tinged with sadness. "The lady of the house hasn't been here for some time," one said. "Sedick...Moved her permanently to the castle."

Vinea knew what that meant. She was very familiar with the dank, lightless smell of the castle's lower dungeons—it was where she had hid herself for several days after the Day of Bluest Blood. She imagined the dungeons could only have gotten worse after Sedick had been allowed to run rampant through them.

Outrage bloomed anew in Vinea's chest. She kept it off her face, though. "Very well then." She strode through the gate and up the steps to the main hall. Once inside, she inquired of a housemaid where 'Lord Sedick' might be. The title left a rancor in her mouth. She silently prayed that he was out on the town, or sleeping, or *anywhere* other than on the premises.

The woman gave her a pitying look. "I suppose it has been a few days since he's had any of you. He's in his study on the second floor. Has been for several days." She grasped Vinea's arm with tight urgency. "Word of advice from one woman just trying to make a living to another? Just do whatever he says. It will go much better for you that way. I've seen countless women come and go, and the ones who fight..." Her face got a haunted look, and her hand shook on Vinea's arm. "They leave here broken." She tapped her temple pointedly. "In un-mendable ways."

Vinea's rage raced like icy fire through her veins for the terror and abuse Sedick spread. And because he had now brought her daughter into it. She clasped the woman's arm. "Thank you." She said. She clung to the woman's fingers with a desperate plea. "Have you seen a young girl here? Blond? Five years old?"

The woman's eyes widened. "The Lorate girl? He took her to be with Lady Milaia weeks ago."

Vinea's throat tightened so quickly she nearly choked. White fury blurred the edges of her vision. "He *what?*"

"Vinea!" Sedick's voice resounded across the hallway like a clap of thunder. All the servants averted their gaze, shoulders hunched as they zeroed in on their tasks as if nothing else in the world mattered more to them.

Lady Vinea straightened her shoulders, though, her righteous fury coursing like acid through her veins. "That is *Lady* Vinea, to you," she said, imbuing all the power and nobility of the Vastir family into her voice.

"I believe I could call you a great many things," Sedick hissed, swooping down his stairs like some butterfly abomination. "Traitor, spy," his lips pulled back in a snarl. "*Princess.*"

Vinea stumbled back as if she had been struck. He *knew?*

Sedick looked at her in disgust, rather than the normal pleasure he got from beating someone out in a mind game. "Osmen and I always knew there was a Vastir brat hiding in the dungeons. It was almost a game, watching you believe you had fooled us and play pretend that you were anyone other than the Queen's sister. Why Osmen let you roam free is beyond me." His face darkened. "But your game ends here."

Faster than Vinea could react, Sedick lashed out and seized her wrist, his grip so tight it made her bones grind together.

Heart pounding, bile pooling in her mouth, and vision turning dark with terror, Vinea tried to snatch her hand away, but Sedick's grip was like iron. She tried to claw away from him, but he wrenched her arm and slipped one of his bangles over her wrist.

"*Indb*!" He barked.

The band tightened around her wrist, searing hot. She gasped in pain and almost dropped to her knees. As if attached to an invisible string, the band moved on its own and forced her arm to twist behind her back, pinning it in place there. "Where is Linae?" she screamed, battling the nausea rising in her stomach and the pain clouding her vision.

Sedick shoved his face in hers. "You have lost the ability to make demands." His spittle peppered her cheeks and lips. Without another word, he dragged her the rest of the way to his study. He threw her inside and shut the door behind them.

Vinea struggled into a standing position with her arm still pinioned behind her back. Tears of rage, fear, and pain coursed down her cheeks. "Give. Me. My. Daughter."

"*Enough!*" Sedick swept his arm across his desk, dumping stacks of parchment and books onto the ground with the sound of bodies hitting the floor. Vinea flinched away from it and hated herself for doing it. That was exactly what he wanted her to be. Powerless and intimidated.

Sedick dropped into his chair behind the desk, his neck colored red with rage. He had dark circles under his eyes. "All you had to do was bring me *one* sword. Your fool husband worships the ground you walk on. He would have *given* it to you if you just asked."

Those words stung like arrowheads to Vinea's heart. She remembered watching Laire's back disappear through the doorway in Vastet, leaving her completely alone. Abandoning her to save their daughter on her own. She clenched her jaw. *Her* daughter. Laire had forfeited his family for the sake of his own pride. He was no father of Linae's.

"It's not *my* fault that *your* control over Sorren made him blow up a village." She snapped at Sedick. "He wounded me, and I couldn't complete my task. You should have never put that spell on him."

"*You* got in the way," Sedick corrected with an accusing finger. "I told you what would happen if you stepped out of line, and here we are." A shudder ran through his body, and he closed his eyes, pinching the bridge of his nose and rubbing it. His shoulders sagged with exhaustion. "Consider yourself lucky that I have been preoccupied with other things. Otherwise, you would have been dead the moment you set foot on my property." He opened his eyes, and they widened fractionally as they focused on the pile of books and documents he had dumped on the floor. His gaze flickered to Vinea, and he put his hand over his mouth in thought, leaning on his elbow. Despite herself, Vinea glanced at the books as well. Although hard to make out in their haphazard state, she saw themes of mountains, a cave, fire, and birds threaded throughout.

Sedick silently leaned forward and picked one up. He shuffled through the pages, and his eyes narrowed as if an idea had just occurred to him. The look he gave Vinea made her blanch.

He stood and paced around the room, his bangles clanking on his wrists. Vinea tried to move to the door, but he spat one of his garbled warlock words at it, and it locked with a resounding click. Vinea's heart stopped beating at the sound.

Sedick faced her, his jaw set tight. His outright anger had vanished, his cool calculations taking its place. A smirk twitched on the corner of his mouth. Whatever he had planned for Vinea seemed to put him in an almost pleasant mood. The thought made Vinea's stomach roil.

"I will give you one more chance," he drawled. He brushed his thumb over the cover of the book, which he had tucked beneath his arm. "In a set of caverns near the Golden Grove, there is an enchanted flame. They call it the Sacred Flame. Bring this to me, and I will return your brat to you. You are on your own for what you choose to do after that."

Vinea gaped at him. He had gone mad. "You expect me to go through the Woods of Desolation on my own, sneak into the Golden Grove, and steal a precious artifact?"

"You're a resourceful woman," Sedick said, his signature smug smile making an appearance.

Despite the pain that still seared through her wrist, and the fear palpitating in her heart, Vinea threw her head back. "I won't make deals with you ag—"

Sedick flew at her. He took her chin in his hand, his long fingernails digging into her jaw, and smashed her into a corner of the room. "Watch your next words carefully, *my lady*," he said, a low growl in his chest. "You are a spy, a traitor and the last of a bloodline our King marked for death. I offered you an easier solution, and you threw it back in my face. The *only* reason you and your daughter are alive today is because of mine and Osmen's mercies." He tilted her chin up, exposing her throat, and pressed her tighter against the wall, the corner forcing her shoulders to cave into her chest. "You have backed your self into a corner, and the only way out is through *me.* "

Vinea swallowed, hating the trickle of cold sweat down her temple. She didn't want to be afraid of Sedick, with his oily smiles and fool's gold words. But as she looked into his eyes, there was nothing but emptiness there. Emptiness and the desire to burn everything that didn't suit his pleasures. No guilt. No humanity. As dark and soulless as the Pit itself. And it terrified her.

Sedick must have sensed her fear, because he smirked and let her go. He took one step back, but was still close enough to keep her effectively hedged into the corner.

"I want to see my daughter," she said, her voice a shuddering rasp in her throat.

Sedick shook his head. "No more bargains. Agree to my terms, and *then* we'll see what sort of leniencies I offer."

Hot tears tracked down Vinea's cheeks, and a helpless, horror-stricken lump formed in her throat. She was out of options. He could rip the most precious thing out of her life in an instant. She had no other choice.

"I will help you," she whispered, broken.

His lips pulled back in a smile. "I knew you would."

Sedick's guard shoved Vinea into a dim room in the palace, with only a table and two chairs.

"You'll let me see Linae now?" she asked.

"No," Sedick answered. "You can see her caretaker." He glowered at her, but a small smirk lingered on his face. "After this meeting, you will leave directly from the palace. Speak to *no one* about your mission. You and I will not speak until you have returned."

Vinea almost cried again, her ear throbbing from the new stud Sedick put there. Her skin still crawled from the feeling of his magic wedging itself into her mind, and the new commands settled over her body like thorns, digging deep into her skin until she knew the only way to relieve the pressure was to obey. She was, well and truly, his pawn now.

Sedick handed her a glass jar, cloudy with an orange haze. "This is what you will store the fire in. There is a guardian over the flame. According to my research, she cannot interfere, but will do everything in her power to make you believe she can." He turned to leave, but stopped in the doorway. "And just remember." He touched his earlobe. "I will see *everything*." He left.

A few minutes after he was gone, the guards let a shambling figure in, her dark face tired and worn and framed with dark coils of hair. Golden bangles glittered on her wrists.

Vinea gasped, her heart lurching at how much the woman resembled Sorren. "*Milaia?*"

Milaia's head snapped up at the sound of her name, her eyes bright despite her haggard appearance. "Vinea?"

Vinea couldn't help herself. She ran to the woman and embraced her, the warmth of her old acquaintance a much needed balm to Sedick's horrors. A guard tried to step forward to break them apart, but Vinea glowered daggers at him. He shrugged and left, closing the door behind him.

Vinea helped Milaia to a chair, taking in the woman's bruises and thin, malnourished body. "What has he done to you?"

Milaia shook her head. "Something I will be sure he answers for some day."

Vinea's mind roiled with questions and fears about Linae. Sedick had said Milaia was her caretaker. That gave her some peace, to be sure, but seeing the state Milaia was in made her fear Linae had received the same treatment. She was only *five*. Vinea should have never put her in the position to be mistreated in such a way.

Milaia must have sensed the anxiety spiraling through Vinea. She took hold of Vinea's hand. "I am keeping her safe," she said.

A shudder of gratitude ran through Vinea. She bowed her head. Milaia shouldn't have to be comforting *her*. By the looks of it, she had suffered much worse than Vinea had. Vinea squeezed the other woman's hand. "I saw Sorren," she said.

The gasp that tore through Milaia's chest was nearly inhuman. She recoiled from Vinea. Tears welled in her eyes and spilled down her cheeks. "He's alive?" A sob broke out, and she covered her mouth to stifle it. "It's been years. He was only twelve when—" A shudder ran through her, and she shut her eyes as if to banish painful memories. "He must be so grown-up now. How is he?"

Vinea wished she could give her good news—that Sorren was

thriving, independent, and happy, but she couldn't lie to her. She told her everything—even her guilt at allowing Sedick to control Sorren for so long without stepping in.

Milaia squeezed Vinea's fingers until her knuckles paled. Her jaw clenched, and there was a flash of fury over her warm brown eyes. Vinea stiffened, but knew she deserved the woman's ire. She would have done much worse if the tables had been reversed.

Eventually, though, Milaia's claw-like grip loosened, and the fury in her eyes subsided to smoldering coals. She took in a long breath. "*Sedick* is to blame for this," she said, his name hissing through her clenched teeth. "And he will have his day. I'll make sure of it." She peered deeply into Vinea's eyes—took in the new stud in her ear. "Sedick was first drawn to me because I have a unique magical ability passed down through my family. I can see the magical threads tying power to certain objects." She brushed her thumb over Vinea's silver stud. A shudder ran down Vinea's spine as if Milaia had touched a nerve. "In recent years, Sedick has used me to make sure his trinkets have sufficient power to control the people he gives them to. If they don't, I tell him."

"Why do you continue to do his bidding?" Vinea asked.

Milaia's face took on a haunted look. "I'm not proud of it, but he hurts me less when I do."

Her eyes focused back on Vinea's stud, and she frowned. "The magic he's imbued in this one is particularly strong," she whispered. "I don't know what business he has with you, but it must be important to him." She took Vinea's hand again. "I can assure you Linae will be safe in my care for as long as you cannot be with her."

"How is she?" Vinea could hardly get the words out through the lump in her throat.

"She misses you," she said simply.

Vinea nodded.

The guards' footsteps approached the door. Milaia looked at her urgently. "If you see my son again, please give him this." She placed a bracelet in Vinea's palm, leather straps woven into intricate patterns around a black dragon scale. "Someday, I hope to find him with it."

The guard entered the room and snatched Milaia way before Vinea could ask questions. "Is the magic sufficient?" he asked gruffly.

"Yes," Milaia said in a flat tone. "She will do his bidding."

The guard whisked Milaia away, and Vinea was left alone again. She hugged her arms around her waist and hummed her daughter's lullaby to herself as tears stained her cheeks.

FOURTEEN

Ro gaped at the wall of mist swirling nebulously in front of them. The black tips of rotting trees and their twisted limbs stuck out like the thorns. Sound seemed to melt into the dead white blanket of fog as if the sound had never existed. A...*presence* emanated from it. Ancient and resentful and inexplicably sorrowful. It seemed to whisper a thousand curses at once. Ro gulped and pulled subconsciously on the ring around his neck. He had a sinking feeling that not even the talisman that had literally saved his life could protect him from whatever lurked in that forest.

Sorren stepped up next to him, desperately trying to look brave, but failing spectacularly. His squared shoulders and puffed out chest were negated by the green tinge in his face. "Nothing to it, right? What's a bit of wet air?"

"Wet air I'd be thrilled about," Styrax chimed in with a hushed whisper. "*That* is not wet air. It's something...*else*. Older and more powerful than I've ever seen."

"Oh." Sorren's voice cracked.

"Legend says this forest hosts the remnants of one of the god-race," Aspen said quietly. She tossed a line of rope to them. "Exactly which one has been lost to time, but its power still lingers."

"Seems like that should have been something someone kept track of," Styrax grumbled, eying the fog like it might jump them while they weren't looking.. "Remnants from the God of Death would be a bit different from the essence of the God of Daisies or something."

Goosebumps stood up like sentinels on Ro's forearms and on the back of his neck. He didn't want to even consider the possibilities.

"Isn't there an easier way in?" Ro's stomach roiled with anxiety as he watched the fog eddy around the trees.

"There are two entrances into the Golden Grove," Aspen said. "One is an old tunnel system that collapsed from root growth. It used to have an exit underneath the heart of the Grove. It would take us days underground in the dark to dig it out."

"I wouldn't mind that," Ash said with a grin.

Aspen rolled her eyes. "Not everyone is part dwarf, Ash."

"All's the pity for them."

Aspen sighed. "Our only other option is the Woods of Desolation. We used to keep part of a magical flame out here that keeps the Sí'Rakk at bay, if you light a torch with it, but with the war, it was safer to use the Woods as an extra layer of protection."

Ro blew out a breath. It made sense, but it didn't mean he had to like it.

Sorren picked up the rope Aspen had tossed them and weighed it in his hands.

"Tie it around your waist." Ash demonstrated a proper knot. "It keeps you from getting separated from the rest of us."

Sorren's eyes bulged, and he gripped the rope tighter. "Is that how bad it is in there?"

"Worse." Aspen's face was grim and matter-of-fact. "Unless you are face-to-face with someone, the only thing you can see in there is whatever images are in your mind. And the Sí'Rakk make those as tempting and horrifying as they can."

Sorren's knees looked ready to give out. His hands shook at his sides. "S-Sí'Rakk?"

"Sirens of the mist. More than likely born of the god-race's magic," Aspen said. "They lure you into the mist with the deepest desires of your heart. Once you're lost, they feed off your despair while you wander aimlessly, starving but still desperately searching for those empty promises."

"You can't be serious." Ro felt a green tinge creeping up his own face, too.

Aspen met his eyes, hers lifeless and haunted. "I wish I were joking, but I would never send someone into danger without letting them know what they were up against."

Ro gulped, wishing he could have held onto the illusion of it all being an elaborate prank a little longer.

"You can turn back now, if you wish," Aspen said. "I have enough supplies to get any one of you to the nearest town. From there, you'd be on your own."

Sorren vehemently shook his head. "There's nothing for me to go back to. Not yet. I...I want to stay with all of you."

Styrax clapped him on the shoulder and smiled at the group. "In all my years of traveling, the Golden Grove is the one place I've never been," he said. "It'd be such a shame to waste this rare opportunity."

"Good answer." Ash winked at him. "I would have dragged you there by your ankles anyway, regardless of your decision."

Styrax's neck and ears turned pink, and he looked down at the toes of his boots as if they had become the most fascinating thing in the world.

Aspen looked at Ro, her eyes piercing through him. He saw it faintly, although she hid it well. The fear that he might leave—that he might disappear from her life like he had the first time. He wished he knew of a way to mend the wound he had inadvertently inflicted. His heart ached, not just for her, but also for what he knew waited for him on the other side of the mist. "I'm ready to go home," he choked out, suddenly finding it difficult to speak past the lump that had formed in his throat.

Relief washed over Aspen's face like rain in a desert. She smiled faintly, her eyes soft. "It's about time, isn't it?"

He chuckled thickly and nodded. There wasn't much more he trusted himself to do.

Aspen nodded back, "All right, then. Let's get going."

They each tied a section of rope around their waists, and Aspen and Ro brought the ends together to make a giant rope loop for the five of them.

"The Sí'Rakk will use any trick they can to get us to wander off," Aspen warned, "including using our own voices. So, to combat that, we have to promise not to speak to each other. That way, we'll know that if someone speaks to us, it's the Sí'Rakk. Understood?"

They all nodded solemnly.

"If anyone needs help, reach out for your neighbor's hand. They'll keep you grounded."

Again, they nodded.

Aspen went around and checked knots one last time. When she got to Ro, she stopped for a moment and lowered her voice. "I don't want to scare you," she said. "But, just before you disappeared, the Sí'Rakk became particularly interested in you. Most of the time, they don't touch their victims, but they tried to grab you on more than one occasion."

"Oh, excellent," Ro said, his voice weak.

"I'm hoping they've given up on their obsession over the last few years, but I'll stay close, just in case," she said. "Just remember to reach out when you need."

"You, too," he said.

She gave him a grim smile and turned toward the fog. Ro watched her tighten her hand around her sword, her fingers shaking. That terrified him more than any words could. Without looking back, Aspen entered the fog, and Ro and the others followed.

The mist swallowed them whole. It settled on Ro's skin like

clammy fingers, and he shivered. Even though he knew Aspen and Ash were only a few feet away on either side, he couldn't see them. He could hardly see his hand in front of his face through the fog. As it settled in, cold sweat broke out on his brow. Claustrophobia huddled on his chest, heavy and immovable. He wanted out. He wanted out *now*.

The deeper they wandered into the forest, the heavier the mist seemed to fall on their shoulders. Styrax had been right. It wasn't the cold and wet mist Ro had expected. It was more the essence of a...*presence*. Ro had no other way to explain it. Echoes of whispers drifted through the flurries. His skin tingled and his hairs stood on end, as if icy fingers had traced trails down his spine. Resentment and betrayal and deep, soul wrenching sorrow formed a heavy pit in his stomach. Feelings more profound and *ancient* than Ro's could ever be. He didn't doubt for a second that whatever surrounded them had once been one of the most powerful beings in the known world. They were surrounded by magic, but magic much, *much* more powerful than anything he had encountered, and probably more powerful than anything else he would ever experience. It made his teeth ache. His ears rung despite the stillness, and his heart raced even while his blood slowed to a sluggish trickle in his body, like a congealed river bed. His limbs simultaneously pulled away from his body—intent on flinging themselves into the murky abyss—and dragged him to the ground. Every fiber of his being buzzed. He had never felt so exhausted and energized all at once. The edge of the wasteland, and their way to freedom, could not come fast enough.

And then someone gasped in pain out in the fog. *Aspen.*

"Aspen? Aspen!" Ro desperately tried to wade back through the mist to get to her. What had happened? Had a Sí'Rakk taken her? He had to get to her—had to save her. He would never forgive himself or her if she died alone.

"Ro, I'm fine," Aspen's voice carried through the mist. "I fought it off. I am capable of *some* things on my own. You know that, right? Help me find you. I can't see through this mist."

Ro's heart leapt, and he almost cried in relief.

"Hang on! I'll come to you! Where are you?"

"Follow my voice! You can't be too far."

Ro fiddled with the rope around his waist. "I'll be right there."

A hand clamped over his mouth while another gripped his hands and kept him from loosening the rope. Ash's face loomed out of the mist, mouth and lips pressed tight in anger and sternness. "Not Aspen," she mouthed. "Don't move."

Ro's eyes widened. He should have known. Should have remembered. Not even ten minutes ago Aspen had told them of the dangers of the forest. Of the Sí'Rakk, waiting to coax them all to an early death. How had he forgotten so quickly?

Ash hadn't removed her hands yet. Ro put one hand over hers and nodded slowly. Ash nodded back and released him.

"Ro? Ro, where are you?" Aspen's voice—the *Sí'Rakk's* voice—called through the mist. "Ro, help me, please! I can't see! I can't find you!"

Ro curled his hand into a fist. Everything in his heart screamed at him to go to her. But his mind knew otherwise. It was the uncertainty between them that killed him. There was always the possibility that it could be Aspen. And what then? What if he genuinely left her to die when he could have helped? It would haunt him forever. An unearthly growl sounded in the direction of Aspen's voice.

"It's back," she hissed in petrified terror. "Ro, it's back. The monster that killed my father—it's coming for me."

Tremors rolled through Ro's body. She sounded so desperate. So petrified. He never thought he would hear Aspen's voice sound like that. And it *was* her voice. The tone. The pitch. Even down to the nearly silent lilt of the Ancient Tongue she had inherited from her elven mother. He would know that voice anywhere. It had been a constant companion for his whole life. That she could be so nearby, so save-able, rather than out who knew where facing a nameless beast on her own and out of reach was something he could only hope for. But the fear of being tricked held him back.

Aspen would have never passed up a chance to save you, his mind whispered. *She wouldn't have cared about the dangers.*

A scream rent through the mist like a dagger through linen. Aspen's scream. It burned in his ears and wracked his frame.

"Help!" she sobbed. "Ro, please help me!"

A sob bubbled up in his chest and tore itself free. All logic rot in the Pit. He couldn't take the chance. He *wouldn't* take the chance. Aspen deserved more than a coward hiding himself in the mist. He would find her no matter the cost and no matter how many Sí'Rakk stood in his way. He would save her, even if it killed him.

Ro drew his dagger and feverishly sawed at the ropes around his waist. Ash batted the knife away. It skittered off into the mist, never to be seen again. She latched onto his hand like a falcon to its prey. "*Not. Her,*" she seethed.

Another hand brushed Ro's arm. He looked and cried out, "Aspen!"

Bloodied nearly beyond recognition, Aspen looked at him with pleading eyes. "It's... coming," she gurgled, blood spilling from her mouth. Her shoulder seemed unhinged from the rest of her body, dragging her sword uselessly behind her. Her ankle had twisted nearly backward. Deep claw marks wrapped around her body, blood oozing from them like sap from a fresh tree. Her clothes hung in tatters around her. Her breath came out labored and halting, her eyes wide and terrified even as the light behind them faded. She was dying. She was *dying,* and Ro was just standing there watching.

Tears pouring down his face and shoulders shaking, Ro wrapped her in his arms, determined to never let her go again. "I'm sorry!" he wept. His breath hiccuped in his chest. "I'm sorry, Aspen! I never should have left you! Can you ever forgive me?"

She picked feebly at the knot around his waist. "It's...still out there," she croaked. "Help me. Please help me. Before it comes back."

Ro nodded, reaching for his dagger, which he quickly remembered was not there anymore. He turned to beg weapons from Ash.

Just in time to see her fist fly into Aspen's face.

The blow landed with such force that Aspen's face audibly cracked beneath it, and she was wrenched from Ro's arms.

An unintelligible roar of fury built in Ro's throat. How dare Ash? How could she look her dying cousin in the face—the one she claimed to love so much—and do something so vile?

Before he could round on her, though—spewing hatred and fury rivaled only by the storm over the Dragon Scales—he saw it. Aspen's image faded for only a moment. Flaming hair and scales like the charred remains of a dead tree. Eyes the color of ash.

Ro recoiled. Aspen's image had returned, but he knew what lurked beneath. He tightened his grip on Ash's hand. She squeezed back.

Tears spilled unabashed down the Sí'Rakk's cheeks. "Why?" It croaked in that horrible, perfect farce of Aspen's voice. "Ash, why? Do I deserve to die like this? Am I your trash, too? To be used and thrown away and never thought of again?" It clawed its way to a standing position with the help of a nearby tree. "Well? Answer me!"

Ash's hand shook in Ro's. She didn't respond, but instead pulled Ro away, deeper into the mist. How she knew where she was going, Ro didn't know, but he trusted her. He wished he had trusted her sooner.

The Sí'Rakk screamed, high and desperate and terrified. Ro clamped one hand over his ear to drown it out. The other he kept firmly in Ash's hand. He didn't trust himself on his own.

As they drew farther away from the Sí'Rakk, the scream turned to a haunting, hideous wail. A laugh followed, almost taunting them.

"Fools," the Sí'Rakk hissed in a voice that sounded damaged by smoke—thin and grating. It hung too long on the 's's. "We are many. You cannot escape us all. How many friends will you lead to their graves?"

Her words hung heavy on Ro's chest. He couldn't breathe fully.

The horrific images of Aspen bleeding and dying plagued his mind. Fingers trembling, Ro pulled out the ring he wore around his neck, waiting for its words of peace—for *Aspen's* words—to thrum through his mind. *For evergreens and aspen trees.*

The moment the ring was out in the open, though, it scalded his palm, the smell of burning flesh rising from his hand. He dropped the ring with a yelp. It glowed bright against his chest, but instead of chasing the fog away, it drew it to Ro. The fog funneled toward him, driving him to his knees as it filled his nose and mouth, strangling him. He grasped at his throat, trying to call for help, but the fog expanded in his chest. Only muted cries eked out. His vision went black at the edges. He clawed at the ring, ignoring the burns it gave him, begging it to save him the same way it had when he had fought the memory eaters.

Aspen's green mist leapt from the ring as if on cue, grappling the fog away. It relinquished its hold on him, and he gasped in precious oxygen. As Ro's consciousness returned, he could have sworn he heard the fog screaming. He didn't have long to register that, though. As he struggled back to his feet, panting and shaking, he saw a line of fire approaching through the mist. A horde of Sí'Rakk, none of them bothering to disguise themselves, all watching Ro with murderous intent.

"He bears the master's treasure," they whispered.

"He dares to bring it here?"

"What was stolen must be returned."

"Give it to us."

"Give us our master's prize."

Ro staggered back, his heart hammering so hard against his ribs they felt as if they would crack. He ran into someone, stumbling over their feet and nearly falling, but they caught him. He looked up, expecting to see a Sí'Rakk, but only saw Aspen. Whole and complete and uninjured. She put a finger to her lips and tugged on the rope between them. Ro covered his mouth in relief. She was *alive.* Really, truly alive! His stomach filling with dread again, he gestured to the line of Sí'Rakk, which was growing by the moment.

Aspen's eyes widened in horror. Without a word, she took Ro's wrist and bolted. There were cries of surprise from the others, but when the Sí'Rakk screamed and chased after them, the others picked up the pace to follow.

"Give it to us!" The Sí'Rakk shrieked. "It does not belong to mortal men!"

Ro was so focused on the Sí'Rakk behind him, he missed the one that leapt at him from the side. He fell beneath her weight, his arm wrenched from Aspen's grip. The monster's burning, scaly skin scraped against his as they grappled. Her flaming hair blinded him, and she scrabbled at his neck. "Give it to me! It does not belong to you!"

"Get off!" Ro bunched his legs beneath her sternum and threw her off. She rolled away, her eyes literally ablaze, and turned to come for another pass at him. But, in the time it took to blink, her fiery hair dimmed, and she looked past Ro with something akin to fear on her face.

And that's when it came. The deep, resonant growl of something that did not belong in the world. Hushed, tortured screams trailed off in its undertones. Screams of people that had met horrific ends.

The breath left Ro's body. What on Mother Night's grave could make a sound like that?

The dead trees rustled, the fog pluming away from them, and a single smooth, white appendage appeared from the shadows—a long, grotesque cross between a paw and human hand. Long and slim, but bent and deformed from years of walking on all fours. Ro nearly vomited in revulsion. It looked like something that belonged to a rotting corpse.

An inhuman cry leeched from the depths of Aspen's throat. She stumbled to Ro, her whole body shaking. "Run." Aspen's voice was hoarse and her face completely devoid of color. She shoved Ro to his feet and dragged him with her, her hands slick and clammy. "Run and don't stop for anything!"

Ro paused. Aspen had told them not to speak. Was this just another Sí'Rakk looking to drag him into the forest?

But then the nightmare beast leapt. Aspen and Ro ducked, and it sailed over their heads before landing atop the Sí'Rakk that had tackled Ro. Her screams shook the trees and the ground beneath their feet as the creature tore into her. The group of Sí'Rakk that had been following them scattered like frightened hares.

Ro didn't need to be told again. Sí'Rakk or no, he had to get away from that monster. He tilted his whole body forward, sprinting half-blind through the jagged forest, his sides heaving with the effort and his head swimming from the exertion. Adrenaline charged through his veins like wildfire, his terror pumping it faster than he knew what to do with it. No matter how fast they ran, though, the monster got closer with every step. Ro felt its breath—cold and rank as death —on the back of his neck. Every fear he'd ever had quailed in the presence of that beast.

Its claws snatched the back of his tunic and tore through the cloth, narrowly missing his skin. He let out an involuntary grunt. Aspen wrenched him into a crouch and swung her sword over him. The creature let out another one of its hideous wails, but the sound retreated a few steps. That gave them enough breathing room to break out of the fog into a grassy alcove at the base of towering, sheer white cliffs. The oppressive silence gave way to rustling grass and the gentle calls of nesting birds in the cliff face.

But none of them had time to take in the beauty. Ro skidded to a stop, panic threading through him like lightning, and tensed himself to the inevitable fight. He quickly counted heads. Aspen, Styrax, Ash, and Sorren. They were all there. They had all made it. And they all watched the edge of the Woods with terror in their eyes.

They heard the creature's heavy footfalls as it came after them. It roared and pounced. But there was a blinding flash, and the creature's roar turned to a scream of agony. They watched its silhouette as it rounded and tried again. Another flash, and a thud as if it had hit a wall. It screamed again before it turned and fled back into the mist.

Aspen collapsed to one knee, her sword plunged into the ground, the only thing keeping her from toppling over. "A shade," she whispered. "There's a shade in the desolate woods."

Styrax muttered a curse and made a warding gesture over his heart.

Memories flooded into Ro with an onslaught of emotion. A shade had killed Aspen's father. He remembered his terror and anger when Aspen's mother had practically beaten down his door, begging him to help her look for Aspen, who had been spouting nonsense about "justice" and "protecting others from a similar fate" all day—the panic as the shadows drew longer with Aspen still missing filled his chest again. He remembered when he found her curled on the ground and weeping, her arms clenched around her body like a shield. Her eyes staring forward, unseeing. Disjointed words and phrases spilled out of her mouth between sobs, filled with nothing but terror. She screamed when he touched her, not seeing him, but something else entirely. He'd had to carry her all the way back home. He had never seen her so broken.

"*That's* a shade?" Ash asked, her voice thready with horror. "What on the Architects kept it out?" She looked at Styrax and Sorren, who just shook their heads.

"The sacred flame." Aspen's voice shook. "They added a new spell to it as a ward against them after...last time."

The silence that followed Aspen's announcement was filled only by the memories still swirling in Ro's mind. He remembered Calla's relief as she gathered Aspen into her arms. He remembered her screams when her husband's bloodied remains were handed to her in a sack cloth. Aspen's trembling as she recounted her story to her mother and the Council of Elders had etched itself deep into his mind, as had her grief and guilt-ridden sobs to him when they had found a moment to themselves. She had tried to do the right thing, but the consequences had been so terrible and irreversible that Ro couldn't be certain if she had ever learned to fully trust herself again.

Exhaustion plowed into Ro like a runaway bull. His eyes widened in shock as his knees buckled without warning beneath him. He turned on his side to avoid falling flat on his face, but that was about all he could manage. His arms hung limp and useless, like a couple of anvils at his side.

"Wha—?" he slurred, his tongue heavy in his mouth.

At the very least, he didn't seem to be the only one suffering from the sudden attack of uselessness. Styrax had his knees propped up, his head resting against them while he draped his forearms over the top. Sorren lay flat on his back spread-eagle, staring wordlessly at the sky. The only one that appeared to have her senses about her was Ash. That shouldn't have been a surprise. That often seemed to be the case with her. She moved gingerly, as if all her joints ached, but she handed out handfuls of nuts and some rabbit jerky to everyone. They took it with silent gratitude. Ro didn't know where they would be without her.

Ash grimaced and cracked her back, dark bags beneath her eyes. "Sunrise won't be for another several hours. We'll be safe here. Let's all rest, and we'll head out just before sunrise."

Ro sat close to Aspen, who hadn't moved from where she knelt in the grass. He tried to put a comforting hand on her shoulder. She immediately shrugged it off.

"Aspen...I..." What was he even supposed to say in a situation like this? "I remembered finding you after your father. I'm sorry that day continues to haunt you." An unbidden lump formed in his throat as more memories flooded him. He remembered her father's warmth —the robustness of his laugh and his genuine smile. In all the years Ro had known Abran, he couldn't think of a time a single unkind word had been spoken, despite how most of the Golden Grove elves treated Abran and his family. He had always been willing to let Ro "help" him in his leather working shop. He had seemed to know that Ro needed a quiet space to work out his feelings, or talk to someone that wasn't Gan. That's where Ro had gone the nights being the true heir to the throne of Loralan felt like too much. It was in that shop, with Abran's quiet, non-judgemental presence, that Ro decided he wanted to *do* something with his birthright, rather than hide it away. Abran's death had bored a hollow wound in Ro's chest that had slowly healed over time. He couldn't imagine having to relive it every day and have that hurt constantly reopened.

Ro wrapped his arms around his knees and looked up at the stars, trying not to think of the mist expanding in his chest and nearly smothering him. It helped to talk to and about someone else to keep his own fear from taking over. "You're a lot like him, I think. You have his heart and forgiving nature." He chuckled faintly and winked. "Mostly."

A wry smile pulled at one corner of Aspen's lips.

"I think both you and your brothers take a lot after him."

The smile slipped from Aspen's face like wet ink off soaked parchment. She turned her back to him and laid on her side. "You should sleep while you can. Morning's going to come earlier than you think." She shifted into a more comfortable position, drew her cloak about her, and said no more.

FIFTEEN

"Ro, Ro! Wake up!" someone hissed.

Ro waded through the fog of sleep and dragged his eyelids open. A blurry face, barely illuminated by the blue-gray of pre-dawn, swirled into focus.

"Aspen?" he croaked, his tongue sluggish and his mouth tasting like dust. "Wassits...wha's wrong? What's going on?"

Aspen put a finger to his lips. She glanced at their sorry excuse for a camp. Everyone else was still asleep. The dusky light cast everything in muted tones.

"What—" Ro's yawn turned into a full-body stretch. He moved Aspen's hands away from his face, sleep tearing up in his eyes. "What time is it?"

"Come with me," Aspen whispered. "I have something to show you."

Ro desperately wanted to ask if it could wait until morning, but his curiosity got the better of him. Aspen had a particular talent for using that against him. He just hoped it wasn't more early morning sword practice. He'd had enough of finding bruises in strange places before he'd even had the chance to fully wake up.

Ro lurched to his feet like a gluttonous noble with too many drinks in their belly. Another yawn leached itself from his throat, and he rubbed crusted sleep from his eyes. "You're lucky I like you," he grumbled.

Aspen smirked. "You'll thank me. Let's go."

Ro extricated himself from his bedroll, grimacing as the wind bit into the skin that had been perfectly toasty only seconds before. He hugged his arms to his sides, the fine hairs along his skin prickly from the cold. He motioned Aspen to lead on.

They crept past the others, careful not to wake them. Sorren had buried himself in his cloak, its folds tucked around him so only the tip of his nose was visible. Ash and Styrax had pulled their bedrolls near each other, their fingertips brushing as they slept. Ro grinned. He couldn't wait to tease Styrax about that in the morning.

Aspen led him to a patch of overgrown brush and ivy clambering up the cliff face. She brushed it aside to reveal a small cave entrance.

Ro furrowed his brow. "What is this?"

Aspen glanced at it. "I believe most people call it a cave." She poked him in the back before he could protest and coerced him into the cave.

He had expected it to be small and shallow, but as soon as he ducked inside, he found a cavern so spacious that the light spilling through the entrance couldn't reach the edges. Aspen followed him in and let the ivy wall fall back into place. She took Ro's wrist and pulled him deeper into the cave. What he expected to turn into stagnant air instead became something fresh and wild, keening through the cave like long forgotten memories. He couldn't tell if that made it more or less terrifying when they walked so far into the cave that it plunged them into complete, heavy darkness.

Aspen stopped and let go of his hand.

Ro couldn't keep the sudden surge of unease out of his voice. "This isn't some sort of elaborate plan to assassinate me and take the throne for yourself, is it?"

Aspen's chuckle rolled out of the dark. "We both know I don't need anything special to kill you."

Ro grinned despite himself. Images of Aspen leaping from the mist and putting a knife to his throat played through his mind. That felt like a lifetime ago. "True."

There was a scratch and hiss, and a torch on the wall flared into existence. Aspen pulled it from its sconce and held it toward the center of the darkness. Ro squinted against the sudden, blinding light, but as his eyes adjusted, his mouth dropped open in wonder. Words failed him as his throat constricted in awe. "What—how—" He couldn't say anything louder than a whisper for fear of breaking the sacred space.

Cavern walls soared up around them, draped in huge, cascading veins of crystals. They glittered in every color imaginable and captured the firelight reflected a thousand times over again. Stone carvings had been hewn from the stalactites hanging from the ceiling, depicting an enormous bird.

"These are the phoenix caves." Aspen stood beside him and held the torch high to take in more of the gem encrusted walls. "This is where they found refuge from the dragons during the Primordial Wars. Before they all became extinct."

Ro let out a long breath of quiet admiration. "You would think I would remember a place like this."

"Not if I never told you about it," Aspen said. She smirked when he gave her an incredulous look. "I think I'm allowed *one* secret place. Even from you." She placed her palm on the crystal walls, running her thumb over the facets. "I would spend hours here, especially after..." The words trailed off into nothing. She was quiet for a moment, but then smiled at him as if nothing was wrong. She pointed to two tunnel entrances. "If you follow the left one, it will take you to the Sacred Flame. It sings, sometimes." She turned and took the right passage, which turned into a long corridor slanted upward. "But we're going this way today. Come on."

The silence stretched out between them like a looming, expectant being. Every fiber in Ro's body itched to say something to fill the space, but he refrained. Something about the darkness felt like it didn't quite belong to him.

To his surprise, Aspen broke the silence first.

"You can't tell Ash this." The snap of Aspen's torchlight echoed more than her whisper did, shattering thousands of crystal glows into millions of pieces on the cavern ceiling and walls. Another long pause stretched out before she spoke again, as if she were choosing her words carefully. "There are so many times I've thought about wandering into these caves and just...never coming back out." She trailed her fingers across the etchings scorched into the stone. "An entire race of the most magical beings known to the world lived and died within these caves. It couldn't be so bad to join them, right?"

Ro looked at her—really *looked*. He hadn't realized how deeply her strong shoulders sagged. How heavy and exhausted each foot-step seemed to be. He could hardly see the little spitfire that used to run as wild as the squirrels around her cottage. Even the woman that had thrown herself at a sorcerer for him seemed to have gone quiet. He knew they were still there, but hidden beneath something tenuous and vulnerable. Ro wished he could fix whatever had broken her, but knew that was not his place. For Sister Earth's sake, he could hardly fix *himself*. "What kept you from doing that?"

"Spite," she said with a mirthless chuckle. The hollow sound bounced into the dark. "I promised myself I wouldn't just leave people behind if given the choice," Ro sensed an aching, jagged bitterness in her voice. "My promise doesn't keep Ash from worrying, though. She's going to keel over from all the grief I give her one of these days." She studied her hand, rubbing the base of her thumb. "I don't deserve her, do I?"

"I think you do," Ro said, his jaw firm. "You deserve to have someone love you fiercely and loyally, especially when you don't feel you can do it yourself." He touched her shoulder. "I'm sorry I couldn't be there for you when you needed that."

"It's not your fault," Aspen said in a guilt-laden voice. "I suppose we all live in a world of experiences no one else sees, don't we?" She took his hand in hers. "Come on, not much farther now."

They emerged into a windswept rock flat. The mountains in the distance drowned in a sea of low-riding clouds, their peaks below Aspen and Ro. The landscape stretched for miles in every direction, the edges still hazy from the light trickling over the world. Ro felt bigger, somehow, as if his body filled the space with no barriers to stop it. They seemed on top of the world. Powerful. Invincible. Untouchable. The only people in all the world. Ro closed his eyes and sucked in the sharp cold of the mountain air until it filled his whole body with its freshness. So this was what it felt like to fly.

Aspen pulled out a heavy cloak and leaned against the cave entrance, the cloak wrapped around her shoulders like a blanket. She motioned him into its warmth. They snuggled close as the sky faded from gray to pink. "They say phoenixes used to take flight from this very spot." Aspen's breath plumed in front of her face and the wind tugged a single strand of hair across her lips. "Can you imagine flying over these mountains every day? Taking in the entire world all at once?"

Ro let the image take hold of him, and it stole his breath away. "Amazing." He snuggled closer to Aspen as the wind plucked at his exposed skin. "Is this what you brought me up here for?"

She looked at him with a quirked eyebrow and a goading half-smile. "Is that a problem?"

He jabbed her in the ribs just a little too hard. "No!"

Aspen rolled her eyes. "Very convincing." She winked. "You'll be happy to know, Mister Ungrateful, that this is *not*, in fact, what I brought you up here for. My vast, archaic knowledge was just a bonus."

"I am *not* ungrateful!"

"Shh! Watch." She gestured her head in the valley's direction. Ro watched with her, not sure what to expect. Nothing moved except for the wind churning the fog in mesmerizing curls beneath them. Moments dragged into minutes as the world eased itself from sleep.

Ro nearly fell asleep with Aspen's warmth next to him, but she nudged him awake. He woke with a start just as the first of the morning sun drizzled its way down the sloping backs of the mountains.

The fog beneath recoiled, drawing back in respect to the morning light. Beneath it, sparkling with what could only have been morning dew, silver trees slowly turned to gold, stretching hungry limbs to the sun and bathing in its light. The entire valley blazed with the golden glow from the trees all nestled into every nook and cranny of the mountainside, as if someone had sprinkled them there. Its very own tribute to the sun. Moors and fields rolled out from the spaces the trees did not occupy. Birds, white as snow, circled over the golden trees like dust particles caught twinkling in the sun. The rush of aquamarine waterfalls dusted the scene in silver mist.

"Whenever you're here to see the leaves turn from gold to silver, you'll know you're home," Aspen said with a soft smile.

CHAPTER

SIXTEEN

Tears rolled, unabashed, down Ro's face. He slipped out of the cloak and picked his way to the edge of his and Aspen's perch like a believer nearing a temple. Chills raced through his body. His heart ached. His breath hitched in his chest. "This—this is—"

Aspen stood next to him, their arms brushing. "Welcome home."

Ro smiled through his tears, unable to pull his eyes away from the Grove. Oh, how he had missed this piece of his heart! "Can we go down?" he asked, dancing on the balls of his feet as excitement built in him.

"It's certainly time, isn't it?" Aspen seemed nearly giddy as well. Much more like the young Aspen he had known. "Let's go home."

Ro practically raced her back to the others. It was a wonder he didn't impale himself on a wall of crystals in his haste to leave. But they made it out without incident. Sorren and Styrax were just beginning to stir, but Ash was pacing frantically around the camp until she saw Aspen and Ro.

"And where have you two been?" Ash demanded like a harried

mother. "I was just about to look for your bodies! You better have a good explanation, otherwise there *will* be bodies soon!"

"We were watching the sunrise," Aspen said simply. "Its been five years since he last saw it."

Ash's face softened and she let out a sigh. "I suppose that's something worth me wasting a little worry over, then." She quickly pointed an accusatory finger at both of them. "*Don't* let this become a habit."

Ro hugged her and hurried the others along.

They followed a winding mountain path up the cliffs, which gave them another wide view of the Golden Grove. Not as spectacular as the view Aspen showed Ro, but even so, Styrax and Sorren stopped to take it in, their eyes wide with wonder. Ro was just tickled to see Styrax rendered speechless for once.

As they trekked, Ro's anxiousness to get to the valley nearly drove him to tear himself out of his own skin. So, he turned to distraction to keep him occupied until then. "What are you all most excited for about getting back to the Golden Grove?" Ro asked.

"I'm excited to learn some more magic," Sorren said quickly, ducking his head when all eyes turned to him.

Aspen raised an eyebrow at him. "I'd say you've got a pretty expert handle on it already, don't you?"

Sorren shifted uncomfortably. "Well, sure, but that's all destructive magic. I want to see how I can fit it into normal life and use it to help people the way *I* want to help them. My ma taught me a few things when she could behind Sedick's back, but this is different."

Styrax wrapped an arm around Sorren's shoulder. "I'm right there with you. It'll be nice to get back into the lifestyle of magic. I don't have to hide my magic anymore or hear about the creative ways townsfolk want to kill Ancient Ones. In graphic detail." He winced, but then grinned at them all. "It'll be nice to be around my own kind again."

Ash arched an eyebrow at him. "Are we not enough company for you?"

Styrax cleared his throat, his ears turning pink. "I didn't say that."

Ash smirked. "Well, *I'm* excited to be back home with proper cooking ingredients. No more of this travel fare." She stretched her arms over her head with a sigh. "It'd probably be a good idea to count my money, too—make sure none of it wandered off while I was gone."

"Or ended up in a certain elder's pockets," Aspen muttered.

"Money?" Ro asked. "Do you have some stowed away somewhere?"

Ash grinned, something deviously mischievous in her eyes. "One acquires a few special things when they're the leader of a group of incredibly successful thieves."

Ro nearly choked on the water he'd been drinking. Instead, he accidentally sprayed it in poor Sorren's face in an effort to not die. "I'm sorry...You *what*?" he coughed out, face red and tears welling in his eyes. He helped Sorren mop himself off.

Ash laughed. "What? You find it hard to believe I'm a hardened, willful criminal? Why else do you think I'm such a crack shot?"

Ro found it hard to believe *anything* she told him at the moment. "I assumed it was because you don't want to *die* in the middle of a battle?"

Ash shook her head. "Nope! No battle for me! I'm the head cook for General Shadowalker, at your service." She bowed deep at the waist.

Ro had to avoid the need to pick his jaw up off the floor. "You're just a *cook*?"

"Not *just* a cook," Aspen cut in sternly, almost passionately. "She keeps everything running far better than I can with just a knife and ladle. Can you say the same?"

Ro watched her with wide eyes. He hadn't expected the tirade, but he saw the glow of pride in Ash's eyes. "No, I definitely can't," he said truthfully.

Aspen nodded emphatically. "I didn't think so. All roles are important in war, and far too many are not given the credit they deserve."

"In fairness," he said to himself after Aspen had turned and started walking again. "I'm not sure I could run anything better than you can, ladle or otherwise."

As they descended into the treeline, Ro was once again left breathless. Seeing the trees from above was one type of beautiful, but this was something else entirely. Gold and silver veins twisted up the bark of each tree like glittering threads. Pygmy dragons slept beneath their canopies in jewel-toned wildflowers, snoring and letting out little bursts of flame.

Something crossed between a gasp and a squeal escaped Sorren when he saw them. He cautiously tried to approach, but they awoke in a flurry of sparks and colors and flew off higher into the trees. Sorren's crestfallen face nearly broke Ro's heart.

Fairies whizzed by on gossamer wings, and dryads watched them from behind the trunks of their trees, their skin nearly the same texture and color as the bark. Pegasi flew overhead, leaving piles of steaming, glittering droppings. Ro accidentally stepped into a pile, but he didn't care. Everywhere he looked, there was another piece of untouched magic. It zipped and fizzed through his veins, making him feel stronger and lighter all at once. This was *magic*. Pure and powerful. This was *home*.

The further they drew into the Grove, the more buildings appeared—winking windows and lights from the hearts of the trees. The trees were still thriving, though, as if the buildings were just a natural part of their structure. As Ro watched them come into view, his heart filled to nearly bursting. He remembered. He remembered running through the paths between the golden trees—remembered watching them change their colors every morning and evening. He remembered the elves and the pygmy dragons and the *magic*. Tears threatened in his eyes at the overwhelm of it all.

Styrax leaned over to him with a smile. "I said you weren't meant for mediocrity," he whispered. "Did you ever think we'd end up in a place like this, though?"

Ro shook his head. "Thank you, Styrax, for helping me get here."

"Hey, I'm the one living off your fame here. I should thank *you*."

Ro rubbed the back of his neck. "Considering I almost killed you with serpent root back in Lorate, I think this is probably the least I can do."

Styrax smirked. "You know, you're absolutely right. What was I thinking? I've *earned* this."

Ro rolled his eyes, but before he had time to respond to that, he caught sight of brightly colored ribbons and bells adorning the trees, tinkling merrily. "Is there a festival?" he asked.

"It's the Goldenlight Festival," Ash said. "It's a renewal of the Grove and those that live in it."

They came upon a large, sprawling camp beside a giant swathe of crop fields growing tall and proud beneath the Golden Trees. Soldiers milled about the tents, running drills, sharpening weapons, and tending the crops.

Ro tilted his head in consternation. "Are those soldiers...farming?" he asked.

"Yes," Aspen said, her shoulders stiff. "We partner with the elves to grow crops faster here so we can—"

"Is that my *idiot* general?" someone roared.

Ro jumped at the sound and saw an elderly, hunched elf marching toward them, a sack of jangling potions slung across her shoulders and her weathered face murderous. Her long, drooping ears poked out from beneath a wild mane of snow white curls.

"Oh, boy," Aspen said under her breath.

"She's *your* healer," Ash said. "It's your own fault for leaving without notification."

"You don't happen to have a healer to save you *from* your healer, do you?" Styrax asked.

"Weeks! *Weeks*!" the woman shouted, not quite coming up to Aspen's chin but radiating a presence so much larger and powerful, jaw clenched and face red. "I didn't know where you were—if you were alive or dead—and then you have the *audacity* to wander back like nothing happened?"

"I'm so sorry, general!" A large elven man ran up to the group, soft-spoken for his massive size. "Grandmother has been...excitable. We're glad you're back safe." He pushed a pair of spectacles farther up his nose and noticed Ro gaping at him. "Oh, hello. I'm Larch. This is my grandmother, Hemlock. I'm her assistant."

"It remains to be seen if she'll *stay* safe when I'm done with her," Hemlock continued to tirade.

"Hemlock, I understand Aspen needs to learn the art of proper communication," Ash said to the woman. "But I was with—"

"Don't even get me *started* on *you!*" Hemlock rounded on Ash. "You enable this bad behavior!"

Ash snapped her mouth shut, looking chastened. Ro marveled at this woman that could so thoroughly cow both of the cousins.

Hemlock crossed her arms over her chest and looked back at Aspen. "What do you have to say for yourself?"

It seemed Aspen couldn't find the words. So, instead, she just gestured to Ro.

Hemlock turned her wrathful eyes on him, and he gave her a nervous smile. As she looked, though, her eyes widened, and her jaw went slack. She whisked her attention back to Aspen. "Child! Is this—?"

Before she could finish her thought, more soldiers poked their heads out of their tents to investigate the commotion. When they saw Aspen, they let out whistles and cheers and came running.

"The General's back!"

"General Shadowalker's back!"

They were mobbed as more and more soldiers surrounded them, each welcoming their general home. Ro had never seen such a motley collection of Ancient Races. He couldn't even name them all. Aspen glowed amid them, though, her smile warm as she greeted each of them by name. Ro watched the tension leave her shoulders and saw a bright, dancing light in her eyes. He couldn't help but smile, too.

The shouts of the soldiers caught the attention of the other elves from the heart of the Golden Grove. They wandered over, trying to get a peek at what the commotion was about.

As they pressed in, a guttural cry sounded through the crowd, as if torn violently from someone's throat. Ro looked up as the crowd parted to reveal a small, slim man. Wisps of silver hair flitted about his mostly bald head, and smile lines creased deep trenches around his eyes. He was not smiling now, though. His skin was pale as parchment, and he looked at Ro as if he were a creature that had clawed itself from the Pit. A basket of peas had fallen from his trembling hands. "Five years," the man whispered. "Five years I lived thinking I would never see that face again."

The world froze, and the crowd seemed to vanish entirely until no one was left except for the smaller man. Ro's heartbeat twisted to a stop. A lump strangled his throat. He knew this man. He knew him from the memories gilded in gold. Knew him from the feelings of love and acceptance and peace—and from his ever-present peas.

Ro cried out, a sound wrenched from his chest, and hurtled toward the man. "Gan!" He nearly fell in his haste, but he scooped his father up and crushed him against his chest, sobbing.

"My son!" Gan sobbed with him. "My son is home!" Gan's tears dripped on Ro's face as he kissed his cheeks and hugged him tight. "That amazing, wonderful girl brought my boy back to me, just like she promised!"

SEVENTEEN

Aspen watched Gan and Ro with her chest full to nearly bursting. Gan had not been the same since Ro disappeared. He had become a shadow of the person Aspen had once known—taken over completely by his grief. He had screamed at Aspen for months after Ro's disappearance. That had been better than the silence that had come after. Now, though, she could see the grief lifting off his shoulders like rain evaporating in the sun.

Arm still wrapped around Ro's shoulders—or what he could reach around Ro's shoulders—Gan looked at Aspen with tears in his eyes. "You kept your word," he said in a thick voice. "Even when I—" He shook his head and hugged her, the embrace deep and full of love and regret. "I am so, so sorry I turned on you when you needed someone the most."

A sudden lump choked in Aspen's throat. She hadn't expected the apology, nor the emotions it would bring with it.

Gan pulled away from her, patting her cheek. "You brought him back to me. Thank you."

Aspen blinked back tears. "It's about time I did something right by you, Gan," she said, her own voice husky. To cover her moment of weakness, she turned to her gathered army. "Soldiers of the Prince's Rebellion, all hail! Your prince has come home!"

A gasp ran through them all. They looked at Ro with awe. He gave them a tight smile and looked down at his shoes. One by one, the soldiers dropped to a single knee, heads bowed. Aspen followed suit, beaming with pride. Ro was back. Their *prince* was back. And it would only be a matter of time before they could freely live in their own kingdom again.

"No, you—I—" Ro stammered, moving as if to make them all stand. "You really don't have to—"

"*What* is this about?"

Any vestige of happiness and hope evaporated in an instant. Aspen's stomach curdled at the voice. She flexed her fingers to relieve the tension that had crawled up her spine and turned. She met eyes with Inula, who threw her proud head back, eyes alight, as her nostrils flared.

"Shadowwalker!" she snapped, summoning Aspen forward with a derisive wave of her hand.

A grumble ran through her soldiers of correcting the missing "general".

"You are called to meet with the Council. *Immediately,*" Inula continued, ignoring the mutters. She turned to Hemlock, who had remained close to Aspen. "All Council members are required to attend."

"Yes, your ladyship," Hemlock said in a mocking tone under her breath.

Aspen stood, and Ash, Styrax, and Sorren all moved with her. Ro hesitated a moment, seemingly reluctant to leave Gan's side. Aspen was about to tell him he had more than earned some time with his father, but Gan patted his shoulder. "Go with her," she heard him say. "It's high time our family started showing her the support she deserves."

Ro furrowed his brow, glancing between Gan and Aspen as if

trying to piece together what Gan had meant by that, but eventually, he also moved to Aspen's side.

Inula's eyes blazed white-hot. "Additional attendees are not required."

"But not forbidden!" Ash said brightly, teeth clenched in a rebellious smile. "So happy to see you again, mother. It's always my highest pleasure." She took Aspen by the elbow and they walked as a group. Aspen felt the shards of Inula's frozen fury as they walked past.

As they paraded into the Golden Grove proper, Aspen straightened her shoulders and marched toward the center square—to the largest building nestled amidst the trees. Her vision tilted. Memories flooded her thoughts as she looked at the Elder's Council Chambers, and her shadow walker mark burned.

When they entered the Chamber, Ash, Ro, and the others went to sit in the audience seats, and Aspen stood in the center of the floor, feeling small and vulnerable as the seats warped around her.

Inula filed into the Council Chamber with two of her guards and sat in the head seat. She glowered at Aspen, but said nothing. Over the next several minutes, the other four elders filed in, each in varying stages of disarray. Obviously, none of them had expected to meet together that day. Most regarded Aspen with an icy indifference. All except for Hemlock. She gave Aspen a wink and a small bow. "About time you came back to us, General," she said loud enough for the rest of the Council to hear as she cast them sidelong glances.

Aspen tried to return her smile, but the cool glares from the rest of the Council froze it. "Hello, Elder Hemlock," she said formally.

Aspen had never interacted with the other three elders in any sort of individual capacity. There was no need when she already knew what they thought of her. Although each of the elders had been elected by majority to serve in the role for the rest of their lives, Aspen knew those three all sat prettily in Inula's pocket. Being the

Council Head came with its perks, foremost of which was the ability to sway majority vote as she chose.

Inula clacked her staff on the floor—the sound pounding in Aspen's ears like a mace to the head—and stood. "The Council of Elders holds this conclave with the purpose of determining the success of General Shadowalker's mission." She cast her eyes around the empty audience hall. "Although, by how few people you brought with you, it is clear that your mission failed. What do you have to say for yourself?"

Aspen nearly dropped her gaze, the weight of guilt bearing heavily on her shoulders. But she couldn't. This was her burden to bear. "The Midnight Fens will not be coming to our aid."

The quiet that rolled through the Elders was deafening. They stared at her without a word, faces grim.

Elder Inula broke the silence first, the knuckles on her pale fingers turning nearly translucent as she tightened her grip on her staff. "And *why* are they not coming, Shadowalker?"

"That's *General* Shadowalker, to you, you arrogant..." Ash's grumbles from the stands faded away to nothing.

Aspen fought to keep a deep, bone weary sigh from coming out of her. Over the past five years, she had learned her script for the show Inula wanted to play. It was always easier if she followed along. "Elders, I believe it will save us all some time if I show you rather than tell you." She glanced at Hemlock. "I will submit myself to Hemlock's scrying magic, if that suits your purposes."

Hemlock pursed her lips, her eyes hardening at the suggestion. She turned and glowered at Inula. "General Shadowalker has already submitted herself to my scrying well beyond the normal limit. We know we can trust her to give an accurate   "

"It's fine," Inula waved her away. "She has submitted to it. Proceed with the scrying."

"What is scrying?" Aspen heard Ro whisper in the stands. Probably to Ash. She almost smiled.

"They'll pick through her memories until they find something they decide to use against her," Ash responded, her tone brittle with anger.

Hemlock huffed and bustled to the center of the Council Room, casting Inula dirty looks as she did so. When she reached Aspen, she turned her away from the Council for a moment. "Are you sure about this?" she asked Aspen quietly. "You know that you're not required to—"

"I have to, Hemlock," Aspen said. "You know they won't believe me any other way." She motioned her head to Ro. "The most important thing right now is getting them to see that Ro is well and truly back."

Hemlock pursed her lips. "You don't always have to sacrifice yourself to get others to appreciate you."

"Do you know of any other ways?" Aspen retorted, her jagged bitterness bleeding through. "Because I've spent my entire life trying them, and this is the only one that at least keeps them mostly civil."

Hemlock sighed heavily, but didn't offer an answer. Instead, she turned Aspen back to face the Council. She placed her hand in Aspen's, and a vision filled the entire room, casting everything else aside. It was of Chaedra, meeting Ash and Aspen on the hill overlooking Lorate. The scene enveloped them completely, settling them into place as if they were there. For hours, Aspen let them see every pertinent detail of her trip to and from Lorate. They saw her break into the fort and the fight with the Midnight Fens' gate-keeper. They saw the fight in Vastet, Tristan discovering who he was, the fight on the Dragon Scales—everything up to the disastrous meeting with Queen Holly. She also showed them the Woods of Desolation, and the shade that had followed them. When its screams pierced through the room, everyone jumped and let out muttered curses.

When the images ended, Aspen and Hemlock had a perfect, golden orb between their interlocked hands, swirling with the images from Aspen's memories. Hemlock pocketed it and then grasped Aspen's hand again, squeezing it gently.

Inula glared down at her. "Elder Hemlock, please return to your seat."

"I'm fine where I'm at, thank you," Hemlock replied in a steely voice.

Inula pursed her lips. "Elder Hemlock, you forget that the Council of Elders must remain unbiased. Standing beside the accused—"

"The *accused?*" Ro called from the stands, outraged. "What's she accused of? She hasn't done anything wrong! She *saved* me!"

Inula cast him a tight-lipped smile. "Prince Ro Edenson, it is a miracle and our utmost pleasure to welcome you back to the home that raised you. However, we ask that you leave elven affairs to the Council."

Ro opened his mouth like he wanted to protest, but Aspen gave him a warning look and shook her head. He clamped his mouth shut, but she could see him still fuming.

Inula's fingers tightened around her staff, and she turned back to Hemlock. "Now, Elder Hemlock, if you will please—"

"The Council forgets that part of my agreement to becoming an Elder and using my unique skills is that I would remain a *healer* first and foremost," Hemlock said coolly. "General Shadowalker is a patient of mine and occasionally requires additional support for her injury. Considering how often she sacrificed life and limb for the sake of her mission, I am, frankly, amazed that she made it all the way back to us with only field medical care." Hemlock leveled an even glare at Inula. "I am staying. Here."

Inula's nostrils flared. Aspen squeezed Hemlock's hand a little tighter in gratitude.

"Very well," Inula said, her tone clipped. "Furthering this argument is pointless. The Council has come to a decision."

Hemlock bristled. "The Council most certainly has *not*—"

Inula rode over her. "Since Elder Hemlock has made it abundantly clear that she is not functioning as a member of the Council today—"

"That has never been a precedent!" Hemlock shouted back at Inula. "It is not required for us to languish away on our fat, cushy buttocks to perform our—"

"The vote is *unanimous!*" Inula continued, ignoring Hemlock entirely. She looked at Aspen, her eyes glittering. "Shadowalker, you have had numerous opportunities to prove your worth to the Golden Grove, and every time, you have fallen woefully short. You were aware that this would be your last chance. And you have failed yet again."

Ro leapt from his seat, hands balled into shaking fists. "It's not her fault!"

"We have seen the memories as well as you have, your highness," Inula said, her voice carefully neutral. "Trust that we have made judgment based on the facts presented."

"I wouldn't trust your ability to *walk* with judgment like that!" He stormed down the audience steps, his face thunderous.

Inula remained unperturbed. "With your repeated interruptions, I'm afraid we shall have to conduct the rest of these proceedings privately. You may rule man's kingdom, but the Council bows to no one." Inula waved to her two guards, who escorted Ro, Styrax, Ash, and Sorren out the door. Ro flung obscenities behind him the whole way.

When they were gone, Inula turned back to Aspen, looking too eager. Too smug. Aspen wanted to wretch. She knew Inula had been looking for any excuse to be rid of her. It was her fault for giving her that excuse.

"I made you aware before you left that you could not fail again," Inula said, leaning back, her fingers drumming on the arms of her chair. "You are a danger to the Golden Grove. If we cannot even trust you to bring *help*, then we certainly can't trust you to remain stationed here." She swept her hair off her shoulder. "If not for the fact that it would take weeks we do not have for a replacement force to take your place, I would have no qualms banishing you now."

"*Banish?*" Hemlock cried indignantly. "This is *absurd!*"

Aspen didn't hear the rest of the argument as Inula and Hemlock fought. She could hardly focus on keeping her shoulders and spine straight—on not betraying any signs of weakness. She battled back the memories from five years ago, when she had been scared and helpless, hardly able to stand. She had come a long way from that girl. But why did she feel as if she were right back in that nightmare all over again?

"*As it stands now,*" Inula barked, over-cutting Hemlock again and breaking through Aspen's spiraling thoughts. "Shadowalker, you and your men may remain in the Golden Grove until this newest threat has passed. After that, you will all be ejected from the Grove and will not be permitted to return—if there is even a Golden Grove left after your failure."

"Oh, so you'll reap the rewards of their work and then turn them out like stray dogs?" Hemlock growled.

Aspen's world spun around her. No. *No.* She knew she deserved it—that she had been lucky to have stayed in the Golden Grove for as long as she had—but the thought of her cottage standing empty and abandoned...of her home being forever out of her reach...

And her *soldiers.* They had made a temporary home here. They were making a difference in the lives of every-day people. "What of the crops that are grown here?" Aspen asked, amazed that she kept her voice even-toned. "How will they get distributed without my soldiers here?"

"That will not be your concern once you have left. I'm sure General Dallowyn and I will find a suitable arrangement to maintain distribution." Inula waved her hand dismissively. "You may leave."

The last phrase felt like the final death knell. Aspen was grateful for Hemlock's help, because she wasn't sure she would have been able to walk out of the Council room under her own power. Her limbs froze in shock and horror. Hemlock guided her outside, where the golden light was suddenly too bright. It raked like claws over Aspen's eyes, and she looked away.

"Hemlock, what am I going to do?" she mumbled, trying to keep the terrified heartbreak out of her voice.

"Well, for one thing, you're going to come with me so we can get your back looked at and take care of whatever other injuries I know you got," Hemlock said. Her stern lines melted away, and she brushed Aspen's cheek. "And after that, you're going to do what you've always done. You will win, beautifully, nobly, and fiercely, and you will make Inula choke on her words."

EIGHTEEN

R o wrenched the guards' hands off and turned to launch himself back into the Council Room, but Ash caught him and hauled him back.

"Whoa, hold on a—" she began.

"You can't seriously think we should leave Aspen in there by herself!" Ro snarled. "She's outnumbered in there! They don't believe a word she says!"

Ash's fingers dug into Ro's arm until bruises formed beneath them. A closed-mouth smile pulled so tightly on her lips they nearly disappeared. She turned to the guards, her grip still fierce on Ro's arm. "Thank you. You boys are always so *gentle* and *noble*." She blinked at them innocently. "I'm happy to see you've finally passed your Gauntlet. Oak, that must mean you're able to pick up a shield without dropping it. And, Lichen, did your archery skills improve, or did the broad side of barns just get, well, *broader*?"

The two elves' faces burned scarlet with rage. "Don't come back!" One of them commanded. They shoved the four along and then stood sentinel outside the Council Room doors. When Ro and the others were out of earshot, Ash relinquished her hold on Ro and rounded on him. "By the *Architects*, Ro, do you really think *I* would just up and abandon Aspen?"

Ro paled slightly in the face of her ire. "I mean, it certainly *seemed* like—"

"*Easy,*" Styrax said, a note of a warning growl in his voice.

Ro mashed his lips together and glared at him. Sorren took a step away from the group, watching them all nervously.

Ash sighed and worried at her braid, casting a look over her shoulder to the Council Room. The guards had gone back inside, but Ro had no doubt they were lying in wait to throw them back out if they tried to enter again.

"My own *mother* is the head of all that mess," Ash said, spitting out the word like it was poison. "I know how their logic—or lack thereof—works." She turned an accusatory finger on Ro. "Riling them up only makes them take it out on their preferred target—who just so happens to be Aspen at this current moment."

"To be fair," Styrax interjected, raising his eyebrow at Ash. "Weren't you the one that started the mildly antagonistic side comments in the first place?"

Ash waved him off. "I don't count. Inula's gotten accustomed to ignoring me, just like everything else that doesn't fit her perfect vision of her life." She let out a bone-weary sigh, and some of the tenseness left her body. "There's not a lot we can do about it now. Aspen might be in there a while. Should we get Ro to Gan's house?"

Ro choked, and he dropped his head in shame. Even after he had been accusing her, Ash was still unfailingly kind.

Ash turned to Sorren and smiled. "You're welcome to come with us if you'd like, but if you'd rather track down some pygmy dragons first, I won't stop you."

If she had handed him the sun, Sorren's face wouldn't have shone any brighter. "Okay!" he was off like a hare, bounding through the trees in search of the brightly colored creatures. Styrax and Ro followed Ash through the streets of the Golden Grove. Ash stayed quiet, her head down, and Styrax walked quietly beside her, his mouth agape as he took in everything. Ro wanted to join him and be excited to be back in the place he'd called home, but the Council had left a rancor in his mouth. Had they always been that horrible? How did Aspen manage it? Why hadn't her family been there to support her?

Now that he thought of it, he hadn't seen Aspen's brothers or her mother since they had arrived.

"Ash?" he asked. "Where's the rest of Aspen's family?"

Ash's shoulder stiffened, and her steps faltered. "For answers to that, you'll need to ask Aspen yourself," she said, her tone leaving no further room for argument.

Ro's heart dropped into his stomach. Something told him he wouldn't like Aspen's answers.

"Where do you live?" Styrax asked Ash, his tone two shades too bright. Ro was grateful for the distraction.

Ash chuckled darkly. "Before or after my banishment?"

Styrax and Ro both froze, looking between themselves and gaping at Ash.

"You were *banished*?" Styrax asked, the hurt somehow personal in his voice.

"*Why*?" Ro asked at the same moment.

Ash's face broke into a grin laced with underlying bitterness. "Every ten years, the best and boldest elven warriors compete in the Gauntlet for the chance to serve as a guard to the Council of Elders, which is just a polite way to say that the Council Head likes to watch people sweat and beat on each other before recruiting them to their personal army."

Ro didn't know if he should be horrified that Inula had her own personal army, or impressed that she maintained loyal soldiers with her less-than-desirable personality.

"The top twenty contenders pass their 'trials', and are generally recruited to serve for the next ten years. Once their service is up, they can either retire or participate in the games again."

Styrax gave her a knowing smile. "I'm assuming you passed your trials, and Inula didn't like that?"

Ash's grin turned diabolical. "Better. I *won*. Four trials in a row." She flicked her braid off her shoulder, looking smug. "The winner is offered the position of the Council Head's personal bodyguard, which comes with a hefty amount of money and no small amount of prestige. It is, of course, offered publicly as a formality, but no elf has ever been insane enough to say no."

Ro grinned despite himself. "Except for you?"

"Except for me," she said with a wink and a nostalgic sigh. "Getting to say 'no' to her face four separate times—and her not being able to do anything about it—was truly worth more than any gold. After I publicly humiliated her for the fourth time, she banished me for 'disrespecting our honored traditions'." Ash shrugged. "I didn't have anywhere else to go. My father was in an accident that altered his mind and made him childlike most days, and violent others, and he disappeared after Inula left him."

She said it so casually that Ro almost didn't pick up on how truly, gut-wrenchingly awful that experience must have been. He shared a wide-eyed look with Styrax, who looked just as pale and shocked.

Ash trekked ahead as if had simply been discussing the weather. "So, I went and made my fortune as a master thief. I had my own crew and everything. And then Aspen needed me more." A sad, far away look came over her. But then she blinked, and it was gone. "But enough about me. Ro, I'm sure your head is full to bursting with everything going on here. Let's get you to Gan's so you can eat and sleep."

WHEN ASH and Styrax took Ro to Gan's house, Ro had to stop and stare. His breath lodged in his throat at the sight, swelling until his

chest felt as if it would burst. Endless rows of pea vines stretched out and away from the small cottage, red blossoms bobbing happily beneath the golden trees. Ro had to laugh, the sound thick with emotion. He turned to Styrax. "Do you see what color the blossoms are?"

Styrax shook his head, rolling his eyes good-naturedly and chuckling. "No wonder you were always so protective of your little vine in Monterro. It reminded you of home. As well as you *could* be reminded, at least."

"And Boff can *keep* his Fernite strand," Ro said emphatically.

At the sound of their voices, the cottage door opened and Gan poked his head out. The smell of something delicious floated out behind him. His smile split his face into bursts of smile lines. "Welcome home, son," he said, his voice wavering. He looked to Styrax and Ash. "There's plenty of food if you'd like to join us!"

Styrax bowed low. "I appreciate it, sire, but I think our prince has earned a night alone with his father."

The pair bade their goodbyes and left. Styrax wrapped his arm around Ash's shoulder and brushed a kiss on the top of her hair before they disappeared around the corner. Ro watched them go, his thoughts drifting to Aspen. Was she all right after the meeting with the Elders? Why had she just let them abuse her that way? But the smell—the *memories*—from his childhood pulled at him, and he let it overtake him. Aspen was home. She would be safe for another night.

Gan had truly laid out a feast. The small table in the center of the cottage was filled to overflowing with trays and bowls of food. The smells made Ro's mouth water. The colors and variety were homey, welcoming, and delicious. He wanted nothing more than to sit and dig in, but the interior of the cottage made him freeze. He had grown accustomed to things being a little fuzzy around the edges—things being just slightly off from how he remembered due to the march of time—but eventually settling into a new normal. This, though, was crystal clear. The scuff marks on the floor. His bed tucked into the back corner of the main room with a wrinkle from where he had placed his hand. The dried flowers hanging on Gan's bedroom door. The two rags—one gray, one brown—hanging next to the washbasin. It was all exactly as it had been five years ago.

"I couldn't bear to move anything around," Gan said quietly, as if reading Ro's thoughts. He hugged him to his side with one arm, the top of his head barely reaching Ro's shoulder. "It made it feel like you could walk through that door at any moment." He looked up at Ro, his eyes shining with pride and relief. "And now you have!"

Ro hugged him with both arms, trying not to let the full brunt of his weight crush Gan's small frame. An odd rush of guilt swept through Ro. Gan had kept everything as it had been before Ro lost his memories. But Ro knew that he had not come back to the Golden Grove as the same Ro that had left five years ago, and he hoped that wouldn't be a disappointment. Not to this man that had loved him so endlessly.

Gan let out a heavy sigh and patted Ro's back. "What are we waiting for? Let's eat before the food gets cold!"

"All right," Ro said, his voice wavering.

They tucked in, and the flavors instantly transported Ro back to the many evenings spent with Gan. Picking peas from the vine. Huddled near their hearth, both sick with a cold but Gan still telling him stories. Singing ridiculous, made-up songs before bed. Talking about life and the pains of growing up. Gan telling him who he was and what he was meant to become.

"What's wrong, son?" Gan's voice cut through the images.

Ro hadn't noticed the tears dripping off his chin until Gan said something. He went to brush them away, but his trembling hand stayed over his eyes, casting him into blessed dark. He leaned his weight against the table, somehow unable to hold himself up anymore. The memories had been so real. He *knew* he had lived them, but they also felt so apart from what he knew of himself, like he was viewing himself in a reflection. That Ro had been so sure of himself. He knew exactly what needed to be done—knew with full certainty that he could become everything everyone expected of him. But *this* Ro had become entwined with Tristan, who had no future or past, and existed with constant fear and worry. This Ro was not the Ro he had been meant to be.

"Gan, I—" His voice broke. He looked at his father helplessly, the guilt and shame racing like wildfire through his body. The love and concern in Gan's eyes nearly broke him. The thought of disappointing him froze all the words in Ro's throat.

Gan leaned back in his chair, one of the legs wobbling as he did so. Ro remembered 'fixing' the chair as a surprise for Gan when he was about ten, but only making the wobble worse. Gan had refused to let Ro actually fix the chair when his wood-working skills improved, claiming he wouldn't know which chair was his without the wobble in it. The memory was a warm pain in Ro's chest.

"You were gone a long time, Ro," Gan said. "Why don't you tell me about the man you've become?"

Ro let out a coarse chuckle. Gan always seemed to know how to get to the heart of the matter. "I don't hardly know anymore, Da," he said. "And I'm—" He swallowed the lump in his throat. "Scared."

Gan didn't move. He just continued to watch Ro, his expression open and gentle. "Scared of what?"

Ro let out a long breath, steadying his nerves. "Of disappointing you. Of disappointing *Aspen*." He ran his hands through his hair, his agitation building. "I'm supposed to be a prince—a *king*. I used to know what that meant, but now—" Laire's words played through his mind. *This is the kingdom you want to lead? Some broken things are better left to burn.* Ro grit his teeth at the thought, even as he wondered if maybe the kingdom *was* better left to someone else. "I couldn't muster the courage to leave a *single* fort to fix myself and find my memories. How am I supposed to lead an entire *kingdom*?" He dropped his hands to his lap, his head hung low. "You taught me so much and built me into someone that was supposed to be a great ruler. But I'm afraid that I will never be that same Ro you lost five years ago."

The cottage was silent, Ro's words hanging in the air like a smothering blanket. Ro couldn't look up. He couldn't see the disappointment and grief had had caused Gan. Gan had already lost his son once. To lose him again...

Gan's chair creaked as he leaned forward. "Ro, do you think *I* haven't changed over these past five years?" he asked, his voice hoarse.

Ro looked at him then and saw nothing but love and understanding. A lump built in his throat.

Gan looked around the cottage. "I didn't let the physical things around me change, because I had too much happening in here." He touched his hand to his chest. "I lost my son—the one thing I thought I had forever after I lost my wife and the kingdom I knew. That changed me. I said and did things the Gan you used to know would never do. Aspen especially took the brunt of that change." He ran his hand along the tabletop. "I've clung to possessions more and lived life less. I have more fear, more anger, and more sadness than I ever did before." He looked up and took Ro's hand in both of his, squeezing tightly. "We are not always in control of the changes life brings our way. But we are in charge of shaping the choices we make despite them."

Ro clutched Gan's hand tightly, wishing for all the world that he could go back to his childhood and bask in the moments where it seemed Gan could control the world.

"I will never again be the Gan that watches you leave without fearing you'll never come back," Gan said, his hands trembling. "But I will choose to let you live your life. I will never again be the Gan that has not lost a son, and because of that, I choose to love you fiercer and openly, because I know there will be one day that I can't." He brushed Ro's hair away from his forehead so that he could look him in the eyes. "Know this—whatever changes life has brought you, I can tell that you are sill someone that chooses goodness, love, and courage. I am and will forever be proud of you for that."

Ro's eyes brimmed with tears again, struck speechless by the warmth and strength swelling in his chest. The only thing he could think to do was lean across the table and hug Gan. "Thank you, Da," he whispered in a husky voice. "I don't know what kind of man I am now, but I know if I'm *half* as wise and good as you are, I'll have a good start on who I want to be."

NINETEEN

Ro was up early the next morning, wandering the Golden Grove alleys aimlessly as the leaves turned from silver to gold in the morning sunshine. He didn't know what he was looking for, exactly, but he had certainly not expected to find Aspen and a group of her men loading wagons full of sacks and barrels. The men nodded and waved to him as he picked his way through the stacks.

"You all going somewhere?" he asked.

"We don't get paid to answer questions," one soldier, a tall, willowy man with green-tinted skin, said, handing him a sack.

"I mean, really, we don't get paid at all." Another chimed in, wiping his brow with the back of his hand. A tattoo of Aspen's Coward's Mark flashed on his forearm. "But we don't sweat the details."

Ro smiled at them and hefted the sack over his shoulder. "Can I at least ask where I'm supposed to be taking this?"

"Now that one we *are* unpaid to answer." The green man pointed to a wagon. "General Shadowalker's over that way. Check in with her, and she'll get that sorted into inventory."

"She doesn't like to answer too many questions, though, so be careful!"

Ro chuckled. "Oh, don't you worry, I'm well aware." He made his way to Aspen as she scratched tick marks on a roll of parchment.

"Can I ask what happened with the rest of the Conclave?" he asked as he placed his load atop similar-looking sacks.

Aspen didn't look up at him, but he could have sworn he saw dread flash across her features. "No. And that's wheat grain you just put on top of all my oats," Aspen said without looking up from her parchment. "That goes over there." She gestured to an identical pile of sacks.

Ro raised his eyebrows, a teasing smile pulling at the corner of his mouth. He bowed deeply and did as he was told. When he stood back up, stretching his back, he took in the clearing, which was full to the brim with boxes, barrels, and sacks. "Are we aiming to feed a small country?"

"It's harvest day." Aspen said, as if that would answer everything. "We've got to haul all of this out so we can make room for more before the Goldenlight festival." She made one final tick, nodded in approval, and rolled up her parchment. "Besides, I wouldn't call Loralan 'small'."

Ro looked at her, his eyes wide with astonishment. "You feed all of Loralan with this?"

"As much as we can." She dug through the back of the wagon, jostling the contents, presumably to make sure everything was fully secure. "We're able to grow a full crop yield every two months, and then we make sure it gets distributed to towns most affected by fallow fields. No sense in saving a kingdom if you just let everyone starve."

The rest of the gathered soldiers checked their own wagons—eight in total—and began harnessing horses to them. Ro watched the efficiency and the sheer amount of food with his jaw open.

"Are there that many towns suffering?"

Aspen nodded, her face grim. "Farmlands have been declining

ever since the war started. Some people think it's because magic's been chased away." She shrugged. "All *I* know is there are a lot of hungry mouths to feed, and there just never seems to be enough to go around."

"You save some for yourselves, though, don't you?"

Aspen shook her head, a wicked grin spreading across her face. "We figure if the supplies ever make it into the King's Men's hands, then it's rightfully ours for the taking. We eat that."

Ro gaped at her, realization dawning on him as he remembered all the stories of the elusive General Shadowalker attacking supply lines left and right before disappearing back into the shadows. The most noteworthy had been at Bael, where the supplies had been meant to go to the front lines. "So you don't attack supply lines just to cause mayhem? You do it so you can eat?"

She tucked her dark hair behind her ear, a wry, smug grin spreading across her face. "The mayhem's a bonus."

Ro shook his head at her, rubbing his forehead at the sheer scope of what Aspen was suggesting. "General Shadowalker's entire duty is to feed the entirety of Loralan?"

"Essentially," she said with a shrug.

"You are absolutely incredible, you know that?"

Aspen shuffled her feet and crossed her arms over her chest, looking away from him. "Like I said, not much sense in putting all this effort into a war only to have everyone starve before it's over."

He smiled. "Yes, General." He saluted her—two fingers to his lips —and bowed. "Tell me how I can be of service."

She rolled her eyes. "Well, for starters, a bunch of rebel soldiers can't very well show up in every town handing out food without drawing suspicion, so we have a fence we'll need to deliver all of this to. Would you like to come with us?"

"I'd love to," he said, grinning. "It's not every day you get to ride with a notorious general on her clandestine schemes."

She smiled, but there was a wicked sort of gleam in her eye. Ro narrowed his eyes, suddenly wary of what he had agreed to, but she waved him off.

"Are Ash and the others coming?" he asked, looking around and expecting them to jump out of the sacks. Aspen had looked far too pleased to have him along.

"Ash has to get her kitchen crew back into shape after being gone so long," Aspen answered, hopping into the wagon. "Styrax and Sorren are probably still sleeping."

"Uh-huh." Ro settled into the wagon beside her, still looking around for them.

"Oh, honestly, I'm not going to eat you," Aspen said, exasperated. "Settle down. We're just going for a ride."

"So you say," Ro countered. "But the last time you said that to me, you had nearly cut me in half. I'm not taking my chances."

Aspen shook her head to the heavens. "And you have come *so far* from being that suspicious soldier since." She clucked to the horse hitched to her wagon, and away they went. A few soldiers rode beside them on horses, weaving between the wagons with lanterns hanging from their saddles.

They rode for only a few counts of silence before Ro asked. "How do we get all of this through the Woods of Desolation?"

"We take part of the Sacred Flame." She motioned to the lanterns the riders carried. A golden flame burned brightly inside. "It keeps the mist and Sí'Rakk away."

Ro gaped at her, shocked into momentary silence. "*Where* was that when the Sí'Rakk almost tore my head off my shoulders?" he finally asked.

Aspen winced. "Sorry. We can't carry them with us everywhere. It's a safety precaution so that others can't sneak into the Grove."

Ro mashed his lips together, shuddering from the phantom traces of the Si'Rakk's fingers on his throat. He toyed with the silver ring around his neck. "Will those lanterns protect us from the shade, too?"

It was like he had cast a shadow over Aspen as soon as he said the words. Her fingers tightened on the wagon reins, and her shoulders hunched as her eyes unfocused. "We're going to have to hope. Of all our current problems, the shade is, somehow, very low on my priority list." Her face was gray as she said it.

Ro chuckled, the sound two octaves too high. "I love it when monsters are the least of our worries. It really helps me sleep at night."

She smirked at him. "At least you sleep." She clucked to the wagon horse, and it picked up its pace to a jaunting trot.

When they reached the Woods of Desolation, the sound of the wagon's jangling harnesses were swallowed up in the silence. Ro held his breath, unconsciously covering his mouth as they drew into the mist. He couldn't tell if it would be worse to close his eyes or keep them open. One hand he kept clenched on the wagon seat as he waited, body tense, for something to lunge out from amid the dead trees.

The lantern riders strung out amidst the caravan formed a sort of light shield around them, their lanterns held high above them. The mist recoiled like some nebulous creature, flinching anytime the circle of light touched it. No Si'Rakk voices drifted toward the group, and no tormented, twisted beasts emerged. Even so, every nerve in Ro's body tingled with the electricity of panic until they emerged into daylight on the other side. He and Aspen shared a sigh of relief.

Outside of the woods, it was a beautiful day. The sun was a soft blanket of early fall warmth, and there was a tiny bite to the air, like a hint of spice in a sweet dish. Grasslands rolled out in every direction, shimmering as the grass bowed with the wind, and there was a sharpness that foretold thunderstorms in the distance. He breathed in, wishing they could have enjoyed the landscape more on their way to the Golden Grove. Traveling throughout the night after a mad man burned down an entire village had a way of putting a damper on things.

A village came into view in the distance, and the lead lantern rider called to two others and they cantered down the road, breaking away from the rest of the party.

"Scouts," Aspen said before Ro could even ask the question. "Although this village is pretty well sheltered from Osmen's oversight, it never hurts to be too cautious." There was a subtle edge to her voice Ro couldn't decipher.

Ro settled back in his seat and watched the village's chimney smoke make lazy curls against the sky. "How long have you been doing these runs?" Ro asked.

Aspen shrugged. "Long time? Ash and I started stealing a few things from supply lines because we saw a need." She tilted her head and smiled to herself. "I also think Ash missed her thieving days, but that's for another time."

One of the lantern riders that had stayed behind—a small, orange-skinned woman with ears like a bat—rode up beside them on a shaggy pony.

"We heard about what two crazy women were doing in the west, and we decided we wanted in on the fun," she said in a low, smooth voice, her eyes twinkling a little too brightly.

"We got so big we made General Dallowyn nervous!" a wagon driver called from the back.

Aspen rolled her eyes. "He wasn't nervous," she corrected quietly to Ro. "He just saw two girls leagues out of their element, and decided to help them out. He invited us to officially join the rebellion, put me in charge of this crew, and now here we are."

Ro just stared at her in wonder. Of all the things she could have done with her time—after nearly losing her life—*that* was what she had chosen to do? "I'm not sure this kingdom would survive without you, Aspen."

She scoffed at that. "You'll find plenty of people that would disagree with you."

"None of them that matter, though," the bat-eared woman grumbled. Ro smiled at her, and she winked.

The scouts returned minutes later, waving the caravan down the road.

"All clear!" Aspen called behind her before urging the cart horse into a faster gait.

The town—which a weather-beaten sign deemed as Alvernet—was perhaps the most thriving settlement Ro had seen in years. Lorate had been happy when he left, but Avernet flew steps above it. The cheeriness almost blinded him. An entire party of townsfolk waited to greet them with cheers as they rolled into town. Their faces were full and bright, not tinged by the realities of war that had started to creep into Lorate. Children laughed and played. Cheery, spiced smoke laden with the smell of food wafted from every house. The adults laughed with each other as they worked and waved to the wagons as they passed.

"Is *this* what Loralan is supposed to be?" Ro hadn't realized he had spoken out loud until Aspen gave him a small, sad smile.

"This is the town my father grew up in." She nodded to a boarded up tanner's shop. "That's where he met my mother. She used to come here to avoid Inula."

Ro snorted

Aspen got a far-off look in her eyes. "Da told me the whole kingdom used to be like this—happy and free." Her hands clenched tighter around the reins. "It's why he was always so proud when we all joined the rebellion. He wanted this Loralan back."

Ro wished he knew how to respond to that without sounding trite.

The caravan rolled to a stop in the town square, and Aspen threw her hood up over her ears. "Oh, one last thing," she said, her eyes sparkling and an impish look pulling at the lines on her face. "Whatever happens today, just go along with it."

Before Ro could ask what that meant, a woman with cropped blond hair and a scar down her cheek sidled up to the carts. "Afternoon, folks," she said with a huge grin. "Name's Selva. You come to join us for our midmonth festival?"

"Naw, it's the mid-*year* festival!" a man called from the crowd, leaning against a shovel.

"Mid year? I thought that was last week!" another woman countered as she bundled laundry into a basket.

Selva chuckled. "Whichever one it is, we have a festival today. 'Fraid nothing's open but my fine tavern, and we're all drunker than fish."

"Well, what excellent timing!" Aspen said brightly. Too brightly. "We're just here to rest our weary bones before we're off to Monterro to sell all this food."

Ro looked at Aspen like she had lost her mind. *Monterro?*

The woman put her hands on her hips. "Well, drat. I know some smaller villages that could really use the food rather than selling it to the fat oafs in the castle city."

Aspen splayed her hands in a helpless gesture. "But the fat oafs have all the money. Whatever would I do if I couldn't sell this for ten times what it's worth?" She leaned forward, elbow resting on the edge of the wagon as she rested her chin on her palm. "Why don't you tell me about those poor village saps, though? I'll be sure to drive by them on my way and laugh at them." Aspen withdrew two pieces of parchment, one her tick mark chart, and another blank. "Start with the most destitute. I like to mock them best."

A slow smile pulled at Ro's mouth. So that was the game they were playing?

Selva blinked up at Aspen, her eyes squinted against the sun. "Ahh, then you'll want to start in Caldrech."

Aspen frowned. Her affected look and tone dimmed. "Caldrech?" she asked, her voice quieter. "I thought they were thriving?"

Selva's face sobered, and she shook her head. "Turns out it was a sprite keeping their fields alive. A soldier killed him not too long ago, and their crops withered."

Aspen hung her head low. "They'll watch this whole kingdom wilt before they learn anything," she muttered to herself. She shook her head and cleared her throat. When she spoke again, it was in that false, bright tone. "How many people should we expect to scorn as we drive by?"

"Eighty-three, m'lady."

Aspen wrote Caldrech and the number eighty-three on her parchment. She then went through her inventory list and crossed off certain items, writing them beside Caldrech's name instead. Once she was done, Selva listed another town and the number of people in it, and Aspen repeated the process. They went back and forth like that for some time. Ro watched in fascination as Aspen deftly divvied out resources, awed at how efficient they were. They really had been doing this a long time.

When the list was finished, Aspen laid it carelessly on top of a box for all to see. "Very well, I believe that is enough victims for one day. We shall stretch our legs and be off. Don't you dare snoop through our wares, either. These are very important things for very important people."

A young girl giggled from amidst the crowd, and Aspen cast her a sharp look. "And there are *certainly* no honey sweets in the box behind the driver's seat. And even if there were, they're poisonous to children." She swept down out of the wagon.

The girl didn't bat an eye and simply grinned, her freckles crinkling across her nose.

Her soldiers approached her. "General," one said loudly. "We need you to look at —"

"*Don't* call me *general*," she said in a broad, affected voice. Ro caught one of the older children grinning and mouthing the words as Aspen spoke them. "You know that in town I'm Cynthia Purplesbottom."

Another peal of laughter rose from the children. A few of the adults quietly joined in as well.

Aspen whirled on them, jaw clenched and nose scrunched with ire, but her eyes gleaming. "You *dare* laugh at me?" She threw her hood off, revealing her finely pointed ears. "I'll turn you all into chickens!"

The children shrieked and ran away. "It was frogs last time!"

The adults waited a few beats before they all drew in a collective gasp. Selva staggered back a pace, a hand over her heart. "Why, they're just a bunch of Ancient Ones! Who ever could have thought?" She pressed the back of her hand to her forehead. "Oh, *oh!* What *ever* shall we *do?*"

"Lock them up!" a child that couldn't have been more than four cried, his tiny fist in the air as he giggled in his mother's arms.

"You're right!" Selva gestured to a few burly men. "We'll have to lock them up and call for the nearest King's Guard. How could they have *known* to come on a festival day when we're too drunk to discipline them ourselves?" She straightened herself and regarded the wagons, folding her arms. "Looks like we'll have to confiscate all these goods, too. Can't have them going to the rebellion when we're all good, king-fearing folk."

Ro had to stifle back a snort, wondering how long it had taken for them all to put their scripts together. His heart filled with warmth, though, as he watched Aspen. She was *playing*, and he loved it.

He waited to see how the others would react as the larger towns-folk approached them, expecting a grand charade of fisticuffs, but Aspen and the others stood patiently waiting as the men stomped toward them. When the men touched the soldiers, they wailed and withered, cursing them for being such mighty warriors. Ro played along, writhing on the ground with the best of them. Loose ropes were tied around his wrists, and they were all marched off to a ramshackle village prison.

"Be sure they can't get out!" The tavern keeper called cheerily. "We're too inebriated to chase after them if they escape!"

Inside was only one large cell with flimsy, rusting bars. The walls appeared to stay upright with strings and prayers alone. The town men hauled them all into the cell and hung the keys haphazardly on a peg, where the keys immediately fell off within arm's reach of the cell bars. The men bowed deeply. "Enjoy your stay. We'll alert the

King's Guard in the morning...If you're still here by then." They winked and left.

One stayed behind, wringing a hat in his hands. "Thank you," he said softly. "My sister and her husband live in a town in the east. I got a letter from her saying she just delivered her first baby. They're both happy and healthy, because some stranger left a pile of food in their town square one night." He put his hat back on, tipped it to them, and then followed his friends. Aspen smiled softly after him before perusing a small board that had been hung on the wall. Scraps of parchment had been attached to it.

Ro folded his arms and watched her work.

"Looks like we've got some highwayman to the east," she said to one of her soldiers, who was scribbling notes. "We'll take care of those once Lorate is dealt with. We can't spare anyone for the trip right now." She pulled another slip of parchment off the board. "And we've got some sabers nearby. We can probably handle those on our way back."

"Whatever you say, General."

Ro leaned against the cell bars and looked at Aspen with a raised, teasing eyebrow. "You went through all that trouble finding me just to get me locked in a cell?"

Aspen handed the rest of the parchments to the soldier taking notes and smirked at Ro. "You *are* a wanted man. You were bound to wind up behind bars at some point."

He leaned into her, his forehead almost brushing hers. "Yes, but that doesn't mean I expected my *general* to lead me there."

Aspen looked up into his eyes, smirking. "You're the one that chose to follow me."

One of the other soldiers cleared their throat. "Friendly reminder that the rest of us are here, too," he said, eying them with barely restrained amusement.

Ro finally registered just how close he was standing to Aspen. He took a step back, his cheeks pink.

Aspen opened her arms to take in the breadth of their terrifying, impenetrable cell. "We've got to give the villagers plausible deniability. They captured us the moment they knew we were Ancient Races. It's not their fault we're hardened war criminals." She reached through the bars and snatched the fallen keys, dangling them from her finger in front of Ro. "It's also not our fault that their prisons weren't meant to hold us."

They waited until dark before they unlocked the prison and slipped into the night. The wagons had been emptied—the inventory parchments taken—and Aspen smiled. "Another successful run," she whispered to the rest of the crew.

They whooped quietly and rode back to the Golden Grove, empty wagons in tow.

TWENTY

Vinea flattened herself into the shadows, her stomach lurching and her heart pounding in her throat. She had lost track of the days since she left Monterro. All she knew was that she was filthy, exhausted, and starving. All she wanted was to curl up in her bed in Lorate with Laire next to her and Linae tucked between them. She had wandered into a small forest off the main road to catch a few hours of sleep before continuing her journey to the Golden Grove, but instead, had caught sight of the men posted in intervals throughout the trees, formless in their shifting armor that nearly disappeared into the background. A camp had formed behind them, tucked against an outcropping of tumbled rocks. The Vanguard.

Vinea stumbled back a few paces. No. *No, not them.* She wanted nothing to do with them—nothing to do with their emotionless, casual brutality—or with the fact that Laire had abandoned her to pursue a station with them.

Even though Vinea was technically now Sedick's subordinate, he had said nothing about immunity or being able to request aid from other soldiers serving Osmen. The Vanguard would most likely kill her if they saw her. She backed farther into the trees. This didn't happen. She was never here. All that mattered was getting into the Golden Grove to save Linae.

"Vinea?"

The voice dripped like ice water down Vinea's spine. Chills raced along her arms, and an involuntary gasp escaped her lips. She turned slowly, not daring to breathe.

A man stood behind her, rigid and wide-eyed. A sapphire-encrusted sword hilt hung at his side, his hand resting on the pommel.

Tears welled in Vinea's eyes. She backed away from him, choking on the lump of both fear and longing in her throat. Her vision lurched, stars dancing in her eyes. She couldn't breathe past the pounding of her heart. "Laire, I—"

He crossed the distance between them in two long strides. Vinea staggered away from him, hands clutching at her chest. "Laire, wait, stop, I—" she stumbled over a tree root and pitched backward.

Laire caught her by the waist before she fell. For a moment, she saw his eyes—the beautiful blue ones she had fallen so madly in love with—and they were filled with nothing but relief. He pulled her to him and kissed her. Vinea's body went numb as he wrapped her in his arms. Tears swept down her cheeks, and she closed her eyes. She hadn't felt so safe—so *loved*—in weeks. She never wanted to leave, choosing instead to stay wrapped in that moment with her husband forever.

Until she remembered why she was in that goddess-forsaken forest to begin with.

Bristling with rage, her vision searing and her blood liquid fire in her veins, Vinea wrenched herself away from Laire. She swiped the back of her hand over her lips and clenched her fists, fighting back the urge to strike him in the jaw.

Laire gave her a wounded look and took a step toward her. "Vinea, what—"

"You *left* me, Laire!" Vinea wanted to scream it at him, but she was too terrified of the other Vanguardsmen hearing her, so she kept her voice to a seething hiss. "I gave you a chance to choose me or this pointless war. You chose the *war*." Her limbs shook with all her pent up terror and rage. She had expected to never see him again—she had even told him as much. But now that he was so close, so *real*...

It enraged her how many times he could break her heart.

"You left, Laire," she said again through clenched teeth. Her hand went to the stud in her ear, the burns from Sedick's band still stark on her wrist. Her charged thoughts raced to Linae, trapped in Monterro's rotting dungeon. "And now—"

Laire ran to her, gripping her by the elbows and examining her injured wrist. She tried to pull away, but he held her tight, his fingers soft and shaking on her skin. "Who did this to you?" he asked, his voice deep and dangerous.

Vinea's resolve was crumbling. She didn't want to answer—wanted to stay true to the decision he had made to abandon her. But he was so *warm*. So solid. And, of anything else she needed in this world, she needed someone on her side.

"Laire, I—"

The moon caught a glint of something on his hands, dark and wet.

Blood.

Vinea recoiled from him, bile rising to her mouth in revulsion. Her gaze darted around the forest, looking for somewhere to run, and landed on a small, bloodied form behind Laire, tied against a tree. *Chaedra.*

"What have you *done*?" Vinea ran to Chaedra, feeling for a pulse and checking to see if she was breathing. Chaedra's eyes fluttered open, bleary with pain beneath the bruises marring her face. Her breath wheezed in her chest, and every movement seemed to cause her pain. Adrenaline poured through every fiber of Vinea's being. They knew. They knew who Chaedra was. Did that mean they also knew—

Laire's presence loomed behind Vinea. "Do you know this woman?"

The fine hairs on Vinea's neck prickled. She looked up at him, and her fear returned anew. Her husband was gone. His eyes had taken on a haunted, gray-tinged quality. The sharp angles of his face seemed as cold and impersonal as blades, and the pull of his mouth was cruel. Bloodthirsty. A grayish glow wafted from the sword at his side. He was no longer the man Vinea loved. A monster had taken his place.

"Of course I know her," Vinea answered in a whisper, her body trembling. She tried not to shrink away from him, but it was a battle she lost. "She works for the bakery in—"

"She's a spy," Laire said, all hints of emotion gone from his voice. Only cold brutality remained. "We caught her snooping at the edge of camp. She will be dealt with appropriately."

"A spy? What?" Vinea tried to make her words sound convincing, but she couldn't get enough strength in them. Laire eyed her, and his hand drifted to his sword. Vinea's heart stopped.

"General Laire!" someone called through the trees. "We found the tunnel entrance!"

Some of the clarity returned to Laire's eyes, and his hand drifted away from his cursed sword. He looked at Vinea with a hint of fear as a shadow crossed over his face. Fear for her.

"You're the Vanguard's general again?" Vinea breathed, the look on his face making her stomach churn. He had meant to hurt her before that soldier had called.

"All for you, my love." He turned away from her, the haunted look still in his eyes. "It's not safe for you here. I'll be back, but you have to be gone by then. Leave the spy to me." He left toward the sound of the voices.

Vinea sat, frozen, as she watched him leave, her heart thundering in her ears. Something was terribly, horribly wrong. And she had no doubt his wretched sword was to blame.

"Vinea," Chaedra said weakly. "Listen to me."

Vinea snapped back to reality. Her jaw clenched with anger at the state Chaedra was in. How dare Laire? She moved to untie Chaedra, but her hands froze in her lap. Sedick's magic swelled in her mind, forcing her to stay put.

Chaedra didn't seem to notice. It appeared staying conscious was already too much effort for her. "You have to get to General Shadowalker." Her words broke between hitching, garbled breaths. "Tell her that someone betrayed us. They're coming through the dwarven tunnels. The Lorate soldiers are under Sedick's control, and the Vanguard will sneak in while Lorate is creating a distraction. Every one of them—Lorate and the Vanguard—will have serpent root nets."

Vinea tried to stop her—the more she knew, the more she could betray. The guilt was already corroding her insides. But Chaedra powered on. "You'll be safe in the Golden Grove. They'll protect you. When you get there, tell the general this phrase: one never knows the trueness of intentions, and can only hope for the intention of truth."

The words slammed into Vinea like a battering ram.

Chaedra repeated the phrase two more times before her shoulders slumped, her head hanging low. "I'm sorry to drag you into this, but you're the only person I can trust to—" Her words cut off abruptly when she looked up at Vinea. Her eyes grew wide with horror and her skin took on a sickly hue. "What's that in your ear?"

Tears of guilt sprang to Vinea's eyes as she brushed Sedick's earring. She saw the recognition in Chaedra's face—the betrayal when she realized she had confided in the wrong person.

"I'm sorry," Vinea said, turning away from Chaedra's accusing face. "He has my daughter." She fled before Chaedra could say anything else that would doom them both.

TWENTY-ONE

A few days after their return from Alvernet, Ro bolted out of bed at the sound of rapping on the door. Gan, it seemed, had already been up for hours to tend to his peas. His bed had been neatly made and a simple breakfast had been set out for Ro. A twinge of guilt prodded at Ro's chest. As a younger boy, Gan probably would have tipped him out of bed for being late for chores. He almost missed that.

More rapping sounded at the door before it was interrupted by Gan's muffled voice.

"Well, aren't you a vision? I'll let you in. I can't imagine my boy should be sleeping for too much longer."

Before Ro had time to react, the door creaked open and in walked Gan, followed closely by Aspen. Ro stared, wide-eyed, at her. The morning sun gilded her simple gown the color of the night sky in a golden halo. Vines had been stitched in silver around the hems of the velvet fabric, and they glittered as it swished around her. Her hair flowed long and free to the center of her back in gentle waves. Her sword was still strapped to her waist. Shimmering, nearly translucent pigment had been applied to the corners of her eyes. Her sword sat low on her waist, cinching the dress just enough to accentuate her figure.

Some sort of inarticulate sound squeaked out of Ro's throat, and he shut his gaping mouth with a resounding clack. Aspen averted her gaze from him, tapping her fingers awkwardly at her side. It was only then that Ro remembered he was still in nothing but his undergarments.

"By the Architects, son! Where's your respect?" Gan asked, trying to sound aghast. Ro saw the twinkle of amusement in his eyes, though, and the smile threatening to break on the corner of his mouth.

Ro quickly tossed a blanket over his lap, scowling at Gan. His face burned. "Aspen! Aspen, what—" his voice cracked. He cleared his throat and tried again. "Aspen, what can I do for you?"

Aspen, at least, had better grace than Gan and looked just as embarrassed as Ro felt. She still hadn't looked him in the eye, her cheeks flushed. "I, um…" she clenched her sword absently and swallowed. "Today's the Goldlight Festival. Would you…could you accompany me?"

Ro gaped at her, uncomprehending. "What?"

Aspen twisted her hands together in front of her as if she didn't know what to do with them. "With coming back and trying to get things sorted out here, and the whole Lorate problem, I completely forgot about the festival. It's this big, grand affair, and even soldiers are supposed to attend, and it might be the last time I—" Her eyes widened and she snapped her mouth shut, shaking her head. It seemed the words had fallen out as quickly as she thought them. She took a deep breath. "Will you come with me?" she asked again, weakly.

Before Ro could answer, Styrax appeared in the doorway, arms laden with a basket of combs and mysterious bottles. He had on a clean white tunic opened slightly at the neck, and a new pair of breeches and boots. His hair had been combed to the side and glistened with drops of water. He let out a low whistle when he saw Aspen.

"Ash told me you two had done an excellent job of putting yourself together, but *this* is truly beautiful." He cast a glance at Ro and winced. "We've got our work cut out for us, don't we?"

Ro threw his pillow at him, which Styrax dodged with ease. "Oooh, and he's got a *temper* this..." He glanced at the sky. "Afternoon. Better run, Aspen. I don't know if he's the one for you."

"If he can handle my temper, I think I can tolerate his every now and again." She winked at Ro, and then her face took on a few anxious lines. "So, will you? Come with me?"

"I...absolutely. Yes, I'd love to." Ro said, still feeling somewhat out of the loop.

"Good. Right." Aspen took a backward step out of the doorway, pulling at the hems of her sleeves. "Well then, I'll see you in an hour...then."

"An hour?" Ro asked, wondering what could possibly take so long that he would need that much time.

A faint smile finally touched her lips. "I assume you don't want to show up to a sacred festival dressed as you are now. Hemlock might break you in half."

More blood rushed to Ro's face. "Good point."

"We might need more than an hour to whip this beast into shape," Styrax said, his hands on his hips as he gave Ro an appraising look. Ro scowled at him.

Aspen left. The three men watched her leave.

"I can't believe you," Gan said to Ro, shaking his head. "You managed to get a woman like that in your patchy underthings. Imagine what could have happened if you'd been wearing your *clean* ones."

Ro felt his blush shoot to the roots of his hair. "Shut up!"

"Right, let's get to work," Styrax said, setting down his basket with a clink of glass bottles. Ro eyed them all dubiously.

Gan chuckled. "Do you have anything to wear?" he asked, as if he already knew the answer.

"No?" Ro answered.

Styrax hit his palm to his forehead. "Oh, sweet Sister Earth, bless this boy."

Ro swatted at him.

"Lucky for you, I had a few things made when you were younger for just such an occasion." Gan rummaged through a wooden trunk in his bedroom to find Ro something suitable to wear while Styrax dragged a comb through Ro's shaggy mane. When Gan re-emerged, he had an armful of clean, expensive-looking clothes. A white tunic with billowing sleeves and a loose leather corset to keep it cinched at the waist. Clean pants. Black boots with silver buttons. When Ro was done putting them on, Gan chewed on his lip, folded his arms, and studied him critically. "If we're not careful, we might have everyone recognizing you as the prince you are, if I do say so myself."

"We can't have that, can we?" Ro asked with a smirk and a wink, covering up the squirming feeling that manifested in his stomach at the thought.

Styrax finished up by trimming Ro's hair, shaving his beard, and dabbing a few drops of liquid that smelled of citrus and spices behind his ears. When he was done, he stepped back and studied his handiwork. "You're passable," he said with a crooked grin.

Gan patted Ro on the shoulder. "It is truly a joy to have you back home, son. For me and, although she won't say it, for Aspen, too. Maybe, when this war is over, we can all sit down to a meal together without weapons or worries."

Ro smiled. "I look forward to it."

"Just make sure you take good care of Aspen," Gan said sternly while he waved him out the door. "Sister Earth knows *one* of us has to do right by her. She puts up a front, but I think we've both hurt her pretty badly."

Ro smiled again, this time sadly. "I know. And I know I've been the one to cause her a lot of that grief."

Gan grabbed him for one last hug and patted him on the back. Despite Gan being nearly a head shorter than Ro and about half his width, Ro still felt safe in his embrace. "I know you'll make it right to her," Gan whispered. He pulled back, wiping moisture from his eyes. He cleared his throat. "And you can start by making sure she's not late for the festival. Get going!"

"And make sure to get close enough that she smells you!" Styrax said. "That smelling concoction doesn't do you any good if you keep her at arm's length!"

Ro rolled his eyes and ran off with a parting smile and wave.

Aspen waited for him on the edge of the Golden Grove proper, absently tracing the stitching of her gown. With the golden glow of the Grove behind her, she looked positively radiant. It caught Ro's breath in his chest. She smiled when she saw him and smoothed out the wrinkles in her silken fabric. "This was my mother's," she said, almost as if she were apologizing for daring to wear something like it. "She is...was much taller than I am, so Ash hemmed it a few inches. Does it show?"

Ro shook his head mutely until he realized more of an answer was probably required. "It looks beautiful on you. I wouldn't have known it was meant for anyone else." He shook his head to wipe the daze away and gave her a crooked smile. "Although you don't strike me as a dress sort of woman. Are you comfortable in it?"

"For special occasions, I don't mind them." She swished the skirts, a soft half smile on her face. "It's nice to forget about the war and just be frivolous for a few hours."

"I couldn't have said it better myself," he said, putting his hands behind his back and rocking on the balls of his feet.

They both stood there for a few moments with nothing to say. It seemed that without the impending threat of death, neither of them really knew how to function.

Finally, Ro cleared his throat. "Well, should we, um, get going?"

"Yes. Yes, we should."

"How does this work? Do I escort you on my arm or hold hands or—?"

"Oh, um, I think just walking together works fine."

"All right, then. Lead the way."

They walked side by side, their only background noise the sounds of the Grove and the bustle of the main square beyond the trees.

"REMIND me what this whole thing is about?" Ro asked as he and Aspen pressed themselves into the crowd gathered at the base of the largest tree in the Golden Grove, which grew at the far edge of the village. Ribbons and glowing lights tended by a myriad of fairies festooned every tree branch, window, and doorway, and tables laden with silver bottles had been set at every entrance to the gathering. Children dashed through the crowd, trailing more silken ribbons behind them. Laughter flooded the crowd, and the air was filled with anticipation. It made Ro grin.

Someone jostled around to let him through, but he tripped over their feet and nearly smashed his face into the dirt. Aspen caught him, though. Her brow quirked. "It's not befitting a prince to fall at others' feet so easily, your highness," she said with a teasing glint in her eyes.

"Ha-ha." He pulled himself up and made sure he hadn't ruined the clothes Gan had given him. "I don't always have to be a prince, do I?" he asked. He had meant it as a joke, but a little too much truth came out with the words.

Aspen tilted her head at him, her brow creased with concern. "It's who you are, isn't it?"

He shrugged, not able to meet her eyes. "Sometimes, I like just... being Ro. Or Tristan, when he's not being an absolute menace."

He expected her to chuckle, but she just continued to look at him with her deep green eyes. "Ro, does it bother you when I call you the prince?"

Ro didn't know how to respond to that. Luckily, he didn't have to. Cheers rose from the crowd as Inula, Hemlock, and the other elders ascended a small stage that had been raised just enough for them to be seen across the gathering. The elders all wore silver robes with gold, shimmering embroidery, and had young golden branches woven into their hair. Inula held a bowl shaped sconce in her hands, where a golden flame danced merrily.

Inula smiled serenely over the crowd. Ro still wanted to punch her in her perfectly unflappable face.

"We welcome you to the Goldlight Festival," Inula said, her voice carrying over the murmuring crowd. "To some, it may feel that celebrations in times such as these are frivolous and weak-minded, but this council could not disagree more." She whispered a few words to the flame, and it rose high into the treetops, its golden light streaked with blue. "Love and laughter protect us from the darkest of times, just as this sacred ceremony, and our Sacred Flame, protects us from the Woods of Desolation and all others that seek to do us harm." He held the sconce over her head, and the flame changed again, transforming into the broad form of a phoenix.

Ro let out an involuntary gasp and took a step closer to Aspen. She chuckled softly and poked him in the ribs.

"Tonight, in the shelter of our great Mother Tree, we celebrate the peace we have savored since the founding of the Golden Grove—as sweet and ancient as the silver wine we make from its sap. And tonight, we toast to centuries more of safety!"

Another cheer rose from the crowd. For once, Ro couldn't disagree with Inula. He knew Aspen. He knew that whatever danger came next, she would handle it. She was the safety of the Golden Grove.

The elders began to sing—a low, wordless note that set a slow, steady beat. The others around Ro joined in, their notes high, bright, and soaring. Free. As one, they swayed, their eyes fixed on the golden flame above Inula's head.

The phoenix grew ever higher, its golden wings encompassing

the entire Grove. Ro tried to follow along with the melody—the memories from his childhood were still hazy—but he stopped the moment he heard the trees. The trees sang, glowing with the Sacred Flame's same light as their canopies broadened, stretching toward the setting sun. The gold and silver veins threaded through their bark spun, dazzling in their glittering movement. More trees joined the others, and soon their harmonies swelled until they resonated through Ro's body and encompassed the entire Grove. Ro smiled, his eyes damp. This was home. This was safety and belonging. He felt as if he could fly. As if he could—

He glanced at Aspen, and the breath was stolen from his lungs. The golden firelight trailed across her skin and set coronas ablaze on the ends of her eyelashes. Her dark hair shifted colors with every move she made—brown, auburn, black, and gold. Her eyes were closed, taking in the music's sound, and a soft smile turned the corner of her lips. Ro didn't think he had ever seen anything more beautiful.

But then her smile faltered, and a single, silver tear slipped down her face. Aspen wiped it away, and when she noticed Ro watching her with furrowed brows, her eyes widened.

"Aspen, what—" he began, but he was interrupted as the trees' singing came to an end. A great cry went up from the crowd, and the phoenix flew overhead, disappearing into the distance in a shower of golden sparks.

"We thank Sister Earth for our home and glorious freedom!" Inula shouted above the crowd.

"For our home!" they cried in unison.

"Come on." Aspen grabbed Ro's hand, all hints of tears gone. "Tonight, we're just Ro and Aspen, enjoying the home we've been blessed with." She dragged him into the night.

A VAST AREA had been cleared beneath the Mother Tree, filled with places to sit and a large space in the middle to dance. The Sacred Flame sat atop the elders' stage, keeping watch over the festivities.

Ro watched Aspen float through the crowd, nodding and smiling —really, *truly* smiling—as she mingled with her soldiers. They laughed and joked, and her cheeks took on a pinker tinge with each new silver wine glass she drank. Her ease radiated from her, nearly as bright as the trees as they turned from gold to silver.

Ro couldn't take his eyes off her.

Styrax leaned against a tree next to Ro, his pose relaxed and effortless as he swirled his silver wine. Sorren sat on a porch beside him, drinking cider and bobbing his head in time with the musicians that had set up beneath the Mother Tree.

"Have you asked her to dance?" Styrax asked Ro.

"What—*no*," Ro's tongue tripped over the words, and he nearly dropped his silver wine as he started in surprise. Was he really that obvious? "She doesn't even like dancing."

"Oh?" Styrax raised an eyebrow. "So you talked to her about that already?"

"Well...No. But she's not usually up for things like that."

Styrax sighed heavily and downed the rest of his wine. "I am *failing* you as a love mentor."

Ro choked. "*Love* mentor? When did I ask —"

Styrax held up a finger. "Shh! This is important." He set his glass down and leaned forward conspiratorially. "When someone you care about gets fancied up for a party, the *least* you can do is ask them to dance. If they say no, they say no, but at least they'll know you noticed them."

Ash approached them wearing a forest green dress with long, trailing sleeves that were slitted high enough to accentuate her muscular arms. Her honey-blond hair had been piled into a series of plaits on top of her head, adorned with several small, glittering gems. "You two seem like you're up to no good," she said. "Anything I can join in on?"

"I was just about to see if you'd like to dance," Styrax said as he offered his arm to Ash.

"Do you think I spent all this time putting myself together *not* to dance?" She accepted Styrax's arm with a small, gracious curtsy. They sashayed off to the dance floor, Styrax casting Ro a smug look over his shoulder. Ro swore they conspired together just to make him feel stupid.

He groaned. "Sorren, what do you think of this whole—"

But Sorren was already on the dance floor. With *Aspen*.

Ro was not prepared for the swell of...*feelings* that bubbled in him at the sight. He couldn't say what those feelings were, but they filled him until he could hardly see straight. He stood up, spine bristling. It was fine. It was *Sorren*. The little brother that he and Aspen had never had. He wasn't jealous. Not at all.

The moment the song was over, he strode to ask Aspen for the next dance, but she was swept away by one of her soldiers, who beamed at her like he was in the presence of royalty.

Sorren sauntered back to Ro, grinning. "Aspen's a really good dancer," he said.

"Shut up," Ro growled, watching Aspen laugh as the soldier pranced her around the clearing.

Sorren's grin widened.

The second dance ended, and Ro nearly ran to Aspen, but she got handed off to another soldier, and away they went. That happened for three more songs. Ro's grip on his wine glass became tighter with each song until he was in danger of shattering it. She had asked *him* to come with her to the festival, for Architect's sake! Surely he should be able to get at least *one* dance with her. But his ire slowly cooled as he watched Aspen enjoy her myriad of escorts. She was so *happy*, radiant in her mother's gown as she talked and joked with her soldiers. It seemed that, for just a moment, the weight of the world lifted from her shoulders, and Ro loved to see it. She deserved to feel this way. He couldn't begrudge her that. So he plunked himself at a table, nursed his glass of silver wine, and smiled.

When Aspen finally tottered away from the dance floor, favoring her feet and sitting at a table, Ro went to her, two glasses of silver wine in his hands.

She looked up when he approached. "You're not going to ask me to dance, are you?" Her voice sounded like she was pleading for mercy.

Ro chuckled and handed her a glass. "Considering what you put me through in our sparring matches, I *should* ask you to dance."

Her eyes widened slightly in quiet dread. "That's...Fair," she said slowly.

Ro let out a dramatic, long-suffering sigh. "You are lucky it's a special occasion. I will spare you. This time."

"You are oh so merciful, your highness." She took the wine glass from him and sipped at it appreciatively.

As he watched her, his one-too-many glasses of silver wine caught up to him. He grinned wickedly at her. "But that doesn't mean *I* can't dance with *you*." Ro chugged the last of his silver-wine for courage and scooped Aspen into his arms. She had just enough time to set her wine glass on the table before he spun her out onto the dance floor, her dress and hair flowing out around her. She let out a soft, giggling gasp and wrapped her arms around his neck. Warmth fizzed down to his fingertips and toes from where she touched him, making him grin like a giddy idiot. He waltzed around the dance floor with her still held close, throwing in a few more extra spins to make her laugh.

She laid her head against his shoulder, her eyelashes fluttering against his neck. "You smell nice," she laughed.

Styrax grinned at Ro from the edge of the dance floor. Ro grinned back at him, feeling like light might explode from his chest at any moment. Being there in that moment with Aspen, beneath the ribbons and lights, felt more magical than phoenixes or singing trees.

When the song finished, Ro completed one final spin and then placed her back in her seat. He sat next to her, laughing and pouring himself another glass of silver-wine. "You seem happy," he said, beaming.

She smiled at him, the tree lights soft across her face. "I am happy."

They sat that way for a while, knees brushing together, fingers only a hair's-width apart. Aspen had a faint, glowy pink on her cheeks from her silver wine. Ro felt it in the sparkling haze at the edges of his vision. Aspen smiled softly at the festival-goers as they twirled around the dance-floor. The shadow of a dimple formed in her cheek, and Ro couldn't pull his eyes away from it. Or from her.

"Look how happy they are," she said, leaning forward and hugging her arms to her sides as she watched Ash and Styrax romp around the dance floor.

"Mmm-hmm," he responded, distracted by the way the silver tree-glow glinted off her eyelashes. He must have had more wine glasses than he had thought.

"And that couple, there." She pointed to a pair of wrinkled elves slowly swaying together, their hair matching the silver leaves. "They've been married since before even Inula was born." She shifted her weight and their index fingers touched.

A surge of sparking, fizzing energy raced through Ro. "Yeah," he said, his mouth dry.

She sat in silence, seemingly unaffected by the touch, but a strange pall fell over her. A melancholy air hung about her shoulders, even as she smiled. Her eyes lost some of their focus and she absently brushed her fingers over her lips. "It must be nice," she said so quietly Ro couldn't be sure it wasn't just to herself. "To have that assurance..."

Ro was too distracted by the shimmer on her lips—was too *drunk*. Too drunk!—to register what she had said for a moment. When he caught himself staring, he cleared his throat and set his glass down. *Far* away from himself. "Assurance of what?" he asked.

"That they'll never die alone."

"Well, I mean, anything could happen, really. One could get in an accident, or—" He stopped himself the moment the weight of her words penetrated his silver wine fog. When he saw the slight tremble in her lip and registered her look of pained regret the moment she spoke the words. Stupid, *stupid* Ro! This wasn't about the elves at all.

A rush of adrenaline from his acutely idiotic error raced through him and chased the liquor fog away. He sidled closer to her and covered her hand completely in his. "Aspen," he asked softly. "Are you afraid of something?"

She didn't look at him, but her fingers curled around her thumb. The happy couple was reflected in her eyes. She took a shuddering breath. "It's odd, isn't it? I'm a soldier. I face death every day, but it doesn't scare me." She let out a hoarse, brittle chuckle. "No, the thing I'm worried about is being surrounded by strangers, or, worse, absolutely no one at all in those final moments. I'm scared I won't be *home*." A single, silver-stained tear slid down her face. She gave him a sad look. "Pitiful, isn't it? The *great* General Shadowalker is just a scared little girl."

Ro couldn't find the words to say. First, that she would relegate herself to "just" anything was absurd. And then *this*...He couldn't find the words to bring any sort of comfort.

"You're right," Aspen continued, folding her fingers over the hem of her sleeve. "Anything *can* happen. My parents were *created* for each other. They were the air each other breathed and the sun and stars. They were never far from each other. But they both died completely alone because of me." She blew out a long, steadying breath and gulped the rest of her wine down. "It would only be fitting for me to pay my sins in kind."

"That's not going to happen," Ro snapped finally, a swell of heated emotions raging through him. "You're not going to die, and certainly not alone."

"You can't promise that," she retorted. "It wasn't your choice to disappear five years ago. Fate doesn't work by choice and promises."

"For evergreens and aspen trees?" he asked pointedly. "Seems to me fate worked pretty well with that." He took both of her hands in his and made her face him. When she did, his breath caught in his throat. He realized the warmth fizzing through his veins every time he touched or looked at Aspen was not from a drunken stupor. In her face, he saw the lines of laughter and worry he had shared with her. He saw her kindness and warmth—her selflessness and intelligence and fiery spirit. He saw her beauty in all its flaws.

"Aspen Tanner," he said quietly, struggling to get enough air to his lungs. "I would tear the stars from the heavens before I *ever* let you feel alone again."

He saw so many things flash across her face—surprise, mulling over the illogic and impossibility of his words, gratitude—until it settled on fear and disbelief. "Ro, you can't—"

"Aspen," he said again, the word a growl in his throat. "You want me to be a king one day. What kind of king would I be if I can't keep a promise to somebody that I...care deeply for?"

Her hands squeezed tightly around his. He drew closer, the perfumes in her hair tantalizing. He wiped a tear from her face, his thumb accidentally brushing the corner of her lip, and became acutely aware of her breath spilling across his hand. Of how it warmed his cheek the closer he drew. Of how pink her cheeks were...

"General," one of Aspen's soldiers emerged from the trees.

Whatever spell had fallen around Aspen and Ro shattered. They practically leapt apart. Ro didn't know what to do with his hands, so he jammed them into his pockets. Aspen folded her arms tightly around her.

"Jardi, what is it?"

"Someone has been apprehended at the border. They say they're from Lorate, and refuse to speak with anyone but you and," she looked pointedly at Ro, "Tristan."

TWENTY-TWO

Vinea stood in the Council Room, her arms folded tightly across her chest and her fingers drumming an anxious rhythm on her elbow. The horrors of the Woods of Desolation still screamed in her mind—Linae and Laire, both happy and healthy and calling to her before being ripped to shreds before her eyes. Her throat was hoarse from her screams, and her body still trembled with the adrenaline coursing through her. She had not intended on being discovered—planning on approaching the Golden Grove on her own terms—but she had collapsed as soon as the cursed woods ended. A scout had stumbled across her, and luckily she had possessed enough of her faculties to mumble that she was looking for Tristan and General Shadowwalker.

And now she was here, her heart threatening to pound out of her throat as she waited to betray the last of her sister's children.

When the Council doors opened and Tristan walked through, Vinea's breath seized in her chest. It was like peering into her memories of her older sister, Eden. He had her same *light*. The self-assuredness that radiated from him like a beacon. He was *happy*.

And she was about to take that all away from him.

His steps faltered when he saw her, his eyes wide and his face growing pale. "*Lady Vinea?*"

She smiled—a ghost of a thing that drove a stake of guilt through her. "Hello, Tristan."

The scout that had found Vinea filed in, followed closely by another woman. Vinea recognized her dark hair and her green eyes. She had seen them reflected in the moonlight that night that seemed lifetimes ago. It was the woman that had helped Tristan escape Lorate. No one else followed them into the room.

Vinea looked at the messenger with a furrowed brow, trying to keep her tone neutral. "I thought I requested to speak with General Shadowalker."

The woman with green eyes folded her arms. "My name is Aspen, and I speak for General Shadowalker," she said tonelessly. Tristan cast her a sidelong glance that seemed to convey some hidden knowledge. Aspen ignored him. "What can I do for you?"

Vinea gazed at her for a moment. "I...Well..." She shook her head. She supposed it didn't matter if it was the general themselves, or their aide. This had to be done. "I come bearing news. About the soldiers coming to Lorate."

Aspen said nothing and waited for her to continue.

Vinea sighed to relieve the tension coiling in her neck and making stars dance in her eyes. She smoothed her skirt with her damp, clammy hands. This was her last chance. Her conscience screamed at her to stay quiet, but the stud in her ear screamed louder, filling her mouth with half-truths that would spell doom for everyone. After this moment, there was no turning back.

But, really, there had been no turning back since the moment Sedick took Linae from her.

"Chaedra sent me here," she said. "She told me you would need to hear what I have to say."

Aspen gestured for her to sit, and Vinea did so. Aspen sat across from her and Tristan followed suit, their shoulders brushing. Vinea tried to ignore the way Tristan looked at Aspen. It only made her heart twist tighter with guilt.

"How do I know Chaedra sent you?" Aspen asked carefully.

Vinea eyed her, banishing images of Chaedra's bloodied and beaten body to the back of her mind. "One never knows the trueness of intentions." She had repeated those lines over and over to herself in the Woods of Desolation. They had been the only things to get her through it. "And can only hope for the intention of truth."

Some of the tightness in Aspen's shoulders relaxed. "That's correct." Aspen sagged in her seat a little. With the new angle of light catching her face, Vinea saw a ruddy glow on the woman's cheeks and her wide, dilated pupils. She was *drunk*, if not tipsy at the very least. "Can you tell me how..." Aspen shook her head, but winced at the sudden movement. "How Chaedra's doing? I haven't heard from her in several days."

Vinea hoped she kept the panic off her face. Chaedra's accusatory, betrayed face floated behind her eyelids. She held back a shudder. "She's in hiding," she said, her mouth dry. "Things have been...Tense, in Lorate."

Aspen nodded as if oblivious to the guilt hovering over Vinea like a personal demon. "I imagine they have been," she said. The light caught her eyes, and Vinea saw beneath the fog of alcohol that there was something more to this Aspen. She got the feeling that Aspen knew more than she let on. "What have you come to say?" Aspen asked.

Vinea had to remind herself that, other than Chaedra, she was not here to lie. She was here to tell nothing but the truth. At least... parts of it. "The Lorate soldiers intend to invade the Golden Grove," she said.

Aspen folded her arms. "We are aware."

Vinea nodded. She supposed Chaedra would have gotten that message across before...everything else. "And are you aware that they intend to use serpent roots?"

Aspen nodded. "We are."

"And that they have woven the serpent root into weighted nets?" Sweat trickled down Vinea's spine. If she had nothing new to offer, they wouldn't find a use for her, and she wouldn't get the access to the Grove that she needed to search for Sedick's precious flame.

Aspen froze with a muttered curse under her breath. "How many?"

Vinea's body sagged with relief. "Too many. They will wipe out whatever magical forces you have."

Aspen rubbed her temples, looking as if she wanted to shove her fingers through her skull. "That will cause some...concerns."

"That's not all," Vinea said quickly, before her courage could leave her. She may not have been able to save much, but at least she could try to garner sympathy for the men of Lorate. "The Lorate soldiers have been put under Sedick's control with talismans. They are coming here against their will."

Tristan blanched, his mouth hanging open as fury flashed in his eyes. Aspen cursed again, her jaw clenched. "Is there anything else I should know about?"

Whatever forces you think you have will never be enough. Your plan is going to fail. You should run while you still can. All those words lodged in Vinea's throat and nearly choked her, but she didn't say a single thing. "No. That's everything I know."

Aspen eyed her again as if she sensed she wasn't telling the whole truth. Vinea relaxed her expression and met Aspen's gaze, even as sweat continued to trickle down the nape of her neck.

Aspen sighed and stood. "Short and to the point. I appreciate these types of meetings." She gestured to the messenger. "Jardi will find you a place to stay. Unfortunately, for the safety of everyone here, I can't let you leave until this crisis is averted."

Success number one. "I understand," Vinea said. "Will I be allowed to roam freely throughout the grove?"

"With supervision, yes."

Vinea kept her disappointment in check and inclined her head. "That is more than generous. Thank you."

"I—I could be her escort," someone said in a strangled voice from the doorway.

Vinea's head snapped up, her heart in her throat. Not him, too.

But there was Sorren, eyes wide and magnified with tears. He dashed them away with his sleeve. "I...Sorry. I didn't mean to eavesdrop. Ash didn't know where you went and wanted me to look for you," he said to Aspen.

Vinea's chest wanted to explode. He looked *happy*. More assured of himself. The gaunt puppet of a boy she had known a few weeks ago had been replaced by a warm, gentle young man. The stud in Vinea's ear burned, and her limbs twitched to jump across the room and strangle him. Hatred, not her own, twisted in her gut. She looked away from him, horrified, and brushed her hair to cover her ears so Sorren wouldn't see the stud. He would immediately know what it was, and what it meant.

"Do you know this woman?" Aspen asked Sorren, her shrewd green eyes flicking between Sorren and Vinea.

Battling Sedick's hatred away, Vinea glanced at him briefly to see his response.

Sorren tugged at his ear. "She was the one that tore Sedick's talisman out of my ear." He grimaced. "That's actually what kept me from killing you in Vastet." He looked at Vinea with a worried frown. "But you were wounded! What are you doing in the Golden Grove? *How* are you in the Golden Grove?"

The frank questions from Sorren's innocent face made a solid lump of guilt form in Vinea's throat, even as another wave of horror from the Woods of Desolation sent shudders through her. She had to look away from him again. "I'm just here to help where I can."

"Well, I'm happy to have you here."

Vinea could hear the smile in his voice, and it drove her deeper into her seat.

"Thank you, Sorren," Aspen said. "If you're all right with being Lady Vinea's escort while she's here, I have no problem with it. Wait outside, and we'll call for you shortly."

He left, and when he did, Vinea raised her head tentatively. Aspen gave her a grim smile. "Well, that's three people now that vouch for you, on top of my own experiences." She blew out a long breath. "Much as I would love for your intel to be false—Sister Earth knows we could catch a break—I believe you. Thank you for bringing us this information. I can't imagine it was an easy journey for you."

The words struck like lightning through Vinea's spine. She didn't know the half of it.

Aspen grimaced slightly and rubbed her head. She looked at Tristan. "It's going to be another long night. Are you coming?"

He touched her wrist. "I'll be there soon."

Aspen scoffed. "Don't rush yourself. Inula is going to throw a fit, and I'd save my eardrums if I were you." She left.

Vinea busied herself with studying her hands and brushing off her skirt, avoiding Tristan's gaze as he approached. Her hands shook, though, so she clenched them tightly in her lap.

Tristan sat next to her with a long sigh. He leaned forward, twining his fingers together. "How much did you know? About the invasion?"

"I found out when you did," she answered, not able to draw enough breath into her lungs.

He was silent for another few heartbeats. "I go by a new name, now," he said. "Although it's not really *new*. Aspen told me you're the one that sent a tip about me, which makes me wonder...How long did you know my real name was Ro?"

Vinea had to look at him then. His expression was unreadable, but looking at that familiar face reopened a deep ache in her chest. "Since the beginning," she whispered. "I knew the moment I saw your face, because you look just like your mother, my sister, Queen Eden."

Before she had even finished the words, Ro had swept her up into a crushing embrace. "Thank you for bringing Aspen to find me," he said, his words thick with emotion. "Thank you for getting me back home."

Vinea wrapped her arms around him and wept, her heart shattering in her chest.

Eventually, Ro had to leave. He helped Vinea up and led her outside, where Sorren waited for her with a wide grin on his face. Vinea had to tamp down Sedick's surging hatred again, reasoning with it that she couldn't hurt anyone. Otherwise, she would never be able to find the flame. That seemed to tame it.

Ro left, and Sorren swept his arm out to the Golden Grove, which was now a bright silver beneath the moonlight. The light blinded Vinea. All she could think of was how it would look crushed beneath the Vanguard's feet. Another treasure brutalized by Osmen.

Sorren walked down the steps from the Council Room, and Vinea followed numbly behind.

"I'm sure you're tired," he said, his voice apologetic. "But with Aspen busy gathering Inula and the others for an emergency meeting, she asked me to take care of an errand before taking you to freshen up and then escorting you to the meeting. Are you all right with that?"

Vinea tried to smile at him, but it felt paper thin. "I don't mind. What's your errand?"

His eyes brightened with excitement. "There's this beautiful golden flame that never dies. They use it for ceremonies. It has so much *magic,* it's absolutely incredible. They just asked me to put it back where it belongs."

Bile churned in Vinea's stomach. No. No, she couldn't use Sorren's kindness and eagerness against him. But she had to. For Linae. "I would love to go with you."

He smiled brightly at her. "Let's go, then!" He held out his arm to escort her, and she took it, hoping he didn't notice her trembling hands.

TWENTY-THREE

"We cannot go off the word of one woman alone," Inula maintained, sneering at Lady Vinea as they all sat around Aspen's planning table. Ro flared his nostrils, clenching his fist as he stood in the corner of the command tent next to Lady Vinea and Sorren. Discussions based on Lady Vinea's report had already gone late into the night last night, and here they were again the following afternoon with nothing more to show for it. All in thanks to Inula. Again.

"I don't have any reason to disbelieve her," Aspen said. Ro almost swore her eye twitched. "She's given us good information before, tipped us off about Ro being in Lorate, *and* gave me Chaedra's pass phrase. I trust her."

Vinea shifted uncomfortably next to Ro. He patted her arm, his conscience smarting when he realized he had forgotten what her feelings must be in the whole situation. "Don't worry too much about it," he whispered to her. "Inula always acts like someone served her manure for breakfast."

Vinea gave him a pained smile.

Aspen folded her arms and sighed, eyes darting across the map of the Golden Grove they had spread out. "Dolo, I've seen these men. They're all just poor villagers that got wrapped up in this nonsense for reasons I still can't fathom. And now they're being controlled by Osmen's personal lapdog. I'd love to avoid bloodshed as much as possible. Any ideas?"

Aspen's tactician, a soft-spoken minotaur named Dolo, shook his head sadly, his shaggy, dark fur swaying with the movement. "Anything we do to drive them back is still going to end up with someone getting hurt. It'll take a miracle or some black magic to even come close to any other outcome."

Aspen chewed on her lip, looking dourly at the table.

Ro leaned over to Lady Vinea again. "It's too bad none of them *actually* have black magic. The soldiers at Lorate would take one look at all these Ancient Ones and go running back home as fast as they could."

The tent had gone quiet. Ro looked up and found the entire tactical council looking at him. He winced. He must have spoken louder than he thought.

Aspen gaped at Ro, her eyes bright. "Say that again?"

The rest of her council looked at him expectantly. He took a step back, hands up in a placating gesture. "It's just a joke. I really didn't mean anything by it."

"No, really. Say it again, please."

Ro puffed his cheeks and let out a breath, not looking the others in the eyes. Had he offended them? He needed to learn to keep his big mouth shut. "I said it was too bad you don't actually have black magic like they think you do. That would scare them away in a heartbeat."

Aspen drummed her fingers on the table, head bowed as she sorted her thoughts. The rest of the council stayed quiet while she thought. Or, at least most of them did.

"Oh honestly," Inula sneered. "We all know we don't have black magic. That's hardly a new revelation to be musing over."

"Hush," Ash snapped from across the table. "You're hardly news, either."

Inula shot a dagger thin look at her.

Aspen motioned Sorren over to the table. "Are there any weaknesses to Sedick's cursed items?"

Sorren gave her an uneasy look and stood a few feet away from the table, hunching his shoulders as he looked at the rest of the council members. "Well, um, *all* magic has weaknesses. What exactly are you looking for?"

Aspen brought him to stand beside her. "What would happen if we scared these soldiers witless?"

A slow smile crept across Sorren's face as realization seemed to dawn on him. "Strong, primal emotions tend to override Sedick's curses. Your thoughts can't be controlled when you're not really thinking."

Aspen patted Sorren on the shoulder and turned to Dolo. "Remind me how many non-magical soldiers we have?" But she already knew the answer and mouthed along with Dolo.

"Fifty-six," he said. "Fifty-seven if you include Ro."

Aspen nodded. "And, Lady Vinea, how many men are coming from Lorate?"

Lady Vinea shifted in her seat, not meeting anyone's gaze and looking uncomfortable. "Approximately three hundred. If they all make it through the desolate woods."

Aspen drew the map of the Golden Grove close to her. Ro leaned in for a better look. She traced a finger from the entrance to the main square. There was really only a single path in, high enough that they would see where to cast their nets for miles, but also narrow enough that none of them would have much chance to wander off. They could keep tabs on all of them entering the Grove.

She tapped her index finger on the parchment. Ro heard her bite back a snort of manic humor.

"If you've got nothing more to say, then I have better duties than sitting in silence," Inula huffed.

"Will you let her think for two minutes?" Hemlock growled.

Aspen turned to Ro while the others will still looking at the map. "This is going to be stupid," she mouthed to him.

He shrugged. "You have my favorite kind of stupid."

Aspen rolled her eyes and turned to the group. "It's true, we don't have black magic," she said. "But these soldiers don't know that."

"Get to the *point,* please," Inula griped.

"We'll use their fears against them," Aspen said. She looked to Dolo and he nodded along, stroking his impressive bovine beard thoughtfully. "We'll dress up the human soldiers to be the most terrifying monsters we can make them to be," she continued. "If we scare them enough, they'll use all their nets, which won't have any effect on our soldiers, and then the magical units can swoop in and capture them before anyone gets hurt."

Inula let out a bark of a laugh. "*This* is what our *grand* general can come up with? This is ridiculous."

But everyone ignored her. Instead, they all watched Dolo. He shook his head, but chuckled. "With our limited numbers, surprise is the best weapon we've got." He looked at Aspen. "General, you may have me out of a job yet. I like it."

Aspen looked grim as Ro walked her back home that night. He tried to pull a conversation from her, but her answers were single syllables at best, and any topic petered out quickly. She wouldn't even look at him. As they walked to her cottage, Ro breathed in the memories. He had spent practically his whole life bouncing between his home with Gan and Aspen's house. He remembered romping through the grass and making general, dirty nuisances of themselves. They had laughed until they cried, cried until they laughed, and everything in between. There had been *life* there. Now, though, it just felt like an empty shell.

Aspen opened the door, but before she could go inside, Ro stopped her with a hand on her arm.

"Aspen," he said firmly. "What's wrong?"

She tried to respond, but he quickly stopped her with a raised hand. "And if you say 'nothing', I'll know you're lying to me. That's not going to fly today."

Aspen raised an exasperated eyebrow. "Has Ash been coaching you on what to say?"

Ro preened, flicking his hair dramatically. "I will take that as a compliment. Ash is very good at taking care of you."

Aspen squeezed his hand, a ghost of a smile on her lips. "You are very good, as well."

Ro's stomach back-flipped a few times as a thrill of warmth traveled up his arm, radiating from her hand in his. His cheeks flushed.

She let go of his hand too soon. "I just worry that I do a poor job of taking care of *you*. Stay here a moment." She disappeared into the cottage and reappeared with a long object covered in dusty linen. "We're going to battle now, and you'll need to protect yourself." She unwrapped the linen to reveal a silver, finely polished and sharpened sword. A single sapphire sat proudly at the end of the hilt.

Ro recognized it immediately. It was *his* sword. The only thing he had of King Salaith's. He remembered when Gan had given it to him, bestowing a private knighting in their home with it when he turned eighteen. The heavy weight of the mantle he would eventually wear settled on his shoulders, but he found it wasn't as heavy as he had previously thought. That filled him with both pride and trepidation.

Ro went to take the sword from Aspen, but her fingers curled around it and she drew it close to her. He looked at her questioningly.

"Ro, there's still time for you to leave," she said quietly.

Ro bristled. "Aspen, I've already told you, I'm not leaving," he said, the words burning with frustration in his throat. Why couldn't she accept that? "I would *never* leave you, and I don't go back on my word." He reached for the sword again.

"Ro, I *need* you to understand!" she shouted, dancing away from his reach again, voice shaking. "The last time I asked you to pick up your sword and fight, you didn't come back! If I ask you to do this again, and you—" her voice broke. "You are far too important to this kingdom. No one would blame you for keeping yourself safe."

Ro's frustration and anger melted as he saw the fear on her face. He dropped his arms at his sides. "Aspen, will you come here for a moment?"

She hesitated, giving him a look of suspicion.

"I won't steal the sword from you. Just, come here," he motioned her toward him.

After a few moments of silence, Aspen took a few hesitant steps toward him. Ro gathered her into his arms and held her close. She stiffened and resisted at first, but slowly melted into the embrace. She rested her head on his shoulder, and the trembling in her body eased. He kissed the top of her head and stroked her hair. "*I* would blame me for leaving," he said. "I may be important to the kingdom for reasons outside my control, but you—" his voice broke, and he cleared it, but the huskiness remained. "*You* are important to *me*, and for a much better reason than being born to it."

She pulled back, her eyes wide, her cheeks flushed. He couldn't tell if she was breathing. Was *he*?

"What reason is that?" she asked hoarsely.

Ro took his sword from her and strapped it to his waist. Before he lost his nerve, he put one hand on her waist and the other on the back of her neck. She sucked in a breath of surprise, her skin warm against his fingertips. He looked into her eyes, knowing that if he looked too long, he would lose himself in that forest of green. He brushed his lips against hers, seeing if she would pull away. When she didn't, he kissed her, deeply and fiercely. Her hands tightened around his arms in surprise. Her breath warmed his cheek. He curled his fingers in her hair as he tried to convey the swirl of emotions that had completely seized his heart and soul. "Because I love you, Aspen Tanner," he said in a low voice against her lips.

He let her go. Heart hammering and feeling light-headed, he watched for her reaction, hoping he would see a similar spark to the roaring flame in his chest. But she just looked at him, her eyes wide and face pale.

That look alone hurt more than any dagger.

He cleared his throat, trying not to betray the lump that had formed there. "Well, goodnight, then." He turned and ran from the house, unable to face the heartbreak of her rejection.

TWENTY-FOUR

Aspen laid flush against Breaker's neck, the mist swirling around them both as he galloped through the rolling moors. Her poor unicorn had been appearing at her cottage for days, pawing at the ground impatiently and gnawing on her wooden fence. There had been so much to do that she had hardly had time to acknowledge him, but eventually her stress became too much—his dark eyes too warm and pleading—and she relented.

She closed her eyes and breathed in the smell of his mane—felt the air rush past her ears and course along her back. His powerful muscles surged beneath her, the rumble of his hoofbeats thundering in her ears in their swift, steady beat. The sunrise peaked over the horizon and tinged everything a blush violet.

Aspen hadn't slept last night. She hadn't slept for days, really, with the looming threat of Lorate hanging overhead. The threat from the men themselves was minor—mind control could not make a weak puppet powerful—and she had received no other correspondences from Chaedra about it, but that was exactly what made her nervous. Something wasn't right with this whole mess. Osmen wouldn't send those men just to die for no good reason. There had to be *something* else. But *what?*

The what ifs plagued her, almost as persistent as the shadows that followed her. But, for the life of her, she couldn't determine any sort of logical reason for Osmen's actions. That had been the main culprit for her sleepless nights, along with the grim knowledge that, no matter the outcome of the battle, the Golden Grove would be forever out of her reach after the whole affair was over.

And then there was Ro's kiss...

So, she came for rides—to clear her head, to be *alone.* To bask in the silence so that maybe—just maybe—an idea would come through its clarity.

Today, though, she wasn't alone. The shadow of a single figure sat amongst the heather, looking out over the Golden Grove.

Aspen was about to find some excuse to tell them off—this was *her* spot—but she stopped herself when she recognized the sandy hair and broad shoulders. She dismounted from Breaker and patted him on the neck, to which he nickered appreciatively. "Styrax, what are you doing out here?"

Styrax jolted. He squinted through the mist, looking harried and sheepish all at once, but his face relaxed when he saw Aspen. "I wasn't expecting anyone out here," he said, sniffing and wiping at his eyes.

Aspen raised an eyebrow at his odd behavior, but chose not to comment on it. "Neither was I." She sat next to him in the grass, the cold, dewy tips brushing strokes of moisture along her skin and clothes and making her break out in gooseflesh. "Does Ash know you're out here?"

He chuckled. "I won't tell if you won't."

Aspen smiled in return. "Deal." She toyed with the grass stems, liking the way the morning breeze combed through the roots of her hair. Styrax didn't force conversation, and they sat in the early silence as the sun rose ever higher, burning away the fog with shafts of gold and leaving the air fresh and warm. The tips of the silver leaves stretched out to the sunlight, their edges burgeoning with gold as the warmth touched them.

Styrax leaned forward with a sigh. "It's really beautiful here, isn't it?"

"Yeah." Aspen barely eked out an answer over the lump in her throat. *When you're here to see the leaves change from gold to silver, you'll know you're home.* She didn't know how many days she had left to appreciate how truly beautiful the Grove was, and that hurt more than she cared to admit.

"Y'know, my sisters and I used to talk about hopping rivers to come visit the Golden Grove," Styrax said quietly. "We thought it would be the ultimate beauty to see the leaves change as the sun went down. Never got around to it, but I wish I had." He clutched a small vial of water in his hand. His fingers tightened around it until his knuckles turned white. "I would have loved to see their faces. Would have loved for them to meet Ash and Ro and seen...Well, *everything* really. Seen me happy." Tears welled in his eyes and trickled down his sleeve as a shudder ran through him. "It's been eighty years, and I still miss them," he said, his voice a hoarse croak in his throat. He mopped at his face with the corner of his sleeve, groaning. "Ahh, Sister Earth, I've made a mess of myself again. Ash took an extra bottle of silver wine from the festival, and we split it last night. It makes her giddy, and makes me..." he gestured to himself, more tears running down a reddened face and hair and tunic in disarray, like he had slept outside. "You should have seen me last night. I was absolutely inconsolable over nothing." He tried to chuckle, but it came out flat and hollow.

Aspen blinked, surprised. "Aren't you...All about feelings? And finding your inner self and all that?"

"That tripe?" He moaned and laid on his back, arm draped over his eyes.

"*Tripe?*" Aspen reared back, a small smile twitching at the corners of her mouth. It made her feel better, somehow, that even someone like Styrax had bad days. "I thought some of it was quite good."

Styrax waved his hand limply in the air. "All right, you're right. It's not tripe. I mean it when I say it to other people."

Aspen cocked her head. "But it doesn't work for yourself? Hmm... Seems to me a sagely naiad once said—"

"Shhh. It's too early in the morning for you to be using my own words against me."

Aspen glanced up and a stray beam of sunlight hit her directly in the eye. She reeled back, blinking stars out of her eyes with a grimace. "Can't argue with you there."

Styrax peeked out at her from beneath his arm. "Couldn't sleep again?"

"No, but I'm almost proud to say I wasn't the one with the worst sleep last night." She gestured to Styrax's disheveled state.

He laughed, sounding congested, but more genuine this time. "We're both a couple of sights, aren't we?" Using his magic, he lifted dew from the grass stems, letting the droplets course over his fingers like glittering, undulating rings. The rims of his irises glowed white. "How are you feeling about all of this?" He motioned vaguely to the tents barely stirring to life—the racks of weapons, provisions, and homespun armor.

Aspen wrapped her arms around her knees. "Can a drunk sage keep a secret?"

Styrax laughed again. "I kept my magic a secret from my best friend for five years. I think I'll be fine."

"Yes, but—and I mean this with all the love and respect in my soul—he's not exactly the observant type."

"True." He gave her a knowing, smug look. "Except with you."

Aspen conceded the point, her cheeks glowing pink. "*Too* observant on that front sometimes, I think." She rested her chin on her knees, watching the Golden Grove with unfocused eyes. The faceless shadows hovered at the edge of her vision, their silent accusations roaring in her head. "I'm terrified, Styrax." She admitted. Flashes of the night at the Dragon Scales, and mirror images in the Golden Grove—all the blood that had been and could be spilt—ate at her mind. "All my life I've been doing what I can to help, but no matter how much effort I put into it, it's never good enough. I fail, and people get hurt. And it's all my fault."

Styrax sat up again. His water droplets had coalesced into a form that fit into his palm. He stroked it like he would a kitten, the morning sunshine dancing through it. "You know, with logic like that, an argument could be made that I let this war happen."

Aspen looked at him in consternation.

He sighed and sent the water droplet wheeling into the grasses. It flew back, dancing around his palm. Aspen envied his precise control.

"I was banished from my river for saving someone," Styrax said quietly. "A young woman I had befriended. She was a sorcerer with minimal power, but I was teaching her a few silly tricks. Like this." The water in his hand shaped itself into a fish and swam in lazy loops around his head. His eyes were sad as he watched it. "One day she got too close to the river to look for me, and my family pulled her in to feed to our life giver." He clenched his jaw, the muscles stark and rigid. The fish dissolved, and the water plopped into the grass. "Thankfully, I found out in time, but it was...*close*."

An involuntary shudder ran through Aspen. She remembered the gray-green glow of the serpent root in the naiad river—the way the light had filtered through the water and glanced off the naiads' scales. The agony of the serpent root draining her magic had only been overshadowed by the terror of the vines dragging her farther into their depths as the last of her air escaped her lungs.

Styrax continued. "When my family found out I freed her, they left me in our serpent root forest to feed it myself." He brushed his hand along his arm, where tiny silver scars stood out in relief against his skin. "When they found me still alive several days later, they didn't know what to do with me. So, they banished me and took away my scales so I could 'live with the filthy humans I so obviously loved more than I loved them'."

The bitterness in his voice pricked at Aspen.

"I went to my sorcerer friend for help, but she'd also decided she'd had enough to do with me. Completely understandable." Even as Styrax said it, though, his face flashed with the pain of old wounds. "I checked on her from time to time, just to see how life was treating her. She married and had children. It was nice, y'know, to see that I had made a difference for someone." He sighed and pulled the dew from the grass again. "But I suppose if you follow a family tree far enough, one branch is bound to make a name for themselves —one way or another." The little water ball spiked around the edges, zooming around like a nervous cat. Styrax cast Aspen a sidelong glance. "One of my friend's children obtained a lordship in Loralan. They had only one son. They named him Osmen."

The words cracked like thunder over Aspen. She felt the emotions flash across her face before she could stop them—rage, horror, sorrow, and guilt at having such volatile emotions toward a friend.

Styrax took in her expression and gave her a small smile. "I can promise you, anything you're feeling right now, I felt it too." He blew out another long breath, his shoulders sagging. Some of the drunkenness had faded in his eyes, but the red-rimmed vulnerability remained. "I went so many years blaming myself for this war. If I had just left things as they were, things could have been *so* different." He looked at Aspen fully, a knowing look on his face. "Sound familiar?"

Aspen's breath hitched in her chest, a lump forming in her throat. "Now, wait, I —"

Styrax held up a hand. "I've learned that we can't control the consequences of our actions. The best we can do is *our* best. And from what I've seen, your best is pretty great."

Aspen's mouth dangled open. To her horror, tears filled her eyes, but she couldn't bring herself to wipe them away.

Styrax just wrapped an arm around her and hugged her. More

thick emotions crept into Aspen's eyes. It felt just like the hugs her brothers would give her, before they…

Styrax said nothing to her. He just let them sit in the silence of that moment. It gave Aspen the time she needed to dash her tears away and get her emotions under control. To cover her moment of weakness, she swerved to a new topic as she pulled herself away from Styrax. "I think I see why Ash keeps you around."

Styrax's eyes shone at the sound of her name, and his alcohol-pink cheeks deepened. "That woman deserves the world, doesn't she?"

Aspen chuckled. The love in his eyes made her heart warm. Ash deserved that. "Are you prepared to give it to her?"

"If she'll let me."

Aspen smiled at him. "I'm glad she found you." She stood and stretched, her back crackling. "Well," she said with a sigh, the sound still raw and vulnerable. "Sun's up, which means it's time to get back to work." She remounted Breaker. "And, Styrax?"

"Hmm?"

"Thank you."

An impish grin spread across his face. "You're *thanking* me?" He asked in an uncanny imitation of Ash's voice.

Aspen groaned. "I take it back. You two are *too* perfect for each other. It's disgusting." With that, she rode back to the Golden Grove, the weight of the day's responsibilities feeling a little lighter on her shoulders.

TWENTY-FIVE

"You did *what?*" Styrax asked Ro, appalled.

Ro groaned and buried his face in the table, hands locked behind his head. The silver leaves had just finished their transition to gold, but already the entire army was up and about, efficient in every movement as they laced on their leather pieces of armor, cleaned their weapons, or filed into line for some food. Ash wielded her soup ladle liberally, divvying out food and gesturing orders all in the same motion. She was completely in her element. Usually, Styrax spent his mornings mooning over her. Today, though, he looked at Ro as if he had affronted every member of his family.

It was too early for this.

Ro sunk deeper into his seat, his face flaming hot. "I kissed her."

Styrax rubbed the bridge of his nose. "No *wonder* she seemed so discombobulated this morning,"

Ro looked at him, eyebrows raised. "What?"

Styrax ignored him. "We all knew a kiss was bound to happen at some point." He motioned for Sorren to join them at the table. "He kissed Aspen," he told the boy.

"*Finally!*"

Ro splayed his hands in protest. "What happened to confidentiality between friends?"

"As I recall, you got mad at me the last time I kept secrets," Styrax said with a smirk. He waved Ro's further protest off. "So you kissed her. But tell me again what you did *after*?"

Ro groaned again, shutting his eyes tight against the humiliation. "I ran."

Ro reopened his eyes and saw Styrax throw his hands up in despair. "Ash is going to blame this on me. I just know it." He turned to Sorren. "Sorren, this is an excellent example of how *not* to woo a woman."

"Should I be taking notes?" Sorren asked innocently, the grin on his face anything but.

Ro massaged his eyes, contemplating shoving them through his skull.

Ash joined them at the table, looking dour.

Styrax furrowed his brow in concern. "Have I done something?"

Ro snorted. "What an excellent 'love mentor' you turned out to be."

Styrax glowered at him.

Ash's cheeks turned pink. She took a spoonful of porridge and worked it thoughtfully through her mouth. "No. You've been...quite lovely." She smiled a little to herself, dreamily stirring her spoon in her breakfast. Styrax beamed.

"Is Aspen with you?" Ro asked, resisting the urge to look around like a deer waiting for a predator.

Ash's sour expression came back. "*No.* She said she couldn't eat. It upsets her stomach if she's going to be training some of the men all morning." She gave Ro an impishly wicked grin. "Why do you ask? Afraid she'll run away from you after such an awful kiss?"

Styrax and Sorren snorted.

"It *wasn't* awf—" Ro gave up and threw his hands in the air with a growl. "Does *everyone* know about this?"

"Aspen gets herself into more trouble than anyone else I've ever known. What kind of bodyguard, secret second-in-command, cousin, and generally concerned party would I be if I didn't have surveillance on her at all times?" Ash raised her eyebrow at him. "So if it wasn't an awful kiss, does that mean it was actually a *good* kiss?"

Sorren, mercifully, took pity on Ro before he had to answer and changed the subject. "Aspen trains all the soldiers?" he asked. "Isn't that a lot of work for just her?"

"*Yes,*" Ash and Ro said in unison.

Ash took another few bites of her breakfast. "But she doesn't teach everyone. She's got a unique style of fighting. She doesn't like to kill people—which gives me a heart attack about every third day —but also doesn't want them to come back to fight another day. So, she maims them just enough that they can't be soldiers anymore, but can still work for a living." She shrugged. "It's much more precise and complicated than stabbing someone and letting the pieces fall where they may, but she's willing to teach it to anyone that has a similar aversion to taking a life."

Sorren looked at her with eyes as wide as saucers. "Aspen can really do that?"

"Do what?" Aspen asked, settling in beside them. Ro nearly leapt out of his skin when he heard her voice. He looked everywhere but at her.

Styrax and Ash shared a look, but said nothing, much to Ro's relief.

Sorren clasped his fingers around his bowl, watching them intently. He got a haunted, faraway look in his eyes. "Can you teach me how to *not* kill people? Even if I've already—?"

He didn't finish the words, but Ro's heart dropped. Sorren was always so happy that sometimes Ro forgot he had been a *child* under Sedick's control. A child forced to do horrific things.

Aspen's face grew soft. She gave Sorren a grim, knowing smile and placed her hand over his. "*All* are welcome," she said. "I will be the first to tell you I have too much blood on my hands. It's never too late to want to make a change."

Ro smiled softly at her. He wished she would allow some of that grace for herself.

"Since you're here," Ash said to Aspen. "This would be an *excellent* time for you to eat some food. Look how accessible it is! You literally walk up, stand in line, and then they just *give* you food! How amazing is that?" She leaned in conspiratorially. "*And* I have it on good authority that the head cook is amazing."

"I can confirm that," Styrax chimed in.

Aspen gave Ash an exasperated side-eye. "I actually came to tell you that Inula will be joining our meeting later this evening, so you better bring a book and something to stuff your ears with."

"Can I bring a gag for her instead?" Ash asked, a little too much sincerity in her voice. "It's always better to stop the problem at its source."

Aspen gave her another look.

"I'll make sure it's a *nice* gag."

Aspen sighed and stood. "Off I go. Training starts soon, and they'll be waiting for me. Sorren, you can come join us now, if you'd like."

"Oh, um. Oh-okay." Sorren inhaled the rest of his breakfast and followed her.

"Welp, gotta follow the boss." Ash downed hers as well and went with them.

Ro watched them go until Styrax kicked him in the shin.

"*Ow!* What was—?"

"Oh, bless. If you were any more dense, you'd be a rock." Styrax flung his arm toward Aspen's retreating form. "*Go with her! Go!*"

Ro scrambled to his feet. "Alright. *Alright!*" He dodged another swift kick from Styrax and ran after the group.

"You better not be running away from a kiss this time!" one of Ash's cooks said cheerily as he passed.

Ro waved his hand, resigned to everyone knowing at this point, and caught up to Aspen's group. When he did, though, he suddenly didn't know what to do with his hands or where to look. *Anywhere,* as long as it wasn't Aspen's face. Or her lips...

"Can I, uh, come train with you?" he asked.

She did a double-take when she saw him next to her. "Oh," she said. "Sure."

Was it Ro's imagination, or did her voice sound strained?

It didn't matter. He followed them, ignoring Ash's and Sorren's knowing side-eyes.

THE TRAINING WAS PHYSICALLY BRUTAL, as Ro had come to expect any of Aspen's training to be. He had new bruises on his tendons and ankle bones, and every time he moved a new sore muscle made itself known. But he was thrilled with the fact that he kept up. It turned out that walking across half a kingdom and fighting off demonic generals was good for physical health.

Aspen smiled proudly at the group of ten soldiers that had joined them that day. "Well done, all of you. Take an hour's rest and then report to your captains for the rest of your assigned duties for the day."

Several of the soldiers flopped on the ground and immediately went to sleep. Ro approached Aspen, taking a deep draught from his waterskin. "Where are you off to next, general?" he asked, offering the water to her.

She took it gratefully. "I've got to check how the fortifications and shelters are coming along, meet with my reconnaissance team, check on progress for the disguises, and then I've got meetings with my war council. Inula will be there, so I imagine that will last long into the night." She gave him a weary, rueful look. "You?"

"Apparently making sure you eat and sleep," Ro said with mild concern. "Can't you pass some of these duties off to other people?"

Aspen shrugged. "I can't sleep anyway, so might as well make those hours productive." She handed him his waterskin. "Besides, I enjoy seeing the soldiers. They chose to be here, and I never want them to feel like that goes unnoticed."

Ro pursed his lips, unable to argue with her reasoning and hating it.

Aspen shifted on the balls of her feet, suddenly not able to meet his gaze. "You know, don't feel like you have to come to every meeting I have. You're the *prince*, and I'm sure there's plenty you'd like to learn or do or..."

"I enjoy coming with you. If I'm going to rule this kingdom someday, I figure I ought to learn how to do that from people better at it than I am. Like you." As he watched her, the reason for her discomfort smacked him across the face like a sack of pegasi droppings. The *kiss*. Sister *Earth*, he really was *dense*. "Uh, um, unless you don't *want* me to come," he said hastily. "If you want me to go somewhere else, I can definitely—"

"No, no, it's fine. I actually don't mind having you around."

"Oh, well, that's good then. I'm glad."

"How many times do we have to tell you? There *are* other people that exist around you!" one of the other soldiers called good-naturedly from the grass.

Ro's blush deepened, and he could have sworn he saw Aspen's cheeks color as well.

TWENTY-SIX

The next morning, Aspen exhaled deeply, trying to dispel her frustrations before meeting Sorren for his training. Her meeting yesterday with Inula and the others had been as productive as she had anticipated—more bickering over nothing and using up time that could have been used elsewhere. Her frustration had kept her up well into the night, half-wishing she had allowed Ash to bring her gag.

The worst part about being left alone with her thoughts, though, was that her mind often spiraled into dwelling on other problems, and the one that had manifested itself last night still sat heavy on her shoulders. She tried to shake it off, though. Sorren didn't deserve to be dragged into her worries.

When Aspen crested the hill of their meeting spot, Sorren was already waiting for her, training sword in hand as he whirled it through the practice motions Aspen had given him. He waved, but his easy smile turned to a frown the moment he saw her. "What's wrong?"

Aspen cursed under her breath. "Nothing you need to concern

yourself with," she said, pulling her hair back and avoiding eye-contact. "We're here to *train*, remember?"

Sorren chewed on his lip and narrowed his eyes. "Is this about the kiss?"

Aspen choked on air as she sucked in a surprised breath. "How do *you* know about—?" Her coughs got the best of her and she bent over, wheezing. "*No!*" she strangled out. "It's not about that!"

Sorren seemed unconvinced. Given her reaction, Aspen supposed she couldn't blame him. She cursed Ash and Styrax and all the rest of her loose-lipped, so-called "friends".

After another moment of slow breaths, Aspen composed herself and wiped her watering eyes. "This is not about a *kiss*," she stressed to Sorren, still wheezing slightly. "If you must know, I'm concerned about reaction times."

Sorren gave her a waterskin. "How do you mean?"

Aspen gulped the water down and then shook her head at herself. How was it that she could never avoid the conversations she actively *did not* want to have? "The time between when I give my orders and when they're acted upon is too great. On normal raids, we've been able to work around it, but with us being so outnumbered and trying to minimize damage, every second counts."

"How do you communicate right now?" Sorren asked, sitting down and resting his forearms on his knees.

Aspen joined him. "The trees, mostly," she said. "It's reliable because it can be heard throughout the battlefield, but it takes time to go from one tree to the next. We're so outnumbered here—any second counts."

Sorren nodded, his face thoughtful. The longer they sat in silence, though, the more his frown deepened, as if he had something he wanted to say but was hesitant to do so.

Aspen tilted her head, smiling ruefully at him. "You have an idea, don't you?"

He looked at her with wide eyes as if he had been caught. "I..." He immediately dropped his gaze. "Well, maybe? Possibly." He doodled in the dirt with his finger. "I don't know. On parchment, it would work, but execution..."

She folded her arms. "Sorren, you know the timeline we're working with. Something that sounds good on *anything* is better than what I have now."

Sorren chewed on his lip, a quiet anguish building in his eyes.

Aspen fixed Sorren with a firm, but gentle, look. "Sorren. Please."

He blew out a short, concussive breath. "There is something we might be able to do." He clasped and unclasped his hands as if unsure of what to do with them. He didn't look Aspen in the eyes. "There are some people that can be taught how to communicate mind to mind. If we had you and some of your captains connect with me, I can take those messages and send them instantly to everyone else I'm linked to."

Aspen gaped at him. "Sorren, what on Sister Earth would make you think this wasn't a good idea?"

"Because it relies on *me*." As soon as the words were out, it looked like Sorren wanted to call them back. He bit his lip again, his face taut. "Aspen, Sedick took control of me *so easily*. What if that happens again? What if you're all relying on me and I fail, or worse, get turned against you again?"

His words struck tender, aching cords in Aspen's heart. She knew those feelings intimately. Nevermind the fact that Sorren had been a *child* when Sedick took control of him. Nevermind the fact that there was nothing he could have done. The pain and fear were real.

"Sorren, do you trust me to tell you the truth?" she asked.

"Of course I do."

She patted the ground next to her, and he sat, but there was a wary set to his shoulders. She met his eyes, green to brown. "What happened was not your fault."

"Aspen, I almost killed you and Ro and Lady Vinea and—"

Aspen held up a hand to stop him. "*Sedick* nearly did all those things. None of that was your fault."

He looked like he wanted to argue more, but he snapped his mouth shut, the look in his eyes a mixture of frustration, guilt, and vulnerability.

Aspen had seen that look before. War did terrible things to people, especially young ones that had to grow with it. She had seen that same turmoil in some of her other young soldiers. "You did everything you could with the tools you had available," she told him. "And the most important part is that you've learned from them. They've shaped you into something new, and I've seen you put in the work to make this new you someone good, decent, and kind. A far cry from the trauma you've been through." Even though the words were meant for Sorren, Aspen felt them release a tightness in her heart and shoulders. Even though she had given similar speeches before, this one hit her differently. Ro must have been making her soft. The vulnerable, wounded girl she had kept tucked away for so long emerged. Instead of shoving her away again, Aspen let her words wash over that broken part of herself as well. "I forgive you. I've forgiven you a long time ago. I wouldn't ask you to do the things I am now unless I trusted you. And I do trust you. Whole-heartedly." The words caught in her throat as they slid like a healing balm over her heart. Her eyes misted over.

Sorren's eyes did, too. "Do you mean that?" he asked, his voice small.

Aspen took his hand and squeezed it. "I do. I trust you, Sorren. Will you be my voice on the battle-field?"

She still saw the doubt and fear in his eyes—the shadows of the trauma he had only ever shared pieces of—but he nodded slowly. "I—I'll try, Aspen. For you, I'll try."

Aspen squeezed his hand again. "Thank you." She stood, stretching her back and rolling her neck out. Presenting the plan to her council—to Inula, really—was going to be another headache, but it would be worth it in the long run. "Take some time to plan how you'd best like to implement this. I've got something to take care of right now, and I'll meet up with you afterward."

Sorren nodded, already lost in thought, and Aspen left him to sort out the details. She had to find Ro—had to act before the vulnerable part of her shut down again. It was time he knew the whole truth.

TWENTY-SEVEN

Ro watched Aspen with furrowed brows as she led him through the Golden Grove, her face set in grim but determined lines. He had been in the middle of putting makeshift costume armor together—mostly consisting of adhering fur, twigs, and other 'ghastly' looking things to already functional armor—when she had come down from her practice session with Sorren and swept Ro away without another word. He didn't want to think about how he smelled, or the glue that still stuck to his hands. All he saw were Aspen's hands balled in fists at her side, and the rigid straightness of her spine.

"Is...everything all right?" Ro asked her tentatively.

Aspen didn't say anything. She just kept walking. After several minutes of his heart rate increasing with every step, wondering what on Sister Earth he had done, they finally reached their destination. Hemlock sat on the porch of a house grown into a short, squat tree. Dried flowers and herbs dangled from the roof and windows, and moss climbed nearly every available surface. She waved when she saw them and motioned them inside.

Aspen only gave her a nod of acknowledgment, though, before

she veered off to a small shed out back. Ro looked at Hemlock, hoping she could give him any clue as to what was going on, but her face had taken on grim lines. She walked into her house and shut the door.

Aspen opened the shed door and they entered. Ro's trepidation shot to the stars. Oh, Sister *Earth*, this had to be about the kiss. That was the only thing he could think of that he'd done egregiously wrong. She must have been *furious*, and had taken him back here to yell at him without making a public scene. He knew he should have been more worried about her complete silence on the matter.

"Aspen, I am so sor..." he trailed off as a golden glow washed over him. The shed was filled with rows and rows of shelves laden with memory orbs like he had seen at the conclave. Each of them swirled with snatches of images that he couldn't make out and cast the shed's interior in a warm light that also sent eerie shivers down his spine. "What are we doing here?" he asked quietly, afraid he might disturb something.

"Hemlock keeps the orbs she makes for the Council here," Aspen said, her voice also hushed. "But she also uses these as a tool to help people that...struggle. She lets them live through their painful memories, and then put them away in this shed for them to access whenever they want. It doesn't take the memory from them completely, but it at least helps compartmentalize how and when to dwell on those memories. Sometimes." She led him farther into the shed. Her hands trembled at her sides. She drew up short at a shelf tucked away in the back corner. An orb labeled *A.T.* sat there.

Aspen let out a long, shaking breath. "After we left the Fens, you asked me why I'm a shadow walker, and I never got to finish telling you."

Ro winced, remembering the haunted look she had given him that night. "Aspen, if it's painful for you to talk about, you don't have to—"

She held up her hand and stopped him. "You deserve to know, Ro, because it's your story, too."

The words settled over Ro's chest like crushing weights. He swallowed and looked at the orb. "Was it...is it the night at the Dragon Scales?"

Aspen nodded mutely. Her lips were pressed together so tightly that they disappeared.

Ro's chest constricted. He wanted to know out of a sense of morbid curiosity, but he saw the anguish in Aspen's eyes. He had already gotten so much of his life back. Did he really need to—

Aspen put her hand on his arm. "It's okay, Ro," she said, trying to smile, her voice wavering and giving her away. "I'm ready to show it, if you're ready to see it. It's beyond time you know the whole truth."

Ro took one long, steadying breath before nodding. Aspen nodded back and took hold of the orb. Its light expanded until it blinded them to the rest of their surroundings. The shelves and the shed faded away, gave way to broken trees and a starless night, and all that was left was the memory.

THE FOUR FIGURES crept softly through the trees as the sun dipped behind the distant mountains and twilight set in. The forest of broken, uprooted trees had no sound. They just stood like brackish, stiff corpses. Nothing moved save for the four figures wending their way through the silence.

Aspen stopped and signaled for the rest of her party to do the same. She listened intently to the night air. All was quiet save for the perpetual crash of waves far, far below. Even so, she pursed her lips. She could have sworn she heard something—or some*one*—out in the broken forest.

She checked over her shoulder at her brothers and Ro. Will and Tarragon didn't show any signs of alarm—their broad shoulders relaxed and their expressions neutral. Ro also didn't seem to sense anything unusual, but at seeing the look on Aspen's face, his expression shifted.

"What's wrong?" he mouthed to her, looking wary.

Aspen shook her head and motioned him to be quiet. After a few moments of tense silence, nothing emerged. No enemies made themselves known. No creatures emerged from the trees' shadows. There was only silence—the kind that pressed on her ears until they rang.

Aspen brushed aside her uneasiness and pressed on. If they waited too long, she was afraid they would miss their opportunity. This war had gone on too long. If their mission were to fail...She shuddered at the thought.

When the night reached its blackest, they reached the end of the treeline and the drop-off into the Dragon Scales. Aspen made them crouch behind a large boulder and poked her head out to survey the broad, windswept plain one last time. They would be completely exposed out there—moving targets for anyone with half a mind and passable aim.

The hairs on Aspen's neck stood on end. She hated this. She hated all of it—the war, this mission, the fact that Dallowyn had put *her* in charge of it. Something still felt off. There was something unearthly about those plains and their inexorable, crashing waves. But she pushed it aside. Her fear of failing was greater than her fear of a bunch of lakes.

"Alright," she whispered to the rest of her team. "Stay behind this rock and don't come out for anything. I'll go down first. When I signal for you, then it's safe to follow me."

Tarragon caught her shoulder before she could swing over the edge of the drop-off. "No, let me go first," he whispered, his grip unyielding on her shoulder.

Aspen shook her head. "I'm the leader of this mission. It's my duty to go first."

"And our duty," he countered, gesturing to himself and Will. "Is to protect you. We don't know what's up there, and you're too valuable to lose just yet."

The girl looked up into his luminous green eyes that almost glowed in the dark. He had gotten the same color from their mother. Her same stubbornness, too. She touched the sword at her waist. "You gave me this sword and promised it would protect me and anyone I chose to protect." She folded her arms. "Are you saying you gave me a fake?"

"You dare accuse us of lying to you?" Will asked with mock hurt, a wide grin on his face.

"The sword's a last resort," Tarragon said, his mouth quirked in a half smile. "We're the first line of defense."

Aspen glanced between the two of them, frustration building in her. She wanted to argue. Wanted to leap over the edge and run off into the night just to spite them, but this was no game. This was war. And they were running out of time.

She sighed, her breath shaky, and reluctantly waved Tarragon past her.

Tarragon squeezed her hand. "You're doing great. We're just looking around for when the *real* soldiers get here. We'll be fine."

Aspen smiled at him, but it came out as a grimace. He chuckled. "Keep our princeling safe. He's a hopeless damsel."

"Hey!" Ro retorted, but he had a smile on his face.

"Well, I'm glad all of *you* are having a grand old time," Aspen grumbled. "Some of us actually have to take things seriously."

"That's why we keep you around, dearest sister," Will said, crushing her to his side with one arm.

Aspen shrugged him off. "Will you get going already?" she snapped to Tarragon.

He grinned and saluted. "Absolutely, captain!" He left them there behind the boulder. A few heart-pounding moments later, there was a low, throaty whistle. All clear.

Aspen let out a pent-up sigh of relief and motioned for Will and Ro to follow her. They met up with Tarragon at the drop-off.

"All's clear," he whispered. "I couldn't see anyone. We should be free to cross."

Aspen let out a long, relieved breath. She felt the tension leave her shoulders and chest. "Thank Sister *Earth*. Let's get this—"

Tarragon's eyes were on the treeline behind Aspen. They narrowed briefly, and then widened. "Get down!" He surged forward and threw Aspen behind him. She fell—hard—her head jarring and her vision skewing so badly that she almost didn't comprehend the arrow that thudded deep into Tarragon's chest.

He tipped to his side, completely silent. Blood pooled around him, thick and scarlet against the Dragon Scales' pale ground.

Aspen couldn't muster the thought to scream. She could only stare, wide-eyed, at her brother's prone form. It wasn't real. He wasn't gone. He couldn't be. He had been standing there only a few seconds before. Her vision swam. Bile rose in her throat.

And then she saw the arrow's fletching—deep, forest green. Her vision tunneled to that and nothing else. It was elven made.

She erupted to her feet, her sword—her *brother's* sword—already in her hands. Her entire body shook with fury. It felt like she was on fire. "WHERE ARE YOU, TRAITOR?"

Ro and Will snatched her and dragged her further out onto the plains.

"We have to get away from the trees!" Will yelled into her ear. "If we get far enough away, they can't shoot us out there!"

Aspen fought against him, her eyes locked on Tarragon. "We can't leave him there! Will, we can't leave him—"

Will shook her and made her look at him. "He's gone, Aspen!" His voice broke and tears welled in his eyes.

The tears finally came for Aspen. She couldn't see past them. The horror welled in her chest, hungry and all-encompassing. Gone. *Gone.* He was gone because of her. He had died to protect *her*.

"Aspen, listen to me!" Will shouted, his teeth clenched so hard she heard them cracking. His fingers dug so deeply into her arms he left bruises. "We have to get out of here. Tarragon would want us to —" Will never finished the sentence. He shoved her aside as an arrow whizzed between them. Aspen thought they had dodged it, but another one followed closely after and thudded into Will below his left arm. It went deep into the side of his chest. He fell with a groan cut short.

"NO!" Aspen ran to him and rolled him on his back. His eyes were glassy, reflecting the nothingness of the night sky above them. Aspen's limbs shook. Her world spun. Not Will. Not Tarragon. She heard their voices—saw the way their eyes crinkled when they laughed, their faces as they looked at her with pride or annoyance, depending on the day. Her sword lay beside her, useless. Her heart was in shattered pieces at her feet. They were dead. They were dead because of *her*. She hadn't protected anyone. She had failed them. The guilt crushed her into the sand, her ears roaring with nothing but the waves of the Dragon Scales.

And then the swell of a battle cry reached her ears. Through her stupor, she looked up and blearily registered a force of a hundred or so men barreling out of the treeline, their armor shimmering and mirror-like. Even through her grief, Aspen felt the quake of fear rattle through her spine. Her heart lodged in her throat.

"The Vanguard!" Ro shouted. He grabbed her hand and tried to drag her away. "We have to leave! *NOW!*"

But Aspen looked at him, heart frozen in terror. She couldn't move her legs. "Ro, *you* have to leave," she breathed, the words hoarse and broken. With each syllable, though, some of the fog left her mind. She was in charge. Dallowyn had placed her in charge of this mission. She would see it through. She would ensure Ro made it out alive. No matter how deeply her brothers' blood had already stained her clothes. "Take a message and get help. Let the Rebellion know what happened. *Go!*"

"I'm not leaving you here! General Dallowyn told us not to engage—"

"Ro, if I don't engage, they'll kill us *both!*" Aspen snapped. She picked up her sword and used it to force herself to her feet. Her arms shook, and her hands were clammy and slick on the hilt. She remembered how proud Will and Tarragon had looked when they told her they made the sword themselves. The memory nearly drove her back to the dirt again. "You're the *prince*! The Rebellion can't lose you, and *I* can't—"

But there was no more time to argue. No more time to escape. The Vanguard swept over them. Ro pressed himself to her side, his sword flashing as he bashed against the roiling mass of bodies. Together, he and Aspen battled them back fairly well, adrenaline and full-blown panic driving every movement. The Vanguardsmen fell back in surprise as the bodies of their comrades littered the ground around them. A large man stepped forward, dragging a bone-white sword at his side.

The soldiers stepped aside for him, and Aspen watched him with wide eyes, her chest heaving. Ro gasped for breath beside her.

"General Laire," one of the Vanguardsmen said, sounding young —too young—beneath his helmet. "There's only two of them. You can leave them to us."

Laire tossed his helmet to the side and sneered at the bodies of the soldiers. "I can see that. You're handling two *children* remarkably well."

"But sir, we can—"

"Enough!" Laire slammed the pommel of his sword into the soldier's chest, making him stagger back several paces. "I'll do it myself."

Aspen hardly had time to prepare before he rushed her, sword circling in long, dangerous arcs. She gave ground to him, shoving Ro out of the way as Laire drove her back. His strikes left her arms shaking, each blow sending devastating shocks through her shoulders and spine.

Aspen threw him off her and managed to get a few steps of distance between them, gasping for breath. He closed the gap in moments, sending a swift, crushing blow to her head.

Despite her shaking limbs, Aspen parried it. The white blade screamed off her black one, and her arms ached from the strain. She fell to one knee, but still threw him off and rolled back to her feet.

She charged at him, trying to keep him as far away from Ro as possible. The night air rang out with the sound of metal clashing against metal.

Laire met Aspen blow for blow, dragging the duel on as Aspen's body slowly broke down beneath his onslaught. Sweat poured off Aspen's brow as her knees started to buckle beneath each new strike. He aimed another blow at her head. She warded it off, her arms and wrists feeling like they might snap. As she struggled to throw Laire off, Aspen saw Ro out of the corner of her eye. He fended off a spear wielding Vanguardsman, bashing and hacking at the shaft even as it scraped along his sides. He finally shattered the spearhead off the shaft. But before he had time to recover, another Vanguardsman snuck behind him, a spiked mace glinting in his hand. Aspen screamed for Ro. It was too late. She was always too late. The mace fell. Ro crumpled.

The cry torn out of Aspen's throat was inhuman. Her vision turned red—red with the blood of her brothers. Red with Ro's blood. She threw Laire off her so violently he staggered back several paces. With no other thought to him, so rushed the two men that had cut Ro down and felled them. They collapsed without a sound. Raging, acidic fury burned through her veins. Not enough. It wasn't enough. They hadn't suffered the way she had suffered. They hadn't lost what she had lost.

She mowed through the Vanguard with no thought to her safety. She had lost everything. What did it matter? Soldier after soldier fell before her. She lost count of the number—didn't care to see the faces. All she saw was the blood that slicked her sword. It would never be the same blood they had taken from her.

She only stopped when one soldier deflected one of her blows. It glanced off his helmet, which skittered off his head. He looked at her with wide, terrified eyes. *Young* eyes. Aspen staggered away from him, her chest heaving. These were not men. These were *boys*, younger than even she was. His brown eyes reflected her in them, blood-soaked with a look as crazed as any demon. Her body shook again as she realized what she'd done. Realized how many she had *killed*—at how much blood had coated her hands.

She took another few steps away, her whole body trembling now. She saw Ro. Saw Tarragon and Will. They all would have died for *nothing* if she didn't do something now.

She turned and ran.

Her hair flew behind her, the dirt churning beneath her boots. She passed the bodies and sobs wracked her body. But she continued to run. She had to get to the trees—had to get a message to General Dallowyn. The rebellion could not come here. They *could not*.

The enemy general was faster.

Laire didn't make a sound as he closed the distance between them and sliced through her back. The agony dropped Aspen in an instant. Her mouth pried open in a silent scream. Her vision went dark. She writhed on the ground, tears pouring from her eyes as she begged for death, feeling as if a deep, internal piece of her had been ripped away.

Someone grabbed a fistful of Aspen's tunic and lifted her until she felt someone else's hot, putrid breath on her face. She made out a dim, hazy outline through her pain. Laire.

"How does it feel, little cockroach?" he crooned. He brushed a strand of sweat-crusted hair out of her face. "To be betrayed by one of your own?"

Aspen mustered up the strength and spat in his face, but he only grinned. "You think you did something here tonight, don't you?" he asked, gesturing to the bodies strewn across the plains. "Think you can mow through some of my men, and you've saved this war?" He yanked on her hair, wrenching her neck back and exposing her throat. "I have the rest of my Vanguard with me. We're going to find General Dallowyn and the rest of his misfits, and we're going to slaughter them *all*. And you, useless, worthless girl, won't be able to do anything about it."

An inarticulate sound of rage and grief pulled itself from Aspen's throat.

Laire threw her away from him like a sack of garbage. "Let's go." He called to his men. "Leave the dead. Crows can feed off their worthless hides." They left, their forms shifting like phantoms in the dark.

Aspen gasped and choked for breath, struggling to find her voice. She couldn't let anyone else die. She *couldn't.* Guilty tears streaming down her face, she dragged herself, inch by inch, to the edge of the Dragon Scales—to the trees that could carry her message. She faded in and out of consciousness, the pain searing across her back nearly unbearable, but she bit the inside of her cheek to keep herself awake.

She stretched her fingers out, weak tendrils of mist trailing from her fingers, and whispered a single message, over and over and over again. The tree was slow to respond, and she wept in frustration. Could it not hear her? Did she not have enough magic? Another failure. More deaths on her conscience. She had been too afraid to let the mission fail. She should have been more diligent. Should have been more careful. And now she had failed everyone.

The tree finally started to move, shaking its dormant branches loose. It whispered to the other trees, and soon the whole broken forest was alive with her message.

Retreat at once. The mission is finished. We failed.

Aspen stayed that way for hours, barely able to breathe and begging for someone to come to save Ro and her brothers. She didn't deserve to live—didn't *want* to live. The pain was too great. The emptiness was too all-encompassing.

When the sky turned to the gray of early morning, a woman bathed in golden light found her. Aspen hardly had time to register that she was there to help before her consciousness finally left her.

CHAPTER
TWENTY-EIGHT

R o expected the memories to stop there. He couldn't breathe. His head still ached from the mace he had watched crush his skull. He staggered a few steps away from Aspen, his cheeks wet with horrified tears. He remembered the gut-wrenching ache of watching Tarragon and Will fall—the terror he had felt standing beside Aspen as the wave of Vanguardsmen approached. She had trembled like a leaf next to him, just as scared as he had been. He wept for the girl he had left all alone.

To his horror, the world spun around him, and another scene surfaced from Aspen's memory orb.

FOR EVERGREENS AND ASPEN TREES...

Blood. There had been so much of it everywhere. She couldn't stop it, no matter how hard she tried. She had helplessly watched the life drain out of their eyes.

Ro, you promised.

The pain was beyond excruciating. Aspen couldn't move. Her

body was on fire, wracked with feverish tremors. It took all her energy to simply breathe, and even that was a struggle. The air rattled in her lungs, and every time her chest expanded, waves of agony raced across her mutilated back.

Hemlock rushed around her, efficiently dabbing her back with a wet cloth and sewing her together. She could feel the needle doing its work, but it was nothing compared to the pain of the wound it struggled to mend.

The smell of blood and burning pine was sharp in the air, mingled with the scent of herbs and spices. Heat washed unevenly across one side of Aspen's body. Wood creaked beneath Hemlock's footsteps, and rain spattered against thick walls as wind howled over the rooftop.

Aspen tried to open her eyes, but her surroundings were nothing but a wash of swaying firelight and indistinct moving shapes. Her eyelids quickly fell shut again.

A door opened somewhere. Wet air forced its way through the entrance before it closed, and the sound of heavy boots entered the room.

"Hemlock, how is she?" a deep voice asked. Aspen's heart skipped a beat with guilt. General Dallowyn.

Hemlock sighed tiredly. "I'm doing my best, general, but these types of wounds don't ever fully heal. Whether she lives or dies is entirely up to her."

"I understand." There was the rustle of a cloak being swept out of the way, and then the groans of a wooden chair as it took the general's weight.

"Shouldn't you be tending to the evacuation?"

"Already done." The man let out a deep, husky sigh. "It would have been a much different story tonight if we hadn't received Aspen's warning. Their numbers had been depleted, but a surprise attack from the Vanguard would have decimated us." There was another creak as he leaned back in his chair. "Osmen would have won if not for those four heroes."

Heavy silence weighed on Aspen's ears. Guilt tore at her soul. No. Not all of them were heroes.

A log collapsed in the nearby fireplace as it was consumed by the flames. Aspen heard the sparks pop as they swirled around her.

"Has there been any word on Ro?" Hemlock asked.

"No. They still haven't found the body." Dallowyn's voice was grim. "Considering who he is, I doubt they ever will."

It felt as if a hand had clenched around Aspen's heart.

No. I promised. I promised I would bring you home! For evergreens and aspen trees, remember?

A door burst open. Bitter wind surged inside. It tore at the walls, howling to be free. Stray raindrops sprayed across the room. The fire hissed in protest, and Aspen flinched at every drop that hit her skin. Gooseflesh rose on her arms and neck, and a shiver ran down her spine.

"Inula!" Hemlock scolded. "This poor girl's been through enough without you bringing that storm in here!"

"That is *Elder* Inula, to you, Hemlock," Inula's voice sneered. The door quickly shut behind her. "Your husband may sit on the Council with me, but you certainly do not."

"You're an *elf*, Inula," Hemlock muttered under her breath. "No one has made you a god yet."

"What was that?"

The general intervened. "Elder Inula, unless this is a pressing matter, I would suggest—"

"Do you see, Dallowyn?" Inula asked, her voice icy and brittle. "Do you see why we did not want to trust your precious half-blood?" Her voice dripped with venom and victory. "Disaster follows this girl like a lapdog. Not only have our months of preparation and resources been wasted, but now our prince is gone as well!"

Inula's words sank like daggers into Aspen's conscience. Their faces swam behind her eyelids—the three precious lives that had trusted her completely.

"Elder Inula, I would ask you to watch your tongue." The chair creaked again as the general stood. "It's not Aspen's fault they were ambushed—"

"Where are they?" A cry broke through the conversation, bleeding through the walls from outside. "Where are my children?"

"It's Calla," Hemlock breathed. "Quickly! Don't let her in here! She's already lost her husband. She can't—"

"Hemlock, don't you dare lock me out!" The voice was warm, but powerful, fueled by the fear of a mother. The door opened to more howls, but quickly shut again. "Where are—" The words sounded like they had been strangled. "No!"

Calla's footsteps rushed to Aspen's side. Soft, trembling hands caressed her face. They were cold and wet, but Aspen yearned for their comfort. "Oh, my sweet girl, what have they done to you?" Aspen felt a kiss on her forehead, and her mother's tears splashed onto her cheeks. She wanted to open her eyes and comfort her mother, but her strength had long since abandoned her. "Hemlock, please tell me you can save her," Calla said.

"She is a fool, Calla. No one can save her from that." Inula's scornful voice broke in once more.

A wounded growl wrenched out of Calla's throat. "You've gone too far, Inula! You will *not* mock my family! Remove yourself from this room, now!"

"I am a member of the Council of Elders! You will not—"

"I am a *mother*, which is more than your poor daughter can say of you!"

It sounded as if Inula had been stunned into silence.

"GO!"

"You never were one to listen to reason, were you, Calla?" Inula's footsteps receded. "I warned you that this would be the price you paid for loving a human. I tried to protect you from this."

"I know you lost something when Jasper had his accident," Calla said, her voice shaking with rage and heartbreak. The silence fell like a pall over the room. "And that's something I wish I could fix for you.

But I am *done* letting you use me, my family, and *your daughter* as whipping posts for your hurt."

Inula said nothing for several heartbeats. "If this breaks you," she finally said, slowly, as if every word cut into her throat. "I will blame your daughter to the ends of her pathetic mortal existence for taking the last of my family from me." The wind roared before the door slammed behind her.

Calla grabbed Aspen's fingers and swept her hair off her forehead. "What happened?" Calla's voice was thick with tears.

"Your daughter was cut down with a blade made from cursed galatite," Dallowyn said.

Aspen's heartbeat quickened in terror at the thought of that nightmarish weapon. Calla choked back a sob and kissed the back of Aspen's hand.

"Was it only one man?" Calla asked.

"No. They were ambushed by the Vanguard. It seems they knew we were coming."

The grip on Aspen's hand tightened, Calla's fingers trembling. "What about...where are my sons?"

Calla's question was met with silence.

"*Where are they?*" Calla released Aspen. "Hemlock, my children are all I have left of Abran. You cannot keep them from me. Where are my boys?"

"They're in the other room," Hemlock said quietly, her tone defeated.

Calla left Aspen's side. There were a few unbearable moments of nothing but the sound of Hemlock grinding herbs, but then an anguished wail pierced the silence.

The sound resonated in Aspen's very soul. Tears spilled down her face as her heart rent itself to pieces.

They had promised. She, Ro, and her brothers had all promised on their sacred childhood oath that they would make it back together.

For evergreens and aspen trees.

Now, she faced nothing but horrible, crushing failure.

A tear fell down her cheek. "It's my fault," she whispered.

Hemlock gasped. "Have you been awake this entire time, child?"

"Supposed to protect them. I—I'm sorry." Aspen's voice was nothing more than a croak, made all the more garbled past the lump in her throat. "Should have died with them."

"Don't you dare say that!" Hemlock rushed to her and shoved herb packets underneath Aspen's tongue. "You are not to blame!"

"Aspen, you're not leaving us!" Dallowyn's and Hemlock's voices floated meaninglessly in Aspen's mind. Those few words had taken the last of her strength. Her feeble grip on consciousness was fading quickly.

Please forgive me.

The last thing she heard before all feeling turned to nothingness was her mother's brokenhearted scream.

As CALLA's screams faded away, the scene changed, and Ro and Aspen were in the Elder's Audience Hall. Ro watched Aspen's unfair trial—saw them burn the marks into her hand while she was barely strong enough to stand. His hands shook with wrath, his stomach twisting itself into a sickened knot. Another image emerged, bright and vibrant.

ASPEN WALKED through the Golden Grove with Hemlock, breathing in the fresh air as deeply as she could. The day was beautiful and mild, with the sun streaming through the Golden Trees. Flowers had pushed their way through the soil, tended by swarms of sparkling fairies, and the trees rushed with a cooling breeze.

Even with the bracing air around her, Aspen leaned heavily on Hemlock as they walked, still feeling as drawn and pale as ever, but a spark of hope fluttered in her chest. Finally, after months of recovery, she could go back to her mother.

"It'll be nice to be home," she said to Hemlock.

Hemlock chuckled. "What, an old woman's company isn't enough for you?"

Aspen rolled her eyes. "You know what I mean." Even as she said the words, though, her voice trembled and dropped to a whisper. Anxiety settled heavily on her chest as she remembered Inula's raging, hateful stare. Of the gasps of horror from the elves in the village and the muttered curses as they moved to the other side of the street. "You're sure she wants me back? Even with—" She clenched her fingers around her left thumb, the shadow walker markings still dark and angry against her skin.

Hemlock squeezed her arm gently. "I know Calla. You are her family. She loves you and is probably in that house right now, waiting for you to come home." She sniffed the air as if expecting to smell something. "She's probably even set out a strawberry tart to cool."

Aspen's stomach grumbled at the thought. "I haven't had her strawberry tart in *ages*. That sounds *amazing*."

"And, of course, as a thank you for everything I've done, it's only right that you share your spoils," Hemlock said.

Aspen gasped in mock disdain. "*Never*. You'll have to fight me for it."

"Oh, please, with all your belly-aching over your medicine, you'd think it would kill you. I slip you a portion of that and you're as good as dead!"

They laughed together and made their way down the path to Aspen's cottage, the small structure just barely coming into view. The house was quieter than usual. That alone sent stabs of agony and guilt through Aspen. She had done that. Her father and brothers weren't there anymore because of her.

But, perhaps, with time, she and her mother could rebuild.

Aspen and Hemlock drew up short just before the door.

"Do you want me to go in with you?" Hemlock asked.

Aspen shook her head, her heart fluttering in her chest and butterflies looping through her stomach. She couldn't wait to see her ma. To hug her and cry with her and just hear her voice. It had been days since she had visited her at Hemlock's. "I'd like to try walking on my own, I think."

Hemlock smiled kindly at her. "All right."

Aspen let go of Hemlock and hobbled through the door. Inside, the cabin was dark, with a fine coating of dust over everything. The curtains had been pulled tight so that only the barest slivers of sunshine forced their way in. A candle had burned itself completely out on the table, wax smudged across the wood.

"Ma?" Aspen called, the sound hollow in the quiet house. The hairs on Aspen's arms and the back of her neck stood on end. Something was not right. Was Calla out? Had she forgotten that Hemlock was bringing Aspen back today? Aspen moved toward the back rooms, leaning on furniture and walls for support, her strides hastening with each step. "Mama?" The terror pounding in her chest felt just as real as when she had faced down the Vanguard. She wrenched a hunting knife off the wall and hurried to the back room as fast as she could.

Aspen flung open the bedroom door. The floor had been covered in her family's belongings—Will's paintbrushes, Terragon's boots, her father's tools—all arranged in a circle around the bed. And in that bed lay Calla, curled in a ball, clutching a white blanket with a burnt corner to her chest—a blanket she had made for Aspen's father when they were betrothed.

Calla wasn't breathing.

Aspen stood stock still in the doorway, taking in the scene with uncomprehending numbness. Outside the bedroom window, the trees whispered in Calla's voice. *I have to be with them. Take me to them. There's nothing here for me anymore. Take me to them.*

Aspen sunk to her knees, silent, numb tears dripping down her face. She had read, once, of an elf that had died of a broken heart. He had lost his lover, and without her the world had become a bleak, desolate place—there was nothing left for him in it. So, he had gathered all of his lover's belongings and placed them in a room, where he waited for her to come to him and take him to the after life. His village had found him several days later, and laid him to rest beside his love.

Before Aspen realized what she was doing, she had carved another mark on her thumb with the hunting knife.

ASPEN RELEASED the orb and stumbled away from it. The vision ended.

Ro stood there for only a moment, mouth agape, tears running down his cheeks. He had *loved* these people. They had been his second family. The grief gnawed a gaping hole in his chest. None of them had deserved that. Especially not—

He turned to Aspen and wrapped her in his arms. "Aspen, I'm sorry. I'm sorry. I'm sorry."

She trembled like a leaf against him, clenching his tunic in her hands. "I wasn't enough," she said in a choked whisper. "I wasn't enough for her to stay. Elves have to believe they have lost *everything* to die of a broken heart. I was her *daughter*, and I couldn't—I wasn't enough. I—" She broke. Her knees collapsed, and she sunk to the floor. Ro went with her, holding her as tightly to him as he could, as if that would keep her from shattering. Heart-wrenching sobs tore out of her throat. Ro pressed his lips to her hair, his heart breaking.

"I lost *everything*," Aspen said through her tears. "And now that I'm starting to get it back...Ro, I'm *so afraid*. I'm afraid that I'm going to lose it all again. I don't know what I'm *doing*! This kingdom deserves and needs *you*, not a scared little girl."

The words hit like darts in Ro's heart. No. No, the kingdom didn't need him. He hadn't been there for *anything*. It needed *her*. "Aspen, look at me."

She did so reluctantly, her cheeks stained with tears.

Ro wiped some of them with his thumb. "You are *blind* if you don't see that those soldiers—*your* soldiers—would go to the depths of the Pit and back for you," he said.

Aspen went to protest, but Ro shook his head. "You know it's true. And it's not because you manipulated them or somehow fooled them into thinking you're someone worth following. They're smarter than that. You *are* worth following. Who else would go through what you have and still decide they had more to give? That they could feed starving families and give back to a kingdom that has done nothing but persecute them?"

She had dropped her gaze again, wiping tears angrily from her cheeks.

Ro took her by the shoulders. "A *long* time ago, you asked an arrogant little twit what he knew about you. Do you remember what he said?"

She chuckled thickly and folded her arms, still leaning away from him. "No, but I remember I was unfortunately inclined to agree with him on a few points."

Ro shook his head. He took a step closer to her, and this time, she didn't pull away. He tilted her chin to make her meet his eyes. "Well, that twit has done some growing up. He got his memory back, changed his name—really turned himself around. And do you want to hear what he knows about you now?"

She watched him, her eyes wide and vulnerable. She didn't say anything.

Ro drew her to him, cradling her against his chest, not caring how quickly his heartbeat must be thundering in her ear. "He'd say you are one of the most intelligent and self-sacrificing people he knows. You will stand and fight when everyone else has already turned and run. You give all of yourself to everyone else, and leave nothing for yourself, which concerns him sometimes." He brushed some of her hair behind her ear. "You will exhaust every option and uproot every mountain to keep the people you love safe, and will protect those that can't protect themselves. You are *endlessly* tolerant and merciful to those that abuse and neglect you." He glanced at the memory orb still abandoned on the floor, his heart aching. "You have a heart that feels more deeply than any other he has ever seen, and that gives you power and strength to do things no one else would dare or *could* dare to attempt. You are determined and passionate and generous and caring and so many other things I can't even *begin* to list. You can and *will* succeed, despite what anyone else thinks. I know it."

He felt her tears soaking his tunic and felt her shoulders shaking with silent sobs. He didn't know how long they sat that way before they slowly petered out. Aspen was quiet for so long that Ro thought she must have fallen asleep. Her tears had stopped, and her body had gone completely still, breathing deeply in rhythm with the rise and fall of Ro's chest. He was caught off-guard when she spoke, her voice soft and mellow.

"I want to forgive myself," she said. "I want to be happy again, for more than just moments here and there. Am I...allowed to do that?"

The words were so delicate that Ro was afraid they might shatter. He curled Aspen closer to him, wishing for all the world that he could shield her from her hurt. "Aspen, you *deserve* that."

He felt her smile softly against his chest. Her body slackened, and this time she really did fall asleep. Ro didn't move. They stayed that way until the sun rose bright and soft the next morning.

TWENTY-NINE

Aspen was softer around Ro over the next few days. She still teased him, and still beat him soundly in every sparring duel they had, but it almost felt as if a door had opened between them. Her shoulders relaxed more when he came around. Her spine went less rigid. He could watch the anxiety in her eyes fade when she saw him walk into a room. The gap they had bridged in Hemlock's memory shed had brought them closer than any kiss had, and warmth swelled in Ro's chest at the thought of it.

Ro pushed Aspen's cottage door open with his hip, trying desperately not to drop the armfuls of food Ash had sent him with. He had the distinct impression that she would know if he dropped even a single loaf of bread. "Knock knock!" he called as he muscled his way in.

A vague noise of greeting floated out from the living space. The smell of wax and candle smoke wafted heavy and thick in the air, nearly choking Ro. The sun had nearly set, but the house was bright as noonday, at least around where Aspen sat at her tiny wooden desk, pouring over pages upon pages of maps and scribbles. Some of the parchment had been glued together by drips of wax from the dozens of candles huddled around her. Her scrawling handwriting went up one page and down the next with no rhyme or reason, but she seemed to understand it, at least, so that was a start. Dots of black ink speckled her lips where she had tapped her quill against them. He could see the gnaw marks on the quill shaft from across the room.

"Been busy today?" Ro asked.

"Uh-huh," she muttered, obviously only half-registering that he was in the room.

"Do you have a few minutes for some food?" he asked.

"Uh-huh," she muttered again, scribbling some more notes for herself and running a hand through her hair to get it out of her face.

Ro raised an eyebrow at her as he set the table. All the dishes were small, but there was a wide variety of them. Ash had most likely sent them all with the intention of getting her to eat *something.* "Can't believe it," he said, watching Aspen for any sign of recognition. "It's snowing red flakes the size of pigs outside."

"Uh-huh."

"What do you think? Should I cut off my left leg or my right?" Ro asked, smirking as he watched her. "I've been thinking I need to change up my image."

"Hmm..."

Ro folded his arms, his eyebrows nearly halfway up his forehead. "I am the most gorgeous looking man in existence."

No response that time. Just more scratching. Drat.

"Such a shame," he said with a dramatic sigh as he caught sight of one dish on the table. "I guess I'll have to eat this strawberry tart all by myself. And Ash had saved it just for you, too."

"Did you say something?" Aspen finally looked up from her notes. She smiled when she saw him, and it made Ro's toes curl in his boots. "Oh, Ro! When did you get here?"

Ro sighed, but chuckled to himself. "You are unbelievable, do you know that? I could have been a pack of sabers tearing up your entire kitchen and you wouldn't have noticed."

Aspen rubbed her eyes, her lips pursed playfully. "I can't help it if I'm better at focusing than most."

"Uh-huh," Ro gestured to the table, which he still only had half set up. "Are you going to come eat before all this food goes to waste? I would prefer not to have Ash fry me up for dinner for not making you eat."

"She wouldn't fry you." She gave him a crooked smile. "You seem more like a stew dish, personally."

Ro gave her a dubious look. "Any particular reason?"

"You just strike me as someone that likes to simmer."

Ro rolled his eyes. "Will you *please* come eat?"

"In a minute. I have a few more notes to finish before I take a break."

Ro sighed, dramatic and long-suffering. He glanced at her candles, one of which was on the last dregs of its life. "You have until that candle burns out before I drag you to the table by force."

She huffed. "Fine, I suppose that's an acceptable arrangement." She went back to work, and Ro finished putting out the assortment of food fit for an entire royal family. The food was all made of simple ingredients, but Ash's ability to season to perfection was unrivaled. It smelled divine, and Ro's stomach rolled somersaults inside him at the very thought of eating it. By the time he had set everything out, Aspen's candle had burned out. "All right, General. It's time I pull rank on you. The prince commands you to join him for dinner."

No answer.

"Aspen, I wasn't kidding when I told you I would drag you to the table by force. I'm under Ash's strict orders, and I'm not about to go back to her with my hands full of food."

Still no answer.

"Aspen?" He glanced at her little work area, and his heart melted. Her head had drooped fully onto her desk, her quill still poised above her, ready to write. Her chest rose steadily up and down, and tiny, breathy snores escaped her lips.

Ro crept toward her and stifled a laugh. Her quill nibbling had gotten the best of her. A long, thin line of ink ran from the corner of her lip, up her cheek, and disappeared into her hairline. She must have been chewing on it when she nodded off.

He wanted to move her to somewhere more comfortable, preferably her bed, which, from glancing at it from the living area, didn't look like it had been slept in for a few days. But he also worried that any adjustment would only wake her. And then she would *stay* awake for days, as she was so aggravatingly prone to do.

So he left her there, nestled into her pile of parchment, and instead retrieved her blanket from her bed. It was white, with tiny, fine leaves embroidered around it. An illuminated C and A had been stitched in gold in the bottom left corner. He ran his thumb across them. He remembered snuggling under that blanket with Aspen and Terragon and Will when they were children, burning tiny candles as they told stories and giggled until all hours of the night. The scorch mark from the one time they had accidentally caught the blanket too close to their candle was still there, faded, but stark against the white fabric. It had been in the house since Ro had known Aspen and her brothers, and they had spent so many hours all gathered around it. How could Calla have forgotten? How could she have just given that all up? He twisted the blanket into his fists and walked out of the room before he could make himself more angry.

He tucked the blanket carefully around Aspen. With nothing else to do, he perused her scribbles scattered around her, trying to see if he could make sense of them all. He couldn't. That became very clear, very quickly. He had no idea how she read anything she wrote. It was like her mind exploded everywhere at once, splattering each page with random doodles that could possibly be construed as words if one squinted hard enough. Possibly.

Either way, it made Ro's head and eyes hurt, and he quickly gave it up, despite his curiosity eating away at him. He trusted Aspen would share it with him when the time was right.

"Enjoying some leisure time, are we?" a voice sneered behind them.

Ro whirled, hand on his sword and ready for a fight. Aspen jolted awake, scattering more of her parchment in every direction. She blinked uncomprehendingly at the blanket Ro had wrapped around her, and then turned to see what he was looking at. All sleep disappeared from her eyes and she hastily stood up, the blanket still wrapped haphazardly around her shoulders and her ink streak now smeared across her face.

"Elder Inula," she said. "I thought you and I had come to an agreement that we would not meet here."

Inula arched a delicate eyebrow, one corner of her lip following its condescending curve. "And I can see why you would want such an arrangement. Is this where you come to slack from your duties where no one else can see?"

Ro balled his hands into fists. Aspen briefly touched his knuckles in an effort to calm him down. "I've been working, Inula. I find it helps me think if I'm in a place where I know I won't be disturbed."

Inula cast accusing eyes at the blanket wrapped around Aspen's shoulders and the food spread out on the table. "Yes, you seem like you've been very busy."

Ro ground his teeth and gestured pointedly at the parchments scattered about the room. "She has been. Very much so. I've seen her working on these plans for the past three days, at least."

Inula's eyes darkened and narrowed at Ro. "Well then, your majesty, let's see these plans, if you're so certain about it."

"Elder Inula, they're not done yet," Aspen said, her shoulders straightening. "I would be happy to show them to you and discuss them tomorrow in the commander's tent."

"I'm sure you would. It would give you more time to slap something together and make it seem like you have indeed been working as you say you have."

Something inside Ro snapped. He felt his eye twitch. "Elder Inula, have you eaten yet?"

Inula and Aspen both looked at him in identical consternation. The only time he had ever seen a family resemblance between them.

Inula looked at the table and curled her lip in disgust. "I have indeed."

She was only adding fuel to the fire. Ro almost welcomed it at this point. Anything he could use as an excuse to punch her right in her judgmental face. "I'm happy to hear you've had a nice, nutritious meal to keep you going. And sleep? Have you slept well?"

Aspen gaped at him like he had taken complete leave of his senses. Inula had a guarded look in her eyes. "Yes, thank you," she said slowly. "I find I sleep quite well most nights with my men guarding my bedchamber."

Ro nearly laughed. Sister Earth, did she think he intended to assassinate her? Considering how angry he was, maybe she wasn't too far off. "Good, good. I'm glad." He folded his arms across his chest. "Would you like to know who *hasn't* gotten either of those things for at least the past three days, if not more?" He didn't give her time to answer. "Aspen. And would you like to know why? Because she has been putting everything she can into helping a village that refuses to give her any sort of support." He gestured around the cottage, where the only thing out of place was her pile of parchment and candles. "Her food is untouched. Her bed has not been slept in for days. I don't know how you elves live—on some sort of high and mighty plane that we humans can't dream of reaching—but for her and I, sleep and food are a necessity. And I suggest that if you want any sort of chance at success with this battle, you will leave her alone and afford her *basic. Necessities.*"

The silence hung thick in the room. Inula had drawn back a little in shock. Aspen still gaped at him, but a hint of laughter sparkled in the corners of her eyes.

"You dare—" Inula started before she trailed off. For once in all the time Ro had known her, Inula seemed at a loss for words. She looked accusingly at Aspen. "You dare let him speak to me this way?"

Aspen took a moment to collect herself. Ro saw a small smile tug at the corner of her lips. Whatever consequences came of his ill-advised tirade, that one brief look had made it all worth it. "I'm sorry, Elder Inula, but I have no say over him. I dare not command above my present station in such esteemed present company. He is the prince, and you are the Council Head. I couldn't *dream* of ordering him to do anything he didn't want to."

The temperature in the room decreased by several degrees. Frosty disgust radiated off Inula in frozen waves. She had nothing to say, though. Absolutely nothing. It made Ro grin inside. Pure, unadulterated bliss. He had her, and she could do nothing about it.

Aspen's shoulders sagged, as if she had suddenly grown tired of the whole mess. "I suppose you won't leave until I show you these unfinished plans, will you?" She asked, mostly to herself.

"It seems you're learning, girl," Inula oozed back.

Aspen dropped the blanket at her feet and turned back to her desk. "I will give you ten minutes to discuss these. After that, you will have to wait until our command meeting tomorrow."

Inula sniffed and settled herself next to Aspen. While Aspen began, Inula absently gathered up the blanket puddled on the ground and folded it neatly over her lap. She traced the gold 'C' in the corner with her index finger while she peered at Aspen's notes.

Tristan was almost taken aback. He never would have suspected Inula to be so...sentimental. Or really have any other emotion rather than disgust and annoyance. He supposed everyone had their secrets to hide and their inner selves to protect. Inula's just made her prickly and ridiculous beyond all reason.

As she and Aspen discussed plans, Ro fiddled with the table placement, unsure of what else to do. He absolutely would not leave Aspen alone with that vile elven nightmare, but he also knew he was well beyond his depth when it came time to discussing plans and battle strategies. Gan had tried to instill a sense of it into him, but he had always been more interested in exploring and spending time with his friends. Some accomplished prince he had turned out to be. Maybe he could ask Aspen and Dolo to give him lessons. At some point in his life, if ever this war ended, he might actually have to rule a kingdom properly, and he would need to know how to do it.

Inula scoffed at something Aspen said and drilled her about a particular detail. Ro was about ready to just shake her and insist she just let Aspen talk, but Aspen had it covered. She answered her question neatly and curtly, and moved on. Inula had nothing to fight back about, because the answer had been so sound. She pursed her lips as if miffed to have nothing to argue about and continued to listen.

This happened a few more times, with her equally shut down every time. Pride glowed in Ro's chest. That was Aspen. Amazing, sensible, intelligent, and firm. He would let her lead him to the Pit, and would still trust her to lead him out of it alive.

"Why have you set up forces by the Mother Tree?" Inula asked, pointing to some more of Aspen's notes. "You're already stretched thin, as is it. It's unnecessary to have them there."

Aspen hesitated to answer this one. "There's still something that...doesn't sit right with me," she finally responded. "I know the collapsed dwarven tunnels lead to there. I know it would take days for anyone to dig through those, but I still want to be cautious. Call it gut instinct or intuition or what have you. I want to ensure that all sides are covered, so we're not surprised by any shady tactics."

"So you're endangering your other men by spreading them unnecessarily to the other side of the battlefield, where they'll be useless and will play no part in the battle at all? That's such a waste of man power to put on a whim."

"Be that as it may, I feel strongly about this," Aspen said slowly. "I trust in my men and their capability on the battlefield. They've proved themselves to me and the rest of the Rebellion more times than I can count. They'll be all right. It's not ideal, but we'll make it work."

"I think you should pull them back to the center line you have set up in the town square," Inula said.

"Your advice is noted, but I'm afraid I'll have to turn it down," Aspen said. Ro could tell she was fighting the urge to roll her eyes. "If there is something that can be prevented by an abundance of caution, I'm going to prevent it. If they end up not being needed, it will be a happy surprise."

Inula folded her hands tightly in her lap, her brow arched and her lips pursed. "You're not going to reconsider at all, are you?" she asked.

Aspen also pursed her lips, her spine straightening as if she expected a fight. "I'm afraid not. I've learned from bitter experience that it pays to be over-prepared."

Inula leaned back, tapping her index finger on her elbow, brows knit in both irritation and thought. Something passed over her face, though, as she looked at the embroidery in her lap again. She brushed delicate fingers over her forehead. "Sweet Sister Earth, I can't believe I'm feeding into your stubborn impertinence." She looked at Aspen. "Would you pull your troops back to your main line if I were to offer my men as a rear guard for the Mother Tree?"

The silence hung thicker than the blanket folded on Inula's lap. Aspen gaped at her like she had lost her senses. Ro wasn't sure what sort of creature had come in and taken over Inula's body.

"You...You want to offer your men as reinforcements?" Aspen asked, her disbelief apparent.

"I don't see why I wouldn't," Inula said with a sniff. "This is their home, too. It would be shameful for its protectors to watch on the sidelines as someone else made a mockery of trying to defend their home."

Ro narrowly avoided pointing out that she had just accused the soldiers already stationed near the Mother Tree of doing just that. But only narrowly.

"It just has never been done before. There's never been a precedent for it," Aspen responded, keeping her voice even, but Ro could hear the pointed note in her words.

"In this instance, a new precedent must be set." Inula straightened and looked down her nose at Aspen. "Will you accept my help or not? You seem reluctant to do so."

"I will happily accept your men's help," Aspen said. "But it must be under the condition that I am in full command of them. They will be returned to you once I have deemed the danger is passed, but I cannot have too many commanders on one battlefield."

Inula opened her mouth as if to say something, but Aspen held up a hand. "I need to know that if I command them to do so, they will act without hesitation and not wait for you to repeat my order."

Inula waved her hand flippantly. "Yes, yes, of course. Whatever you say."

Aspen straightened her shoulders, looking Inula straight in the eye. "I am serious, Elder. They will be a liability rather than a help if it is any other way."

Inula sighed heavily and stuck her left hand out. "If you are so suspicious, fine. I will shake an oath, and then we may be done with this matter."

Aspen shook Inula's with her left hand, her dark coward's mark stark against the candlelight. Inula curled her lip at it as if it were some filthy, rotting disease, but said nothing about it.

Shortly after, Aspen finished up the rest of her once-over of the plan, and then Inula left. Aspen followed her to the door and watched her go. Ro continued to sit at the table, stunned. When Aspen returned, she looked as if she weren't fully present. Her eyes were far off in disbelief, and she swayed on her feet.

She sat into a seat—or more like flopped—and stared at a spot on the wall just above Ro's right shoulder. She sat that way for a moment, her lips moving without words coming out, before she ran a hand through her hair and looked at Ro in consternation. "I'm not mad, right? Inula really did just agree to sign her men over to me temporarily, of her own will and choice?"

Ro shrugged helplessly and chuckled in disbelief. "I think so."

Aspen shook her head and took an absent bite of bread. "I'm losing my mind," she said with a small laugh. "It's amazing what war will bring out in people."

Ro nodded. "Are you worried she might renege on her promise?"

Aspen's face turned somber. "That will always be a worry, particularly where I'm concerned. I fear she may hate me more than she loves anything else." She chewed contemplatively. "But I think she does still have the Golden Grove's best intentions at heart. I think she'll choose the right thing." She took another bite of bread and chuckled. "Ash won't believe me when I tell her."

"*I* hardly believe it, and I was sitting right here the whole time!"

Aspen's chewing slowed and her eyes widened to take in all the food. "This...This is really good, but does Ash think I'll be able to finish all of this?"

Ro laughed. "I think she just wanted to make sure you actually *ate*."

"Well, I can't disappoint her, can I?" Aspen responded, her eyes twinkling.

They dug in and forgot the world for a moment. They broke into peals of laughter as Aspen recounted a time when Ash had hidden Inula's staff out of spite. Ro told of the time two sweet ladies had set up courting dates for him and Styrax with their granddaughters, but had forgotten to inform their granddaughters of it, so he and Styrax just stood in Lorate square for an hour, looking pitiful with their slowly wilting flowers. Ro couldn't remember the last time he had seen Aspen cry so hard from laughing.

The night waned, and eventually Aspen nodded off to sleep, the food too much for her to handle. Ro carried her to bed and tucked her in. She smiled faintly and nuzzled into the pillows. Ro smiled and brushed some hair from her forehead.

He doused her candles before he left, but left her mess of parchment as it was. He might mess up whatever sham of a system she had, and he did not want to be in her line of fire for that. He packed up the leftover dishes, closed the door behind him, and walked off into the silvery trees of the night, whistling softly to himself.

THIRTY

"I don't like it," Inula growled, her lip curled in disgust. "Filthy sorcerer magic will not be permitted anywhere near my men."

Ro barely withheld an eye roll. Every time? Did it have to be *every* time Aspen introduced a new idea?

Aspen looked like she had sucked on a lemon, and was desperately trying not to betray how sour it was. "*Elder Inula,*" she said, her nostrils flaring as she drew in a long breath. "I will not have you insulting any of my soldiers that way, particularly when they are offering to help."

Sorren looked at Aspen with wide eyes and pink cheeks. "I'm one of your *soldiers?*" he asked quietly, awe-struck.

A small smile tugged at the corner of Aspen's mouth.

"Mind magic is an invasion of privacy," Inula snapped. "I will not permit my men to have their minds *linked* to yours in such a way."

Aspen raised an eyebrow. "Please explain to me how scrying is any different."

Inula's lips pressed into a thin line, and she said nothing.

Dolo sighed and rubbed his furry face beneath his eyes. "Elder

Inula, *please*, we've been at this for hours. I'm tired and would like to go home to my wife." He leveled a flat stare at her. "Using Sorren's magic is the most efficient and error-free way to communicate on the battlefield. You know this, but are just choosing to be stubborn about it."

"The answer is. Still. No." Inula ground out. "Find some other way."

"You are the most *pig-headed, vile—*" Ash began.

"No one asked for your opinion," Inula shot back.

"Enough!" Aspen barked. She looked ready to strangle someone. "Fine. *Fine*! Inula, you can have your ridiculous communication methods. We will put *one* signal tower where your men will be stationed so they can let us know if anything goes wrong."

"There will be no need, because *nothing* is going to happen out there."

"There. Will. Be. A. Tower," Aspen growled. "Now, can we *please* move on to other subjects?"

Ro watched Aspen through the rest of her meeting, not entirely picking up on everything that she said. His brain was too frazzled and too tired for that, and he had no idea how she kept it up. He chewed on his lip as he kept an eye on her. Even with the sleep she had finally managed to get at home, she still looked exhausted, body and soul. He could see her brain frantically sorting through her list of responsibilities as the time ticked away, absorbed into Inula's stubbornness. Her leg bounced beneath the table, and she kept scribbling notes to herself as Inula droned on.

Ro ground his teeth. Even the people Aspen could delegate tasks to had been sucked into the hostage situation. Sorren had trickled out as soon as discussions about his mind magic were over, but Ash, Dolo, and the others all stayed. Aspen had always made it clear that Ro was welcome at the table as well, but he often relegated himself to the outskirts to observe. That worked in his favor today, and he snuck out while everyone bent their heads over yet another map of the Golden Grove.

He wandered through the camp, scuffing the dirt as he lost himself in thought. There had to be *something* he could do to help Aspen. Whether or not he liked it, he was the prince. Eventually, he would have to stop hiding from the title. Loralan deserved something better than Osmen, at the very least. If he wanted to achieve that, he'd have to get some practice in. Who better to do that under than Aspen?

As he wandered, he looked out over the moors and spotted Styrax and Sorren there. Flashes of purple swept around Sorren as Styrax sat in front of him, arms crossed. Ro approached them, curious.

"Show me what you *feel* about that!" Styrax called to the boy as Ro came into earshot.

"It's a *rock*. I don't feel anything!" Sorren shot back, looking unusually irate. His hair was plastered to his red, sweaty face as a rock the size of his head zoomed in circles around him, propelled by his magic. When he saw Ro, he started in surprise, and the rock dropped—right on his toe. He yelped, spouting expletives that would have made Lady Vinea blush, and the rock exploded.

"There, see? Now you're feeling something," Styrax said with a grin.

Sorren shot him a murderous scowl.

"What's going on here?" Ro asked as he sat next to Styrax in the long, soft grass.

"Well, look who finally escaped the beast's den." Styrax turned his grin on Ro. "I'm so glad I'm not important enough to go to those."

Ro pursed his lips and gestured to Sorren, who was now hobbling in circles and still cursing to himself. "How long have you been in the business of abusing children?"

"Not long." Styrax stretched his arms over his head, back arching, and yawned. "You all right?"

Sorren waved a dismissive arm even as he continued to nurse his foot. A leather bracelet with something smooth and shimmering inside it flashed in the sun from where it rested on his wrist.

"He asked me to teach him more magic," Styrax said when Ro continued to look at him for an explanation.

Ro gave him a dubious look. "And you do that by making rocks float? When he can already level entire towns if he really wants to?"

"It's not about the rock. He could do a tree branch or a leaf, too, or really anything he wants. What's most important are the movements he does with them. They're meant to be long and methodical to help him meditate and tune into himself." Styrax plucked a blade of grass and let water coalesce around it. It floated above his palm, and Styrax sent it out into long, curving arcs, changing direction with every long inhale and exhale he took. Ro watched it, entranced, as it caught the sunlight. "Magic is as much a part of us as breathing," Styrax said. "It ties directly to our emotions, and if we are not in tune with those, our magic suffers for it." The water droplet froze, its edges jagged and razor sharp. Styrax let it fall back into the grass, where it shattered.

Sorren had picked up another rock with his magic and guided it through a similar sequence to Styrax's water droplet, this time much farther away from his feet.

Styrax's jaw was unusually tight, his eyes hard, when he spoke again. "From what little Sorren's told me, Sedick is, well, *Sedick*. He beat and broke all the emotions out of Sorren until his magic was nothing but clinical, empty destruction. And now he's afraid to incorporate that back into himself." He blew out a long breath, eyes still flashing. "Magic is meant to add depth and joy to the beauty of life. It's not meant to destroy it." Styrax sat back with a wave of his hand, as if warding off evil spirits, and stared up into the clouds. "But enough of that. You didn't come here to hear me rant. What can your resident sage do for you?"

Ro watched Sorren, his problems suddenly feeling trite in comparison. So what if he didn't feel useful? At least he hadn't had his entire personality beaten out of him as a child.

"I don't like that face you're making," Styrax said, looking at Ro with raised eyebrows.

"What *face*?" Ro asked, splaying his hands in consternation.

"It's the 'my-problems-aren't-big-enough-to-share' face. You and Aspen both have it. You get this sad little crease between your eyebrows and look down and to the side like you're trying to study just one nostril." He demonstrated the look, which made Ro snort despite himself. He looked positively pathetic. Styrax gave him a lopsided smirk. "So, are you going to tell me what's on your mind?"

Ro rolled his eyes. "It's stupid."

"I seem to recall a very similar conversation, where we determined we are never *not* stupid."

Ro gave him a sidelong look. "Fair enough, I suppose." He tucked his knees closer to him and sighed. "I'm feeling pretty useless right now. Everyone here seems to have magic or some other vital skill, and I'm just...me." He held up a hand, cutting off Styrax as the naiad opened his mouth to say something. "And I don't want to hear any of that 'but being you is the best thing you can be' nonsense today," he said in a remarkably fair impersonation of Styrax's voice. Styrax reluctantly closed his mouth again. Ro watched Sorren move his rock around, and noticed that the grass around the boy had started to grow, twining around his legs and blossoming. "I float around Aspen and watch her do the incredible things that she does, but I don't have anything I can do to help or add in meaningful ways. I'm supposed to be a *king*, but right now I just feel like a glorified errand boy."

Styrax stayed silent for a long time. Too long.

"No words of wisdom?" Ro asked, partially teasing, mostly desperate.

Styrax splayed his hands. "As a self-taught sage, I have learned that silences can sometimes be just as helpful as words."

"Silences are sometimes *more* helpful," Aspen chimed in, making Ro jump as she approached.

His heart dropped into his stomach, hoping she hadn't heard much else of their conversation. When she looked at him, there was no pity or the look of wanting to make him feel better, so he supposed he was safe.

Aspen sat on the grass beside them, her spine slowly relaxing as she massaged her temples. "Do you know how helpful it would be to have Inula lose her voice? Just for a few days?"

Ro patted her arm in sympathy. "Things work out with her today?"

"I got my signal tower, if that's what you're asking," she said with a scoff. "I wish she would let Sorren work with her men, but I only have the capacity for so many battles at a time." She nodded toward Sorren. "What's going on over here?"

Styrax leaned forward and watched Sorren as well, nodding in approval. "He asked me to help with some additional magic exercises."

"That's good. I know he's been concerned about the mind links." Aspen watched Sorren thoughtfully, her eyes losing focus for a moment. "I ought to have you help me with magic at some point, too," she mused.

"Oh, Sister Earth help us, a more powerful Aspen," Ro said, throwing his hands up in mock despair.

Aspen elbowed him while rolling her eyes.

"I could give you a quick tip or two right now, if you'd be open to hearing them," Styrax said.

Aspen tilted her head, her expression guarded but curious. "All right," she said slowly. "What do you suggest?"

Styrax met her gaze with a flat but honest stare. "You have too many emotions that you keep locked away. That's why all your magic comes spilling out of you when you start feeling deeply, and why you're exhausted all the time after using your magic."

Aspen opened and closed her mouth like a suffocating fish. "Oh," was all she said.

Ro grimaced. "You couldn't have added just a *little* sugar to that statement, Styrax?"

Styrax shrugged. "She wanted to know. I gave her fair warning."

"You did." Aspen turned back to Sorren, brushing her fingers through the ends of her hair. "If that's the case, I suppose it's a good thing we're not relying on my magic to win this."

And that was when the thought hit Ro, so powerful it nearly knocked him on his back. He had known all along that magic was not required for this fight, but he had forgotten that all of Aspen's inner council and captains were magical in some capacity. He didn't need magic. He just needed sheer, dumb luck. Something he seemed to possess in abundance.

He faced Aspen. "Can I ask you a favor?"

She furrowed her brow, giving him a wary look. "Perhaps?"

"Will you let me train with and lead the non-magical unit when Lorate gets here?"

She looked at him like he had grown an extra head and placed a hand on his arm. "Ro, I want you to know that I would absolutely trust you to do that."

He sensed a 'but' coming.

"But it's too risky. What if something goes wrong? You can't be king if you're dead."

Ro stood up and paced, running his hands through his hair. "Aspen, you're always telling me I'm going to be king someday. That it's my birthright and that I'll be the king everyone needs me to be and..." he trailed off, trying to avoid rambling as much as possible. "But here's the thing. I don't *feel* like a king—I don't even feel like a *prince*. I've done nothing for this kingdom—"

"That's not true," Aspen interjected, her eyes ablaze.

"It *is*." Ro crouched and took her hands in his. "I appreciate so much that you see the best in me. I treasure that more than you could know. But, all I have done since surviving the Day of Bluest Blood is hide and have others take care of me. What kind of king would I be if I wasn't willing to sacrifice my life for the people that have done the same for me my entire life?"

Aspen opened her mouth, but no words came out. He could tell she still wanted to argue, though. He squeezed her hands. "Aspen, *please.* Let me be useful to you. Let me do this and take it off your shoulders. Please."

Aspen looked to Styrax as if expecting some support. He just shrugged. "I know I'd much rather follow a king that I knew wasn't afraid of conflict."

Aspen compressed her lips and looked back at Ro. He could see the worry lines between her brows—the fear of him leaving again.

He brushed his thumbs over her knuckles. "I said I would tear down the stars before I left you again, remember?" he said quietly. "For evergreens and aspen trees."

She sighed, the sound hollow. "All right," she said. "I trust you."

Ro hugged her. "Thank you."

THIRTY-ONE

Ro stood in the predawn light a week after Aspen turned over control of the non-magical unit. He bounced from one foot to the other, letting his arms swing loosely at his sides as he moved. He knew he should stay calm—should portray a sense of stillness and composure. He was the prince, after all. But blood and adrenaline raced through his veins, tendrils of electricity that scorched through his body and made his limbs tremble. This was war. And he was right in the middle of it.

The call from Aspen's reconnaissance team had come through only a few hours earlier. The Lorate troops had made it to the Woods of Desolation. They would be upon the Golden Grove at any moment.

Ro's armor weighed on his shoulders, the ruff of fur itching his nose, neck and ears. He prayed he would not have to test its mettle against arrows or swords. He hoped the mere picture of his presence would be enough to stop the coming battle. These men were farmers —superstitious and afraid of shadows. If he could play the part and be a big enough monster, maybe no one would have to die today.

As he sat with his crew, all waiting with bated breath, the fog swirled and lifted as the sun stretched out over the valley. The Golden Grove's leaves melted from silver to gold, blinding him with their brilliance, and with the sun came the first specs of human life emerging over the crest of the mountains.

"Here they come," Styrax said in a whisper.

Ro nodded, not trusting himself to speak

Are you ready? Sorren's voice came to his mind. Ro didn't know if it was Sorren asking, or Aspen. He pondered the question for a moment and then nodded.

Yes, he said, squaring his jaw. He maneuvered himself to the front of the gathered men. "Form up" he hissed.

As quietly as they could with their cumbersome armor, they did as he ordered. He was about to follow them when someone approached him from behind, and a soft hand touched his wrist. He turned and saw Aspen. His heart flipped in his chest while a quiet, warm calm spread through his limbs. "Aspen what—"

Her grip on his wrist tightened. "I just wanted to say…" she said, almost not loud enough for him to hear. She let out a huff of self-deprecation and shook her head, not meeting his eyes. "I wanted to let you know before you go down there and before anything could —" She couldn't finish the sentence and chuckled wryly to herself. "I don't know what I'm saying." She looked him in the eyes, her gaze soft. "Do you remember that kiss at my cottage?"

Ro tried not to grimace. The memory still haunted him and yet was still so tender in his chest that he couldn't bear to talk to her about it. Especially knowing that she didn't feel the same and how much he'd humiliated himself. But, as she looked at him, he knew he couldn't refuse to answer her. He never could refuse her anything. "Yes," he said sheepishly.

"I just wanted to tell you—" Her voice broke as if strangled in her throat. She growled and pulled his face to hers, kissing him roughly on the lips as if frustrated with herself. She pulled away just as quickly, leaving him dazed and seeing stars.

Her face flaming with blush and her eyes darting to anywhere but his face, she said, "I just want to let you know I feel the same. Be careful out there." She turned and left, her hair flicking his face.

Still dazed, Ro turned around. Pax gave him a look with one arched eyebrow.

"I've heard of battlefield confessions," Styrax said. "But that one was just *sad.*"

"Shut up," Ro groused, but his lips still tingled. The only thing that kept his giddy heart from leaping out of his chest and floating away was the weight of the enemy soldiers making their way into the Golden Grove.

"Let's go," he said to the men behind him, not trusting that other thoughts of Aspen wouldn't slip past if he sent a mental message to them instead. His voice still cracked, though.

A light chuckle ran through the men, and Ro felt some of their tension ease. He blew out a long breath. *We've all got something to come back to,* he projected to them. *So let's make this count.*

They all nodded in unison, their faces taught with determination. Ro put his headpiece on, minotaur fur tickling his face and threatening to make him sneeze, and they made their way into the center of town.

Ro glanced at the long line of black dots as they made their way down from the cliffs. He counted them off as he wound his way through the village. *How many do you see, Sorren?* he asked.

Two-hundred and thirteen, came Sorren's quick reply.

Those are not great odds.

It's less than what Lady Vinea predicted, Sorren pointed out. *Aspen has faith in you. You'll be fine.*

Ro chuckled mirthlessly, more to get his nervous energy out than anything.

He called for the soldiers to halt when they surrounded the main square of the Golden Grove. He monitored the number of soldiers spread across the cliff-face to make sure no other surprise troops came over the ridge. None did.

When the Lorate men had gotten within range to throw their

nets, Ro leapt from the treeline, letting out the most primal, unhinged sound he could muster. The other soldiers did the same, letting out wild sounds that reverberated through the trees and made Ro's hairs stand on end. A slurry of dark storm clouds—Styrax's doing—rolled over the group, flashing with ribbons of lightning. Ro and the rebel soldiers took off at a dead sprint for the men, waving their weapons above their heads and chanting nonsense—guttural, terrifying-sounding nonsense.

Ro watched the Lorate men, waiting for their reactions. At first, they all just stood there with their mouths dangling open, their eyes glazed over. Ro's heart dropped at the sight. Did they know that this was all a sham? Had someone finally trained the fear out of them? If this didn't work, the rebels had no other recourse. They *had* to get those nets away from them.

For a few heart-stopping moments, nothing changed. Ro was running Aspen's men into a fight they couldn't win—not with their limited numbers.

It wasn't until the rebels were practically on top of them that the Lorate men reacted. Their bland expressions turned to ones of pure panic. They nearly trampled each other in their rush to shove themselves as close to the cliff face and away from the rushing group of "monsters" as possible.

"They just forced us through the Woods of Desolation! Now *this*?"

"Retreat!"

"We can't!"

"Use the nets!" Ro called, casting his voice to the Lorate soldiers.

In their panic, they didn't pay attention to where the order came from. But they latched onto it like a lifeline. One after the other, the nets fell into the crowd of soldiers. The rebels fell beneath them in dramatic cries of pain, flailing for all they were worth. Everything was chaos. Ro danced out of the way and veered to the side so he could watch for all the nets to be thrown. He grimaced as helmets and armor clacked together while the soldiers went down beneath the nets. There'd be some concussions and heavy bruising from this ordeal, but if that was all they got, it would be a miracle.

Although the chaos made it feel much longer, it was only a matter of moments before Ro saw the last net thrown.

The Lorate men looked down at the carnage below them in shock and awe. And then a great cheer rose from them. Some collapsed to their knees or raised their arms to the heavens.

"Thank Mother Night!"

"We didn't die!"

NOW! Ro called mentally to Aspen's waiting forces, rushing out of his cover to free the men from the nets and get the serpent root far, *far* out of the way.

Aspen's unit leapt from the tree canopies, ropes trailing behind them. Before the Lorate men knew what hit them, the rebel soldiers bound them in groups, overwhelming them with sheer surprise. There wasn't even a scuffle. One moment, the Lorate soldiers were celebrating their victory. The next, they were being frog-marched down the rest of the cliff-side trail and made to sit in the middle of the village square, surrounded by horrifying monsters.

They gaped at their captors in terrified silence for a long moment. Ro and the others gaped back at them. Ro glanced at the sky. The sun had hardly shifted from its position. In less than an hour, they had nullified the threat to the Golden Grove.

Ro glanced at a soldier next to him. "Was that it?"

The soldier removed his wolf's-head helmet. "I think so?"

Ro looked around the clearing, his adrenaline pounding through his chest and making him grin. He ripped the helmet off his head. "Sweet Sister Earth, it *worked*!"

A cheer rose and rattled the trees overhead.

THIRTY-TWO

Hair trailing out behind her, leaping over debris and dodging silent, staring prisoners, Aspen bolted for the motley crew of rag-tag fighters in mismatched armor, headdresses, and fur. Face nearly splitting in two, she launched herself at the figure standing in the middle of the pile of trussed up King's Men, directing others on where to dispose of the serpent root nets appropriately.

"You did it!" Aspen practically sang as he stumbled under her weight. "You big, beautiful idiot! That harebrained scheme of yours actually worked!" She planted a giddy kiss on his cheek and surveyed the surrounding carnage. "Just *look* at them all! Barely a scratch on either side! How did you—" Her emotions caught up to her, and she choked on the sudden lump in her throat. She gazed at Ro, her heart full to bursting. The golden trees glimmered in his clear blue eyes, and realization enveloped her like a torch in a cave. *He* was home. Not her cottage. Not the Golden Grove. Just Ro. Inula could banish her all she liked—as long as Ro was with her, she could be happy. "It doesn't matter. Just...*thank you.*"

Ro brushed his fingers across his cheek, looking dazed and starstruck. "I will accept more kisses as payment for my contribution to this success."

Aspen smiled sheepishly at him. "Don't get your hopes up. That was a one-time deal."

Someone called for Ro to help with a stubborn net, and he gave her a wounded look. She smiled at him. "Go on. Come find me later."

"With more kisses?" he asked.

A blush spread across the bridge of her nose, but she couldn't stop smiling. "We'll see."

He grinned and left.

Aspen sat down hard on the ground before her knees could collapse beneath her. Cheers and relieved tears rippled through the air and shook the golden leaves, which sparkled and danced in the sunlight. Their whirring sounded like the applause of thousands of hands.

Aspen looked out, wide-eyed, over the battlefield. No blood—no bodies. No screams and cries of grief. Only happiness. Relief. Safety. *Peace.* She covered her mouth with a shaking hand, her lips pulling apart in a smile of disbelief.

"We did it," she breathed, a half-laugh, half-sob pulling itself from her chest as tears pricked her eyes. "We *actually* did it." She watched and basked in the surrounding happiness, not trusting her legs yet to stand and join in. There were too many emotions running through her all at once for her to trust herself with much of anything. It had actually worked. Nothing had happened. No one had died. Maybe really, truly, her curse was over. Just like Ro said it was.

"I told you there was no need for the troops near the Mother Tree," a clipped voice sounded at Aspen's right. Inula, a sneer still on her face as she looked out over the churning, sweaty mess of soldiers. It seemed nothing could completely wash that look from her face. She stood just far enough away from Aspen to ensure that no one misunderstood she did not view Aspen as anything other than filth.

Aspen stood and looked Inula directly in the face. She smiled. A real, genuine smile that didn't pull her face too tight and didn't make her teeth grind together. There was a comfortable warmth in her cheeks. Almost a glow. Inula squinted as if it was too bright.

"You are absolutely right, Elder Inula," Aspen said. "I'm sorry to have wasted my time and yours arguing over the importance of putting extra precautions in places we didn't need them. I'll rectify that mistake right now." She turned to leave, but Inula stopped her.

"That won't be necessary," Inula said, catching her by the shoulder, her face pulled tighter than usual. "I am more than capable of recalling my own men."

"Oh, no, I insist." Aspen gave her an earnest look, clasping Inula's hand in hers tightly. Inula tried to wrench away, but Aspen held tight. "I have burdened you with such a terrible inconvenience. I must, of course, fix it myself."

Inula finally extricated her hand and took a step away, massaging the knuckles as if Aspen had bruised them. "Fine," she said with a scowl. "Do what you must. Just know that I will not miss these ridiculous antics when you are banished."

If she expected a reaction from Aspen at the reminder, Aspen did not give her the satisfaction. The people she cared about were safe. There was nothing to do but enjoy it and celebrate. After she released Inula's men from their post, of course. Even they deserved a chance to be happy. Sister Earth knew they didn't get much chance to feel that way around their mistress. Or maybe they all basked together in their misery. She may never know nor care. She chuckled to herself and continued on her way.

"Always a pleasure seeing you," Aspen called over her shoulder.

Through the crowd, she caught Ro's eye. His smile nearly split his face, and he lit up at the sight of her. Aspen's heart melted into her fingertips and toes, making them tingle. He motioned her over, but she shook her head. "Later," she mouthed as she motioned toward where Inula's men had been stationed.

"Hurry!" he mouthed back with a wink before getting practically mobbed by an over-eager Dolo.

"My fur doesn't look half bad on you!" he bellowed. "We'll make you into a minotaur yet!"

Aspen watched the Lorate soldiers as she passed by. Most hung their heads in defeat, eyes wide open and staring at nothing. A handful glowered at her with all the hatred they could muster. Others, though, wept openly, their faces turned toward the golden canopy of trees. As Aspen got within earshot, she heard their muttered prayers of thanks and relief for not dying that day. She allowed herself another smile. It was rare that both sides could celebrate together. Today was a special day indeed.

The lightness across Aspen's shoulders spread throughout her whole body until she felt weightless, as if her feet never touched the ground. She couldn't stop smiling. She tilted her face up and basked in the Grove's golden glow. For the first time in years, it felt safe. Really, truly safe. And it was time to spread that feeling to the rest of Loralan. It was time the kingdom's true heir reclaimed his throne.

THE ROAR of cheers made Vinea's head swim. Her stomach lurched, and nausea clawed its way up from her gut. Every smile was like a physical blow to her. And the worst of them all was Ro, shining like a beacon of happiness as he crushed Aspen to him—smiling with a smile so like Eden's it made Vinea want to weep. Vinea had failed her sister in every way imaginable, and now she would leave Eden's son to the same fate.

No. No, she had to do *something*. Even though Sedick watched her every move—even though his cursed stud seared in her ear—surely she could find *some* way to warn Ro of what was coming.

Vinea waited to approach Ro until Aspen left. She touched him on the arm to get his attention and he turned to her, beaming. She saw so much of Linae in him—her smile, her goodness, her sheer exuberance for life—in that moment that her heart stopped.

"We did it! We *did* it!" He crushed Vinea to him, Vinea swamped in his bulky armor and fur. His grip was tight and trembled with what must have been relief. He drew her away from him. "And it's all thanks to you!"

She let out a hollow chuckle, his words a dagger to her heart. Her fingers dug into the bracers on his arms, her teeth grinding together. She had to tell him. She *had* to.

His smile grew quiet, and he tilted his head. "Is something wrong?"

The words were on Vinea's tongue. Her heart hammered to their rhythm. *Be ready to fight. Be ready to run.*

But Vinea's courage failed her. All she saw in Ro was Linae, locked away and waiting for Vinea to come for her. She couldn't risk her. Not for anything. Not even when she felt as if she was selling her soul to save her.

Vinea touched Ro's cheek. It took all her power to keep her fingers from shaking. "I am so proud of you." The words were traitorous ash in her mouth. She motioned with her head in the direction Aspen had gone. "It seems she makes you happy."

The warmth in his eyes colored his cheeks like one too many drinks of silver wine. "She does."

Vinea remembered when Laire used to look at her that way. Looked at her with warmth, kindness, and *love,* and not the haunted eyes of a hollow monster. "Keep her close, Ro," she said, pouring as many of her thoughts into the words as possible, hoping he would understand the underlying warning. "Love like that needs to be kept close—kept safe from anything that may come to steal it away."

But victory was too potent a drug. Ro simply grinned at her. "I know." He leaned forward and kissed Vinea on the cheek. "Thank you for everything. If you don't mind me saying so, I've always viewed you as the mother I never had."

Vinea gave him a smile that broke her. She turned away and fled into the crowd before he could see the tears of regret that bled down her face, weeping as she made her way to the caverns and the Sacred Flame they held. Her heart fell in shattered pieces behind her.

THIRTY-THREE

Aspen rounded the bend to the Mother Tree, marveling at how quickly the side streets had emptied out as everyone left for the square. Ribbons and lights from the Goldenlight Festival still dripped from the tree branches. It felt fitting to have them there. The main hub of celebration had faded to nothing but a distant rumble, and the quiet swept a calming breeze over her. She hummed tunelessly to herself as she walked.

That peace broke when the Mother Tree came into view. Aspen's body seized. All the blood fled her face, and her ears rang. Her mouth went dry. Her heart stopped beating.

Inula's men were gone. In their place was the shifting, mirrored armor she had prayed never to see again. The Vanguard—the phantoms from her nightmares. They emerged like cockroaches from a black void beneath the newly cut, mutilated roots of the Mother Tree. The old dwarven tunnels.

The Vanguardsmen turned their faceless, phantom helmets toward her, and she saw an immediate ripple go through them as their hands went to their weapons.

Aspen's body shuddered. Her hand shook as she laid it on the pommel of her sword. The Vanguard. The Vanguard was here. She had known the invasion from Lorate had been too easy. Her teeth ground together as she tried to force her body to move, but it stayed rooted to the spot. Clarity spread through her, carrying with it the poison of fear. She knew what would happen next. She couldn't run —the Vanguard would shoot her down and then flood into the main square where everyone had gathered. It would be a massacre. No. This was her fight. Just like that night on the Dragon Scales.

A wave of fear rushed through her. Alone.

She ground her teeth and drew her sword. The sound of steel against leather echoed a hundred times over as the men pouring from the Mother Tree followed her lead. Her heart pounded in her mouth, her throat dry. Her stomach twisted in so many knots she almost vomited.

No. She bit it back. No. This was the life she had chosen.

Sorren! she screamed mentally. *Get the soldiers on alert! The Vanguard is here!*

She received only silence in return.

The first wave attacked. Arrows screamed around her as a line of soldiers charged her. She darted forward, dodging through the arrows as they shrieked past her eyes. Her heart thudded in time with her footsteps.

Sorren!

Still nothing.

Aspen clashed with the first soldier. The blow jarred through her arms and shoulders, but she used the momentum to fling herself away from the first soldier and onto the second, driving him back as well. She mentally drew a line across the clearing where the silver wine tables had been placed. The Mother Tree had grown tucked into a mountain alcove of sorts, and that was the only way out. It didn't matter how many she had to fight. They would not cross that line—not while she was still alive. Not when she had people to protect.

She whirled from one man to the next, blow after blow beating them back, but only by a step. She couldn't read their faces behind their helmets. The hairs on Aspen's arms stood on end as she was reminded of the faceless, nameless phantoms that never stopped following her—the soldiers she had felled at the Dragon Scales.

Even as she beat the Vanguardsmen back, more continued to pour out of the entrance. It had never been an entrance meant for an army, but with everyone distracted by the Lorate soldiers, they had bought all the time they needed to file into the Grove. Aspen clenched her jaw, sweat already dripping down her temples and her body shaking from the coursing adrenaline. She should have trusted her gut and stationed her men here.

Sorren! Listen to me! SORREN!

The soldiers converged as one on her. They stopped trying to force their way past and circled her, all swinging in unison. Aspen battered them away. She seized the tip of one of their spears. The soldier held fast to it, which was exactly what Aspen wanted. She rammed her body weight against the shaft. It threw the soldier off-balance and flung him into two of his comrades. An image flashed across her mind, bright and vivid, of Ro tripping in the golden-lit festival crowd.

Aspen leapt through the opening, but not before another soldier swiped at her. It was a lucky blow and grazed her side just beneath her arm, where the leather breastplate she wore didn't cover. Another flash—Ro's hand wrapped around her waist as he spun her across the dancefloor. She ground her teeth in pain but shook it off. The wound wasn't deep.

She glanced back in the direction of the village, hoping someone was coming. Where were Inula's men? Why couldn't Sorren hear her? It didn't matter. It *didn't matter*. What mattered was keeping the Vanguard out of the Golden Grove, and if she was the only one there to do it, so be it. More images swam through her vision—Ash and Styrax spinning together, grinning like idiots. The crowd singing as one as the trees joined their voices to the song. The Sacred Flame flying overhead as a phoenix. Ro. *Home*. Her home.

Her green magic bled out of her skin and pooled at her feet, whisking away to the alcove entrance and blooming into a thick, latticed rosebush that cut the Vanguard off from the Golden Grove. And cut her off from any help. The vial she always kept tucked in her breast pocket burst and wreathed around her, lashing at the Vanguard soldiers that drew too close.

"Isn't this familiar?"

Aspen's back erupted with pain when the voice spoke. Her skin felt as if it had caught fire. A gasp wrenched out of her throat, and she nearly fell. Only sheer force of will kept her upright. Laire stepped out from between the Vanguard, his blasted, bone white sword dancing in his hand.

Flashes of the night at the Dragon Scales blinded Aspen and made bile build in her throat. She parried more blows from the Vanguardsmen, but her movements were slow and ragged. Rather than stopping the blows entirely, they only slid off her blade and dragged more gashes across her skin. Her rose vines were the only things that kept her vitals safe. She looked at Laire, panting but throwing her head back defiantly. "What is this, rematch number four?" she asked, her voice firm and steady even as her body quaked with pain. "If I had known you cared so much about winning, I would have thrown a fight a few rounds ago." She had been much closer to the cursed galatite without issues before. Had something about the sword changed?

"I'm going to kill you today, wench," Laire said, as mildly as if he were discussing a summer day. "And I'm going to enjoy it."

Aspen gave him a bright smile she didn't feel. "We've been through this. I'm not going to die here, and I'm not going to let you kill anyone else, either."

Laire said nothing. Only smirked.

A spiked club smashed into Aspen's midsection. Her vines protected her from being impaled, but the impact shattered her ribs. Her vision went white with agony. The blow threw her across the clearing, where she slammed into her wall of roses. The thorns tore through her tunic and when she staggered to her feet, blood dripping from her mouth, the fabric tore more and exposed her jagged scar to the crisp air.

Laire charged at her. Aspen raised her sword to parry him. Just as she had done so many times before. She was prepared for the agony to tear through her back. She knew how heavy his swing would be as she came to meet it. But Laire dropped his shoulder and drove it into Aspen's side. Aspen's jaw fell open in a silent scream as her already broken ribs shattered inside her. Blood welled up from a punctured lung. She couldn't make her eyes focus. Her vision stained red. Her body seized, panicking that it couldn't get enough air. Her stomach heaved, and she vomited, sending every part of her agonized body into a frenzy. Still, she forced herself to stand.

When her eyes refocused, Laire stood over her and swung his blade. She raised her blade to parry it, the voices of her brothers floating through her mind.

So long as you have this sword, it will protect you and everyone you choose to defend until it's time for you to retire and pass the fight to someone else.

"I'm not done," she hissed to herself, the taste of blood thick and sickening in her mouth. "*Not. Done.*"

Laire grinned, the sapphire eyes in the hilt of his sword glittering. A surge of grayish miasma blasted from the blade—a flash of power that robbed Aspen of her breath and strength, and made her soul feel as if it were going to rip out of her body. The single, minuscule chip on her sword shone in the light.

Her galatite blade—the strongest metal in the world—shattered on impact.

Sorren tapped on Ro's shoulder while he celebrated with Styrax, Ash, and the others. Ro had taken off his bulky, fur-lined armor and basked in the cool breeze of relief washing over him. He turned to Sorren with a grin. "You did great today!"

Sorren acted as if he didn't hear the compliment, brow furrowed. "Have you been hearing anything?" he asked, tapping his forehead.

"No, why?"

"I keep thinking I might be, but with everything being so loud, if I'm not focusing, I can't tell for sure if it's an actual message or just my imagination." He bobbed anxiously on the balls of his feet, purple magic zipping between his fingers as he rung his hands. "Have you seen Aspen? She'll know what's going on."

Ro frowned. He couldn't remember the last time he had seen Sorren so shaken. "She went to go relieve Inula's men of duty. She should—" He caught sight of Inula through the crowd, surrounded by her soldiers. He pointed them out to Sorren. "There they are. I'm sure Aspen'll be back any minute. Go and celebrate. If I see her before you do, I'll send her your way."

Sorren still seemed out of sorts, but thanked Ro and wandered off.

An odd pit formed in Ro's stomach, and he continued to frown as he watched Sorren leave. He turned to Ash, who sat on Styrax's knee. "You haven't seen Aspen recently, have you?"

Ash shook her head. "Last I saw, she was headed to Inula's men."

Ro nodded. "That's what I thought."

Ash gave him a concerned look. "Is everything all right?"

Ro spread his arms wide to take in the surrounding celebrations. "How could it not be? We've *won*! Everything went as Aspen hoped it would. She's incredible that way." He smiled at Ash, and she went back to enjoying the celebration. Even with his extra reassurance, though, something still sat fretfully in his stomach.

Aspen watched the pieces of her sword explode around her. A gasp rent out of her throat. That sword had been at her side for five years, never wavering. Never failing her. Its loss felt as if one of her arms had been torn away—as if her brothers had been taken for a final time. Errant shards of the black metal sliced down the length of her hands and arms.

She didn't have time to grieve. Laire came in for another pass, roaring in triumph. She dodged away, her ribs screaming at her and her body nearly collapsing from the agony. Her limbs dragged behind her like leaden weights, and her vision roiled. Fevered sweat dripped down her brow. Awake. She had to stay conscious. The entire Golden Grove had fallen squarely on her shoulders.

Sorren!

She had flung herself far enough away that she had a space to get her bearings, but she knew that would be short-lived. Think. She had to *think*. Brain fog, heavy and impenetrable, flooded through her thoughts. Her hands and feet went numb. Her lung fluttered uselessly in her chest as stars danced in her eyes. She scrunched her eyelids shut and tried to force some of the stupor away. Her protective rose wreath had withered. She had a few knives hidden on her, but with her ruptured lung and broken ribs, she wouldn't have the strength to maintain close combat for long. Some of the Vanguardsmen had already started hacking away at her rose hedge. She had to think of something *now*.

Aspen opened her eyes again. Laire approached her languidly, the shattered pieces of her sword protruding from a pouch on his belt. He smiled at her, his cursed sword swinging in casual arcs at his feet. It was in that moment, all alone, with the nightmares she had never been able to escape closing in on her, Aspen knew. She knew that her brothers had been right—her sword had protected her until it was time to retire. Out of the corner of her eye, she saw the single signal tower. It was time to let the others know she had passed on the torch.

Aspen took off toward the signal tower, shoving fear, logic, and pain to the darkest recesses of her mind as she forced her legs into long strides. Blood poured from the nick on her side. She coughed out more blood with every half-breath she could pull in. Her vision narrowed into a tunnel, the only thing visible from the signal tower. She knew she shouldn't have been able to push her body like that, but she didn't care. It didn't matter. She didn't matter anymore. It was freeing, in a way.

Sorren! Ro! ANYONE! she shouted mentally, the words the only thing keeping the fog of agony at bay. *Hear me!* She took a running leap onto the signal tower scaffolding. The jolt through her body made her lose her vision entirely for a moment. Her grip loosened. She teetered back, but caught herself at the last moment, forcing herself back into consciousness. Growling, she dragged herself up from the tower.

"Shoot her down!" Laire roared. "And someone set fire to those hedges!"

Aspen was too slow to dodge the first arrow. It struck just beneath her left shoulder blade, slamming her into the scaffolding with the force of it. Her vision went black again for a heartbeat, but she maintained her grip and kept climbing, her screams for Sorren still playing through her mind. The Vanguard would breach the Golden Grove. She knew she couldn't stop it. But it wasn't about her anymore. The village needed to know. They needed to prepare. Ro and the others would take care of it. She knew it. She just had to let. Them. Know.

Smoke had started to rise from Aspen's hedges when the second arrow hit, sinking deep into her lower back. Her arms almost gave out on her then. She kept on by sheer force of will, tears of frustration and anger building in her eyes. No. This would not end with her mission only halfway complete. She kept climbing.

The third arrow came quickly after the second. Aspen could hardly feel where it hit. Her limbs were like lead. She only saw through a pinprick of her vision. Magic bled out of her almost as quickly as her actual blood. Her consciousness felt disconnected from her, somehow, floating away on the breeze. She thought of Ro tucking her into bed and kissing her hair—of how he looked at her like she was the most beautiful woman on earth. He had always deserved so much more than her, but she had been his choice. She had just gotten used to that.

Aspen clamped her jaw and leapt the last few yards to the top. Her fingertips scrabbled for purchase. More arrows hissed past, but somehow missed.

"HOW HARD IS IT TO KILL A HALF-DEAD GIRL?" Laire's voice roared from below.

Aspen finally got a grip on the upper platform and hauled herself up. Blood slicked the wood where she dragged herself over. She coughed, and more blood spattered beneath her. Her entire body shivered as sweat poured off her. Half-stumbling, half-running, she forced herself to the signal horn.

"Go to the *Pit.*" She directed every fiber of anger, resentment, and protectiveness in her to flow into her magic, funneling it toward Laire and his Vanguard. *HEAR ME!* She blew the last of her breath into the signal horn. The sound ripped through the forest. Anything that could fly erupted from the trees, swirling in the air and crying out in alarm.

Aspen released all control of her magic. It exploded. Monstrous rose vines smothered Vanguardsmen beneath them and cracked through the foundation of the tower scaffolding. From her vantage point, she saw other rosebushes erupting from the ground, setting up shields around the village.

The tower began to sway and crumble. The Vangaurdsmen had burned a ragged hole into her wall big enough for them to fit through. They shoved their ways through, ignoring the flames licking at their armor, and ran for the village, carrying more serpent root nets. Aspen blew into the horn again, the sound peeling strident and desperate over the Grove. *I have done enough,* she thought to herself as tears finally spilled down her cheeks.

A fourth arrow finally cut the sound short.

The rosebushes convulsed, breaking the last of the tower's supports. Scaffolding collapsed beneath Aspen. She fell with it, the arrow shafts in her back snapping against debris as she crashed through it. She couldn't bring herself to scream. The rubble buried her and left only a single opening for her to see the trees above.

Aspen heard the rest of Vanguard spilling out from the Mother Tree. Her heart ached and screamed at her to get up. To keep fighting. But she knew she couldn't. It was up to the others now.

Darkness encroached like a shroud over her vision. Her faceless phantoms leaned over her, their fingers outstretched. She strained to keep her eyes fixed on the trees and thought of Ro, selfishly wishing he was there with her. A sob gurgled its way out of her chest.

As Aspen's world faded around her, she heard the trees above whispering in her voice.

THIRTY-FOUR

Ro heard the bell. He heard Aspen's scream in his mind. He staggered away from the group, clutching his head, his heart wrenching in two. Rose bushes erupted around the Grove —*Aspen's* rosebushes. Huge, vibrant, and more powerful than Ro had ever seen them. Before he could comprehend what was happening, the signal horn's sound abruptly ended.

And then the world shattered.

It seemed as if Mother Night herself had scooped her horrors from the Pit and hurled them over the Golden Grove. Aspen's rosebushes caught on fire and were trampled beneath hordes of soldiers that cut through rebels and the Lorate soldiers alike. They didn't give any thought to the fact that many of them were either bound or unarmed. They simply slaughtered them. Serpent root nets fell from the treetops. Screams of agony tore through the village as the soldiers from Lorate and Aspen's soldiers alike fell beneath the Vanguard's onslaught. The sounds were like arrows to Ro's heart. His whole body trembled with adrenaline, fear, and rage. How could they do this? How could they do this to their *own* kingdom?

And where was Aspen?

"Architects have mercy," Ash breathed, watching the sky with wide eyes. Styrax leapt up and immediately took off toward the fires, water swirling around him.

Ro ground his teeth and whirled to Sorren. "Where are they coming from?"

Sorren gave him a haunted look. "The Mother Tree, Ro, where Inula's men were stationed."

All the blood in Ro's body fled. No. *Aspen—*

"Look out!"

Ro's breath exploded out of his lungs as Ash knocked him away. An arrow sunk itself deep into her shoulder, and she grunted in pain.

"No!" Ro dragged her out of the line of fire behind a wall. She groaned, blood dripping down her arm, but grit her teeth and drew Ro close to her. "You have to get away from here!"

"I'm not leaving you here!" Ro motioned Sorren over to help heal the wound. The boy's eyes went round at the sight of the blood, and he barreled for them, sliding on his knees next to them and immediately placing his glowing purple hands over the wound. Ash flinched and tensed at first, but relaxed as Sorren continued to work.

Ro brought her attention back to him, afraid of how much color she had already lost. "Listen to me. Aspen would *murder* me if I left you by yourself. You know that! Styrax would, too."

Ash shook her head. "Sorry, your highness. These are General's orders. You're to be protected at all costs in case...anything happened to her."

Ro shared a looked with Ash, his whole world stopping. He saw the tears swimming in her eyes. "Ash." He couldn't get enough breath to support the words. "You don't think that—"

"*No!*" Sorren shouted, a wave of purple magic wafting from him in his vehemence. "She's *fine*! She'll be fine! She's *Aspen*!" He looked at Ro with a pleading look. "Right?"

Ro took in the surrounding chaos. The screams. The clash of weapons. The sobs and cries for help. Fires had sprung up somewhere, and they roared like dragons as they devoured the golden trees around them. The Vanguard closed in from either side, tightening the noose around the people Aspen was so sure had been safe. And he *knew* she would *never* give up until that surety became truth.

"She *is* fine, and we'll find her." The conviction filled his whole body until he shook with it.

Ash grinned, even as cold sweat dripped down her brow. "That's what I wanted to hear." She sat up, shooing Sorren away. "That's healed enough. I'll take care of things here. It's about time I got a chance to *actually* be second-in-command." She forced herself into a crouch, wincing as she rotated her shoulder. "Firing an arrow's going to be fun with this," she grumbled before turning to Sorren. "Can you help Styrax put out those fires?"

Sorren hesitated, but nodded. "Of course."

"Good." Ash looked at Ro, unstringing her bow off her back and firing over their protective wall. Someone screamed. She hadn't even looked to aim. "You bring our girl home."

Ro balled his fists, his jaw clenched. "I will."

They split up, each running to their respective tasks.

Our mind link is still open, Sorren spoke to their minds. *If you need to relay orders, you know what to do.*

Tell everyone to get to cover, Ash responded. *Homes, businesses, rocks, caves...anywhere. I don't care. They need to get out from under those nets.*

Ro saw the others' response almost immediately. They disengaged from whatever enemies they were fighting, eyes to the sky, and ran for cover. He marveled at Sorren's power.

We have to find where they're coming from and put a stop to it, Ash continued. *Non-magic users, I know you're all tired, but cut those that have been captured free and get them to the medical units. We're not done yet!*

A rousing cry rose up from the Shadowalker soldiers, and they came together in comprehensive units again, rallying with their new orders. They looked ragged—their numbers significantly less than what Ro remembered seeing from around the camp. But they had

Aspen's same determination in their eyes. A grim smile pulled on Ro's mouth as he ran by. He trusted them to do what needed to be done. He had a general to save.

A net hissed past him, lashing at magic users as it fell. He immediately looked for where it had come from. Rooftops empty. No movement on them. Something flashed in the leafy ends of one of the trees near him. He clambered up the trunk until he saw the shifting, reflective glaze of one of the Vanguard's helmets—the same ones he had seen in Aspen's memories of the Dragon Scales. The soldier turned to look at him, the movement only visible in the shifting images of the leaves across it. Righteous fury fueled Ro on.

They're in the trees! he yelled at Sorren.

He leapt from the trunk to the branches, knocking the soldier from his perch. They both fell, crashing through gold and silver leaves as smoke billowed around them. They landed hard on one of the thicker branches and fell apart from each other. Ro bruised his shoulder and side. The Vanguardsman lost his helmet. Ro flipped him over and sat on his chest before he could move. The face behind the mask was just a young boy, hardly older than Sorren. Ro wanted nothing more than to throw him from the tree and watch him crumple on the ground, but he couldn't bring himself to. Aspen would never do something like that.

Instead, he gathered the net and bound the soldier in it before he came to. He leaned him against the trunk of the tree and then ventured out to the end of the branch. If he got a running lead, he could jump to the next tree without a problem, and then continue that way to the Mother Tree. And Aspen.

He took a few shuffling steps back, breathing deep and preparing himself for the leap. He bunched his muscles and leaned, feet planted firmly against the wood. Before he could take that first running step, though, a body shot out of the leaves to his right. It plunged headlong into him, and they both plummeted.

Adrenaline coursed like liquid fire through his veins. He flipped his body and caught onto a branch with one arm as it flashed past him. His shoulder wrenched out of its socket, but he tightened his grip and clenched his teeth. How did Aspen *do* things like that and make it look so easy?

His sweaty palm started to slip, but he curled his wrist tighter. *I will not die here. I WILL not. Aspen's waiting for me!*

He glanced down at his ambusher, who'd wrapped himself around Ro's waist to keep from plunging to the ground below. Ro's eyes widened. *"Boff!"* If Ro had expected anyone, it had not been the wizened farmer that had fought with him over pea plans back in Monterro. He had so many questions—namely, how someone so old had moved so *fast,* and *why*—but it would have to wait. He was too focused on the creaking sounds of his handhold breaking.

Boff looked at him with crazed eyes and drew a knife from his waist. He raised it, eying a spot beneath Ro's ribs. The movement put more strain on the snapping branch. Boff's hand shook. A cruel grin split his mouth, otherworldly on his normally curmudgeonly but placid face. Ro blanched. Even through the adrenaline and throbbing ache in his dislocated shoulder, he recognized the symptoms of warlock magic. A brand new silver stud in Boff's ear caught the light.

"Boff, listen to me," Ro panted, sweat dripping into his eyes and collecting particles of acrid smoke. "You're not yourself. You kill me here, we'll both fall, and you'll die with me. I don't think you want to do that." His hand slipped down the tilting branch. He strained to keep them from falling any further.

Boff hesitated. His feral grin pulled down at the corners.

"That's it," Ro said. "Now, if you just give me...a moment to think, we can probably—*you piece of goblin sludge!"*

Although Boff had elected not to kill Ro, he still stabbed him in the fatty part of his calf. Blood flowed freely into Ro's boot when Boff wrenched the blade free.

In the same instant, the branch snapped. Ro's stomach hovered somewhere between his chest and stomach as they dropped. He cast around for something—*anything!*—to land in. And then he saw it. A patch of Aspen's rose bushes. It was better than nothing.

Ro hardly had time to shield his eyes before they smashed into the plants. Brittle thorns bit into his skin and tore his clothes as if they were nothing but parchment. Even with the rosebushes slowing his fall, he landed hard and fast on his chest. Ribs cracked. His breath vanished. The world went dark for a moment.

Tristan tried to suck in breath, but his ribs crushed against his lungs and felt like they would drive right through. Gasping in ragged, shallow breaths, he glanced blearily around for Boff, worried the old-timer had fared much worse. Boff had glanced off the bushes and laid completely still. Ro thought he could see his chest moving, though.

"Boff?" he called, the sound raspy in his throat.

Boff moaned, but otherwise didn't move. He was alive.

That would have to do for now. Ro didn't have time to worry about him—or himself, really. He had to get to Aspen. They had to save the villagers and the crops. The rebellion would not be dealt a fatal blow tonight. He wouldn't allow it.

Tearing himself out of Aspen's rosebushes, he dragged his protesting body to where his sword had fallen, silently thanking Aspen for saving him again. Hot lances of pain shot through his chest as he crawled the distance. He grit his teeth. His body shook. "Almost...there..."

He curled his fingers around the hilt just as someone else stomped on the blade, effectively pinning him.

"Well, looks like I found myself a wayward son."

A face loomed in Ro's face, a bone-white blade flashing past. The liquor on the man's breath made Ro's head spin. "How has your *family* been treating you, *Tristan*?"

Ro's mouth ran dry. No. *Anyone* but him. "Much better than you treat yours," he spat. "Do you want to explain why your wife is *here* instead of with you?"

It took a moment for the words to register in Laire's ale-tainted mind, but Ro saw the instant it connected. Laire's face twisted in on itself, and he howled. He kicked Ro's face with the stiff tip of his boot. Ro moved his face in time, but the blow connected with his dislocated shoulder. Ro screamed and his vision flickered with the new surge of pain.

Aspen. Have to...get to Aspen.

Laire teetered off-balance and took one steadying step. That gave Ro the opening he needed. He snatched his newly freed sword and rolled out of reach. His entire body screamed in outright rebellion. He shoved the agony away. He didn't have time for it. Aspen had forced herself to push beyond much worse odds. It was the least he could do for her. He forced himself to a somewhat standing position —his damaged calf couldn't support much weight—and faced Laire. His sword trembled in his weakened grip, and he could barely keep himself from toppling over sideways.

Laire glowered at him. "You took them when you left," he growled. "Vinea and Linae *left me* because of you! You had a family in us and you *destroyed it!*"

"They left because of *your* choices!" Ro spat. "And you will have to live with that for the rest of your life."

Laire laughed, a crazed, maniacal sound. "No. I have my Vanguard back. And with it, the last of the rebels will be crushed beneath my feet, and I will build the life Vinea always deserved." He gave Ro a grin that threatened to pull the skin from his cheeks. "But, first King Salaith's final heir must fall—killed at the hands of the Ancient Ones while he tried to broker peace." He tilted his head toward his sword, as if listening to something from it. "And Loralan will fall."

The words coursed through the fog of pain in Ro's mind, and it took him a moment to string them together. "B-broker peace? I was here to *protect* them! From *you!*"

"And who will they believe? A King's Man that saw it all happen, or a dead prince that can't speak for himself?"

Ro could only gape. The pieces started to fit together. Why Laire had kept him alive so many years ago. "That's what you wanted? This whole time? For me to just *die* to further your agenda?"

Laire didn't even hesitate. "Yes," he said with a feral grin. "Same with those poor, hometown souls from Lorate that were *mercilessly* and *needlessly* mowed down by a far superior enemy. The outrage that will sweep the kingdom will incite the people to action again. They will rise up against the Ancient Races once more, and then this war can finally *end*."

Ro saw the Lorate men's terrified faces as the Vanguard mowed them down. He knew some of them—knew what women and children would never see their husbands and fathers again. The thought of more families suffering the same fate for no reason sent fury coursing through his veins. No. *No.* "I won't let that happen!" Ro trained his sword on Laire. "I won't die here, and I won't let you kill anyone else!"

"Funny," Laire said, licking his lips and prowling closer like a caged animal. "I seem to remember a filthy half-blood saying the same thing not even an hour ago. It didn't go so well for her."

He threw a broken sword at Ro's feet. The black pieces glittered with flecks of silver, like shards of the night sky.

Ro's world stopped spinning. He lost sight of everything else except for the sword. He saw the chips on the edges. The smaller fractures among the pieces. And the blood.

He screamed—something feral and broken—and charged at Laire. Laire swayed out of the way and missed losing his arm by only a hair's breadth. He dragged his blade along Ro's forearm, carving a long, jagged path there. Ro's vision turned white—all sound leaving him. His insides felt like they had been fractured in two. Someone screamed, and it took a few moments for Ro to realize it was his own scream—tearing brutally through his throat. The world lurched beneath him, and he fell.

Get up. Get. Up! his mind feverishly tried to tell him. *You promised! You promised Aspen she would never be alone!*

Ro tried to stand, his entire body convulsing. But he pitched forward again. Blood dripped down his arm. He couldn't see straight. No breath actually seemed to stay inside him. His minutes of any sort of consciousness could be numbered on one hand.

They've found the safe-houses! Ash's voice swam in his mind. *All able-bodied fighters converge on those locations. Civilians take full priority. We cannot lose them!*

The world was falling apart around him, and all Ro could do was bleed.

He used his sword as a crutch and propped his trembling, feverish body up. The world spun and jumped with multi-colored spots, but he stayed upright. The moment he moved the blade, though, he would topple over again. He coughed up bile.

"You're not looking well, boy," Laire said. "Any final words for your kingdom?"

"Aspen's *not* dead," he rasped. "And this is not over. She'll save the Golden Grove, and you will have failed."

Laire smirked. "Say hello to her in the afterlife."

Six other men emerged from between houses and trees, their faces nothing but shimmering, shifting helmets that blended into the background. Emotionless. Cruel. They looked like nightmares.

"Anything else can be beaten to a bloody pulp," Laire said to them. "But leave his head intact. We need *something* people will recognize."

Without thinking, Ro hurled his sword. It thudded into a burning branch just above Laire and the other soldiers. The branch screamed as it broke free of its tree and plunged toward them. The soldiers lunged forward, and Laire jumped back. As he did so, though, he tripped over a piece of debris, and his sword skittered out of his hand as he tried to regain his balance. Laire's face blanched, turning a sickly gray, as if all the life had been drained out of him. He jumped toward the sword, practically throwing himself on top of the burning branch, but Ro managed to be faster. He snatched the bone-white sword away from Laire. Immediately, his wounded arm felt like it was being slashed open again and again, tearing him apart from the inside, but he maintained his grip on the sword. He couldn't let Laire have it, no matter the cost. Laire screamed, a haunting sound that sent chills down Ro's spine. The general tried to leap for him one more time, but his subordinates caught him and hauled him back, dragging him away from the flames and back into the center of the village. Laire howled the whole way.

The remaining men charged at Ro, weapons spinning. Ro grit his teeth against the agony coursing through his arm and turned to face them, Laire's weapon drawn in front of him. A strange buzzing sound filled his head. He rushed forward to meet their attacks.

Two of them lost weapons and use of their arms within the first few moments. They reeled back, clutching their wounds in silent agony. The next few put more caution in their step and managed to maintain their grips on their weapons when Ro blocked them. Every blow he parried jolted and tore at his body. His ribs felt as if they had turned into a monster intent on eating his insides. His dislocated arm hung at his side like a leaden weight. His stabbed calf muscle felt like it had torn itself away from his bone. However, every time his attackers swung at him, it felt as if Aspen's hands guided each of his strokes, saving his life again and again with the dance she had trained in him.

With every successful strike, the pain in his arm lessened, too. The buzzing grew in his mind and turned into something akin to whispers, urging him to fight faster, harder—more brutally. Ro leaned into it, grateful for the extra surges of strength filling him.

Until his blood-loss finally caught up to him.

His reaction time slowed. His head buzzed and he couldn't see straight from pain and blood loss. The men kept gaining ground.

Fear began to set in. Dragon fire blazed through the village. Screams were cut short. The sounds of battle slowly diminished as cries of triumph took their place in voices he didn't recognize. They were losing. For all his promises, Aspen's people—*his people*—were all being overrun, wounded, and carted off. He was failing, and he could do nothing about it.

He chewed the inside of his cheek, fighting back the panic. "No... we're not done. Not done yet!" he said under his breath.

"Praying does you no good now." A soldier blindsided him while he was locked with another opponent. The soldier buried a knife deep into Ro's side and drove his heel into Ro's ankle. It snapped, and his whole body gave way. He crumpled, the knife still in his side. His sword fell out of his senseless grasp.

Ro heard their shouts of victory as a muddled din as the agony raced through his body. Despite the fires raging around him, he couldn't stop shivering.

"Kill him already!" he heard them scream. Something loomed over his head. He tried to reach for his sword, but couldn't make his arm move. Tears of frustration rolled down his cheeks. *Come on. Come ON!*

Whatever hung over him cast undulating shadows from the firelight as it swung toward him.

"*RO!*"

He knew that voice. It cleared enough fog in his brain for him to get his weapon in hand again. Something collided with the group of King's Men around him, showering droplets of water, and metal shrieked on metal. Bodies collapsed around Ro.

Shaking hands propped Ro up. "Sweet Sister Earth, Ro! What—"

Ro tried to focus his eyes, but couldn't. "Styrax?" he croaked. That was a mistake. It felt like he had swallowed fire.

"Don't talk. I'm getting you out of here. It's a good thing Sorren told me where you were headed."

Ro was too tired to comprehend what he'd said. He tried to sit up on his own, even though it was a futile effort. "Aspen. We have to get to--"

His words were cut off as he heard shouts from the Vanguard.

"We've won!"

"The Golden Grove has fallen!"

"The rebellion's been crippled!"

"Long Live King Osmen!"

Ro's grip tightened around his sword. "*NO*—We're not—Aspen wouldn't—" He tried to shove himself free of Styrax's grip. "It's not...over!"

Styrax shoved him flat on his back again. "Ro, stop! You've lost too much blood!"

Ro continued to fight him. "Have to...find Aspen. Have to save them!"

"Ro, there's no helping them right now. We have to leave before they find us."

Ro grit his teeth and shook his head. He wrenched one of his arms free, but accidentally punched Styrax in the face with it.

"All right, that's it." Styrax bound Ro's wrists in a globe of water. "Ash! I need you!"

Footsteps ran to them. "Sister *Earth*, Ro! What have you done to yourself?" Ro felt Ash's magic cover his mind and heard a single Ancient Word. "*Sleep.*"

Ro's body stilled. The surrounding sounds swirled into nothingness, and his eyelids fell shut like stone doors. "I'll...I have to find her." The darkness came for him and let him forget the burning buildings, the raving soldiers, and the elves being herded to their doom.

The last things he saw were the shattered pieces of Aspen's sword, glinting in the fire of the Golden Grove's downfall.

THIRTY-FIVE

Vinea stepped into the antechamber, her cheeks wet. The screaming echoes ricocheting through the caverns had gone quiet, but phantom sounds still played in her mind. She knew what was out there—knew exactly what was happening. She knew what she could have stopped.

"Oh, Ro, Eden, forgive me," she whispered to herself, wiping her tears away.

She strode to a dais, where the Sacred Flame glowed bright and fierce. It almost spat at her as she approached, as if it knew her intentions. Vinea couldn't help but feel how pointless this whole journey had been. She had put herself in danger to protect Ro, and then had put Linae at risk to protect him, and now here she was again, sacrificing one for the other. No matter how much she tried to break it, this war had ensured a pattern that would see her continue to lose her family.

A lump swelled in her throat. She wanted nothing more than the comfort of her husband at her side—to feel his arms around her and hear his voice in her ear—but she had lost him forever. The half-man she had met with the Vanguard proved that. She grit her teeth. She *would not* lose her daughter as well.

Vinea stepped onto the dais, the golden warmth washing over her and glinting on the dusty golden urns tucked into the walls. In the quiet, she could almost swear the fire sung, nearly silent but pure tones resonating deep in her bones. It was an achingly beautiful, lonely sort of sound. Vinea clenched her hand around Sedick's jar and reached for the fire.

Golden light erupted from the flame with such force that it knocked Vinea on her back. She struck her ribs on the edge of the dais, the blow driving all the air from her lungs. The entire cave was illuminated in blinding clarity for a moment, making spots swim in her eyes. It dimmed eventually, but only slightly. Vinea fought to regain her breath, blinking away the light stains, and dragged herself back to her feet. She checked the jar, afraid it had broken, but it didn't have a scratch. Sedick must have reinforced it.

A golden specter had emerged—the hazy image of a woman with a scar across both eyelids. She was somehow both warm and terrible to look at, her light blinding but soft. Vinea's knees trembled at the sight of her, overwhelmed with the urge to bow. She didn't know this woman, but every fiber in her body screamed to fear her.

The woman stood between Vinea and the flame, her stance neutral but serving as a potent shield, nonetheless.

"I know why you've come." The specter's words reverberated through the cavern and echoed back in whispers that pounded into Vinea's skull. "You've come on an errand you do not fully understand."

Vinea's voice caught in her throat, and she watched with wide-eyes as the specter motioned to the flame. "The Demon Queen seeks this flame, and only those that serve her would have need to steal it."

Vinea took a step back, the blood draining from her face. A demon? Sedick may have been a monster, but even he could not compare to the evil, depravity, and sheer power of a demon. She opened her mouth to protest, but the words died in her throat, evaporating like frost in the morning sun. She did not pretend to know much about magic, but in the months leading up to her and Laire seeking Sedick's magic to help them conceive, she had learned one thing. Warlocks did not have their own magic. They instead borrowed from others.

So why not borrow from a demon?

"You are not the first nor the last to seek this flame," the specter continued as the crushing, horrifying reality settled over Vinea. "The Demon Queen will stop at nothing to achieve her ultimate desire, which will do nothing but invite the end of this world. This flame will bring her one step closer to her success."

"That means nothing!" Vinea's vision went black at the edges. A demon. She had left Linae with a *demon*. Terror clawed up her spine and took a choke hold around her throat. She had to get to Linae. Get to her *now* and take her somewhere no demons could ever touch her again. She dug her nails into her palms until they bled and turned toward the specter—the thing keeping her from her daughter. "You will not stop me!"

The specter's eyes seemed to pierce through to her very soul. Vinea's heart quailed at the sight, but she clenched her jaw in resolve. Linae couldn't protect herself, and Vinea would brave any danger to keep her safe.

"Will you bring an end to all you know and love?" the specter asked.

A sob hitched in Vinea's chest, resentment, fear, and rage burning through her like hot coals. "It *has* already come to an end," she said through her clenched teeth, hot tears threatening to spill. "My husband left me, my home is no longer safe, my daughter is being held captive by a demon, and," Ro's face swam in her vision for a moment, and some of her ire fell beneath her crushing guilt. "My nephew," she whispered. "Oh, goddess, I might as well have killed him."

The specter didn't seem to hear her. It only stood, silent, and waited.

The specter's apathy broke something in Vinea. All she saw was Laire, deaf to her pleading, leaving her alone in that room in Vastet, choosing his ambitions over her and Linae. *He* had left them in this predicament. He was the reason she was not at home with Linae at this very moment, tucking her into bed and singing lullabies. He had taken their happiness away, and she hated him for it.

With a growl deep in her throat—of anguish, terror, and broken resolve—Vinea surged forward, throwing herself at the specter. It exploded. Vinea was ready for it this time and dropped to her stomach to avoid getting thrown back.

The specter's golden light swirled in a roar of fire, surging into a black form that seemed to fill the entire cavern. Monstrous wings beat against the cavern air, golden flames flaring from their feathered tips, and a bird-cry lanced through Vinea's eardrums. A phoenix.

"I will not let you do this." Its voice was sad and heavy, but filled with the power to follow through with its claim. A jet of golden flame peeled away from one of its wings and raced toward her.

Vinea rolled out of the way, but not before the flames engulfed the entire lower half of her body. She screamed, her mind going white with fear.

It took her several moments to realize there was no pain. No searing heat. No smell of burning flesh.

Her eyes grew wide as she looked at her legs. Untouched. Perfectly safe and uninjured. She remembered Sedick's words. *There is a guardian over the flame…She cannot interfere, but will do everything in her power to make you believe she can.*

The phoenix let out another cry, a piercing sound that flooded the entire chamber and tore at Vinea's breast. It was a beautiful, hauntingly lonely sound. The phoenix circled for another pass.

Vinea choked back the fear. *For Linae.*

Vinea gathered her feet beneath her and sprinted for the flame. She knew the phoenix bore down on her, but she didn't dare turn around. Every hair on her body stood on end in terror. What if the first had only been a warning shot? What if this time the flames *did* engulf her, and she died a slow, horrific death?

She couldn't think of that. Only Linae. Only her little girl—who needed her mother to *live*.

"Millions will die if you do this!" the phoenix cried.

"My daughter will die if I don't!" Vinea leapt as the phoenix swooped overhead. The rush of its wings battered against her. Vinea's heart froze as she heard the rush of its fire.

She swept the glowing flame into her jar and stoppered it shut.

It was as if she had snatched the breath from the mountain itself.

The flame's light died, and with it, so did the phoenix and all other light. All in an instant, snuffed out like a candle. A chill swept through the mountain, so cold that Vinea could see her breath pluming from her by the dim light of the flame. She felt her tears freeze on her cheeks and hugged the jar to her chest. The flame was still there, faint and listless, and fluttered against the edge of the glass like a frantic heart. "I'm sorry," she whispered to the silent darkness.

THIRTY-SIX

S orren blasted another Vanguard soldier away from him, choking on the raging emptiness in his chest. The space Aspen had occupied in his mind had fallen quiet. Too quiet. And Aspen would never have let the Vanguard through. Not unless she was—

The truth weighed on his limbs like lead. He knew. He knew from the emptiness that consumed his mind where his link to Aspen had been, but that didn't make the grief any easier to bear. He should have heard her. Should have felt her attempts to reach him. He had suggested they use the links—*his magic*—for exactly that purpose. If he had responded sooner, none of this would have happened. He had failed yet another person that had shown him nothing but kindness.

How was he going to tell Ro?

An arrow glanced off his shoulder. He whirled, all his broken anger crackling from his hands in arcs of lightning, and released that magic into a group of three Vanguardsmen. It hit the middle man square in the chest and illuminated him in a halo of purple before he crumpled without a sound. The arcs leapt from the fallen soldier and blackened the other men. They fell with screams of anguish, clutching their seared flesh.

A stab of nausea tilted Sorren's vision on its head. He had nearly exhausted his magic. But that didn't matter. It wouldn't have mattered to Aspen. She would get the job done, no matter the danger to herself.

He balled his fists and turned to run back into the quickly deteriorating battlefield. He wasn't sure if he could even call it that anymore. More just stragglers defending what was left of their home.

A young elven girl staggered through the murk just as a branch screamed overhead as it broke free of its trunk. Sorren flung his hands out, two pillars of magic lurching from the ground to catch the branch before it smashed the girl, but the crushing weight against his already depleted magic nearly snapped his spine in two.

"Run to me!" he screamed at her. Although glassy-eyed and bleeding from a wound in her shoulder, she luckily had the where-withal to register his command and follow. As soon as she was out of danger, he let the massive branch crash to the ground in an explosion of hissing sparks and golden ash.

Sorren crouched—more like collapsed—to his knees to be at her eye level. "What are you doing here?" he asked between panting breaths. "Why aren't you safe in the caves with the others?"

She bravely tightened her jaw, but tears welled in her eyes. She mumbled something Sorren couldn't hear.

Sorren leaned forward, every joint screaming at him. "What?"

Tears fell freely down her ash-stained face. "They found us. They're taking them all away. Mama and papa and all my brothers... They're all gone!" She crumbled into Sorren's arms, wailing and shaking.

Questions and dread zipped through Sorren's mind, but he could tell the girl had reached her limit. She wasn't in any state to answer more questions.

Instead, he healed her shoulder enough to stop the bleeding and then drew a rune circle in the dirt with enough room at the center for her to lie down and rest. He handed her the last of his food and water and then stepped outside of it. He imbued the last of his magic into the rune and it formed a glowing purple dome around her.

"Nothing can come in there to get you," he said, sweat dripping from the end of his nose. He couldn't tell if he had any blood circulating in his face or not. "You'll be safe in there, and can leave any time, all right?"

She nodded, a look of relief washing over her face.

Sorren turned toward the caverns, where everyone was supposed to have been safe. If they couldn't even protect everyone that was depending on them, what had been the point of it all? What had been the point of Aspen's—

No. He couldn't think like that. It's not what Aspen would have wanted him to do. There was a job to do, and he would do it, magic or no. He would save the villagers. For Aspen.

The Vanguard's trail wasn't hard to follow—they had left a gaping wake of destruction through the Golden Grove. Sorren took one last look at what he had hoped would be a safe place, and then followed after them.

CHAPTER

THIRTY-SEVEN

Waves crashed against the jagged shores of the Dragon Scales, lapping at the bodies piled in its surf. The clash of swords rang across the plain, echoing with cries of pain. He'd seen this before. He'd lived it—the fear, the panic, and the grim realization that he would not leave alive. His heart pounded as he glanced around, waiting for the mace to fall. Waiting for the agony that would turn his world dark. But it never came. Instead, the swords continued to ring out with their keening, strident notes.

He stepped forward, intent on finding the swords and the people that wielded them. He had to stop them before...

Before what?

Terror lurked on the edges of his mind, coupled with a loss so deep it burrowed a hollow, freezing cavern in his chest. But he didn't know what he had lost.

The moment the thought struck him, the scene blurred around him, streaking away into the night, and a jagged, colorless forest took the Dragon Scales' place. Blackened, burnt branches crumbled to ash as he watched, swirling away on a smoke laden breeze. The brittle ones left behind scratched against each other in a chorus of hissing whispers. He *squinted against the smoke, coughing. The sword strikes were closer now, even though the Dragon Scales had long since vanished. Heart in his throat, he followed the sound.*

A woman wreathed in green light—the only color in the lifeless forest—appeared through the trees, locked in a treacherous dance. She had a black sword in her hand, fractures of light snaking along its blade. The smoldering trees leapt at her, their branches like pikes as they aimed for her heart. She battered them away, each branch collapsing to ash the moment her blade touched it. But more took their place, with hundreds waiting behind them. They drew ever closer, the limbs cracking like dark laughter. They drew bright streaks of blood across her skin as they inched forward. She was all alone.

Fear raced through his heart as the trees hedged her in. He had to get to her—had to save her. He lunged forward, but the trees had come for him, too. A branch curled around his ankle and snapped it. Another gouged a deep wound in his forearm. A scream of agony and frustration tried to tear itself from him, but the trees wrapped around his limbs like rope and tightened around his throat. Silencing him. Immobilizing him. He could do nothing to stop what came next.

Something moved through the trees, massive and sinuous. It scraped against the bark with a sound like plate mail. Branches cracked and fell as it passed. Scales flashed in the woman's green glow, reflecting it with a sickly imitation. Silver eyes glowed from the shadows, changing to sapphire in the uncertain light. Its breath sent waves of scorching heat across the scene.

The woman hadn't noticed the encroaching beast. Another branch swept at her, and she moved to parry it. Upon impact, the branch—pale white and jagged—remained intact. The woman's sword shattered, glittering like so many stars in her green light.

He tried to scream for her, but the trees had muzzled him. Tears raked down his cheeks. He strained against his bonds, his muscles screaming at him. He could not let this happen. The woman could not die.

Before the shattered sword had time to touch the ground, the silver eyes moved out of the shadows. It raised its head far above the trees—a massive black dragon that cast its shadow over the woman. She turned to look, even as the branches tore at her, and raised her broken sword to the beast.

He managed to loosen the branches around his mouth. "NO!"

She looked at him, her green eyes as wide and deep as a forest. His heart stopped beating. Sound stopped. The army of branches froze as they whipped toward her.

She smiled. "For evergreens and aspen trees."

The dragon's black maw snapped shut around her. Her light vanished, and the world plunged into empty darkness.

The dragon's voice came as a deep rumble—hissing with cruel mirth.

"I told you to keep her close."

RO GASPED HIMSELF AWAKE. Sweat and tears poured off his face and pooled at his temples. He barely registered the burnt and blackened trees above him—the air gritty with smoke and ash as thick as in his dream—before he staggered to his feet. "Aspen." Pain lanced through his sides and forearm like a branding iron, and the world swooped in dizzying arcs around him. He shut his eyes and grit his teeth against it. Images of the woman in the colorless woods flashed across the inside of his eyelids. The loss drove stakes into his heart. No. *No.* He drove himself up and off his bedroll.

"Where do you think you're going?" Hemlock's voice carried to him. Strident. Scolding. Exhausted.

"Where's Aspen?" Ro asked, the words ragged and labored. A small, ragged crew of battered soldiers milled about a makeshift campsite, tending to injuries or laying too still bodies beside each other—the remains of Aspen's troops. "What happened?"

Hemlock ignored the question. "It's hardly been more than a day. I can work miracles, but not *that* fast. You need to lie down and rest."

"Son, thank the Architects you're back with us. Gan's face floated into view as well, looking disheveled but otherwise unhurt as he stood behind Hemlock.

Ro fought off Hemlock's hands, which were fussing at his bandages, and kept plodding forward, stars swimming in his vision.

"Ro, stay put! That's an order!" Hemlock snapped.

"I'm a *prince*," Ro growled back. "I don't take orders from anyone." More smoky ash swirled into his nose and down his throat, sending him into a coughing fit. Agony raged through his ribs, and he bent over double. "Where's Aspen?"

"What did I tell you, you stupid—" Hemlock tried to help him back to his bedroll, but he fought her off again.

"Gan, do something about your boy!"

"There's nothing wrong with telling him—"

Hemlock growled and turned away from both Ro and Gan. "Ash! Come help me with this idiot!"

Footsteps approached, slow and heavy. "Ro, what are you doing?" Ash's voice. Or, at least, a hollow, almost lifeless shell of it. Ro looked at her and nearly recoiled. She looked like she had aged decades—all the stress and worries of lifetimes pulling taut across her face and leeching the light from her eyes. "You almost died. You can't be—" A shadow crossed her face, and she covered her eyes with her hand, bracing herself against a tree. "You can't be up and about like this," she finished with a croak.

"Ash, where's Aspen?"

Ash didn't look him in the eyes, but her body tensed. "You shouldn't be moving around. The Grove is in shambles, Sorren's missing, Styrax is still dousing fires, and there are so many wounded that need help. Clearing things up is hard enough without you—"

"Ash," Ro took her hand, squeezing it as tight as he could. The Grove and Sorren panged in his chest, but his dream still resonated through every bone and fiber. The fear gripped him just as tightly as the phantom branches. "Where. Is. Aspen?"

Ash's lower lip trembled, and a shudder ran through her. It looked like her knees would give out at any moment. She looked at him, her eyes wide with terrified tears. "I haven't found her, Ro," she said in a hoarse whisper, the bags under her eyes giving her a deathly, haunted look. "It's been a day and I still haven't —"

Ro squeezed her hand to cut off the words—to stop them from feeding the terror in his heart. *You should have kept her close*, the dragon whispered. He buried the thought, even as his whole body trembled with its poison. "We're going to find her," he said to Ash, his lips numb and hardly able to form the words. "You've got me now. Where do we start?"

Hemlock placed her fingers on his wounded forearm, the brief touch sending currents of pain flooding through his body, nearly making his knees give way. "You aren't doing anything, your highness," she said, though it was a feeble, hoarse attempt.

Ro ignored her. "We're going to find her," he said again to Ash, the words stronger this time. "She's Aspen, remember?"

Ash just looked at him. Ro saw a fluttering of hope in her eyes, fading fast. He saw the heartbreak taking over, and he clenched his jaw. *No.* There was no need for grief. Aspen was *alive.*

"Let's go find our girl."

Ash nodded slowly and pushed herself away from the tree with some effort. They trekked deeper into the forest, leaving Hemlock behind them in silence.

Ro took in the desolate scene. The scorch marks. The collapsed homes. The ash swirling mournfully through the air. The silver of the leaves that hadn't been burned cast the only light, eerie against the black soot. Ro's heart had stopped beating in his chest, and only silence remained. The images of the darkened, lifeless forest in his dreams haunted him, but he shook them away.

She has to be here, he told himself with each step he took. *She's here somewhere. She is. It was only a nightmare.*

Ash's voice shook when she spoke. "I've looked practically everywhere except for..." she swallowed, her face pale. "Except for the Mother Tree."

Ro clenched his shaking hands. Aspen had been heading that direction when he last...

And that had been where the Vanguard entered the Grove.

He took Ash's hand. "Come on."

When they got to the Mother Tree, the forest was in shambles, even more so than the rest of the Grove. Wood and scaffolding had collapsed like haphazard piles of kindling, scorched beyond recognition. Withered rose vines climbed every available surface or had been trodden underfoot. The Mother Tree's roots flailed helplessly, sap dripping from them like blood. The signal tower was gone.

Ro approached the nearest wreckage tentatively, almost fearfully. What if she was in there? And what if...No. He couldn't think about that. Wouldn't think about that. He would have known. He would have felt it. She was alive. Hurt, injured, and unconscious, maybe, but alive.

He pawed through the wreckage. The inner parts of the wood still glowed with heat, as if protesting the abuse and trauma it had been through. It scalded his hands, but he hardly felt it. Dust and ash billowed into his nose and mouth. He hacked and coughed and could barely see, but continued anyway. If she was there, he would find her. He had to find her.

Each failed attempt to find her—every piece of wreckage turned over with nothing to show—made Ro even more desperate. The blood had drained from his face. His heart thundered in his ears. His wounds throbbed and his body shook. He tore down support beams and tossed aside wreckage like it was nothing, his hands blistered and burnt beyond the point of recognition and his clothes black with soot.

"Aspen!" he roared, tears of frustration and fear building in his eyes and choking in his throat. "Aspen, by the Architects, *answer me!*"

Nothing. Still nothing. His panic rose. Each moment he couldn't find her was another moment that she didn't get help. She needed help. Hemlock would be able to save her. He knew it. *She's fine. Everything will be fine. She's FINE.*

And then he heard it—whispers cutting faintly through the ashen quiet.

I can't do anymore…Someone save them, please.

Every part of Ro froze. His limbs went numb. Every breath felt like shards of ice cutting through his body. He couldn't hear his heartbeat anymore. He locked eyes with Ash, who had gone white. Slowly, mechanically, she turned to a tree huddled low over the wreckage of the signal tower, rustling quietly with no breeze. "That's Aspen's voice," she whispered, her voice terrified.

No.

An inarticulate cry wrenched itself out of Ro. He rushed to the wreckage, tearing apart what was left of the structure. He shoved aside the massive horn, his muscles and injured ribs screaming at him. As soon as he threw it aside, he dug through the shattered wood beneath, the tips of his fingers tearing as he scrabbled against the bark. Stars swam in his eyes, mingling with the image of silver eyes watching him from the shadows. He shook his head, fury rising like a storm in him. He would have *known!* He would have! She wasn't— She couldn't be—

His hand brushed against something soft. Smooth.

And cold.

Heart seizing in his chest, Ro heaved the rest of the logs aside, his ribs shrieking in agony. Beneath them was a dark-haired woman, smeared with soot.

Ro sobbed in relief. "Aspen!" He scooped her up and held her to him. "Thank goodness I found you! I—" his voice choked in his throat. She was cold. So very cold. There was no movement as he cradled her. "A-Aspen?" He tried to smile. Tried to tell himself she was sleeping. Exhausted. Wounded. Something other than—

He listened for a pulse.

Nothing.

He checked for breath, his hand shaking as he held it beneath her nose.

Nothing.

And then he saw the blood. So much blood. Everywhere.

Ro's knees collapsed, grinding into the debris beneath him.

I told you to keep her close.

Should have kept her close.

Keep her close, boy, before she's taken from you forever.

"Aspen, please," he sobbed in almost a whisper. She didn't respond—didn't move. She just laid there, broken, in his arms. He brushed strands of hair and streaks of soot off her face, his soul feeling disconnected from his body. This wasn't real. It couldn't be. He would have *known*. "You're *Aspen*. You've been through worse than this."

But he felt the arrows bristling from her back—four of them buried deep. He saw the blood crusted to her side and dribbling from the corner of her mouth.

He turned to Ash, helpless. "You can save her, right?"

Ash collapsed, her whole body shaking as silent sobs tore through her.

The world shattered around Ro, and there was nothing but horrible, empty darkness left in its place.

CHAPTER
THIRTY-EIGHT

Ro cradled Aspen to his chest and trudged back to the main camp, the weight of her loss wrenching against his spine. His ribs screamed at him, but he didn't feel it. He didn't feel anything. Hollowness had enveloped his shattered pieces—a vessel with no spirit inside. The world passed by him in a murky haze, lightless and colorless. Every breath he took felt stale, threatening to choke him as he breathed it in.

Styrax saw them first. He froze, his eyes glowing white as listless storm clouds gathered overhead, drizzling faintly. "Oh Sister Earth, no." He looked at Ro like he might a drowning man, stuck in his own grief but also grieving for Ro. That look nearly broke Ro again. Styrax went to Ash, wrapping her in a tight embrace as she collapsed against him.

Gan was not far behind Styrax. When he came upon the scene, he fell to his knees, his shoulders hunched as his body shook from weeping. "Oh, sweet girl, I am so sorry."

Aspen's remaining soldiers came next. Their small groups fell deathly silent as Ro passed them.

"Is that—"

"Not the general. It can't be."

Even with their broken words of disbelief, they each took a knee, bowing their head in respect to their fallen general as tears streaked their faces. They choked back sobs, and the camp fell into complete, enveloping silence. Ro felt the soldiers' grief wash over him. Their general was dead. Their leader that had led them through to so many victories—had kept them safe and trained them and taken them in when no one else would. The general that had seemed indomitable and invincible. She was gone.

Hemlock and Inula approached the group, drawn by the sudden stillness. Hemlock's sternness melted, and her face twisted with grief. She bridged the distance between herself and Ro, her advanced age seeming to catch up to her in moments, dragging her shoulders and spine toward the ground. Slowly, hands shaking, she placed a hand on Aspen's forehead, saying quiet prayers to Sister Earth. Inula stood apart and away from the rest, refusing to make eye contact. Ro couldn't have cared less. She didn't deserve to be anywhere near Aspen.

But then it struck him like a bolt of lightning. He remembered. He remembered seeing her in the crowd after Aspen had left, surrounded by her guards. Guards that could have saved Aspen's life.

The realization shattered Ro's empty vessel, and the fire of blinding, searing fury consumed it instead. Ro's vision centered on Inula, the world tinted red and the blood burning away from his face. "YOU!" He clasped Aspen's broken frame tighter to him. "YOU DID THIS!"

Inula looked at him as she might an injured deer. Pitying. Ready to put him down if his wounds were too great. But uncaring. "I don't know what you mean, your highness. I believe your grief has made you delusional. I am not the one that killed her—you have the Vanguard to thank for that." She gestured to the whole desolate scene around them. "You have them to thank for all of this! Place your anger where it will be more useful and retaliate against the king and his followers."

Rage burned through Ro's skin. "I saw them, Inula," he spat, rising to his full height, his chest swelling and his shoulders tight. "I saw you with your soldiers."

"I don't know what you're implying," she said coolly.

"That night you agreed to have your men under Aspen's command, I was there, remember? You swore only Aspen would be able to command your men away from the Mother Tree. But she never got that chance, did she?"

The group had gone silent. They turned wide, accusatory eyes to Inula as the implications of Ro's words seeped in. Hands went to weapons, and the soldiers drew in closer as a supportive wall behind Ro.

"She never did like the general."

"I never thought the *mighty* elders would stoop so low."

Ash had stiffened in Styrax's arms, her hand gripping a fistful of his tunic, her knuckles white. "Mother, you didn't."

"Do *not* call me that, Ash." Inula didn't even look at her. She continued to glower daggers at Ro. "How many times do I have to say it? I am no one's mother, and certainly not yours."

Ash lifted her chin, eyes blazing as they reflected her tears. "Aunt Calla would be ashamed of you."

Inula's eyes darted to Ash then, her face pulling taut with anger.

"Inula, when Aspen went to relieve your men of their duty, thinking the battle had been won, they weren't there, were they?" Ro growled. He couldn't stop shaking. Laire's sword thrummed white-hot on his waist. If he weren't carrying Aspen, he would have drawn it.

Inula looked away from Ash and raised herself up. Her attention did not stay on Ro, though. It darted to all the spectators, who looked at her with equal amounts of horror and hatred. "I do not know what that girl did with my men. They were under her control after all, not that it helped us in the end."

"INULA!" Ro screamed, veins bulging in his forehead and his throat torn raw. Styrax drew a few steps back from him, eyes wide, turning his body to shield Ash. Aspen's soldiers flinched, but their grips on their weapons tightened. "I SAW them! You called them away! You left us unprotected, and all of this...Aspen..." His voice broke as he looked down at Aspen's face. He saw the ghost of pain permanently etched into her face. She had died in agony and *alone*. Venomous anger swelled in him again, and he looked back at Inula. "You WILL tell me the truth! I am the rightful heir to the kingdom of Loralan, and you bow down to me!"

The words rankled in his mouth the moment he said them. That was not the power he wanted to wield, but it seemed to be the only one he could. No one wanted to see reason. No one wanted to own up to the mistakes and bigotry and lies that had poisoned them. No one had listened to Aspen's quiet, patient power. And now Aspen...he nearly choked on the lump in his throat. Irreparable damage had been done, and he would no longer tolerate others refusing to take the proper accountability for it.

Inula met his gaze with fire in her eyes. She gestured to the desolation around them. "And see what inheritance that kingdom leaves in its wake," she hissed. "Hatred, destruction, violence, and arrogance," she gestured broadly at him. "If this is what your reign will bring—if this is the portent of things to come—then I want no part of it. We would have been safe if we had not tried to interfere with the workings of men—if we had not sheltered you and that pitiful pea farmer. We could have hidden ourselves away, as we had done for hundreds of years. We could have had peace."

"And watch the rest of the world and the Ancient Races fall to extinction?" Hemlock growled.

"Perhaps. But what are they to the mighty Golden Grove that we have preserved for so long?" Inula opened her arms wide to the golden trees. "We live beneath the last remains of the Phoenix Clan, the very symbols of rejuvenation and rebirth. We could have come back and righted the wrongs against us and our fallen brethren, and we could have begun again. Nothing would have been truly lost, because we would have been there to rebuild once the hatred was over. But now, now no one is safe. We are all doomed. It does not matter where my men were. We were doomed from the start, particularly under that cursed girl's command."

Some broken things are better left to burn. Laire's sword pressed into Ro's ribs, something hissing in his ears. "ENOUGH!" His vision went white with vehemence. "It was YOUR stupid pride that killed her and the Grove!"

"Calla would have *never* left the world to burn around us!" Ash shouted, almost as loudly as Ro. "She would have thought you were a monster even *before* you killed her daughter! How can you stand there and say you've done nothing wrong?"

Inula's face paled. For the first time, Ro saw her truly angry. Her eyes were wild, her cheeks devoid of color, and her jaw ground so tightly that her face looked as sharp as a blade. "Do *not* bring my sister into this!" she screamed at Ash, rushing at her with staff brandished and robes billowing around her. Styrax stepped in front of her, eyes glowing and jaw clenched as a shield of water materialized between them. Inula swung at it, but her staff shrieked off the wall of magic. "You were not there when she died! You did not see the *wretchedness* your beloved cousin brought upon her! If you are to blame anyone, blame the filthy half-blood. If the battle was over, as she said it was, there was no reason for my men to stay at the Mother Tree, and no reason for them to be under her control anymore. I kept my end of the bargain! I moved them as soon as the battle was over! She is the one that went there on her own!"

Ash smiled. A tight thing that showed nothing but contempt, fury, and brokenness. "Thank you for your testimony, Elder Inula."

The silence rang, heavy and deafening, as everyone stared at Inula. She had admitted it.

But that could not fix the damage done.

Ro's body shook with rage and grief, the emotions pressing so hard against his chest he feared he might burst. What now? What could he do now? Nothing he did would bring Aspen back.

But surely a king can claim justice? a voice whispered in the back of his mind.

The words sent a shudder of truth through Ro. He laid Aspen gently on a bedroll, folding her hands one over the other, and unwrapped Laire's sword. What did it matter anymore if he maintained a relationship with the Golden Grove? It had fallen. He had no interest in working closely with bigots and unapologetic murderers. Aspen would have been patient. She would have forgiven and forgotten even as it ate her away from the inside. But she was gone. And Ro found himself much less inclined to be merciful. The kindness and forgiveness had died with Aspen.

Inula's rage had subsided, replaced by her cool, heartless neutrality. She raised an eyebrow at Ro. "Do you intend to kill me, boy? Will that save you? Will that save your misplaced love?" Glowing green magic wound its way up her staff. "Perhaps you are more fit for the blood-stained throne of Loralan than I originally thought."

Ro clenched his teeth and nearly drew the sword completely, but Hemlock placed a gnarled hand on his. She said nothing to him, but gave Inula a flat, emotionless look. "You say that, according to the stipulations of your agreement with Aspen, your men were rightfully under your control **again** when you called them away from their post."

Inula pressed her mouth together in a thin line. "That is correct. The battle had been won. I had agreed to lend her my men for one battle, and that was all."

Hemlock nodded once. "Understood."

Ro looked at her, outraged. "Hemlock, this is *her* fault! You know it is!"

Hemlock squeezed his hand so hard it nearly collapsed in on itself. Otherwise, she ignored him.

"I was afraid they may get complacent," Inula said, her magic still burning bright on her staff. "They are warriors of the highest caliber, and cannot be left idle for long."

Ro practically ground his teeth to nothing. "That's your excuse? Worried that your bodyguards might lose years and years of practice in the span of, perhaps, an hour?"

Inula sneered at him. "Perhaps if you put in the effort to be as skilled as they are, you would know."

"And yet here I am, and they're either dead or captured." Ro spat at her feet. "A fat lot of good your training did them."

Inula's eyes blazed again.

Hemlock stepped between Ro and Inula so that neither could see the other. "Enough!" She glared at Ro. "You, stand over there." She gestured to Ash and Styrax. "I'll deal with you later."

"With *me*?" Ro gaped at her like she had lost her mind. "I am not a willful murderer!"

"And you are also not an elder in the Council!" Hemlock roared. "Leave our politics to us."

Ro was left speechless, appalled at how similar her words sounds to Inula. They plowed into his gut like physical blows. His face darkened. They were all the same, every one of them. He glared at her until he found his voice. "And here I thought you cared for Aspen and what she stood for. It appears I was mistaken." He whirled and stood next to Ash and Styrax as she had ordered, his entire body vibrating with rage.

None of them spoke. Hemlock seemed unphased by his accusation. It didn't surprise him anymore. None of them cared about anyone other than themselves.

Hemlock turned back to Inula. "You were afraid they might lose the edge from their rigorous and endless training, correct?"

Inula's eyes narrowed. "I see no point to this line of questioning."

Hemlock waved her hand. "I am working to absolve your guilt."

Inula snorted. "I highly doubt those three will take any sort of 'fact' to heart with whom they choose to accuse of this mess," she jabbed her chin in Ro's direction. Styrax and Ash each held one of his wrists as he nearly lunged at her. A smirk curled at the corner of Inula's lips. "To answer your question, Hemlock, yes."

Ash let out a sound somewhere between a sob and a growl, her face contorted in rage as she fought back tears. She had bitten her lip hard enough to draw blood. Styrax had tightened one arm around her, a scathing glare fixed directly on Inula. Droplets of water floated around him, flickers of lightning racing through them.

Hemlock had shoved one of her hands deep into her apron pockets, her fingers balled into a fist. "Were you concerned because they are meant to protect the Golden Grove?"

Inula nodded once. "Of course. That is always my main priority."

"And were you not advised that keeping them at their post near the Mother Tree is likely where they would have been the most help in defending the Golden Grove?"

Inula pursed her lips. "I'm not sure I would consider that girl a proper means of counsel."

Hemlock didn't react. "She was a general in the Prince's Rebellion, was she not?"

"Much to my chagrin, yes."

The other soldiers had released their weapons, but murderous rumblings rippled through them at Inula's words.

Hemlock, again, remained unphased and kept up her line of questioning. "Therefore, in matters of war, she would outrank you, would she not?"

Inula's lips had nearly disappeared with how deeply she pursed them. "Again, that anyone would put that girl in such a position after all she's done is beyond me."

"Yes or no, Elder Inula?"

"Hemlock, this is asinine. Our home has burned around us. What could these questions possibly—"

"Yes. Or. No?"

Inula pinched the bridge of her nose, her eyes shut and her lips compressed. "Yes."

Hemlock let that single word ring out over the onlookers, maintaining a stony silence for several breaths. Ro watched her closely, his heart still thudding painfully against his ribs. His ears rung with...anger? Anticipation?

Hemlock drew herself to her full-height, her stooped back unfurling. She was taller than Inula, and her eyes flashed with terrifying power and wisdom. Even Inula seemed to shy away from her. "So, if you are to be understood correctly," Hemlock said, each word methodical and perfectly articulated. "You are telling me you ignored the counsel of a ranking official—causing deaths that should not have happened—because you were afraid?"

It was as if the air stopped moving in that moment. Ash sucked in a breath, her eyes wide with shock. Ro covered his mouth as his jaw dropped. He remembered those words. He remembered them from the images in Aspen's memory orb. They had been the same words to condemn her as a shadow walker.

Inula's face went white. Her face contorted in barely controlled fury. "That is not what I said, Hemlock. If you consider the context—"

"As I seem to recall, Inula, from a similar trial five years ago, you insisted that context does not matter. Only facts. You then sentenced that girl to the only punishment suitable for cowards of the highest order."

Inula's fists shook. She took long strides to Hemlock, her face burning with a mixture of emotions. "You wouldn't *dare*. Your accusations are unfounded and biased—"

"It seems you have also said that the Council of Elders is bound to a rule of unbiased equality. No matter the person or circumstances. Precedent made by one is rule for all." Hemlock lifted her hands to Inula, her eyes glowing. "And I am sorry to say, the precedent has already been set."

Inula screamed and lunged. Rose bushes—*Aspen's* rose bushes—erupted from the ground, coaxed awake by Hemlock's magic. They entangled Inula and caught her in place. She spat and fought, but they held her fast. Blood oozed from the thorns she had worked deep into her skin, stark against her pale complexion and flaxen hair.

"You will regret this, Hemlock!" she shrieked. "No one will believe you! I am innocent!"

"You told me this as well, Inula," Hemlock said quietly, the words fierce and pointed. "The spell only works on those that are guilty, whether real or perceived. If you are as innocent as you say, perhaps you should not have so much fear in your eyes."

Inula, for once in her life, was struck speechless.

Hemlock looked to Ash, Styrax, and Ro, all standing there frozen with mouths agape. "Collect the names of every fallen soldier," she commanded. "Bring me the list when you're done. I'll stay here to monitor her."

Inula spat in the dirt, curses rolling off her tongue in a constant stream.

The three left to do her bidding. Ro staggered behind them, disbelief leaving him senseless. He stopped and looked at Hemlock. Unassuming. Humble. She had loved Aspen just as much as he had. He should have remembered that.

"I'll be back," he said to Ash and Styrax. He rushed to Hemlock and hugged the old elf tightly. "Hemlock, I'm sorry," he whispered. "I should never have doubted you. I hope you can—I should never have said—"

Hemlock shook in his arms, her emotions finally spilling down her face. "I can forgive you," she said thickly, pulling away and wiping at her damp eyes. "But you had better not forget that I am wiser than you will ever be. And you had better remind me of that fact often. Do you understand?"

Ro nodded somberly. Hemlock got quiet again. "Whatever shall we do without our girl keeping us on track?"

Ro shook his head, unable to form a coherent or complete thought. He tried to say *something*, but words failed him. All he saw was Aspen's still form on the bedroll. The wound torn into his soul was too much to bear, and he turned away. He left Hemlock where she stood and went back to the others, and they left together to count the dead.

THEY BROUGHT the list back to Hemlock several hours later, exhausted emotionally and physically. So many dead. Too many friends. Too many futures and lives cut short.

Ro had ground his teeth raw. This all could have been avoided. They all would have survived and been fine if not for Inula's pride. He glared openly at her as he handed the list to Hemlock, the roll of parchment long and thick. Hemlock took the document soberly. She traced a circle of curling runes around herself and Inula, who made no attempt to hide her contempt and fury. Hemlock sat down, opened the parchment, and settled her palms down to the earth.

She closed her eyes, and the runes glowed. "*By Law you are bound,*" she chanted. "*By Law, what is done cannot be undone. We present you, coward and fiend, to be judged by the Earth.*"

The ground rumbled beneath them. The tree branches bent and swayed, scraping together in accusatory, rushing whispers that filled the camp. Gooseflesh appeared on Ro's skin, but he folded his arms tight over his chest.

"Hemlock, stop this! You will regret this! I will have your seat on the Council! You will never practice medicine again, and you will be banished from the Golden Grove!"

Hemlock ignored her. The runes glowed brighter around her, and her white hair thrashed around her face. Her eyes glowed like a vengeful deity. "*An act of fear has led to death uncontrolled by others. I, Sister Earth's handmaiden, present the names of the dead for judgment. Should their blood be on the hands of the accused, whether in mind or in truth, their marks shall appear on the skin of their killer, forever remembered and stained.*"

"HEMLOCK!"

Hemlock read the first name. A name that Ro didn't recognize, but he knew Aspen would. He knew she would be standing next to him, jaw tight and shoulders stiff, blaming herself for a death she couldn't control. For a soldier she should have been able to save if she had done her part.

Inula screamed, this time in pain, as a single stark, black mark seared its way onto her hand. The smell of burnt flesh made Ro's eyes water, and he looked away. Ash stood, resolute, and watched, her expression unreadable. He had to remember this was her *mother*. He wondered what was going through her mind.

Hemlock tightened her jaw and continued despite Inula's cries. She read name after name, each one burning another mark into Inula's skin. They completely covered her left hand, making their way farther and farther up her arm. Once they had reached her elbow, Inula's screams had stopped, and she only stared blankly into the trees. They covered her arm up to her shoulder and the side of her neck. There had been at least a hundred names on the scroll. Ro remembered how repulsed the Queen of the Midnight Fens and others had been at Aspen's mark of five. He couldn't imagine what Inula's life would be like now with so many of her sins on prominent, permanent display.

Hemlock reached the last name, her hands shaking. Her impassiveness had gone, and pure anger took its place. "*Aspen Tanner,*" she said, the words charged with fire and vindication. A mark burned itself beneath Inula's left eye. The only scar on her face.

"These marks shall bear the names of the slain," Hemlock finished. "*When gazed upon by their killer, their faces and names shall etch ever deeper into their mind and heart. Never to be forgotten, never to be silenced. The guilty shall never be free from their sins.*" The spell ended. The runes faded, and Hemlock released Inula from her thorny bonds.

One by one, they left her there, crumpled in her pathetic heap. Ash helped Hemlock to her feet and guided her away, Styrax trailing close behind. The soldiers left as well, their angry muttering taken over by bereft sounds of grief. Gan hugged Ro before leaving as well. Soon, Ro was the only one left.

Inula's hair hung plastered to her skull with sweat. Her breathing was labored, and her left arm spasmed uncontrollably. She gave Ro a half-conscious look, obviously fighting to keep her eyelids open. She scoffed. "Have you come to claim your justice?" she asked in a halting, rasping voice. "No one will stop you now. No one would care."

Ro's hand twitched momentarily to the sword at his side. But, instead, he squatted in front of her, his eyes boring into hers. "No," he said, the words icy. "Anything I could do would be a mercy. And I am nowhere near as forgiving as Aspen." He gave her a ruthless smile that made his face feel like it might split in two. "I want you to live a long, miserable life. You deserve to live with every wretchedness you sentenced Aspen to. She would have tried to help you—would have fought for a lesser sentence, saying that no one deserves that same fate. But you killed the only person who would have fought for you." He tapped the dark mark beneath her eye. "*That* is justice."

An inarticulate sound of rage gurgled in her throat. She swiped at him, but he just stood and walked away. She was too weak to follow him.

When she disappeared that night, no one cared to look for her.

CHAPTER

THIRTY-NINE

The next few days passed in an empty haze. Ro hardly slept or ate, but followed along meekly when Hemlock came to tend his injuries. The wound on his arm from Laire's sword splintered arcs of pain through his body, leaving a void behind. The sword glittered a few feet away from him, it's sapphire eyes always watching him. He knew the stories behind its powers, but it felt like the sword had taken so much more than just a portion of his soul. Aspen's absence made it feel like his entire world had been ripped out from under him.

Hemlock had just finished another round of ministrations—most of his wounds were healing well with her magic, except for his arm, which was to be expected—and Ro was sitting, staring into nothing, when Ash crouched next to him, a parchment and quill clutched in her hands. She looked tired, her honey-blond hair stringy and her eyes dull. There were bags under her eyes, and her cheeks were drawn.

"We need to collect Aspen's last..." her voice broke, and she waved vaguely to the trees.

Ro hardly registered the words. He blinked at her several times uncomprehendingly.

Tears welled in her eyes, and her face flashed with anger and desperation. "Ro, don't you leave me, too," she said, her lower lip trembling. "By the Architects, Aspen didn't do what she did for us to just give up and fade away! Aspen, Sorren, and, Mother Night curse her, even Inula..." she glared daggers directly into Ro's eyes. "I'm not going to lose someone else, do you hear me?"

Ro swallowed and nodded, his heart hovering somewhere in his throat.

"Good," Ash said, her voice wavering again. She stood and offered him her hand. "Let's go."

He stood and followed her, his joints creaking from misuse. As a last thought, he wrapped Laire's sword in a blanket and then strapped it to his waist. He didn't want it leaving his sight and falling into someone else's hands.

Ro and Ash wound through the remnants of the Golden Grove, every tree blackened and dying. There was no silver, no gold. Just... nothing. They didn't speak to each other as they walked, but kept a steady pace through the ruins of their home.

Ro balked before the last curve to the mother tree, though. The image of the rubble—of Aspen—was burned in his mind as permanently as the carvings in the phoenix caves. His limbs shook. His knees threatened to collapse. He staggered back a few paces, chest heaving with ragged breaths, searching for somewhere to run to while tears burned like acid in them. He hadn't expected the visions to hit so deeply. Hadn't expected his body to lock itself in place. "I can't," he gasped, clutching his chest and Aspen's silver ring beneath his tunic. "Ash, I—I can't. I can't."

Ash gripped him by the shoulders and made him face her. Her jaw was clenched tight, but her eyes and cheeks were red and soaked with tears. "Yes, you can," she said, her voice thick and fierce. "You can, because you loved her, and you would never let her final moments go forgotten like those poor souls in Brahmon." She watched Ro and waited for the words to sink in.

Aspen crouched beneath the keening trees in Brahmon played through his mind, her eyes closed and her hand pressed against their bark as she translated the words no one else had bothered to. He had seen the pain on her face—the angry acceptance of the half-bloods' mistreatment. She had been hurting and terrified, but she still took the time to help them. The very *least* he could do was give her the same respect.

Ro took a deep, bracing breath. Ash was right—she was always right. But that didn't make the next part any easier.

Ash's face softened and she squeezed his shoulders. "Are you ready?"

"No," he said hoarsely.

She let out a watery sound that wasn't quite a laugh. "Me either." Her body swayed for a moment as she looked down the silent path to the Mother Tree. "Can we—can we hold hands?" she asked in a small voice.

"Yeah," Ro said. He took her hand—both of them hanging onto the other for support—and together they walked the rest of the way to where Aspen's final words waited.

The first whisper of Aspen's voice through the trees nearly broke Ro. They brushed the edges of his mind, as if she were talking with someone just around the corner. Instinctively he looked to find her, and finding nothing but a wilting tree shot daggers to his heart. She wasn't there. She never would be again. Her body was back at camp with Hemlock, awaiting a proper burial.

Ro stumbled into a sitting position beneath the tree that carried Aspen's final thoughts, his entire body shuddering with grief.

Ash knelt next to him, her knee pressed against his, her skin cold and clammy even through the material of her trousers. Her body trembled. She laid out the parchment and placed her hand on the tree.

"*Guardian spirit,*" she said, "*I thank thee for preserving the memory of my brothers and sisters. Relinquish thy burden. Thy work is done. We are the fallen's closest kin."*

Ash's gray-green magic swept up the tree's trunk, and Aspen's words rushed from the tree in a flood.

It's up to you, now. It's all up to you. I can't do anymore, and I'm at peace with that.

The sorrow slammed into Ro like a physical blow. Even Ash stopped writing, her hand shaking. Ro had seen Aspen fight—had seen how little regard she gave to exhaustion. She pushed beyond any limits presented to her. Knowing that she had finally been pushed too far—imagining what that must have looked like for her—wounded him worse than any cursed blade.

Someone hear me. Ro, Ash, someone, please save them. Please. Don't let the Vanguard take them away. Don't let them get to the capital.

There was a long silence after that—so long that Ro thought that might have been the end of her thoughts. But then her voice came back, so soft that he had to strain to hear it.

Ro, I'm scared, the tree whispered in her voice. Broken. Lingering on choked back emotion. *I don't want to die here alone. I don't want to lose the family I've gained in Ash, Styrax, Sorren, and you. I wish you were here so I wasn't alone. So I could tell you how much I love you.*

The tears fell, thick with bitter guilt, down Ro's face. Heaving sobs wracked his body, and he didn't hear anything else. He had failed her. He had made her one promise—that she would never be alone again—and he couldn't even do that one thing for her.

Ash finished transcribing the message and rolled the parchment. Her shoulders curved in on themselves, and she rested her arms over her stomach, as if trying to keep herself from falling apart. Tears streamed down her cheeks.

"This is my fault," Ro whispered through clenched teeth. "I should have been here. I shouldn't have left her. I could have protected her."

"No," Ash's hand fell heavy and sudden on Ro's shoulder. He could hear her teeth grinding. "You stop that *right* now." She made

Ro look at her, her eyes bright with fierce tears. She still curled into herself with her grief. "You and I both know that Aspen lived the past five years of her life with that kind of guilt. She could never do enough or be enough to make it right."

Ro tried to argue with her, but she held up a hand to stop him. "You can't keep everyone you love safe forever. Life is beautiful because it ends." Her voice broke again, and she choked back a sob. "And we never know when that will be." She released Ro. "Aspen may have lived with that guilt, but she never, *ever*, would have wished that on anyone. And I think—I think you, of all of us, helped her the most in moving past that guilt and living the life she deserved and wanted." She smiled at him, even as her lower lip trembled. "So live with her memory, and let this guilt wash away with your sorrow as time moves on."

Ro gaped at her, flooded with the righteous fierceness in her voice. He knew that she believed her words with every fiber of her being, and he wanted so desperately to settle into their comfort. But, his guilt was still there, eating away at him just as insidiously as the memory eaters had picked away at his past. He should have been there for Aspen. He had promised her—had vowed he would tear the stars out of the sky before he would ever let her be alone again. And he had failed. Wholly and completely. That had not been the ability to choose Gan had promised him. He could *want* to be someone that was there for Aspen, but it wouldn't change a thing. He would always be that failure.

Ro didn't have the energy or words to explain that to Ash, though, so he swallowed the feelings back and simply nodded.

Some of the tension eased from Ash's shoulders. She slipped the scroll of parchment into Ro's hands. "What now?" she asked.

Ro wanted to ask her why she expected him to have the answers, but weighty responsibility fell on his shoulders. He was the prince. Now that Aspen was gone, decisions regarding the war would have to fall to him. It didn't matter how shoddy a prince he was. The thought settled like sawdust in his mouth. "Aspen died trying to keep the villagers safe," he said, slogging through the panic rising in him. "And I won't let that be in vain. We'll follow Sorren's lead and go after them. We'll rescue them before they reach the capital." He half expected her to ask if there was anything else. Laire's sword pressed into his hip, somehow warm and cold all at once. Another idea swirled, bright and hot, in his mind, but he wasn't ready to share it yet. He wasn't sure if he would ever be.

But Ash didn't ask him anything. Instead, she seemed relieved to have a job to do again. She stood and patted him on the shoulder. "I'll let Styrax know." She motioned to the scroll with her chin. "As part of the magic, if you brush your fingers over the words, you'll hear their voice," she said. "Read the last part. She meant it to be for you." Without another word, she left him there.

With shaking fingers, Ro unrolled the parchment. He skimmed over Aspen's words of fear and regret, his heart shattering all over again, until he came across words he didn't recognize.

I know you promised me the stars, Ro, Aspen said. *But, I'm glad you're not here. You have a duty to fulfill that's so much bigger than me.* There was almost a laugh in her voice as the next words came. *A long time ago, there was a bitter, broken young woman that believed you to be arrogant, bigoted, vindictive, and a nuisance. Well, that young woman has done some growing up, and do you want to hear what she knows about you now?*

A raw chuckle pulled from Ro's throat. "Always have to use my words against me, don't you?" He clenched his jaw as his lower lip trembled, wishing he could gather Aspen into his arms again.

You are kind. You are intelligent. You are willing to hear and learn and change. You love fiercely, and are resilient in the face of insurmountable odds. You have the capacity to be the greatest ruler Loralan has ever known. Claim what is yours and turn this kingdom into a place where we can all live in peace. I know you can do it. I believe in Ro Edenson, son of Gan the pea farmer. Her voice faded, the words trailing off as if she were struggling to stay awake. But, her last words pierced to his core. *I love you. For evergreens and aspen trees.*

Ro sat in the dead stillness of the forest, golden ashes swirling around him as tears swept down his cheeks. He read those words over and over again, seeing the soft looks Aspen would cast him across the command tent. The subtle ways their hands brushed as they walked through the Golden Grove together. The wine-drunk pink on her cheeks as her eyes reflected gold and silver leaves. "I love you, too," he wept, the world turning an even deeper shade of gray around him. "I want to be the man you see me to be." The emptiness her absence left engulfed him. Gan's voice shuddered through his bones. *We are not always in control of the changes life brings our way. But we are in charge of shaping the choices we make despite them.*

"I can't do it without you, Aspen." Laire's sword dug into Ro's side. He grit his teeth, gripping the parchment so hard it crinkled beneath his fingers. His choice ripped like fire through his being. "I *won't* do it without you."

CHAPTER

FORTY

Vinea drew up just short of Monterro, filthy and aching and nauseous from her boat ride to the island. The sand dragged at her boots, and the water caught the lantern lights glowing from the city. Memories of the day the castle had been overrun flooded her—the hopelessness and grief and feelings of failure only compounding on the ones she felt now. White hot anger flared in her chest and roared through her ears, pulling fire into her cheeks and neck—anger at Sedick, at Laire, at the war and the king it served, and at herself. She knew Sedick would be waiting for her in his grand mansion, built on his lies and manipulation and gross misuse of power.

She ground her teeth and plunked the jar of fire in the sand. Her days of powerless, dutiful obedience were over. She had done everything asked of her and had earned this one small act of defiance. If Sedick wanted his prize, he would have to come to her.

Vinea unscrewed the jar lid, letting the golden glow send its warmth and magic to the surrounding space, calling to anyone searching for it by the sheer magnitude of its magic—although that had seemed to be fading with every step of her journey. Vinea sat next to it, waiting in silence as the ocean washed against the beach, foaming and hissing.

As Vinea had expected, it didn't take long for someone to come for her. Except, it wasn't Sedick. It was a figure wrapped in a black cloak, its cowl drawn up to hide their face. Strange figures appearing from seemingly nowhere were disconcerting enough, but this being had a dark presence that flooded Vinea's senses. Loneliness. Desperation. Terror and fear. And cold, dead cruelty, the kind that made every nerve ending in Vinea's body shrivel away.

Vinea plucked the jar from the sand and held it tight to her, rising and taking a step back. "Who are you?" she asked. Her voice came out shrill and terrified rather than the demanding tone she had hoped for.

A thin smile flashed from beneath the cowl. "You have done surprisingly well, Lady Vinea," the figure said in a man's voice, soft and somehow all the more terrifying for it. "I had my doubts when Sedick pawned his duties off to you, but it seems they were unfounded." He held out his hand, the fingers long, pale, and skeletal. "The flame, if you please."

Vinea took another step back, her heart pounding and her throat dry. She couldn't suck in a full breath as adrenaline raced through her veins. Something about this man's presence terrified her. More than Sedick's ever had. It was as if all the light vanished around him, replaced only with death and suffering. And he knew about her deal with Sedick. What else did he know about her? The questions left her feeling naked and vulnerable. Shivers and gooseflesh raced across her body.

"Who—who are you?" she asked again, her voice small and fragile.

He raised his pale hand to his cowl and threw it off, revealing a face covered in dark, swirling markings. His milky eyes darted sightlessly back and forth, but Vinea got the feeling he could see *all* of her. "I am the demon, Ambrose," he said, his voice as quiet and piercing as an assassin's knife to the back. "I am Sedick's master and, in turn, a servant to my great mistress." A smile pulled at his lips like skin peeling away from a rotting corpse. "And you have brought something that will make her *very* happy."

Vinea clenched her fingers tighter around the jar. A thousand questions piled in her thoughts, but they all stuck to her throat. All save for the most important one. "My daughter?"

A mirthless chuckle spilled from his bloodless lips. "You have done well, and I like to reward those that serve me well." He vanished, and the hairs on Vinea's neck stood on end. She looked around, waiting for him to leap from the shadows and attack her. But he did not. Instead, he reappeared only moments later in the same spot he had left, Linae's wrist clutched in his hand.

"MAMA!" Linae screamed, tears pouring down her face.

Vinea's knees nearly collapsed beneath her. A strangled cry of relief tore itself from her. She ran across the beach, stumbling through the sand to reach Linae. She had gotten so big! She looked healthy and well taken care of. Milaia had kept her promise. Vinea's arms ached to hold Linae close again.

She drew up short, though, when Ambrose curled his bony fingers around Linae's shoulder, too close to her neck in a silent threat.

"The flame," he hissed.

Vinea hesitated only a moment, the specter's words haunting her thoughts. But it took only one look at Linae's face to banish any doubts. It didn't matter. Not when she had her daughter to protect.

She handed over the golden flame, and in that same instant Ambrose shoved Linae away from him.

Vinea scooped her up, laughing and crying all at once as she crushed her to her chest. She stroked her curls and peppered her with kisses.

"I—I missed you, mama!" Linae cried, burying her face in Vinea's shoulder. "I thought you were never coming back for me!"

Vinea wiped Linae's tears from her cheeks. "I know, my love. I know. I'm sorry. But I'm here now, and everything's going to be all right." She cradled Linae close to her again, Linae's head resting on her shoulder, and looked at Ambrose. "What about Milaia?"

Ambrose didn't answer her for a moment. He stroked the jar with a single finger. The flame guttered and trembled, pressing itself against the far side of the jar as if repelled by him. He capped the jar and tucked it into his robes. "Milaia is Sedick's prize," he said, neutral and uncaring. "Despite his arrogance, he has been a faithful servant. I will not take her from him unless you can provide me with something exceptional." He turned his head in her direction, his eyes still staring sightlessly past her. "I'm afraid the only thing tempting enough for me to pull her from Sedick is information regarding my mistress' sword, which no mortal has yet been able to provide."

"Your mistress' sword?"

"A bone white blade," he said, his voice hollow and bereft. "Razor straight on one edge and as jagged as dragon's teeth on the other. The most beautiful weapon you have ever seen." He waved his hand through the air as if clearing away unseen phantoms. "But it has been lost for centuries."

Vinea's brow furrowed. Surely there couldn't be many blades that fit that description. The only one she knew of…Someone else was after Laire's sword? That wretched thing could elicit so much interest? "I know where this sword is," she said tentatively.

Ambrose's face turned stormy. "Do not mock me, woman."

Vinea back-pedaled, squeezing Linae tighter to her. "But I—I do. You can ask Sedick. He sent me to retrieve it, and—"

She stopped at the look in his eyes. Ambrose's expression had turned from storm clouds to raging thunderstorms. He vanished again, and in a moment was back with two other people.

Milaia stumbled away from him, her eyes wild as the golden shackles fell off her wrists. She looked at them, her hands shaking. "I'm…I'm free?"

But Vinea's attention was rooted on Ambrose and the other person he had brought with him. Sedick dangled from Ambrose's clutches, scrabbling at the pale hand wrapped around his neck. His eyes bugged from his skull.

"What is the *meaning* of—"

Ambrose squeezed tighter, and the rest of Sedick's words strangled in his throat.

Milaia scrambled over to Vinea, her entire body trembling. "*What is going on?*" she hissed.

Vinea shook her head mutely, her hand pressed to Linae's head to keep her from looking up. Linae whimpered and nuzzled deeper into her.

"You *knew!*" Ambrose seethed, his eyes two white flames of fury in the dark. The shadows on the beach seemed drawn to him, writhing like eels at his feet. "You *dare* to hide things from me? *Me?* Who gave you your power?"

Sedick shook his head and tried to speak again. "I don't—"

Ambrose shoved his face in Sedick's. "Lie to me again, and I will tear out your throat." He shook him. "The *sword* Sedick! Where is it?"

Vinea had never seen fear on Sedick's face until this moment. It spread across his face like a blood stain on a white shirt, visceral and stark. It filled her with a sick sense of satisfaction.

"Lost—in the—battle," Sedick croaked, his face turning purple from lack of air. "Lost prince—has it, now,"

Ambrose screamed—an unearthly sound that sent arcs of panic through Vinea's spine—and threw Sedick into the surf. "You are too entrenched in my mistress' plan for me to kill outright, but I *can* promise you that death would be a mercy compared to what I will do to you."

He turned his face toward Vinea, his expression feral. The moonlight caught the designs on his face and almost made them look alive, writhing across his features. "You have what you want, and have given me a most precious gift," he said to her in a soft, silent voice that crawled across her skin like spider silk. "In return, I will give you two final gifts." The silver stud in Vinea's ear dissolved, and the pressure of Sedick's magic in her mind disappeared. "If you wish to cling to your short, miserable lives for as long as possible," the demon said. "I suggest you forsake this kingdom and its people. Death is coming to Loralan, and my mistress will rise from its ashes to achieve her divine revenge. With the Sacred Flame now in her possession, it is not a matter of if, but when." His corpse-grin peeled his lips apart again. "Cherish the moments that matter while you can." He turned away and strode to Sedick, who sat floundering and gasping in the surf. Ambrose's tongue slicked across his lips. "And I shall greatly cherish *this* moment."

Milaia's eyes widened, all the color leaving her face. She gripped Vinea's arm so tightly that bruises appeared beneath her fingers. "Run."

Vinea didn't have to be told again. They all turned and fled as Sedick's screams tore across the ocean.

ALSO BY A. L. LORENSEN

For Evergreens and Aspen Trees: The Songs of Loralan, Book 1

The Land Built by Giants: A Songs of Loralan Anthology

Acknowledgments

This book did not take me nearly as long as the first (although fourteen years isn't hard to beat), and that is largely in part to the absolutely incredible people I have in my life.

Ryan, as always, thank you for supporting me in going after my dreams. If it weren't for your love, support, and partnership, I would not be a published author today.

To all my family, both blood and chosen, thank you for encouraging me to live my dreams. I am living them now, and it's all thanks to you.

Cassandra Caswell-Stirling and Aria Carpenter, my absolutely *amazing* editors, thank you for saving this manuscript. I, really truly, sent you a dumpster-fire of an original draft to work with. After your help and guidance, I am so proud of how this book came out. You are the real heroes!

Timea Schweiger, you stunned me again with this cover. I was beside myself when you sent it to me, and it keeps getting better every time I look at it.

And, as always, my readers, thank you for following along to this next installment. I am blown away by your outpouring of love, encouragement, and support. I write these books for you, and I am beyond thrilled that it made it into your hands. Thank you for reading, and for being you. You make the world a better place.

ABOUT THE AUTHOR

 A. L. Lorensen has had a lifetime passion for writing and the art of storytelling. She graduated from Utah State University with a Bachelor of Science in Social Work and maintained her writing on the side. A. L. mainly writes fantasy, but has dabbled in fiction, mystery, comedy, and anything else that may strike her fancy. *For Evergreens and Aspen Trees* is her debut novel.

A. L. Lorensen currently resides in Logan, UT with her husband, their cat, Muse, and their many, many bookshelves. If you would like to keep in touch with A. L. Lorensen (and get a free short story), you can join her newsletter at www.allwrites.com.

facebook.com/allorensen.writes

instagram.com/authorallorensen